broken *playboy*

A WINDSOR
ACADEMY NOVEL

LAURA LEE

BROKEN PLAYBOY ©2021 Laura Lee

Editor: Ellie McLove of My Brother's Editor

Proofreader: Christine Estevez of Haven Author Services

Cover Design: Lori Jackson Designs

Cover Photographer: Scott Hoover

To Alley and Julia : This book wouldn't be out in the world without you.

Also, to Kristen: Bentley's IRL girl.

chapter one

BENTLEY

"The family would like to thank all of you who have gathered here today to celebrate the life of Carissa Lynn Marquart. To bid farewell to a young woman taken from this earth far too soon. To support one another in your grief from Miss Marquart's passing..."

"God, this is lame."

My head whips to the right, where the girl I've loved almost my whole life stands. The sun glints off the charm bracelet she always wears as she tucks a lock of her long, blonde hair behind her ear.

"Wh—" I fling my hand toward the people gathered around, all dressed in black. "But, you—"

Carissa lifts a delicate brow. "Died?"

I swallow, watching as the polished wood casket is lowered into its grave. "Yeah."

Her pouty lips form into a smirk. "Yeah. That part kind of sucks, huh? Puts an end to that whole, we'll get married one day and be together forever *dream of mine."*

"I don't..." I shake my head. "I don't understand. How are you here?"

"Because I had to tell you."

"Tell me wh——" My eyes fall closed when pleasure shoots up my spine. I plant my feet more firmly on the ground so my legs don't give out. "Fuuuuuck."

"Bentley, pay attention."

My brown eyes meet her baby blues. "Huh? What were you saying?"

A wail pierces through the air, and I look up to find my best friend's sister, Ainsley, holding on to my other best friend for dear life.

Carissa nods to the mourners. "They're here because of you."

I moan as warm, wet lips meet my skin. As a tongue traces the vein on the underside of my shaft. I lean back against the tree trunk, looking down on a head of long, black hair.

What the fuck?

I try pushing her away, but instead, I wind up wrapping

those curls around my fist as she starts bobbing up and down, applying the perfect amount of suction.

Jesus fucking Christ, she's good at that.

"This is your fault, Bentley. Everything is your fault."

I watch as the mystery girl works my dick over like a pro, trying to get a glimpse of her face, but my eyes won't seem to focus.

"Bentley!" Carissa shouts. "Look at me!"

I turn my attention back to her, my vision perfectly clear. Carissa's so damn beautiful, it hurts sometimes. And that beauty is one-hundred-percent natural. She never felt the need to keep up with all the plastic girls in our social circles. She's tiny in stature, but she has long, lean muscles honed from years of ballet. Her hair is the perfect shade of golden blonde, which complements her creamy skin and light blue eyes. She could easily be a model if she were taller and interested in shit like that.

I give her my signature panty-dropping grin. "What were you saying?"

"That." She nods to the girl on her knees. "That is why it's all your fault."

We both watch for a moment as the girl sucks me off. There's no way I'm going to last much longer.

"What do you mean? You're the one who said we needed to see other people. To sow our wild oats."

Rissa's eyes fill with tears. "I didn't mean it. I was coming to that party to tell you I didn't mean it. I was done pretending, Bent. I didn't want anyone but you. But then I saw you with her."

"I didn't want anyone but you either, Riss. But you made it clear you had no interest in being in a relationship until we were in college. You told me I had to see other people. How was I supposed to know you didn't actually mean what you said? I'm not a goddamn mind reader."

I look down again at the dark head of hair as my balls start tightening. "Oh, shit, honey, I'm gonna come."

Mystery Girl's nails bite into my ass as she pulls me closer, moaning her intention to stay right where she is. Mind-numbing pleasure ricochets throughout my entire body as I explode into her mouth. She bobs on my cock, working me through the final tremors before swallowing my load. Christ, I swear that almost made me come again.

Carissa sniffles. When I look up at her, tears are rolling down her cheeks.

"Riss—" I reach for her, but she pulls away before I can touch her.

"It's your fault, Bentley! I killed myself because you broke my heart into a million pieces!" She throws her hands out. "That's *why I ran off that night.* That's *why I tried finding someone to replace you."* Rissa scoffs. "A lot of good that did me."

Murmurs roll through the crowd of funeral-goers as our voices rise.

The girl in front of me stands. I band my arms around

her back, nuzzling my face into her neck. Damn, she smells incredible, like baked goods or some shit. I suddenly feel the need to trace every inch of her skin with my tongue.

"What are you talking about?" I ask. "I don't even know this girl."

Carissa releases a sardonic laugh. "Yeah, you do, Bent. Look at her. Really look at her."

When I pull back, the girl's face finally comes into focus. My God, she has the prettiest eyes I've ever seen. They're bright bluish-green, which might not seem so unusual, but her complexion is similar to mine, so the light color really stands out. There's a scattering of freckles across the bridge of her nose that, for some reason, I find really sexy. Everything about her is sexy, really. She's much taller than most girls in our school; I'm guessing maybe five-foot-nine, five-ten. Her lips are full, she's got curves in all the right places, and when she smiles, it takes my fucking breath away.

"Bentley!" *Carissa yells.*

The other girl frowns, backing away.

"Wait!" *I reach for her.* "Don't go. Hold up a sec."

She shakes her head, taking another few steps backward.

"Did you hear me, Bentley?!" *Carissa tugs on my arm.* "I'm dead because of you!"

"Fuck." I bolt upright in my bed, scrubbing a hand over my face.

It was just a fucking dream. It didn't really happen.

Man, that was intense. I take a few deep breaths

5

until the sleep fog clears. Then I throw my covers off and head into my attached bathroom. After turning on the shower, I strip out of my boxers and brush my teeth, allowing the water a moment to warm. I stand under the spray, for I don't even know how long, running the dream through my head.

That wasn't a dream. It was a goddamn nightmare.

I haven't dreamed about Carissa for months. In a way, it was nice seeing her again, but at the same time, it gutted me and ripped apart old wounds. We were never technically together, but we did have sex often, and there were definitely feelings involved on both sides. She was the one who insisted we screw other people, but we kept those casual fucks completely separate from our relationship. Or non-relationship. Whatever the hell it was.

I stay in the shower until the water runs cold before drying off and heading into my walk-in closet to get dressed for school. I hate wearing a lame-ass uniform every day, but at least it's high-quality shit—the spoiled assholes at our private school wouldn't have it any other way. Plus, I look damn good in it, if I may say so myself. With a quick glance in the mirror, I grab the keys to my Porsche off my dresser and head out.

"Bent, honey, aren't you going to eat breakfast?"

I come to a stop in the foyer as I hear my mom's voice. When did she get back from her trip?

"Hey." I let her wrap me in a hug. "When did you get home?"

My mom smiles. "About an hour ago. I took a red-eye."

"Huh. I didn't realize you'd be back so soon."

She chuckles. "Bentley, I sent my itinerary to you, just like I do every time your father or I leave town. Did you even open the email?"

I shrug, not bothering to respond because she already knows the answer to that. "How is everyone?"

"Great. Although, your grandparents wouldn't stop nagging me about how long it's been since they've seen you. We should fly over there during your spring break. I think it'll be good for us to have some mother-son bonding time before you venture off into the real world."

"Maybe."

She rolls her eyes. "Oh, don't tell me you're getting to be like your father."

My mom is half Hawaiian, and she grew up there, so she really embraces the culture. I don't think she's ever enjoyed living in the chaos that is LA, but she deals with it because she loves my dad. She does, however, fly to Maui every few months to visit her side of the family. My dad rarely accompanies her because, being the workaholic he is, the slow pace of island living drives him insane.

I'm pretty sure the man is actually more stressed out when he's lying on the beach with my mom than he is working eighty hours per week as a venture capitalist. They really are polar opposites, but for some reason, their relationship works. I think I'm the only high schooler I know with somewhat normal parents.

I smile. "Nah, I see no problem with the aloha lifestyle. I think it's pretty fucking smart, actually."

My mom scowls. "Bentley Fitzgerald! Watch the language."

I give her a wry look. "Mom, I'm eighteen."

"And you're living in my house, so you'll abide by my rules."

I bend down to kiss her cheek before heading toward the front door. "Well, it's a good thing I only have a few months until graduation then, isn't it? I'll be out of your hair in no time."

She shakes her head. "Smartass."

"Mother! Language!" I gasp dramatically.

"Okay, okay, I get your point." My mom props a hand on her hip. "You're not going to eat?"

I shake my head. "I've gotta get to school. I'll grab something there."

Luckily, the food at Windsor is the shit. Seriously. I think they have three-star Michelin chefs who prepare the menus.

"All right. Have a good day, honey."

I give her a half-assed wave as I step out the door. "Yep."

On the short drive to school, I tell myself that the dream didn't mean anything. That it's simply my mind's way of coping with my grief. But I know that's not true. I know there's a damn good reason why those thoughts slipped into my subconscious last night, and there's only one person to blame: Sydney-fucking-Carrington. The new girl. The headmaster's daughter.

My greatest mistake.

chapter two

SYDNEY

"Crap, I'm going to be late if I don't hurry up," I mutter under my breath.

As I pull on my blazer, I take one final glance in the mirror at my new uniform. Like my old school attire, it's very *Gossip Girl* chic, except with a red, black, and white color scheme instead of Cambridge's emerald, navy, and gold. I can't say I hate the flirty plaid skirt or thigh-high stockings one bit. Nor the chunky-heeled leather Mary Janes that make my calves look awesome. Tucking an errant curl behind my ear, I grab my bag and make my way out the door.

As I pull through the iron gates of Windsor Academy, I take a fortifying breath and give myself another pep talk. Maybe yesterday was a one-off.

Perhaps this won't be as bad as it initially seemed on my first day. Oh, who am I kidding? I'm no stranger to entitled teenagers, but I'd swear the students here are worse than any I've ever encountered. I spent all day yesterday feeling like I was under a microscope. Being looked down upon. I lost count of how many times catty girls glared at me or turned their noses up when I smiled at them in greeting.

Not a single person my age spoke to me yesterday. They talked *about* me in not-so-hushed whispers, but never *to* me. Just because I don't have a trust fund waiting to be spent doesn't mean I'm lesser than, but it seems as if these pricks have missed the memo. The class separation struggle is real, yo.

My parents' income is more than decent, but it doesn't go far in Los Angeles, where the cost of living is obscene. We're not poor by any means. We have a lovely home in Woodland Hills, and it's well cared for in a safe neighborhood. But we live in a three-bedroom mid-century modern ranch instead of a grandiose mansion like these assholes. My Audi Q5 is almost ten years old with over a-hundred-K miles, instead of the brand new vehicles valued at a-hundred-K minimum filling the student parking lot. I rode with my dad to school yesterday, so we parked in the teacher's lot, where the vehicles are more comparable to ours. But today, as I'm sliding into a spot next to a matte black it's-so-fancy-I-don't-even-know-what-kind-of-car-it-is, I realize how much my used vehicle sticks out, and not in a good way.

God, this sucks.

I was perfectly happy at Cambridge Prep. Now, in the middle of my senior year, I have to start over. All because my father decided to take a new job at his beloved alma mater. I begged him to let me stay at Cambridge, but he was so in love with the idea of me graduating from the same school as him, he wouldn't cave.

I don't see the big deal; it's only a few months until graduation, and the distance between each school and our house is almost identical. Plus, my annual tuition was already paid in full because my dad got such a steep discount as an employee perk. But he *insisted* I transfer to Windsor anyway, and what my father wants, my father gets.

There are plenty of privileged kids at Cambridge Prep, but the school awards dozens of scholarships each year, so their students come from various backgrounds. According to my dad, Windsor Academy has *never* and likely *will* never offer scholarships to less fortunate kids. The school prides itself on its *selective admission process*, whatever the hell that means. Personally, I think it's a fancy way of saying *we think we're better than you.*

I make a point to keep my chin up as I get out of my car. I take no more than two steps before I'm forced to stop as a silver Porsche 911 Turbo whizzes past me, sliding into the spot on the other side of the black car. "VIBEZ" by DaBaby blasts into the parking lot as the driver opens the door before killing the engine. This douche can't drive, but at least he has good taste in music.

When the driver stands, confirming my assumption it's a dude behind the wheel, he towers over the vehicle, affording me a glimpse of broad shoulders stretching the limits of his white dress shirt. When Idiot Driver turns around to address the guy getting out of the black sports car, I'm frozen for an entirely different reason.

The first thing I think when his captivating brown eyes lock on mine is, *damn, he's pretty.* The second thing is, *oh, my God, I thought I'd never see him again.* And the third, *why does he look like he wants to off me?*

Seriously. Why?

I stand here, dumbfounded, as the guy next to him glances at me over his shoulder before hunching down and saying something to his passenger. I mold my body to my SUV as the strange door opens vertically and a beautiful brunette climbs out. She gives me a brief smile before joining the two guys waiting for her on the other side of the vehicle. Shitty Driver hasn't stopped staring at me this entire time.

Glaring is more like it.

The brunette touches his arm, which breaks his focus as he looks down at her and shakes his head before stomping away. She and the other guy hurry to catch up with him as they walk toward the center building. The same building I'm about to head into since my first class begins in three minutes.

Awesome.

The remaining students still loitering in the parking lot, watch me as I make my way toward Lincoln Hall, turning their noses up as I walk by. What the hell ever. If these people don't want to be my friends, fine. I don't need more anyway. If they think they're better than me simply because they have Mommy or Daddy's Black cards in their wallets, so be it. One thing I won't do, however, is cowering down to them. As long as they don't mess with me, we won't have a problem. If they do... well, let's just say I'm not afraid to stand up for myself.

Thankfully, my class is in the middle of the first hallway, so I don't have to haul ass in heels to beat the tardy bell. The school held an assembly yesterday morning to introduce my father as the new headmaster, so this is the one class I didn't get to attend. Assigned seating seemed to be hit or miss yesterday, so I approach the teacher's desk as soon as I walk into the room.

Fine lines form around her mouth as she smiles. "Welcome to statistics, Miss Carrington."

"Uh, thanks." I tuck an unruly curl behind my ear. "Do you have assigned seating in here, or may I take any desk?"

She inclines her head toward the left. "We do. There's an empty seat with your name on it in the last row, fourth one down."

"Thank you."

I pretend I don't hear the snarky comments as I approach the indicated desk. The brunette from the parking lot is sitting at the desk behind mine, so I give her a small smile while hanging my bag on the chair.

She lightly pokes my shoulder the moment my butt hits the chair. "Hey. I'm Jazz."

I turn around to face her. "Sydney."

She tugs her bottom lip between her teeth. "I know. I was at the assembly yesterday when your dad introduced you."

My face warms when I recall having to stand up

in front of the entire school, trying not to squirm as their eyes looked my way. "Yeah, that was loads of fun. Nothing like being put in a fishbowl on the first day of school." I eye her warily when she chuckles, trying to figure out this chick's intentions. She's being, dare I say, friendly, but I've learned from past experiences that not everything is as it seems. "Jazz, huh? Like the music?"

"It's short for Jasmine."

I nod in understanding. "Ah."

I leave it at that, but the girl doesn't get the hint. I start wondering if I have something in my teeth as she just watches me like she wants to say something, but she's holding herself back.

She mutters a curse before finally speaking again. "Look, Sydney. I know what it's like being the new kid on the block around here. Trust me when I say *it blows*. Most of the people are..."

"Pretentious assholes?" I helpfully supply.

She laughs, and that's when I notice how much attention we've drawn. All of the seats have been filled, and almost every one of their occupants are looking our way. "Yeah. *That.* I told myself I'd stay out of it, but—"

The bell rings, prompting me to face forward, leaving me to wonder what Jazz was going to say. For the next forty-five minutes, I listen to the teacher drone on and on, trying to keep up. Thankfully, the curriculum at my old school was pretty challenging, so it didn't take much effort to figure things out.

As class ends, Jazz drops a folded piece of paper on my desk as she's walking by. "Here."

I nod to the little white square. "What's this?"

"My number." She shifts to the side to avoid being trampled. "I won't take offense if you choose not to use it, but if you want to meet up and talk more at lunch, text me."

With that, she files out of the classroom with the others. When I step into the hall, I spot Jazz across the way, being pulled into a hug by the same guy she rode to school with. He looks familiar, but I can't figure out why. Then again, if you've seen one rich preppy boy, you've seen them all. As if Rich Boy can sense my gaze, he turns his head, immediately homing in on me. I'm not gonna lie; the dude's fine as fuck, but he's also a little scary. Okay, maybe *more* than a little scary. His eyes remain locked on me as he leans down, saying something to Jazz. She looks over her shoulder briefly before turning back to him. Their discussion becomes more animated, and if I'm not mistaken, *heated*. I feel dumb just standing here watching them argue, so I head off toward second period.

There isn't assigned seating in this class, so I take one of the two empty desks in the back and pull out my Chromebook. As I'm typing in my login credentials, someone takes the seat next to me. I glance up out of curiosity and turn to stone when I see who it is.

"Hey." I offer him a shy smile, deciding to be the bigger—a.k.a. less intense—person. "Brantley, right? I'm Sydney. Do you remember me? I mean... from before today?"

His jaw tics as he continues to stare, not saying a word.

We met once at a party sophomore year, but now I'm legitimately wondering if he remembers that. I don't recall everything that happened that evening for reasons that still make me nauseous whenever I think about it, but I *do* remember flirting with him and laughing *a lot* in between some *really great* kisses. He must've been absent yesterday because there's no way I would've missed him. The dude's a walking, talking thirst trap. If he has no recollection of meeting me, I'd be lying if I said I wasn't a bit hurt. I really thought we vibed that night. I've thought about him more than a few times over the last two years, disappointed with myself for walking away without getting his number.

Brantley still hasn't replied, so I wave my hand in front of his face. "Um... hello? Did you hear me?"

He's still staring at me like he's cursing my existence.

What's this guy's problem?

"Rude much?" I face forward, trying to figure out what the hell is going on. "O-kay, then. Never mind. Forget I said anything."

"It's *Bent*ley," he finally grits out. "Not *Brant*ley."

Is that why he's so salty? Because I bruised his precious ego by getting the name wrong? Geez, buddy, give me a break; I was close enough.

"Yeah, uh-huh," I mutter. "Sorry to bother you, *Bent*ley. Won't happen again."

I can feel his gaze drilling into me, which is equal parts arousing and irritating. Ugh. Infuriatingly sexy jerk. Why do I have to be so attracted to him?

"Good." He scoffs, lowering his voice. "See to it that it doesn't. I'm over my whore phase, so it's a lost cause, sweetheart."

My head snaps to the side. "*Excuse me?!* Did you just call me a *whore?*" My volume matches his, but I make sure the quietness of it in no way reduces the rage infusing my tone.

The jackass shrugs. "If the loose pussy fits..."

My jaw drops. "Who in the hell do you think you are?"

"Didn't we just cover this?" Bentley gives me a snide smirk. "Since you're obviously a little slow, I'll indulge you one last time. It's *Bentley*. Try not to scream my name when you're working later. I'm sure whatever loser is paying you might take offense."

My nails bite into my palms as I clench my fists, trying to incinerate him with my eyeballs. This asshole doesn't shy away from my contempt one bit. In fact, he seems amused by it, which only makes me angrier. By the time I have enough of a leash on my fury to respond, the bell rings, indicating the start of class.

Throughout the rest of the period, I do my best to ignore the prick on my left and pay attention to our lesson, which is, ironically, on human behavior and sexual attraction. It's pointless, though, because I can't stop wondering why Bentley is being so mean to me. I can't help feeling like I did something wrong, but my brain won't produce a single thing that would warrant his hostility. Maybe he's just a jerk by nature. Maybe the charisma he exhibited during that party was bolstered by my inebriation and dicey memory. Hell, maybe he has a twin named Brantley, and he's sick of being mistaken for his brother. That last one is a little farfetched, but what the hell do I know?

I watch the clock, waiting for the moment when I can get out of here. I plan on bolting the second the bell rings, but the dick next to me beats me to it. He's out of his seat before anyone else, storming toward the door like his ass is on fire.

And what a fine ass it is. Goddammit! Shut it, stupid hormones.

Fuck. Why do I suddenly get the feeling I just opened a giant can of asshole-ish worms?

chapter three

BENTLEY

By the time lunch hits, I feel like I'm crawling out of my skin. I really need a joint, or a drink, or anything that will help me chill the fuck out. I consider finding someone to blow me in an empty classroom—because, let's face it, it wouldn't be difficult to find a willing female—but that only lasts half a second before I remind myself that easy pussy no longer has that effect on me. Quite frankly, it never really did, but I pretended otherwise a lot longer than I should've so people wouldn't ask questions. So they wouldn't dig too deep. So they wouldn't *see*.

People expect me to be the joker. The flirt. The one who's always down to fuck or get wasted. They definitely don't want to hang out with the loser who feels like he's floating aimlessly through life. The asshole who's insanely jealous of his best friends for finding their soul mates. The man who's responsible for killing the only girl he's ever loved.

The guy who, most days, wishes he died instead.

"Fuck," I mutter, scrubbing my hands down my face.

"Bent! Hold up."

I pause mid-stride when I hear my buddy Kingston's voice. I turn around to find him and Reed, my other brother from another mother. They're both eyeing me cautiously like they're about to start psychoanalyzing me or some shit. That's one downfall of having someone in your life who knows you so well. I'm convinced these fuckers can read my mind more often than not, and sometimes, that doesn't work in my favor. Especially on days like today, when I'm feeling extra unhinged.

I lift my chin in greeting. "Whassup?"

Kingston inclines his head to the right. "Why don't we grab lunch off campus today? Just the three of us."

I narrow my eyes. "Why?"

Now, don't get me wrong, I'm always down for off-campus lunch, especially if we're heading to In-N-Out, but the fact that Jazz and Ainsley aren't coming along is suspicious as fuck.

"What do you mean, why?" Reed grabs on to the back of his neck. "Because we're hungry."

My eyebrows lift, not believing that bullshit answer one bit. "What about the girls?"

"What about 'em?" Kingston shrugs. "They're perfectly capable of getting their own food."

Okay, now I *know* something is up. Kingston Davenport would spend every waking moment with Jazz if it were up to him. Shit, they're already shacking up, playing mommy and daddy to her little sister, yet he still can't get enough. I one-hundo-percent believe he would surgically attach himself to her if it were possible. I can't exactly blame him; Jazz Rivera is pretty fucking spectacular, and God knows they've had their share of challenges to get to this point. But still, the dude's eighteen going on forty, and he couldn't be happier about it.

I flip him off. "Fuck off, dude. Why don't you tell me what's *really* going on? Better yet, do it while we're standing in line because I skipped breakfast and need to eat. We're already late; our food options are getting slimmer and slimmer the longer we stand here."

Kingston pulls on the back of my blazer when I start walking toward the dining hall. "C'mon, Bent. I'll explain on the drive."

I shake him off. "What's your problem, bro? I

don't *want* to go for a drive. I want to fucking *eat*." I point to the double doors ten feet away. "And there's a ton of bomb-ass food right behind those doors."

"Bentley, *don't* go in there. Not without being prepared." It's my other friend who speaks up this time, and considering Reed Prescott is not a man who says *anything* without reason, it gives me pause.

I lean back against the polished mahogany lockers and cross my arms over my chest. "Well? Are either one of you going to explain?"

Both guys share a loaded glance. I'm guessing Davenport drew the proverbial short straw because he gets a strange look on his face right before dropping the bomb.

"Jazz invited someone to have lunch at our table. A chick from her first-period class."

"And?" I don't see the problem. The dining hall tables seat eight, and there are only five of us combined.

Kingston pulls on the ends of his dirty blond hair, something he does when he's agitated. "*And*, it's someone you don't want to be around. I told Jazz to stay out of it, but... I'm sure you can imagine how well that went."

I stare him down, decoding his cryptic statement. When it hits me, I start marching toward the doors. "Oh, fuck no." I shoot him an accusatory glare. "Tell me she didn't do what I think she did, dawg."

Kingston's reply isn't necessary because, in the next moment, the three of us are stepping into the dining hall, and I have a clear view of our table. Like every day, Ainsley and Jazz are sitting there eating lunch, but today, a third person is occupying the chair to Jazz's right. The chair where I usually sit. I watch in shock as the three girls chat about who knows what, smiling and laughing as if they've been besties for years.

My teeth are grinding together so hard, I'm surprised they're not cracking. "What. The. Fuck."

Kingston throws his arm out when I charge forward, blocking me. "Calm down, dude. You don't want to go over there half-cocked and cause a scene."

"The fuck I don't." I scoff. "I love Jazzy to death, man, but you and I both know she crossed a line, and I'm not going to stand here pretending like it's fucking okay! What was she thinking?"

"She was thinking about how bad it sucks to be the new girl, and..." Kingston nods to them. "It seems like they're getting along pretty well. You know Jazz, nor Ains, have much luck making female friends."

"Yeah, because most of the girls here are jealous, petty bitches," Reed offers.

As if they can sense us, all three sets of eyes turn our way. When Ainsley and Jazz spot their significant others, they smile brightly before shifting their concerned gazes to me. The third girl narrows her gorgeous eyes when she notices my glare.

Jesus. Did I really just compliment her?

At least I kept that shit inside my head, but still. I don't like it. This bitch is the enemy. I can't afford to forget that.

"Fuck this." I shake my head. "I'm out."

"Dude, wait!" Kingston calls.

Both assholes follow me down the main hall.

Reed curses under his breath. "Bent, you can't keep taking off every time you see her. You won't graduate."

Yesterday, when I first spotted Sydney at the assembly, I couldn't get the fuck out of Dodge fast enough. I needed time to process the deluge of memories that assaulted me.

"For the record, I had to sit *right next to her* during second period, and I didn't take off then." I slam my palms against the heavy wooden doors that lead to the parking lot. "I know I can't do anything about the fact that she's here, especially considering who her father is. And when I saw her in the parking lot this morning, I was prepared to suck it up and deal."

But when I sat next to her in psych class, I remembered how she's even more beautiful up close. How easy it can be to get lost in her sea-green eyes, fascinated by how they stand out against her light brown skin. Of how she's the one person on Earth who knows exactly why I hate myself so much.

I shake my head, stuffing that line of thought to the back recesses of my brain where it belongs.

"Bent—" Kingston starts to say.

I hold my hand up to cut him off. "If Jazz insists on inviting Sydney-fucking-Carrington to our party of five, you can count me out. It's her or me."

Kingston's lips thin. "Dude. That's not fair."

I open my car door, looking him dead in the eye. "I can't do it, man. Look. I'm not trying to put you in a difficult situation, but I just *can't*. So, do whatever you need to do to make Jazz and Ainsley understand. If you can't... well, I don't fucking know. Just figure out a way to make 'em understand. *Please, Davenport.*"

I don't like the way my throat clogs on that last sentence.

His eyes bounce between mine for a moment before he nods. "I'll try."

I slide behind the wheel and start the ignition. "I'll be back. I need... I just need to breathe for a minute."

I peel through the gates of Windsor with no real destination in mind. I roll down my windows, allowing the breeze to hit my face as I speed through the winding roads, cornering much faster than I probably should. I know what this fine piece of German machinery is capable of, though, and despite how miserable I am most days, I'm not suicidal. I would *never* dishonor Carissa's memory like that. I just hate living with this crushing guilt day in and day out. I honestly don't know how much more I can take without losing my fucking mind.

When I realize where I'm at, I pull off on the side of the road and kill the engine. It fucking figures I'd end up here without thinking. Thankfully, I always keep a bag of athletic clothing in the trunk in case I get an itch to play ball. Using my car as a shield to quickly change out of my uniform, I make the short hike over the dirt trail that leads to Topanga Lookout. As my feet hang off the edge of the colorful platform, I look down, remembering the last time I was here. Rissa loved hiking around Los Angeles, and I loved seeing her skin glistening in tiny workout clothes, so I'd join her any chance I could get. This place was one of her favorites. We sat in this very spot, watching the sun setting over the valley only a few days before everything went to hell. Before life as we knew it would never be the same.

Before I met Sydney Carrington... the catalyst that set everything in motion.

chapter four

SYDNEY

As the beginning notes of Hozier's "Take Me to Church" thrums through my veins, I inhale deeply, inviting the haunting melody into my soul. My muscles are infused with the emotion of the lyrics, prompting my limbs to move on their own accord in a series of long lines, leaps, twists, and twirls. I tell a story with my body of oppression and irreverence. Resentment and shame. Sensuality and longing for intimacy.

This is why lyrical is my favorite style of dance. You're combining the grace and athleticism of ballet with the fluidity of jazz, but you're doing so in a way that conveys the passion behind the song. To properly execute the choreography, you need to pour your heart into it. Your soul needs to *bleed* onto that stage. If you're hyper-focused on technique, you're missing the most essential part. You're missing the key component that breathes life into the dance.

When the song ends, I take a moment to collect myself before standing to address my small audience.

"So? What'd you think?"

"It's *perfect*, Syd," my best friend, Cameron, assures me. Her blonde ponytail swishes from side to side as she bounces on the balls of her feet. "There's *no way* the Los Angeles School of Performing Arts won't accept you after *that* audition."

My eyes flicker to my mom. "What about you?"

My mother presses an open palm to her chest, her dark skin contrasting beautifully against the pale pink of her leotard. "It was absolutely stunning." She holds her forearm parallel to the vinyl floor, showing me the fine hairs standing to attention. "Look. I have goose bumps. You should use it for your solo during our spring recital."

I grab a hand towel off the nearby stool and wipe my face. "Yeah, maybe."

My mom was a professional ballerina—a rather

successful one at that—but when a freak accident resulted in several shattered bones and subsequent surgeries, she retired and moved back to California, eventually opening this studio. I've been studying here since I learned how to walk. My strengths definitely lie in lyrical, hip-hop, and jazz, but I'm not too shabby with ballet or polyrhythmic tribal dance either.

Despite my natural talent, I have no desire to join a professional company. I don't know... maybe it's because I've seen firsthand how demanding it is on your body. Knowing what my mom went through, the time commitment and sacrifices she made, how her lifelong dreams were ripped away in an instant at the height of her career... it doesn't seem worth it to me. Don't get me wrong; I *love* to dance, but teaching and choreography are where my true joy comes from. I want to attend the LASPA simply for the esteem a degree from such a reputable academy would give me when I want to take over this studio one day, or maybe work behind the scenes on movie and television sets.

A bell dings over the lobby door. Through the large observation windows, I can see students arriving for the next class. My mom teaches barre for adults on Tuesday evenings because it's a popular form of exercise, and she says you have to diversify.

"Duty calls," my mom singsongs as she shoos Cam and me out of the room. "Why don't you two go have dinner or something? I can shut everything down when class is over."

I raise my brows. "Are you sure?"

"Yep," my mom insists. "Everything else is already taken care of for the night. I'll lock the front door after the last student arrives, and as soon as class ends, I'll be following them out to the parking lot."

"Okay." I bend over to kiss her on the cheek. I definitely take after my dad when it comes to height. "Thanks, Mom. I'll see you at home."

She smiles. "Bye, girls."

I hit the button on my key fob to unlock my car. "What do you feel like eating?"

Cam shrugs. "Sushi?"

I nod. "That works."

Our favorite sushi place is located in a nearby outdoor mall, so we hop in my Audi and make the short drive from Woodland Hills to Calabasas, rapping along with Megan Thee Stallion and Queen Bey about being a savage.

"Bitch, you my boo," we both point at each

other, half-singing, half-laughing like we always do when it gets to that part in the song.

When we arrive at the restaurant, Cam and I order several different cut rolls and start chowing down the moment the plates hit the table.

"So, how was your second day?" Cameron asks through a mouthful of crab.

"Better, I guess. I made a couple of friends." I frown. "I think."

She chuckles. "What do you mean, you *think*?"

I sigh. "These two girls, Ainsley and Jazz, the former of which is really into ballet. You should've seen her when I told her who my mom was. She totally fangirled. It was adorable. She's actually applying to the LASPA like me. Overall, they both seem pretty chill. It was refreshing to find other students who don't perpetually have their noses in the air."

"What's the problem then?"

I think about how to explain it. "Do you remember that frat party I went to sophomore year? The one where my cousin, Lindsey, um... you know."

Cam gets a disgusted look on her face. "God, I hate that skank. I'm sorry; I know you're related to her, but what she did was completely unforgivable, Syd."

"You're preaching to the choir, girl. Whenever we're at the same gathering, I go out of my way to avoid her, so I don't *accidentally* punch her in the throat and have to explain to my entire family why."

She takes a sip of water. "Why are we talking about crazy relatives anyway? How does that relate to my question about your new school?"

I bite my lip. "Because... the two girls I mentioned earlier seem to be good friends with the guy I made out with at that party."

Her blue eyes widen. "Isn't that a good thing? That means you know who he is now. I thought you said he was hella fine."

"He is. Even hotter than I remembered. God, *so*, so hot. But... no, it's *not* a good thing." I shake my head. "Brother's got anger issues. For whatever reason, he's giving off major hate vibes. Like, *major*, major."

A crease forms between Cameron's light brown eyebrows. "Why?"

"Your guess is as good as mine." I dab some wasabi on my roll and pop it in my mouth. "He's in my psych class, and he was so freakin' mean this morning. I just said hello, asked if he remembered me, and he instantly went into douchecanoe mode. Legit called me a whore."

Cam gasps. "What?!"

I nod. "I know, right?"

Cam waves her hand dismissively. "So, the guy's a jerk. Whatev. Fuck him. That doesn't mean you can't be friends with some of his friends."

I point my chopsticks at her. "See, that's the thing. I think it might. I haven't quite figured out the Windsor hierarchy yet, but I get the impression that Hella Fine Party Guy—his name is Bentley, by the way—is top tier. I didn't want to seem weird and ask Jazz or Ainsley, but I can tell he's someone important. You should've seen how the other students watched him and his friends. Plus, the boy's got swagger. I saw him in the hall between third and fourth periods. He walks around like he's got the biggest D in the joint and doesn't give a shit what anyone thinks about him."

Cam wiggles her brows. "*Does* he have the biggest D in the joint?"

"We made out *one* time *years* ago." I give her a wry look. "Do you really think I'd know whether or not he's packing?"

"It was worth a shot." She shrugs. "I still don't understand why you had to transfer to that place."

"My mom and I tried talking him out of it, but you know how relentless my dad can be when he gets an idea in his head."

Cam pouts. "Well, I miss you. *Everyone* misses you."

"I'm sure Olivia doesn't miss me *at all*."

She scrunches her pert nose. "Well, that bitch can eat a bag of dicks with a side of sweaty, hairy balls."

I laugh. "Thanks for that colorful—and disgusting—visual."

Cameron winks. "Anytime, babe."

"Enough about me. What's new with you?"

"Um... my mom has a new boyfriend again, but I haven't met him yet. We're supposed to have dinner with him and his kids tomorrow night. Woo-freaking-hoo." She waves her imaginary pom-poms in the air.

I raise my brows. "Didn't she *just* break up with that Darren guy?"

"She claims this one is *special*." Her baby blues roll back as if she doesn't believe that one bit. "I guess they used to date in high school or something, but they lost touch. Evidently, he's *the one that got away*. Who knows with her? She could be grabbing on to the first dude who made eye contact. You know my mom doesn't feel complete without a man in her life."

I shake my head. "Bitch slap me silly if I ever get like that."

Cam's dad has been out of the picture her whole life. The poor girl's had to watch her mom suffer through one toxic relationship after another, simply because she's deathly afraid of being alone.

"Fabulous example she's setting, right?" Cam mockingly raises her voice a few octaves. "You can be anything you want, Cameron. The sky's the limit... as long as you have a man who'll take care of you."

When Cameron and I were thirteen, we made a vow we would never be like her mom. That we would grow into strong, fierce women who didn't take shit from anyone. Thankfully, we had *my* mom to lead us in the right direction. Daphne Reynolds knew she wanted to be a dancer from a very young age, but the odds were stacked against her as a Black girl from Compton, raised by a single mother who was barely making ends meet. But she refused to believe she couldn't do anything she set her mind to.

My mom didn't even receive formal dance instruction until she won a scholarship to a performing arts academy based solely on raw talent and determination. That's where she worked longer and harder than anyone else to perfect her craft. And when Juilliard came calling, she leaped at the opportunity, which eventually led to a prestigious career with the New York Ballet.

"Well... good luck tomorrow night. I hope it's not too much of a shit show."

Cameron laughs. "Thanks. You going to Skyler Roosevelt's party with me on Friday?"

"She's the junior that lives in Malibu, right? The one with the red hair?"

"Yep." Cam nods. "I heard her house is pretty sick and right on the beach."

"Do you know if Zach will be there?" I take one final bite and lean back in my chair, waiting for her answer.

She scrunches her face. "Would it be a deal-breaker if I said yes?"

"No." I shake my head. "I just want to be prepared."

Cam straightens in her chair. "Yeah, I'm pretty sure he will be. I heard Austin and Sky are smashing."

"Fine," I sigh. "But I won't hold my tongue if that dipshit begs me to take him back again."

Zach Harper is my ex who refuses to accept he's been canceled, and Austin McCarthy is his boy. One rarely goes somewhere without the other.

"Do you *ever* hold your tongue?"

My lips curve. "Every once in a while."

She snorts. "Sure, Syd. Whatever you say."

"Oh, screw you, bitch." I flip her off, laughing.

"Hey! You should invite your new friends. It'd be a good opportunity for me to see if they pass inspection."

"I guess it wouldn't hurt to ask." I shrug.

"Okay, it's settled then." Cam dabs the corner of her mouth with a napkin. "You ask the Windsor girls if they want to come, and then figure out what you're going to wear that'll make Zach Harper rue the day he decided to be a two-timing sleaze."

"Did you really just say, 'rue the day'?"

"I sure as shit did." She gives me a, *what are you gonna do about it?* look.

I chuckle. "God, I love you."

"I love you too, bitch." Cam smiles. "I'll love you even more if you get the check. I don't get paid until Friday."

I shake my head as I dig out enough cash to cover the bill. "Fine. But you're getting the next one, and I am *not* accepting Taco Bell."

"You're so high maintenance." She sticks her tongue out. "You're lucky you have a great rack, or I wouldn't put up with your crap."

I roll my napkin into a ball and throw it at her. "You're such a little shit!"

"You wouldn't know what to do without me." Cameron beams, showing off her pearly whites.

She is right, though. Cam was my lifeline when I was going through some pretty tough shit. I would be lost without this girl in my life.

chapter
five

BENTLEY

Fucking great. Just what I need to top off this shitastic day. I take a deep breath as I pull up next to the white Range Rover sitting in my circular driveway. My shoulders stiffen when its driver gets out and leans against the car. My headlights are shining right at her, so I can see the pity on her face as she waits for me to exit my vehicle. I don't want anyone's pity, especially *this* girl's.

She's the strongest, most resilient person I've ever met. There was a time when I thought she'd be the one to pull me out of my guilt-laden misery. I thought I was falling in love with her and that maybe she could one day feel the same. Then, after one of the hottest nights of my life, I knew I never had a shot because the woman is head-over-heels-no-turning-back in love with my best friend, and he feels the same about her.

I push the button to kill the engine and climb out of my Porsche, ready to face the music, no pun intended.

"What are you doing here, Jazz? I'm pretty sure it's against the rules to drive alone with a learner's permit."

"Kingston didn't tell you? I got my license on Saturday."

I shake my head. "Believe it or not, Davenport doesn't tell me everything."

"It doesn't matter anyway." She shifts a little on her feet. "Can we talk?"

I scoff. "I'd rather not."

I can see the crestfallen look on her face under the outdoor lighting, and I have to remind myself not to let it get to me.

"Bentley, please."

I shake my head. "Not tonight, Jazzy. I can't do this right now."

The girl's easily a foot shorter than me, but she looks awfully mighty when she stands tall and levels me with a glare. "I wasn't going to pull this card, Bentley, but you're forcing my hand. I seem to remember giving *you* a chance to plead your case when you'd given me no reason to. You could at least afford me the same courtesy."

Goddammit.

I hate it when she's right, which, let's face it, is almost always.

I release a harsh breath. "Fine, but I need a smoke, so let's go out back."

Jazz nods and follows me down the path along the side of the house. I lead her around the pool into the private grotto that houses our hot tub. The only lighting back here is the soft blue glow from under the water, so it's perfect.

"What are you doing?" Jazz asks the second I start stripping off my clothes.

"Relax, Jazzy Jazz. I'm not trying to seduce you; just wanna take a dip." I dig the small metal case and a lighter out of my pocket before dropping my pants. "I'll even leave my boxers on to protect your precious virtue."

"I think we both know that ship sailed a while ago, Bent."

I smirk. "Nah, baby, I don't think so. You're still a good person. You just like to get dirty every now and then. Nothing wrong with that."

Jazz smiles softly as she removes her shoes and socks and pushes her joggers up above her knees before taking a seat on the ground, dipping her feet into the hot tub. She watches me while I stick a pre-roll in my mouth and light it up. My head falls back on the ledge as I exhale, willing the weed to do its thing sooner rather than later. I'm gonna need it for this conversation.

"No, I'm good." Jazz shakes her head when I offer the joint to her. "Can I talk now?"

I take another hit and wave my hand dismissively. "Might as well, since I know you're not leaving without saying what you came here to say."

"First of all, I'm sorry for inviting Sydney to lunch, Bent. I really am because I knew it would bother you, but I need you to listen to my thought process behind why I did it."

I hold the smoke in my lungs a little bit longer on the third hit, which is when my buzz finally kicks in. I close my eyes as my head falls back to the concrete again and wait for her to continue.

"When I saw how the Windsor assholes were treating her, I couldn't just sit by and not say something. Look, I know you hardly remember the night you met her, or whatever, but she seems really cool. You obviously saw something in Sydney if you hooked up with her. I think if you just gave her a chance—"

I hold my hand up. "I'm gonna stop you right

there, Jazzy. If I saw *anything* in her that night, it was a pair of great tits and blow job lips. That's it. I'm *never* gonna give Sydney Carrington a chance. I don't want her in my life."

"Why not?"

Because I wasn't nearly as fucked up as people think I was, and I remember *everything* about the night we met.

I shake my head. "It doesn't matter."

"The hell it doesn't, Bent!" Jazz throws her hands up. "You've gotta give me something better than that because I like her, and Ainsley does, too. We want to hang out with Sydney and get to know her better."

"How nice for you two." I scoff. "If that *like* happens to turn into a little three-way pussy licking, I wouldn't be opposed to watching some video footage, but I'm still not going anywhere near Sydney-fucking-Carrington."

"Don't be a dick, Bent."

"Aw, what's the matter, baby? Are you getting tired of playing house? My boy not taking care of your needs?" I grab my dick through my shorts, which is admittedly getting hard from the hot girl threesome I just planted in my head. "You know, if you want some of this, all you gotta do is ask. We don't even have to tell Kingston. I know you've been gagging for it ever since—"

I'm not even surprised when Jazz kicks her foot, spraying water all over my face, extinguishing my blunt. I know that shit was over the line, and I honestly didn't mean a word of it, but I couldn't seem to help myself.

She points a stern finger at me. "I'm gonna let that slide because I know you're hurting, but don't think you can get away with it again. *Not* cool, Bentley." Jazz sighs heavily. "Sydney told us how you behaved in second period today. What you called her."

I try lighting the soggy joint again, but it's a lost cause, so I toss it on the ground. "Nice to know she's a narc on top of being a lying whore."

"C'mon, Bentley." Jazz throws her hands up. "This isn't you! What's going on inside that head of yours that's making you act this way?"

Fuck. Sometimes I hate how perceptive she is. Jazz can see straight through someone's bullshit from a mile away.

"Why don't we cut the crap, and you can just tell me what you want from me, then? *What the fuck* do you want from me, Jazz?"

Jazz scoots her ass along the concrete until she's sitting right next to me. "I want you to talk to me,

Bentley. If not me, Kingston or Reed, or hell, even a therapist. You can't keep blaming yourself—or Sydney—for Carissa's death."

I give her a sardonic laugh. "The fuck, I can't."

"Quit being such a stubborn ass." She reaches out and pinches me really hard.

"Ow!" I rub my arm, narrowing my eyes. "What the hell?"

The ends of her chocolate-colored hair dip into the water as she bends down far enough to get in my face. "Listen to me, Bentley. I know what Carissa experienced was awful, and no one should *ever* have to go through something like that. But regardless of what happened the night of that frat party, it's not your fault. Carissa's death was on her. Not you. Not Sydney. Not anyone but *her*."

I look away, hating the pussy-ass tears welling in my eyes. "You weren't there, Jazz. You have no idea what you're talking about."

She tries turning my chin toward her, but I resist. After a few failed attempts, Jazz curses, tosses her keys on the ground, and steps into the water fully clothed, right in front of me.

"Goddammit, Bentley, look at me!"

When I finally turn my gaze in her direction, I see that she looks almost as broken as I feel. "Baby girl—"

She holds her hand up, cutting me off. *"Don't you dare* tell me I don't understand because you *know* I do. My mom died because she was trying to do something good for me. If she would've never come to see my father that day... she would no doubt still be on this earth. At least I had almost eighteen years with her. Belle didn't even get *half* that, and now, she never will. Do you think I don't feel guilty every time I look at my sister? Every time she asks me questions about growing up with our mom because even though it's only been six months, she's so young, she's already forgetting? I'm doing the best that I can, but that's something I'll have to live with for the rest of my life."

"Jazz—"

"Shut up. I'm not done." She narrows her brown eyes at me. "Now, taking all of that into consideration, taking the emotion out of it, I *know* I couldn't have done anything to prevent it. My mom's decisions were her own, and there were consequences for her actions. *Really shitty consequences.* Regardless, it was *her* decision that led to her death, just like Carissa's decision led to hers. Stop being such a goddamned martyr, Bentley."

I shake my head. "It's not that easy."

Jazz pulls me into her, and since I'm sitting on the bench and she's standing, my head rests against her abdomen. "I never said it was easy, Bent. But you've gotta stop torturing yourself. And you've gotta stop taking it out on a girl who doesn't deserve it."

I wrap my arms around her waist and hold on tight because, sometimes, you just need a hug, and this is one of those times. I know Jazz is trying to make me feel better, but she doesn't really understand because she doesn't know the whole truth. None of them do. And I'm scared to fucking death that if Sydney Carrington tells them what really happened that night, they'd realize that I'm not a martyr. That my guilt isn't unwarranted.

That I'm the fucking villain in this story.

chapter six

TWO YEARS EARLIER

BENTLEY

"Holy shit."

Goddamn, she's fine as fuck.

Reed follows my gaze, taking in the group of sorority girls standing against the opposite wall. "What?"

I take a swig from my bottle of beer, seemingly unable to tear my eyes away. "The one wearing the Delta Pi top. That girl is straight fire."

"Absolutely." He nods. "You gonna go for it?"

I shrug. "I don't see why not. I mean, according to Rissa, this is what I *should* be doing, right?"

Physically speaking, the Delta Pi girl is pretty much the exact opposite of Carissa. The petty part of me wants her even more because of it. Every dude Carissa has ever hooked up with besides me has had light features with a California surfer vibe. Sometimes, I seriously question whether or not that's the type of guy she's really attracted to, which is the real reason she refuses to be in a monogamous relationship with me.

I am way too sober to handle the sympathetic look he gives me. "Dude——"

I shake my head. "No way, bruh. None of that shit tonight. I'm here to get fucked up and have a little fun. I'ma go talk to her. Why don't you come with me? You know, the little brunette to her right sorta looks like Ain——"

"Don't fucking say it, man." Reed's eyes narrow.

I laugh. "What's the problem, buddy? It's not like she's *actually* her, so you wouldn't be breaking any of your lame-ass rules."

Reed downs the rest of his beer and kicks off the wall. "Okay, fine. Let's do this."

I dig the little baggie out of my pocket and pull out a capsule. Reed lifts his eyebrows in question as I swallow one.

"Molly," I explain, holding the bag out to him. "Care to partake, fine sir?"

He reaches into the baggie and retrieves a pill. "Where'd you get this?"

I nod to Grady Anderson, the future politician-looking douchebag standing in the corner. I met him last year through a mutual friend at Windsor. I was shocked when I found out what he does for a living. I swear the dude's a genius with that cover. Who would ever suspect *him* of supplying high schoolers throughout the greater LA area with the finest illegal substances? He's got the innocent pretty boy look on lock. Whatever your pleasure may be, Grady, or one of his popped-collar associates, can usually hook you up.

Reed nods in understanding. "I didn't realize he was hitting up frat parties now, too."

I shrug. "Guess so."

Or, I *may* have mentioned to Grady that I was coming here and that he could make some serious bank if he did the same. What can I say? It saved me the extra stop.

I incline my head toward our targets. "C'mon, man. We've got some pretty girls to talk to."

I pause mid-stride when I get close enough to see Hot Girl's gorgeous eyes. She's obviously a mixture of races like me—I'm guessing two of my three—but where my brown eyes are several shades darker than my skin, her eyes are significantly lighter, the bright bluish-green color giving them an almost ethereal effect. I've never seen a color quite like it before. Not on a human being anyway.

"Did you know your eyes are the exact color of the tropical ocean where blue bleeds into green?"

"What?" She laughs.

I scratch the side of my head, feeling like a complete dipshit. "Uh..."

I usually have much better game than this. Reed must be wondering the same thing because his lips are twitching as he's working the cute brunette like he's trying not to laugh at my stupid ass. What the hell is wrong with me? Maybe it's because I've never hooked up with a college chick before.

Well, that's changing tonight if I have anything to say about it.

"You said something about my eyes, but it came out so quickly, I'm not sure if I heard you correctly." Said eyes twinkle with amusement as she takes a sip from her red Solo cup.

Damn, even her voice is sexy. It's undoubtedly feminine but also a little raspy.

Instead of repeating my statement, my eyes slowly peruse her body, making my interest crystal clear. The top of her head is level with my mouth, so based on my six-foot-three, she's well above average height for a girl. She legitimately has one of the most unique and prettiest faces I've ever seen.

No girl has *ever* competed with Rissa in my eyes as far as beauty goes. But... why does this chick feel like the exception?

Because she is, the voice in the back of my head says. *She's absolutely stunning.*

I have an irrational urge to kiss the scattering of freckles that run across the bridge of her nose. My eyes continue their exploration, roaming over high cheekbones, a pert nose, and plump lips that are *made* for sucking cock. I have to will my dick to calm down when my gaze dips below her delicate collarbone to a pair of more-than-a-handful tits. I'm almost positive they're real because she's not rail thin like most girls I encounter in LA. This girl's painted-on jeans do nothing to hide her thick thighs and hips, for which I am incredibly thankful. She's fit, as evidenced by her toned arms and the little slice of rock-hard abs peeking out from the hem of her white tank, but she's certainly got curves I'm dying to explore.

"Hello?" She waves her hand in front of my face. "Anyone home?"

I finally pull out of the weird trance she had me under and flash my signature panty-melting grin. "What's your name, beautiful?"

She laughs at me again, which is *not* the reaction I usually get when hitting on someone.

"Wow... so, that's the approach you're going with, huh?"

I frown. "I'm not following."

"Well, first the cheesy comment about my eyes..." She rolls the eyes in question. "Then, instead of course correcting and coming up with something a little more original, you decide to go with, '*What's your name, beautiful?*'" She gives me a quick once over. "You're fine; I'll give you that. But I'm not interested in chillin' with someone who has a big vacancy sign hanging between his ears. Sorry, bud."

After giving me a condescending pat on the cheek, she spins around, giving me a fantastic view of her perfectly heart-shaped ass as she walks toward the kitchen area.

I stand there, slack-jawed, processing what just happened. I don't snap out of it until Reed—*perpetually stoic Reed*—starts howling in laughter.

I turn my head toward him. "Did she just... call me a moron?"

Reed nods. "She sure did. I like her."

I flip him off. "Oh, screw you, man. I didn't exactly see you scoring either."

"That's because your pathetic bumbling was distracting me. What's the deal, man? I've never seen you act so nervous around a girl before."

"Fuck if I know." I scoff, pulling my mini pipe and a bag of flower out of my pocket. "Whatever. College chicks are hell on the ego. I need a smoke."

Reed laughs again. "Christ, Bent, how many varieties of drugs are you smuggling?"

I give him a wry look. "Keep it up, and I won't share."

He puts his hands up in surrender. "I take it back."

"Uh-huh."

I look around the room, searching for the other people we came here with. I'm pretty sure I make a face when I spot Kingston and his girlfriend, Peyton, sitting on the couch arguing about something. I can't hear them, but her flailing arms and Kingston's glare are pretty good indicators their conversation is far from pleasant. God, I seriously hate that bitch.

Kingston's going through some crazy shit right now, so all he does lately is get fucked up, fight in this underground circuit he found, or fuck. Peyton *is* smokin' hot, and from what I hear, down for virtually anything in bed, so I suppose she's suitable for the latter if nothing else. I'm not sure that would even be worth dealing with her high-maintenance ass, though. Have I mentioned how much I hate her?

After my lovely pals, Molly and Mary Jane, kick in, I'm in a much better mood than when I got here. In fact, I'd go as far as to say I'm feeling *pretty fucking good*. Reed and I have been lounging on the couch for the last thirty minutes or so while a different set of sorority girls show off their lap dancing skills. I can't say I hate the attention per se, but I can barely manage more than a semi despite how many asses grind against my lap. That suddenly changes when I spot Lil' Miss Attitude in the middle of the crowded room, busting out some hella impressive hip-hop moves.

"Dayum, girl knows how to shake what her mama gave her," I mumble under my breath.

"What's that, sexy?" Drunk Chick Number One asks, using a whiny baby voice. "Did you say something?"

I pat her hip. "Nah, baby. But while I have your attention, why don't you turn around and shift just a little to the left?"

She doesn't even question it, giving me her back before she resumes twerking over my denim-clad cock. As Drunk Girl does her thing, I watch Pretty Eyes rub up against her cute friend from earlier. They both look like they're enjoying the high life as well, sporting glazed eyes and perma-grins as they dance with one another. When the song switches to

"Skin" by Rihanna, I spring off the couch faster than should be possible with all the weed in my system. I barely notice Twerky Tina bitching at me from her spot on the floor.

I'm across the room in a few long strides, sliding into position behind Pretty Eyes. She stiffens when I bracket her hips with my hands and press my front to her back, but it's only a matter of seconds before her body molds to mine. We move our hips in time with the beat for a few moments before I lower my mouth to her ear.

"You gonna tell me your name?"

I'm fairly certain she just moaned, but it's a little too loud in here to be sure.

"Mmm... you keep moving like that, and I just might." She turns her head back and flashes a toothy smile. "Show me what you've got."

I smirk. "Gladly, honey."

Kingston and Reed give me shit for it all the time, but I love dancing at parties because I can move, and I know damn well girls relate that to sex. It's a preview, if you will, of how much I'm going to rock their world when our clothes come off. I like to think I'm a bit ahead of my time in that regard because I haven't failed to deliver yet. It hasn't even been two years since Riss and I punched each other's V-cards, but I watch a lot of porn, and I've had a lot of practice. There's not much in this world I enjoy more than getting a girl off.

My hands wander over her body, careful not to directly touch any of the really good parts, but *fuck*, I want to. I don't think I've ever danced with someone so tall before, but when she backs up, and my dick is suddenly nestled between firm ass cheeks instead of someone's back, I can't complain. God, this girl and I are so perfectly in sync, it's unreal. I've never had such an instant connection with someone, and we've barely spoken a word. I can tell she's enjoying it just as much as I am. Possibly even more.

I don't get this with Rissa. As obsessed as she is with ballet, it's the *only* kind of dancing she likes. Carissa has no interest in anything that involves moving in time with a beat or simply going with the flow of the moment. She's all about gracefully extended limbs, perfectly executed twirls, and carefully crafted choreography. There's nothing wrong with that. She's an incredible ballerina; I call her my tiny dancer for a reason. I could watch—and have watched—Carissa for hours on end, completely mesmerized. But this... what I'm doing right now... vibing with Pretty Eyes... feeding off of each other's sexual energy... I didn't realize how much I was missing out on until this very moment.

There are many things you miss out on because of Carissa, my inner voice reminds me.

Fuck.

Why am I even thinking about her right now? I have a gorgeous girl in my arms who's becoming more touchy-feely as the song continues. When Pretty Eyes drops to the floor in time with the lyrics, turns around, and slowly climbs up my body, I could kiss whoever controls the music. I groan when her tits brush over my very interested dick. I nearly come on the spot, imagining sliding my erection between them.

When Pretty Eyes is fully standing again, she wraps her arms around my neck and closes the scant distance between us. Our lips are no more than an inch apart as her lush curves press against my hard edges. She smells incredible, like a donut shop or some shit. I don't think I've ever wanted to devour someone so badly in my life.

I hold completely still as she lifts up on her toes and presses her mouth to my ear. "It's Sydney. My name is Sydney."

I band my arms around her waist and lean into her ear. "Bentley."

Sydney gasps when my fingers flirt with the tops of her ass cheeks. "You wanna grab a drink with me and cool down for a bit, Bentley?"

I don't think anything will extinguish this heat between us, but our skin is coated with a thin sheen of sweat from dancing, so we could probably both use a break.

"Sure. I think there's a bunch of seating in the backyard. You wanna check it out?"

She nods, pulling out of my grip. I have to stop myself from reaching out and bringing her closer. Reed gives me a shit-eating grin as he catches sight of Sydney and me walking toward the kitchen where all the liquor is stationed. I give him one right back when I see the Baby Davenport lookalike on his lap. I guess he decided to take another shot and actually dunked this one.

I laugh when I see the irritation on Kingston's face as he watches them. I've no doubt he knows exactly why Reed went after that particular girl. The dude's been hung up on Kingston's twin—or *baby sister* as he calls her—for a while now. Reed won't nut up and admit it, though, even though it's painfully obvious to everyone in our circle. One of these days, Reed's bound to figure out that nothing but the original will do.

"What's your pleasure?" I lift a bottle of vodka. "Liquor? Wine? Beer? It looks like they've got a bit of everything."

Sydney fishes through the cooler and grabs a

pineapple hard cider. "My cousin told me not to accept any open drinks from anyone but her."

"Your cousin?" I quirk my head to the side.

"Yeah, my cousin, Lindsey. She's around here somewhere, probably hooking up with a guy." Sydney twists the top off the bottle and takes a swig. As she swallows, I may imagine those lips wrapped around something much thicker. "Or girl. Or possibly both at the same time."

I laugh, grabbing my own bottle and popping the top. "She sounds adventurous."

She gets the most adorable little crinkle between her brows. "Or something."

I nod to the Greek lettering on her shirt, lingering for a beat on her peaked nipples. "So, you're a Delta Pi girl? What year are you?"

Sydney looks down at her top, momentarily confused. "Oh. Um... I'm a sophomore. You?"

"Same." I smile. "You seeing anybody?"

She tucks a curl behind her ear. "No. You?"

"Not exclusively." I shake my head. "Now that we've got that out of the way..."

Her ocean eyes round as I move closer, caging her in against the cabinet. She shivers as I run the bridge of my nose along the curve of her neck. It's probably the Molly in my system, but I can't seem to stop touching this girl. She feels too good.

Sydney gasps when my hand grips the side of her waist, slipping beneath her cotton shirt. "Bentley, what are you doing?"

"Your skin is so soft." My lips brush against her jawline. "I love touching you." I press into the small of her back, pulling her flush against my body. "Do you want me to stop?"

Her tits press against my chest when she arches her back, and it takes everything in me not to bury my face in them. "No."

I nip the shell of her ear. "Good. 'Cause I really want to keep touching you."

Sydney moans when my tongue sneaks out, licking her delicate lobe. "Bentley?"

"Mmm?"

"Kiss me."

I pull back with a smile. "You don't need to tell me twice." When I look into her aqua eyes, I see the same desire burning through my veins reflected back at me.

The moment my mouth presses against her pillowy soft lips, my self-control snaps. I'm vaguely aware of the raucous laughter or the idiots cheering us on in the background, but mostly I'm consumed by everything Sydney. The vanilla scent wafting from her skin. The sweet pineapple taste on her tongue. The softness of her curves pressed against me.

I've never admitted this to anyone—not even the guys—but Carissa is the only girl I've ever kissed on the mouth before now. To me, kissing is too intimate; I wasn't willing to give that part of me to someone else. But the moment this girl mentioned it, I couldn't think of anything I wanted more. I'm not sure how much time passes before we come up for air, but by the time we do, Sydney's lips are swollen, and I'm guessing mine are, too.

Neither one of us says a word when I rest my forehead against hers and take a few deep breaths. The chemistry between us is off the charts, but there's something about this girl that goes beyond physical attraction. I'm sure I'll have all sorts of confusing thoughts about that later, but for right now, I allow myself to get lost in the moment. To get lost in Sydney.

chapter seven

SYDNEY

"Hey, so there's this party on Friday night, and I was wondering if you and Ainsley would like to come. A girl from my old school is throwing it. It's in Malibu right on the beach."

Jazz's brown eyes light up in interest. "Yeah? I think I could manage that. Maybe we could meet at Ainsley's and my house since we also live in Malibu on the beach. Depending on where this girl lives, we might even be able to walk to the party."

"No shit?" My eyebrows rise. "I can't imagine living right on the beach. It must be pretty sick."

"No shit." She nods. "We haven't been there long, and it's much smaller than most of the beach-front homes, but I love it."

"My girl, Cameron, is going, too. Would it be okay if she came with me to your place?"

"Of course," Jazz replies. "I'd love to meet her."

I hold up a finger. "Wait. You said *yours and Ainsley's house*, as in singular. You two live together?"

"We do," Jazz confirms. "Kingston, and my little sister, too. Well, technically, Belle—that's my sister—is only with us on Sundays, but she has her own room because I'm trying to get partial custody."

I'm sure I look as confused as I feel, trying to click all the pieces into place. "I'm sorry, but what about your parents?"

She sighs. "It's a really long story—maybe I'll tell you about it later—but our parents are out of the picture. Well, Belle's dad is still around, but he's not much of a parent, so he doesn't really count. Kingston took some money out of his trust fund and bought this place so we could all live together. We're all eighteen, so there wasn't really anything stopping us."

I take a moment to digest that. "Wow. So you and your boyfriend are legit shacking up. You two are pretty serious, huh?"

"About as serious as it gets." She smiles fondly. "I know on the surface it might seem crazy, but... Kingston and I had to grow up really fast from a young age. We may only be eighteen, but let's just say our life experiences belie that. If you stick around, you'll learn Kingston can be a little intense at times and fiercely protective, but there's good reason for it."

The bell rings, ending our conversation for now. When class is over, she pulls me aside as we walk out of the room into the hallway.

"Hey, there's one more thing I wanted to say."

"What's that?" I ask.

Jazz chews on her bottom lip. "I know Bentley Fitzgerald is in your next class, and... um... if he seems, I don't know..."

"Like he has a massive stick up his ass?" I offer.

She smirks. "Yeah... that. Please don't hold it against him. That's not who he really is, and I'm working on it. But... just keep that in mind, okay?"

I nod, catching her boyfriend watching us in my peripheral. Man, she wasn't kidding about that fiercely protective thing. He looks like he's ready to fight to the death on her behalf at a moment's notice. Have I mentioned that the dude's a little scary? Because he totally is. I'd be lying if I said it didn't make him even hotter, though.

Clearly, I have issues.

I sigh. "I'll keep that in mind, but just a head's up—I'm not a doormat kind of girl. If he's going to be an ass for no apparent reason, I'm not going to let him walk all over me."

"I wouldn't expect you to, and quite frankly, I think I'd actually enjoy seeing you spar with him." She shrugs with a smile. "Bentley needs a woman who won't take his shit."

"Hold up, there." I make a time-out gesture with my hands. "Who said I'm interested in being his woman?"

Her eyes widen. "Uh... that's not what I meant. I just—"

"Jazz, you're going to be late for second period if we don't get going." Kingston wraps a hand around her waist, eyeing me warily.

Damn, that boy is stealthy. I didn't even see him crossing the hall.

"Hey, I'm Sydney." I give him a lame wave.

He juts his chin out. "Kingston Davenport."

"Oh, I've heard *all* about you, Kingston Davenport." I smirk when his eyes narrow. "I'll see you at lunch, Jazz?"

She chuckles. "Sounds good."

I smile to myself when I hear Kingston asking Jazz what the hell that was all about. I'm still smiling when I get to my psych class until I see there is only one desk left, right next to none other than Bentley-whose-last-name-is-apparently-Fitzgerald.

"Fuck my life," I mutter.

His deep brown gaze drills into me the entire time I'm walking down the aisle toward the back of the classroom. I refuse to be intimidated, though, so I stare right back. I even take it a step further and put a little extra sway in my hips, not missing the way his eyes trace my every move nor the unmistakable heat behind them. I take my seat and stare straight ahead, completely ignoring the asshat to my right. Cameron would be high-fiving me for being such a badass bitch. As a matter of fact, I'm going to text her right now and tell her.

His dark chuckle as my thumbs fly across my phone screen make the hairs on the back of my neck stand on end. "So, it's gonna be like that, huh?"

I turn my head and quirk a brow. "Excuse me? Were you talking to me?"

My phone vibrates with Cam's reply, and when I look down, I laugh.

GBOAT: *Jim and Pam from The Office air high-fiving GIF*

I reply to her before turning my attention back to this idiot.

Me: *Amy Poehler and Tina Fey high-fiving GIF*

GBOAT: *Hailee Steinfeld woo GIF*

"Who the hell is G-boat?" Bentley's deep voice growls.

I scoff. "You really have no manners, do you? Didn't your mommy ever teach you that it's rude to eavesdrop? That applies to text conversations as well, you know."

"That doesn't answer my question."

"A, if I don't *want* to answer your question, I don't *have to* answer your question." I roll my eyes when a collective gasp fans out throughout the room. "And B, since I'm feeling generous, I'll tell you anyway. It's not G-*boat*. It's G-B-O-A-T as in, *greatest bitch of all time*. Also known as my bestie."

If I didn't know better, I'd swear he was fighting a smirk. I must've imagined it, though, because when I blink, he's back to being Mr. Stupidly Sexy Scowly again.

I pretend not to notice how his eyes fall to my mouth as I wet my lips. And I *definitely* don't notice when his tongue peeks out and mimics the gesture. Neither one of us says a word as we stare at each other for a good thirty seconds before the bell rings, breaking the spell. We both face forward and proceed to ignore the other throughout the rest of class. This time when we're dismissed, I'm the first one out the door, leaving him choking on my dust. I don't dare look back, but I could swear his eyes were on my ass the entire time.

As I'm on my way to Lit class, I can't help but wonder why the other students reacted the way they did when I was talking back to Bentley. It's almost as if they were shocked I would have the nerve to do such a thing. He's obviously a big deal around here, but as I'm dodging the multitude of strange looks and whispers in the hall, I think I may have underestimated *how much* of a big deal he is. I decide I'm just going to ask Jazz about it. She seems pretty forthcoming about everything so far, and at this point, what do I have to lose?

When it's time for lunch, I stop for a quick pee break on my way to the dining hall. As I'm exiting the bathroom, I pull my phone out of my bag to text Jazz and let her know I'll be there in a minute. As I'm typing the message, my head is down, so I don't have a chance to brace for the impact. One second, my thumbs are jabbing letters, and in the next, my phone is flying across the white marble floors as I'm falling forward.

"Dumb bitch," some girl spits out. "Not such tough shit now, are you?"

I instinctively throw my hands out, which I quickly regret. I cry out in pain upon impact, clutching my aching wrist. Everything happens so fast; by the time I recover from the shock of being assaulted and look up, there's no one close enough to blame. Just a few small clusters of people snickering at my expense. I refuse to let these people see me cry, so I grab my fallen bag and phone and pick myself off the floor, trying not to wince as a sharp pain shoots up the side of my forearm.

My wrist really freaking hurts, so despite my pride's adamant refusal, I make my way to the nurse's office to get an ice pack. When I explain what happened, she immediately calls my dad, who comes rushing into the health room no more than a minute later. He must've run here because his chest is heaving as he tries to regulate his breathing. A bit of an overreaction, in my opinion, but I can't fault him for caring. Even though we don't always agree, he's a great father.

"Sydney, what happened?" My dad nods to my left wrist, which currently has an ice pack wrapped around it.

I recap the whole event for him, watching his expression quickly morph from concern to rage.

"This is unacceptable," he huffs. "Why would some girl just randomly attack you?"

I shake my head. "Like I said earlier, I was minding my own business, leaving the bathroom, and whoever it was, just came out of nowhere. I have no idea why."

My dad's carefully styled blond hair sticks up as he rakes a hand over his head. "It doesn't make any sense. Did you have some sort of confrontation I should know about?"

"No, Dad."

He eyes me dubiously. "You're positive? There's not a single girl you can think of who would be upset with you for some reason? No one who seemed... angry with you over the last few days?"

I suck in a sharp breath when a thought hits me. Sure, there've been catty comments from several girls this week, but nothing that would indicate they had a personal beef with me. There *is*, however, one person who *definitely* has a problem with me, despite my inability to figure out why, but there is nothing feminine about him. Would Bentley Fitzgerald sic another girl on me? Is he *that* type of guy?

"What are you thinking?" my father presses. "I can see your mind working, Sydney."

"Nothing," I lie. "I was just spacing out."

He sighs. "Honey, I can't help if—"

"Dad, it's nothing. Really. Can't you just check the security feeds or something?"

"I certainly will," he assures me. "But unfortunately, if it happened close enough to the ladies' room, we won't get anything. The cameras are aimed away from the doors to avoid any accidental invasions of privacy."

"Well, that's awfully convenient," I grumble.

"Look, Sydney. Why don't you take the rest of the day off? I'll be sure to let your teachers know why you're gone, and they can send your assignments to you through the class portal. I think we should take you to the hospital to get X-rays just to make sure nothing is broken. I'll call your mom and—"

"Nuh-uh." I shake my head. "If I run scared, whoever did this is going to think they can do it again."

His face falls. "Sweetheart—"

"Dad, I said, *no*." I flex my hand, biting back the pain the movement caused. God, I don't even want to think about what effect this will have on dance if it doesn't heal quickly. "Look. I'm fine."

He rubs his temples. "I swear, sometimes you're too much like your mother for your own good."

My lips curve upward. "I'll take that as a compliment."

"You should." His eyes soften. "Your mom is pretty remarkable."

Gah! They're so in love, it's almost sickening sometimes.

"I'll be fine, Dad. I swear. Maybe someone just accidentally bumped into me and knocked me off balance."

I don't believe that for a second, and if the look on my father's face is any indication, neither does he.

"Fine," he concedes. "But if there are *any* other incidents, no matter how small, I'm getting involved. If you won't let me step in as your father, it's still my responsibility as the headmaster of this academy. You promise you'll tell me if anything else happens?"

I nod. "Promise."

As my dad kisses me on the forehead before heading back to work, I really hope I don't have to break that vow.

chapter eight

BENTLEY

"Hey, fucker. We need to have a word."

I turn around at the sound of Kingston's voice. I barely get a chance to blink before his fist connects with my face.

"Shit." I rub my aching jaw.

His nostrils flare. "You deserved it, and you damn well know it."

"I'm aware." I move my jaw from side to side, testing its soreness. Jesus, this fucker can throw a punch. "Is that why you asked me to meet you here before lunch? So you could get it out of your system? Did it work?"

Kingston scoffs. "I don't know. You plan on ever saying shit like that to Jazz again?"

My head slowly slices to the left, then the right in reply.

"Good." He nods. "Then, yeah, it worked."

"For what it's worth, I'm sorry, man. I didn't mean a word of it."

Kingston's golden-green eyes bounce between mine. "You've gotta sort your crap out, Bent, because I have a feeling Sydney is sticking around. Jazz and Ains invited her to lunch again. They love you, man, but they're not gonna bend on this. They see something in her they really like. You know how rare that is. And let's face it; you're being an unreasonable ass."

"I know." I release a heavy breath. "I also know it's not fair for me to put you guys in the middle of this. I was just... caught off guard, maybe."

"So, we good?" He lifts his brows.

"I guess." I shrug.

He assesses me carefully, obviously trying to read my thoughts.

"Look, dude. I'm not asking you to like it, but I *am* asking you to let this play out for their sake. Think you can do that?"

I honestly have no fucking clue. I've been thinking about it nonstop since Jazz left my house last night. I only know that I don't want to lose time with the few people who matter to me because Sydney-fucking-Carrington has decided to worm her way into our group.

"I'm not going out of my way to be nice to her. The best I can offer is... to not be an outright dick. But I make no promises there either."

I think I can handle this as long as Sydney doesn't start dredging up the past. All bets are off if that happens.

Kingston combs his hands through his hair. "I don't get it, man. I know Sydney reminds you of a night you'd rather forget, but it almost seems like you have an issue with her directly. Like, she actually did something to piss you off, or whatever."

I didn't hear a question in there, so I don't bother responding.

"Bent? What am I missing here?"

Of course, he wouldn't leave it at that.

I groan. "What?"

"Did she?" Kingston frowns. "Did the new girl do something that pissed you off? Because from what I remember, you two seemed to get along *very well* that night. As a matter of fact, I seem to recall you beating yourself up afterward for not getting her number because you dug her so much. It wasn't until we found out what happened to Riss that you dropped the subject."

I laugh sardonically. "Excuse-fucking-me for no longer wanting to talk about how much I wanted to bang one girl when I was trying to figure out how to fix the one who was broken beyond repair because of me."

His face falls. "Bentley. It wasn't yo—"

I hold up my hand. "Don't fucking say it. I already went through this with Jazz. Carissa would've never been at that party if it weren't for me. And *my actions* caused her to run out of that room and straight into trouble."

"You weren't doing anything wrong by fooling around with Sydney that night," he argues. "Rissa told you to go find someone else. I was *right there* when she said it; she couldn't have been any clearer. Besides, you had no idea she was even at that party. If you had, you would've dropped Sydney right away and gone to Carissa."

I have nothing to say about that. Well, that's not entirely true. I have *plenty* to say, but I'm not going to.

I kick off the side of the brick building I was leaning up against. "Can we go eat now? I'm fucking starving."

Davenport inclines his head to the double glass doors leading into the library. "You wanna grab a bite in the café?"

Not only does Windsor have a top-notch dining room, but they also have a full-service café in the library. As much as I'd like to avoid what's about to happen, I know I need to nut up and get it over with. I'm not doing anyone any favors by delaying the inevitable.

"Nah, dawg. There's no time like the present, right?"

He slaps me on the back. "Right here with ya, man."

As we walk into Lincoln Hall, I put my ever-present cocky asshole mask back in place as Kingston dutifully dons his *I hate people, don't talk to me* mask. I take a deep breath as we open the doors to the dining hall, my eyes instantly searching for one person in particular. When I don't see her at our table, my gaze wanders over to the buffet line. I frown when I don't see her there either, although I'm not sure why, because I should be relieved.

Kingston and I get in line for food and grab trays from the attendant.

"I thought you said Jazz invited her to lunch."

He selects a bowl of orange chicken and rice while I choose a delicious-looking cheeseburger on a pretzel bun. "I did."

I jerk my head back to our table, where only Jazz, Ainsley, and Reed sit. "Then, where is she?"

My best friend shrugs. "No clue. I guess we'll find out when we get over there."

After loading up our trays, Kingston and I make our way to the table, taking our usual spots on either side of Jazz.

Jazz bumps her shoulder into mine. "I'm glad you came, Bent."

"Where's your new bestie?" Okay, so that came out a little harsher than I intended. Based on the glare Kingston is giving me, I'd say he agrees.

"She's not my new bestie. I barely know her." She rolls her eyes. "But to answer your question, your guess is as good as mine. I texted her about five minutes ago, but I still don't have a reply. Maybe she decided to have lunch with her dad."

I scoff. "Why doesn't it surprise me that Sydney-fucking-Carrington's a daddy's girl?"

"Be nice, or I'm going to start calling you Bentley-fucking-Fitzgerald," Ainsley scolds from her seat directly across the table. "Side note: a lot of people would *love* to have a healthy relationship with their parents. I think you take that for granted sometimes."

I take a bite of my burger to avoid replying because now I feel like a total dick. Ainsley, Kingston, and Jazz are all orphaned, and Reed's parents are judgmental über conservative pricks. He avoids conversations with them at all costs ever since they disowned his sister for being bisexual. My parents may be gone a lot for my dad's business, but they're good people.

"Sorry," I mumble around a mouthful of food.

Jazz holds up a finger as her phone buzzes from its spot on the table. When she unlocks it, my shoulders stiffen when I see who the incoming message is from. "She says she got tied up with something."

"Tied up with what?" Ainsley asks.

"Dunno. She didn't say." Jazz shrugs, typing out a reply before setting her phone back on the table.

Reed swings his arm over the back of Ainsley's chair. "Why does it look like there's a bruise forming on your cheek?"

Jazz gasps as she turns her attention to me. I haven't looked in a mirror since Kingston clocked me, but it's pretty tender, so I'm sure there's a noticeable mark. "Damn it, Kingston, you said you were just going to talk to him!"

"We *did* talk," he argues. "Right, Bent?"

I smirk. "Right."

"You two are idiots." Jazz huffs. "Bentley, you should really ice that."

I bump my shoulder into hers, suddenly feeling a bit lighter. "Nah, baby girl. It's all good. I deserve the hurt."

Her full lips twitch. "Yeah, you kinda do. But you should still ice it."

The tightness in my chest loosens slightly when Jazz rests her head on my shoulder. This right here is my little slice of normalcy. The five of us, giving each other shit, knowing not one of us means to harm the other. These people aren't just my friends; they're my family. I don't know what I'd do if I ever lost them.

I surreptitiously try to peep Jazz's phone screen as she gets another incoming message and subsequently types her reply. I guess I'm not as sneaky as I thought because she gives me the side-eye as she hits the send button.

"Nosy ass. If you want to know what I'm saying to Sydney, you should just ask."

Oh, fuck it. I've already been caught.

"What are you saying to her?"

I narrow my eyes when Jazz gets a little victorious smile on her face. "I asked if she wanted to hang after school, but sadly, she's teaching from four to seven."

A crease forms between my eyebrows. "What do you mean she's *teaching?* What the fuck does she teach?"

Jazz hesitates for a moment, but I can't figure out why. "Uh... dance."

Ah. *That's* why.

"You've got to be kidding me," I mumble.

I'm not surprised, though. It's been two years, but I can still remember exactly how well Sydney's body moves on a dance floor.

Ainsley's eyes light up. "Get this—her mom was a professional ballerina. An *amazing* one. I legit watch her old performances on YouTube all the time. She owns that studio in the Woodland Hills Plaza. Oh my God, if I didn't love Madam Rochelle so much, I'd totally switch. Daphne Reynolds is practically a legend. She has this really inspiring story about how she went from being a poor girl from South LA to the youngest principal ballerina the New York Ballet has ever had.

"I had no idea she moved back to California. Can you believe it? She's been this close the whole time! Anyway... that's where Sydney teaches class three days a week. But not ballet, oddly enough. She says she can fill in when she has to, but it's not really her thing."

Ainsley has been training to become a professional ballerina almost her entire life, but she doesn't limit herself like Carissa did. She loves all forms of dance. Christ, now I know I don't have a chance in hell of Sydney just fading away after the newness wears off. Ains will keep her around for that alone. I know she misses having someone to share her passion with. I file Sydney's workplace in the back of my brain, just in case I need to have a little talk with her about keeping her mouth shut.

Ainsley turns her attention to Jazz. "Did you find out what time this party is on Friday?"

"What party?" I ask.

Kingston and Reed both watch me warily, so I have a feeling I'm not going to like the answer.

Jazz sits up straight. "Sydney invited Ains and me to a party someone from her old school is throwing. It's only five houses down from ours, so we're all going to walk there along the beach."

I look over at Kingston and then at Reed. "Are you two going?"

Reed shakes his head. "Nah. They're making a girls' night out of it. We were thinking of hanging at Kingston's so we can be close if they change their minds. You in?"

"I'll get back to you."

I start inhaling my food because lunch is almost over, and I don't really want to continue this conversation anyway. I pretend not to notice as they all exchange concerned looks with one another. Why am I suddenly so out of touch with my closest friends? Fucking hell, as if it didn't already suck being the constant fifth wheel.

Yet another reason why Sydney Carrington needs to go. Now I just need to figure out how to make that happen.

chapter nine

TWO YEARS EARLIER

SYDNEY

"Sydney!" Lindsey singsongs. "I brought you another one of my Aphrodite cocktails!"

Bentley loosens his hold around me so I can take the plastic cup from my cousin. "Thanks. These things are yummy."

Lindsey gets a sly smile on her face as she checks out the guy behind me. "And who might this fine brother be?"

Bentley's deep chuckle sends a shiver down my spine. "I'm Bentley. I've heard... interesting things about you, Lindsey."

My cousin preens, twirling a braid around her finger. The bright pink threads woven into it really pop against her black hair. "Oh, really, now? All good things, I hope."

I take a sip from my fruity drink. "I told him you were probably off having a threesome somewhere."

"Nah, that fell through." She pouts. "But the night is young."

Bentley's breath warms my neck as he laughs, likely surprised by the bluntness of my statement or the lack of shame in Lindsey's reply. You'd think my comment would embarrass my cousin, but I knew it wouldn't, which is why I said it. I don't have a problem with my cousin's casual attitude toward sex. Provided she's safe, and it's consensual, Lindsey can screw whomever she wants without any judgment from me. She does, however, seem to take issue with the lack of sex in *my* life, even though I'm a few years younger than she is. I swear the girl has made it her personal mission to get me laid.

I lean into Bentley as he trails a finger down my bare arm. The boy can't stop touching me, and I can't say that I mind. He hasn't skimmed over any intimate areas, but I don't think I'd object if we had privacy. I've never been so attuned to someone like I've been with him tonight. Every little caress, every breath, every kiss is amplified. It's like all of the nerve endings in my body are electrified. The weirdest part of all is I feel like I've known him for years instead of hours.

Lindsey smiles and raises her own cup. "Well, I'll leave you two alone now. Drink up!"

I raise my cup. "You too, Linz."

"Is it just me, or was that odd?"

I turn around to face Bentley. "Not just you. But that's how she rolls."

His hand reaches out to smooth some hair away from my face. I close my eyes, leaning into his touch. When I reopen them, Bentley is staring into my eyes like he's trying to unravel some great mystery within them.

"What is it about you?"

I bite my lower lip. "What do you mean?"

Bentley pulls my lip free and traces the contours with his finger. "Why do I want to kiss you so fucking bad? I don't..." He shakes his head. "That's not normal for me."

"What do you mean? You don't like kissing?" I smile. "'Cause I've gotta say, you're pretty damn good at it."

He flashes a megawatt smile, showcasing his sexy as hell dimples. "I *do* like kissing. A lot. But..."

"But *what?*"

"But... before tonight, there's only one girl I've

wanted to do that with. You're only the second girl I've ever kissed on the mouth."

"I find that hard to believe." I give him a good once-over. "Don't take this the wrong way, but you look like you're no stranger to the female body."

His lips kick up in the corner. "I didn't say I wasn't familiar with the female body. Only that I've avoided mouth-kissing for the most part."

"What makes this mystery girl and me so lucky?"

Bentley ducks his head and starts peppering kisses along my jaw. "Carissa—that's her name— was my first everything. I've known her almost my whole life."

I gasp when he moves down to the slope of my neck.

"*You* are... gorgeous, funny, down to earth, *sexy as fuck*, and... I don't know how to articulate the rest. I guess I just feel like you get me, which I know sounds dumb considering we just met, but that's the easiest way for me to explain it."

"It doesn't sound dumb." I moan when he slides the strap of my tank to the side and places a kiss on my shoulder. "Hey, Bentley?"

"Hmm?"

"You wanna see if we can find somewhere a little less crowded?"

He stands to his full height and gives me one of those piercing stares again. "Yeah?"

I nod. "Yeah."

He takes my hand and starts leading me toward the back of the house. "I think I saw a staircase to a basement. Let's go check it out."

I pull him to a halt when we pass a garbage can. "Hold up a sec." I down the rest of my drink and toss the cup in the trash. Bentley does the same with his beer, then we're on our way again.

The basement is just as crowded as the main floor, so we check the upper level and hit one locked door after another. Even the bathrooms have mile-long lines to get in. Geez, this house is huge; it feels like we've been walking around forever.

"Fuck," Bentley mutters in frustration as the final door we check is also locked.

He pulls his hat off, runs a hand over his cropped hair before putting it back on. With Bentley taking the lead, we head back to the main level, resigned to the fact that this place is packed, and privacy is pretty much impossible. I'm a lot more disappointed than I'd like to admit. The longer the night wears on, the more and more I feel like I'm crawling out of my skin if he's not touching me. I've never felt such a strong attraction to someone before.

Bentley jerks his head in the direction of the kitchen. "You want to get another drink?"

I smile when a new song starts playing. "I have a better idea."

Bentley's dimples pop as I drag him to the temporary dance floor. "I like this idea."

In a sea of writhing bodies, we lose ourselves to the sensual beat. One thing's for damn sure; the boy knows how to dance. It's rare for me to encounter someone who can move the way Bentley does outside my mom's studio. And let's be honest; ain't nobody dancing like *this* in a studio. I swear the heat building between us right now could impregnate any child-bearing female within a five-mile radius.

It feels like Bentley has four sets of hands as he runs them along every inch of my body within reach. Goose bumps scatter across my flesh, my nipples become painfully hard, and my panties shamefully wet. I close my eyes, tuning into the lyrics. As Ariana Grande sings about feeling like a dangerous woman, I swear every lyric speaks to me as if they were plucked straight from my head. Something about this boy makes me want to be bad in all sorts of deliciously wicked ways.

As Bentley's hands brush the underside of my boobs, I decide to do just that. I turn in his arms and pull his mouth to mine. Our kiss is intoxicating, filled with this crazy desperation, unlike anything I've ever experienced. There's nothing gentle about it. Our teeth clash, our tongues duel, our hands wander, finding purchase wherever they can.

I moan as he wraps his fist around my curls and gives them a solid tug. Bentley pulls my neck back at an awkward angle, causing my spine to arch. His lips travel down the column of my neck, across my collarbone, to the swell of my breasts. My hand reaches forward, rubbing his impressive erection through his jeans. His groan rumbles against my skin as he buries his face in my cleavage.

A sense of urgency rolls through me, needing more of him right this very second. When Bentley's large hand creeps under my shirt and cups my boob, my knees buckle. His other arm bands around my back, holding me up as his thumb brushes back and forth over my nipple through the lace of my bra.

"God, Syd."

"I know," I pant.

I'm faintly aware of the song switching to "Bom Bidi Bom" as we continue moving our bodies in time with the new rhythm. I can't help thinking Nick Jonas has a solid point. Every one of Bentley's kisses, every touch, *is* like a hit, and it feels like I'll never get enough. The rest of the world has disappeared. It's just him and me and the inferno blazing between us. I feel like I'm floating, high on this incredible feeling, in no hurry to ever come down. I need more of him; I can't bear being without him for another moment, so I paw at his belt buckle and pop the button on his jeans. His brown eyes widen when I drop to my knees and slide the zipper down. As I reach into his black boxer briefs and pull out his more-than-impressive cock, my mouth waters, dying for a taste.

"Fuck, honey, you sure you wanna do this?" He gathers my hair, pulling it away from my face.

I smile up at him. "Right now, I can't think of anything I want more."

chapter ten

SYDNEY

"Here we are." Our Lyft driver shifts her car into park in Jazz and Ainsley's driveway.

"Thank you." After handing her a tip, Cameron and I climb out of the lady's Ford Escape.

Jazz said we could crash in her guest bedroom tonight if we wanted to drink, but I wanted a backup plan if Cam and I didn't feel comfortable doing that, and I didn't want to leave my car here. I've known these girls for less than a week. They seem cool, but past experiences have made me really cautious when putting my trust in someone.

"This is cute," Cam says as she looks over the front of the house.

The sun's already gone down, but the front of

the house is well lit. The small Spanish-style home is exactly as I pictured it from the little Jazz told me.

"It is."

"So, they really don't live with their parents?"

I shake my head. "Nope."

"What's the deal with that?"

I shrug. "Jazz said maybe she'll tell me the story sometime, but I get the feeling it's not a pleasant tale. Not exactly an ice-breaking-getting-to-know-you kind of conversation."

We briefly check out the little courtyard off to the side before ringing the bell. The dark wooden door swings open a moment later, with a smiling Ainsley on the other side.

"Hey, Sydney." Ainsley gives a little wave. "You must be Cameron. I'm Ainsley."

"I am." Cam smiles. "Nice to meet you, Ainsley."

Ainsley steps aside to let us in, gesturing toward the small staircase off to the side. "Jazz should be down in just a bit."

The front door leads into what looks like the main living area. The light gray couches are stylish but built for comfort, and the hardwood floors are rustic. On the opposite end of the room, there's an oversized archway with beautiful cobalt tiles serving as a border. In between is an entire wall of windows bookending French doors that I'd imagine let in a lot of natural light during the day.

"Would you like a tour?" Ainsley asks.

"Sure," Cam and I reply in unison.

Ainsley takes us down a hallway I didn't notice at first, where she points out three of the house's four bedrooms along with two bathrooms. Cam gives me a questioning look when we get to the princess-themed room that obviously belongs to a child. I make a mental note to tell her what I know about Jazz's little sister later. We then cross the living room into a cute kitchen that has white shaker cabinets on top, navy on the bottom, and butcher block countertops in between. The kitchen is connected to another living area with a massive TV on the wall and multiple gaming consoles. A black leather couch with matching recliners on each side takes up the majority of the small space. This area is incredibly masculine, in stark contrast to the rest of the house's beachy boho vibe.

Ainsley rolls her eyes. "My brother staked a claim on this room. When Bentley and Reed come over, this is where the guys usually hang out. Jazz and I got to decorate the rest of the house, but this space was all Kingston; hence, the major man cave vibes."

"Total man cave vibes." I laugh but quickly

sober when I think of something, berating myself for not considering it earlier. "Do you think they'll be hanging out here tonight?"

Bentley Fitzgerald's presence would definitely influence my decision to stay over. Now, I just need to figure out if it would be a pro or a con. He's been a total ass to me this week, but for some reason, I can't forget the pull I felt between us on the night we met. Thanks to my ho-bag cousin, I may not remember much that happened that evening, but I do remember that.

"Well, Kingston lives here, so he'll definitely be around. Reed, too, because he almost always stays with me on weekends." Ainsley nibbles her lower lip. "As for Bentley... I honestly don't know. The three of them are together more often than not, but..."

"But *what?*"

"But he knows Jazz and I are hanging out with you, so that might cause him to stay away."

I shrug when Cam gives me a *what's that about?* look. "I don't get why he's so hostile toward me. We hung out *once* two years ago and didn't see each other again until this week. The little I remember from that night, we seemed to click, but it's been the exact opposite since I started at Windsor. The guy acts like he despises me. I keep racking my brain, but I'm coming up empty. Is he just naturally a dick or something?"

Ainsley tilts her head to the side. "The exact opposite, actually. Everyone loves Bentley. It's almost impossible not to."

I scoff. "I find that hard to believe."

She sighs. "Bent's been through a lot over the last two years. Sometimes... especially lately... I think it's getting to him. He's having a hard time being the carefree guy everyone expects him to be."

"I don't expect him to be a carefree guy. Or anything, really." I shake my head. "I just want to know why he seems to hate me so much."

I'm still trying to figure out if he had anything to do with that girl pushing me down. I've been avoiding him entirely over the last few days. I've hauled ass to get to second period as early as possible, so I didn't have to sit by him, and at lunchtime, I've been eating in my dad's office. Every time I saw Bentley, whether in psych class or during passing time, he stared me down, the threat of something hanging in the air, although I don't know what that could be. When I wouldn't take the bait, it only seemed to incense him further.

"Hey, guys."

I look up at the sound of Jazz's voice and find her standing under the arch that leads into the kitchen. She looks absolutely gorgeous as always with her long dark hair and golden complexion, but there's something extra about her tonight. I don't know... it's almost like she's glowing. A moment later, Kingston comes up behind her, giving her a solid smack on the ass as he makes his way into the kitchen, heading straight for the fridge. I smirk as I realize that *glow* is most likely post-coital if the look he's giving her or his messy sex hair is any indication.

God, I'd love to have someone look at me like that one day. Like they could never get enough, no matter how recently they had you.

"Jazz." I nod my head toward Cam. "This is my girl, Cameron."

Jazz's face lights up in a genuine smile. "Hey, Cameron."

Cam smiles as well. "Hey, back."

Kingston pops the lid off the Gatorade he just retrieved from the fridge, making no attempt to introduce himself.

Jazz shakes her head. "And that anti-social ass is Kingston."

Cameron's lips twitch. "Whoa there, buddy. No need to bombard me with your life story all at once."

"No shit," I agree. "We've got time, dude. Chill."

The four of us laugh at Kingston's expense while Ainsley holds her hand up to Cam for a high-five.

Holy shit, he's actually cracking a smile. "Yeah, you'll get along just fine." Jazz leans into him for a kiss as he's leaving the room. "Be careful and have fun. Text me if you change your mind and want us to come down."

"I will," she promises, closing her eyes for just a moment as he holds her close and whispers something in her ear.

Damn, they're the real deal, all right.

Jazz inclines her head toward another set of French doors in the kitchen. "It'd be easier to get there if we just walked along the beach. I checked earlier and confirmed that the house where the party is being held has direct beach access."

All four of us are dressed pretty similarly in jeans and fashionable boots without heels. Jazz and I opted for baggy, off-the-shoulder sweaters, while Ainsley and Cam wear cropped sweaters that hit right around their navels. I like that they didn't feel the need to get all glammed up like many girls our age do. It's late January, but this is Southern California, so temperatures are still mild, nixing the need for coats as long as we're not outside too long. At least until the liquor warms our bellies. We all file out the door onto the large elevated deck and make our way down the stairs to the beach.

"So, tell me about the people that will be at this party," Jazz says as we start walking toward Skyler's house.

I take a deep breath, inhaling the briny air as a light breeze blows.

"It should be mostly kids from my old school, Cambridge Prep. Maybe some recent graduates. Cambridge has a lot of scholarship students"—Cam raises her hand, indicating she's one of those scholarship students—"so the pretentious bullshit among the student body isn't nearly as extreme as it seems to be at Windsor. There are definitely exceptions to the rule, but for the most part, they check their elitist attitudes." I cringe when I realize how judgmental I sound. Jazz and Ainsley are so down to earth, I almost forgot they're loaded. "Sorry, I didn't mean to sound like such a bitch. I wasn't trying to imply that all people with money are jerks. Cambridge has plenty of assholes—they're just not as focused on the class divide, I guess. If they want to be dicks, they do it just because."

Jazz laughs. "Sydney, you have no reason to apologize. Girl, I grew up in Watts and lived there until six months ago. I am *well* versed in economic stratification."

My brows lift. "Really? My mom grew up in Compton, so I've spent a lot of time in the area. My grams and Auntie Chelle still live there, a few blocks down from Walmart."

"Small world. I shopped at that store regularly. Who knows? Maybe I've seen them around." Jazz jerks her thumb to Ainsley. "Quite frankly, Ains and the guys are the only people I've met at Windsor who don't base someone's worth on their bank accounts."

Ainsley slings her arm around Jazz's shoulder. "Love you, girl."

"Love you, too," Jazz replies.

"Aw, don't feel left out, Syd. I love you more than all the chocolate and lattes in the world." Cameron tries putting her arm around my shoulders, but because I'm a good six inches taller, I have to bend sideways to make it happen.

"Damn, that's a lot of love."

We all dissolve into a fit of laughter when I trip and take Cam down with me.

"Get off me, bitch!" she half-screams, half-laughs. "I'm getting sand in unmentionable places!"

I stand up, extending my arm to help Cameron off the ground. "Drama queen, much?"

Cam huffs as she brushes herself off. "Bitch, if I wanted sand down my crack, I'd like to have a *much* better reason for it than your clumsy ass. I will never understand how someone so talented on a dance floor can be such a klutz off of one."

"What?" Ainsley laughs. "How is that possible?"

I shrug. "No clue, but it's totally true. I have an affinity for walking into walls and tripping over absolutely nothing."

"Like when you fell outside of the bathroom at school and hurt your wrist?" Jazz nods to said wrist.

I took the Ace bandage off this morning, but she saw it in class and asked what happened. I wasn't exactly forthcoming about being pushed, though, considering her friend is a suspect.

"Yeah." I laugh awkwardly, nodding to the house with a bunch of teenagers spilling off the deck, desperate for a change of subject. "I'm guessing that's Sky's place."

"Yep," Jazz confirms. "This is the fifth house down from mine."

"Well, what are we waiting for?" Cam asks. "Let's go find the liquor."

"You'll have to excuse Cam. She's young, so she still gets overly excited about the prospect of underage drinking."

Cam smacks my arm with the back of her

hand. "Oh, shut the fuck up, Syd. I'm not that much younger; I'll be eighteen in October."

I laugh. "Ah, but you're the only junior here."

"You're a junior?" Ainsley asks.

"Yep." Cam jerks her chin to the partygoers. "But I guarantee I won't be the only one here tonight who is. Skyler, the girl throwing the party, is also a junior, as are many of her friends."

"And on that note..." I start climbing the stairs to the deck. "Let's get in there, shall we?"

chapter eleven

SYDNEY

The party is in full effect when we walk in. It's your typical rich kid gathering—lots of bodies, booze, questionable activities, and loud music. Cam and I say hi to several people we know as we make our way to the kitchen, where someone mentioned the drinks were located.

"I'll only drink out of containers that I can open myself," I explain as I'm looking through the coolers, trying to find something I like.

Jazz nods. "Me, too. I had a bad experience once, and ever since, I'm extra careful."

I'd be lying if I said I wasn't curious, but I have no intention of digging my skeletons out of the closet, so I won't ask her to expose hers.

"Me, too, actually." Ainsley grabs a White

Claw and hands a second to Jazz. "Some asshole tried dropping a roofie in my cup once. I didn't drink it—thank God—but I could've if Reed didn't watch the whole thing go down and beat his ass."

I release a startled laugh. "Really? Reed seems so... reserved. I can't imagine him starting a fight."

"Oh yeah." Ainsley nods furiously. "Bent and my brother jumped in, too. It was a crazy night, in more ways than one."

Loud catcalls draw our attention to the living room, where a girl is perched on the coffee table, her dirty blonde hair whipping around as she shakes her ass.

"Is that Kelsey Cartwright?" I nod to the dancing queen.

Cam's lips curl. "Sure is. Girlfran is loaded, no doubt."

The four of us find an empty corner to continue our conversation.

"So, I've gotta ask. What's the deal at school?"

"What do you mean?" Jazz asks.

"Well..." I take a moment to think of how I want to phrase this. "So, you know how every school has its social hierarchy, right? I could easily spot the jocks, nerds, and mean girls from a mile away, but I don't know where you and your boyfriends fit into the mix. I get the impression you're important somehow."

Neither Jazz nor Ainsley misses the fact that I leave out Bentley Fitzgerald, but they're kind enough not to call me out on it.

"Well... the dynamic has changed quite a bit since Jazz showed up." Ainsley giggles.

A crease forms between my brows. "How so?"

Jazz sighs. "To make a *very* long story short, Windsor has a long-standing archaic ruling system in place among the student body. Each year, three guys and three girls are crowned the kings and queens of the school, essentially making them untouchable as they sit on their thrones. The six of them rule from their dais, not really allowing anyone else into their social circle. Nobody dares to question it; they just follow along like brainless little sheep. This year's been... different."

"What changed?" Cam takes a giant gulp of her hard seltzer.

Ainsley shrugs. "I mean, I guess that system is still in place, but... it's been modified. At least until we graduate. Peyton Devereux, one of this year's queens, was ousted and moved to a boarding school in Paris over winter break. Thank God, because that bitch is cray. As for the guys... I can't say they don't enjoy the power trip, but they also aren't afraid to shake things up; hence, where Jazz and I come into play."

"What do you mean?" I ask.

"My brother, Bentley, and Reed are this year's kings. Typically, in years past, kings and queens were coupled up. Sometimes they had casual hookups, and other times, legit relationships. This year started out that way, but the guys canceled that real fast. After shit went down with Peyton, the boys agreed to let the two remaining queens, Imogen Abernathy and Whitney Alcott, do their own thing as long as they don't mess with Jazz or me. The whole situation caused quite the scandal." Ainsley punctuates the last sentence with an eye roll.

"Huh." I can't think of anything else to say to that.

"Anyway..." Jazz waves her hand dismissively. "Now that you have the CliffsNotes version, I will say don't let Bentley try to scare you off just because he's a king, or whatever. I absolutely adore Bent. He's one of my favorite people in the world, but he's not acting right, and he knows damn well where I stand on the subject. That doesn't mean my opinion will convince him to stand down, though, so if he gives you shit, you make sure to give it right back. He needs to know without a doubt you're not going to cower down to him."

I smirk. "I don't think you have anything to worry about there."

Ainsley laughs. "And this is why we like you."

"Hey, what about me?" Cam whines. "I'm feeling left o—" She frowns when something grabs her attention. "Oh, you've got to be kidding me. What in the hell is *he* doing here?"

My head swivels in the direction of Cameron's glare, along with Jazz's and Ainsley's.

"Who?" I ask.

Cam crosses her arms over her chest. "Hayden Knight."

"Who's Hayden Knight?"

"My mom's new boyfriend's shit-for-brains son."

My eyebrows lift. "The one who was a total jerk at dinner the other night?"

"One and the same," she confirms.

"He looks our age. Does he go to your school?" Ainsley asks.

"No, thank fuck." Cam shakes her head. "He's also a junior, but at Beverly Prep, because according to his dad, they have one of the best football teams around. Evidently, the fuckwad's fairly talented at throwing a ball."

Jazz smiles knowingly when she sees how hard

Cameron is staring him down. "He *is* pretty, too; you've gotta give him that."

Cam may not like this Hayden guy, but she can't deny she's attracted to him. She looks like she's debating whether or not she should punch him in the throat or jump his bones.

"That's about all he's got going for him." Cameron tilts her head back, chugging the rest of her drink. "I'm gonna go give him a piece of my mind. Be right back."

Ainsley, Jazz, and I all watch with amusement as Cameron stomps over to him. You can tell Hayden's not pleased to see her. The two guys standing next to him look just as entertained as we are as she goes off on him about something. I'm so enthralled by the drama unfolding before me, I'm not paying attention to my surroundings. So, when the one person I was hoping not to see approaches me, I startle.

"Syd. Can we talk?"

I sigh as I turn toward my ex, Zach. "I'll pass. Thanks."

He tries tugging on my arm, but I pull away in time. "C'mon, Sydney. Just a few minutes." He flashes a cocky smile in Jazz and Ainsley's direction. "'Sup? I'm Zach."

Jazz's lips turn up at the corners. "I'd say it's

nice to meet you, but... you're giving off major douche vibes, so it's not."

I bust out laughing. Damn, I really like this girl.

Zach glares at Jazz before turning his attention back to me. "Sydney, please."

"Fine. You can have five minutes." I turn to the two girls at my side. "I'll be right back. You good staying here by yourselves?"

"Yep," Ainsley and Jazz reply at the same time.

I walk toward the back deck without checking to see if Zach is following. There are way too many people on the deck itself, so I walk down the stairs leading to the beach. There are still some people below, so we won't be alone, but it gives us a bit more privacy. I'm not the kind of person who enjoys drawing the attention of gossip mongers.

I prop my foot against one of the pillars supporting the deck. "What do you want, Zach? I think I was pretty clear when I said I never wanted to speak to you again."

I turn my head away, narrowly avoiding his lips as he leans into me. "I miss you, baby."

I press my hand to his chest to push him back some. "That's not my problem."

He fingers a lock of my curls. "C'mon, Sydney. I said I was sorry a million times."

I bat his hand away. "And you can say it a

million more. I don't care, and I don't accept your shitty apology."

There's just enough light shining through the cracks in the deck to see the angry slash to his brows. "Don't be a bitch, Syd."

I scoff. "Wow. You're batting a thousand, aren't you? Go away, Zach. I'm done with this conversation."

He leans into me again, this time not relenting when I try pushing him away. "Fuck, I miss the way you smell." He cages me in against the pillar, nuzzling his nose into my neck. "I miss the way you feel." He presses forward until his body is flush with mine, and I can feel his erection against my hip.

"Zach, get off of me."

His warm breath reeks like whiskey as he releases a dark chuckle. "C'mon, Sydney. Don't you miss me, too?"

I try pushing him off again, but he grabs both of my wrists, pinning them to my side. My left wrist is still pretty sore, so I whimper a little as he squeezes.

"Zach, I mean it. Get. Off. You lost your shot with me when you decided to dip your dick into someone else."

"Sydney, Sydney, Sydney." He groans when he presses his hard-on into me even more. "You know

Olivia didn't mean anything to me. I was wasted, and she was a warm hole. You're my girl. I want *you*, not her."

"You must be wasted now if you think I'm still your girl."

I wriggle my arms, but his grip is too tight. I'm not tiny, but Zach's stacked. He easily has fifty pounds of muscle over me. This isn't typical behavior for him, though. In the year we were together, he never tried to assert physical dominance over me. He wasn't a gentleman by any means, but he wasn't forceful either. *It's because he doesn't like losing*, my brain supplies.

"Why don't you give Olivia a call? I'm sure she'd be more than willing to wet your dick."

"I don't need to call her. She's inside the house. If I wanted Olivia, I'd *have* Olivia. She already made that very clear tonight." He adjusts his hold, so both of my wrists are shackled with one hand while the other pushes my sweater down, baring my shoulder even more, so he can kiss my bare skin. "C'mon, baby, let's go find an empty room. I'll eat your pussy so good, you'll forget all about that little mishap with Liv."

"Not likely. I hate to break this to you, buddy, but you're not nearly as great as you think you are in the pussy eating department."

He bites my shoulder, causing me to cry out. "Watch your mouth."

"Zach, I'm not kidding, and I am *not* picking up what you're throwing down. If I wasn't clear before, I don't want you to touch me *or* talk to me. I'd be perfectly fine if I never saw your cheating ass again." I struggle harder because this asshole is actually starting to scare me now. There was nothing playful about that bite. "Now, let go."

"You fucking bitch," he spits out. "Obviously, I need to teach you a les—"

"I really wouldn't finish that sentence if I were you," a deep voice growls. "I believe the lady said she wanted you to let go."

I gasp, quickly turning my head to find Bentley Fitzgerald looming over us with a thunderous expression on his face.

Zach releases me and takes a step back, puffing his chest out. "Are you shitting me right now, Sydney? You're hooking up with this guy now? Of all the fucking dudes in LA, you choose *this* guy?"

Bentley looks as confused as I feel. "You okay, Syd?"

I rub my aching wrists, ignoring the warm feeling I get when he shortens my name with an affectionate tone. "Yeah, I'm good."

Bentley lifts his eyes to the deck above. "Maybe

you should head inside and find your friends. I'll take care of this."

Oh, hell no.

While I appreciate the rescue, I'm not going to forget how much of an asshole he's been to me all week, nor the fact that he may have sent that girl to hurt me. He needs to learn that I'm not afraid to fight my own battles.

I fold my arms over my chest. "Again, *I'm good.*" The *now get out of here* is implied in my tone.

Zach's fists clench at his sides. "You're a real piece of work, you know that?"

I park my hands on my hips. "What's that supposed to mean?"

"You know, the only reason I asked you out was because you're hot, and I thought you were a sure thing. Austin tried talking me out of it because you were such a frigid bitch at school, but the evidence was right there in front of me. My brother was in that frat, Syd. He invited me to that party. I saw everything in living color *with my own two eyes!*" Zach throws his hands out toward Bentley. "How could you not be an easy lay after seeing what you did with *him* in the middle of a crowded room? I mean, if you did that shit in public, you *had* to be a freak in bed, right? I guess the joke's on me, isn't it?"

Bentley stiffens at my side, making me wonder

what that's all about, but I have bigger fish to fry at the moment.

"I'm lost. What are you talking about? I've never done any*thing* with any*body* in public. What evidence do you supposedly think you have?"

"Oh, that's right; you have no idea, do you? Because that's the same night your cousin spiked your drinks. Maybe that's my problem. Maybe your inner slut only comes out when you've been drugged."

Bentley lunges for him. "You motherfucker."

I step in the middle of these two assholes, determined to figure out what the hell is going on. I don't even care about the audience we've gathered at the moment.

"Bentley, stay out of it. This is *my* problem, not yours."

Bentley's jaw clenches in irritation, but he's smart enough to keep his mouth shut.

"*Explain*, Zach."

He laughs. "Nah, I don't think I will. You'll find out soon enough, and I'm going to really fucking enjoy it when you do. Later, Syd. I'm gonna go see what Liv's up to."

Bentley lunges for him again when Zach starts to walk away, but I grab on to the back of his shirt. "It's not worth it."

Bentley's nostrils flare. "The fuck it's not."

I narrow my eyes. "Why do I get the feeling you know what Zach was talking about?"

"*You don't?*" He stares at me for a moment. "Seriously? You have *no* idea?"

I rub my temples, suddenly feeling a headache coming on. "Look, I know you don't know me, but I'm not a liar. What you see is what you get, and I don't like playing games."

Bentley clasps his hands behind his head and starts pacing back and forth. "I don't fucking believe this."

I throw my hands up. "You don't believe *what?* What's going on?"

"I suppose the next thing you're going to say is you're a virgin," he mutters. When I don't utter a word, his jaw drops. "You're a virgin?!"

Snickers ring out behind us, reminding me we have an audience.

I grab his arm, pulling him away from the small crowd, totally ignoring the energy sparking between us. "First of all, that's none of your damn business. Second, if I was—which I'm not admitting shit— there's nothing wrong with being a virgin."

I can see his mind working overtime, but I have no idea what's going on inside that head of his.

"Sydney, I—"

"There you are, bitch!" Cameron runs down the last few stairs with Jazz and Ainsley right behind her. "We've been looking for you."

Jazz's eyes dance between Bentley and me, no doubt sensing the tension in the air. "Everything okay here?"

When neither Bentley nor I say a word, Cam pipes up. "Syd? Are you okay? I saw Zach a few minutes ago, and he looked pissed."

"Yeah, I'm fine," I assure her. "But you know what? I'm not exactly feelin' the party scene anymore. My head hurts." I pull my phone out of my back pocket and open the Lyft app to order a ride. "Would you mind if we go home now, Cam?"

"No, girl. That's totally fine."

"You're more than welcome to come back to our place," Ainsley offers. "I'll get you some Advil, and we can just chill. Watch movies or something."

Yeah, right. There's no way I could relax with Bentley present. I have a feeling he has no intention of leaving, which is why it's up to me to remove myself from this equation.

"Thank you, but I'm not in the best mood right now. Can I take a rain check?"

Ainsley nods. "Sure."

"Sydney—" Bentley tries again.

I hold up my hand. "Nuh-uh. Not now. I've met my bullshit quota for the evening."

I loop my arm through Cameron's and start walking toward the stairs. "I ordered a ride. We're just going to cut through the house to meet the driver out front. It says he's only a few minutes away, so we need to hurry. I'll talk to you later, Jazz. Okay?"

"Okay. Text me to let me know you got home all right."

I nod. "'Kay. Night. Sorry for bailing."

"It's fine," Ainsley says.

As Cameron and I weave through the throng of drunk teenagers, I'm not surprised in the least when I see Zach and Olivia making out on a couch. Hell, based on the way she's grinding on top of him in her short skirt, they may be doing more than kissing. I flip them off just for the hell of it right before leaving through the front door.

Cameron tugs on my arm as we wait at the end of the driveway for our ride. "You gonna tell me what that was all about? I'm guessing Mr. Tall, Dark, and Broody was Bentley, huh?"

"Sure was." I sigh. "And honestly, I have no fucking clue what just happened. Not even a little."

chapter twelve

BENTLEY

"C'mon, Bent, let's go back to my house." Jazz loops her arm through mine as we start walking along the beach. "What are you doing here anyway?"

"I wasn't trying to crash the party or anything." I gently shake out of Jazz's hold so I can grab a J from my pocket and light up. It takes a few tries with the wind, but I finally get it.

"Then why were you there?" Ainsley asks. "Where'd you come from anyway?"

I take a long drag. "Your place."

"When did you get there?" Jazz grabs my arm again like she's afraid I'll run off or something. "We haven't been gone very long."

I shrug. "Kingston may have mentioned which

direction you were headed, and I may have wandered this way when I went outside for a smoke."

Ainsley steps in front of me, causing me to stop in my tracks. "Hold up. You said you weren't there to crash the party, yet you intentionally went to the house where the party was located? You're contradicting yourself, Bent."

"Fuck. Hold this." I hand the joint to Ains and dig through my pocket until I find what I need. It's dark, so I can't quite see their faces clearly, but I suspect they're both frowning as I pop two pills and swallow them. I grab the blunt back from Ainsley and take another big hit.

"What did you just put in your mouth?"

I can't stand the concern in Jazz's tone. She seems to think I'm her problem to solve, but she'll be sorely disappointed when she finally realizes I'm a lost cause.

"Relax. It's just a couple of Xannies."

"Why do you have Xanax? Where did you even get it? And should you really be taking it with weed?"

"Christ. What the fuck is this? Twenty questions?" I snub the joint out with the bottom of my shoe and put it back in the metal case. "Sorry, Mom. Is that better?"

Ainsley sighs. "Bentley, what's going on with you?"

I pull my hat off and flip it around before putting it back on my head. "It's not a big deal. I've been having trouble sleeping lately, and the pills help me relax."

"Doesn't flower do the same thing?" Jazz asks.

I scoff. "Not when you've built up a tolerance to it like I have."

A chill breaks out over my skin when the surf crashes against the shore. We're close enough to the ocean that tiny droplets of cold-as-fuck water spray onto my forearm.

Jazz grabs my hand and twines our fingers together. "Bentley, please talk to me."

It should feel weird holding hands with my best friend's girl, but it doesn't. The situation between the three of us is... unique. Don't get me wrong; Jazz is one-hundo-percent Kingston's, and I am well aware. I'm holding out no hope Jazz and I'll be a thing one day. I won't pretend I'm not attracted to her because I'm a dude with a fully functioning dick, and she's fine as fuck, but what we're doing right now is purely platonic, and it always will be. I don't look at her like that anymore.

Jazz just has this uncanny ability to read people. She knows I'm a tactile person, and I find comfort in simple touches. Kingston knows this as well, which is why he allows it, even though it goes against every alpha asshole instinct he possesses. And okay, maybe I push his buttons sometimes just to be a prick, but it's all in good fun.

Ainsley takes my other arm. "Why were you heading to the party, Bentley?"

"I *wasn't* heading to the party," I insist. "Not really. I guess I purposely went in that direction, but I was looking for some space to think. I definitely didn't plan on running into Sydney, but she was right there. I couldn't just stand by when I saw what that fucker was doing to her."

We've reached the house, so Jazz releases my hand and takes the lead up the stairs. "That Zach guy? What was he doing to her?"

I clench my jaw. "He was restraining Sydney and pawing at her. She clearly told him to let go multiple times, but the shithead wouldn't listen, so I made myself known. The pussy backed off, but it didn't stop him from running his mouth."

Jazz unlocks the back door so we can all walk inside. "What was he saying?"

"Hey. You're back early." Kingston crosses the room from the kitchen and pulls Jazz into him. "I see you found Bent. Where's Sydney and her friend?" He's eyeballing me over the top of Jazz's head like he thinks I have something to do with Sydney's absence.

"They left from the party. Syd ran into her asshole ex and wasn't in the mood to hang around." Ainsley looks around the room. "Is Reed here yet?"

Davenport shakes his head. "Not yet, but he should be soon. He was picking up pizza on the way."

"Awesome." I bypass Kingston and Jazz and make my way into the TV room. I kick back in what I've deemed *my* recliner and stretch out. "I'm fucking starving."

Ainsley takes a seat on the couch closest to me. "Bent. Finish what you were saying. What do you mean Sydney's ex was running his mouth?"

Jazz and Kingston also park their asses on the couch, except Jazz is on Kingston's lap because sitting next to each other would apparently be too far away.

"You run into some trouble?" Kingston lifts an eyebrow. "I told you to stay out of it, man."

I flip him off. "For your information, *I* didn't run into any trouble. Sydney's douchebag ex was getting handsy, and she wasn't feelin' it, so I told him to take a hike. That's all."

"But he said something to her," Jazz reminds me. "What was he saying?"

I scrub a hand down my face. "When he saw me, he started going off. Dude acted like he recognized me."

"Have you met?" Ains asks.

"Nah." I shake my head. "But... he claimed to be at the frat party where I first met Sydney. That house was *packed*. Even if Sydney did know him back then, it's possible he could've blended in with the crowd and gone unnoticed. I didn't exactly ask clarifying questions, but he alluded to the fact that he saw the two of us together. Or at least one of the pictures that were floating around a while back."

Ainsley's hazel eyes widen. "Of you and Sydney, um... you know?" She mimes giving someone a blow job with a raised fist and her tongue pressed against her cheek.

"Yep." I pop the P for emphasis. "Here's the real kick in the nuts: When douchenugget mentioned the... event that took place that night, Sydney seemed completely clueless. Genuinely perplexed, like she had no memory of the whole thing."

"Do you think it's possible?" Kingston asks. "Was she that fucked up?"

"Not *that* loaded, from what I recall."

I need to tread carefully here. As far as these guys are concerned, I have virtually no memory of that night. The only reason I supposedly even know what Sydney looks like is that people took pics of her blowing me and thought I'd like a little memento, so they sent them my way.

"The dude mentioned something about Sydney's cousin drugging her that night." I force back the stomach acid threatening to surface.

Ainsley gasps loudly while the other two are deathly silent. When I look up, all three of them look as horrified as I feel.

"Bentley." Ainsley's eyes are filled with unshed tears, and her voice is so quiet, I have to strain to hear her. "Do you think... is it possible Sydney *was* drugged? With the same stuff that was used on Rissa?"

"I have no clue."

At least that part is true. Sydney wasn't stone-cold sober—nobody was—but I would swear on my nuts, she seemed cognizant enough to be fully in control of her actions. I would've *never* touched her otherwise.

"Fuck, man." Kingston rakes a hand over his freshly cut hair.

I blow out a breath. "Yeah."

There's not really much else any of us can say. The events that transpired that evening lit the match that caused my whole world to burn to the ground. Ever since, I've been wading through endless piles of ashes, trying to purge the bitter taste from my tongue. I've spent the last two years of my life drowning myself in copious amounts of liquor, weed, and as of late, pills. Hiding behind stupid jokes and an endless supply of pussy, praying that something—*anything*—would make the pain stop. Take this pressure off of my chest, so I could finally breathe again.

"Bentley, you have to talk to Sydney," Ainsley insists. "You have to find out what she remembers."

Baby Davenport's right, no doubt, but I don't think I want to know. Suppose Sydney doesn't remember what happened that night. In that case, she doesn't remember me confessing my deepest, darkest secrets, which would generally be a good thing. But if the reason she doesn't remember is that she was drugged? I'm pretty sure that makes this whole situation even worse. Because if that's the case... that means I'm no better than the bastards who raped Carissa. And that very well could be the one truth that pushes me off the edge.

chapter
thirteen

SYDNEY

"So, are we gonna talk about what went down tonight, or are we pretending it didn't happen?" Cameron jumps onto my bed, making the mattress bounce beside me.

I groan. "Do I have to? My head is still spinning. I can't make sense of it."

"You know what I can't make sense of? The fact that Zach put his hands on you like that." Cam scrunches her face.

"Me neither." I gave Cam the rundown on how Zach manhandled me on the ride home. "I think he may have been on something. Not that that's any excuse."

"Like what?"

My shoulders lift. "Dunno. Maybe powder?

Football season is over, so he doesn't have to worry about random testing."

"Since when does he partake in anything beyond weed?"

I sigh. "Who knows? I feel like I don't know him at all after earlier. I mean, he's obviously a cheating jerk, but I've never seen him so aggressive or mean-spirited before. And then he had to pull out all that crap about asking me out only because he thought I was a sure thing? What would've ever given him that impression?"

"I don't know, girl." Cam arranges her body so she's sitting cross-legged like me.

I throw my arms over my head and fall backward. "Boys are dumb. Is it too late to switch teams?"

She giggles. "I don't think it's ever too late, but I'm pretty sure you like putting the P in your V too much for that to ever happen."

"I don't even know what real peen feels like." I raise my hand. "Virgin here, remember?"

"Honey, did you forget about the fact that I know *all* about your collection of goodies hiding in the fun box? You already know what dick feels like. If anything, you'll be totally bummed when you get the real thing because they rarely measure up." Cam snorts. "Literally."

I laugh, throwing a pillow in her face. Okay, fine. I may have an extensive collection of vibrators in my arsenal. What can I say? I was curious once, and I was hooked as soon as I discovered what all the fuss was about. Thank God for the internet and discreet shipping.

"I know what went down at that party made you gun-shy for a while, but you're not in that same headspace anymore, Syd. You've run all the bases with a few guys since, and you were fine with doing that, right? I think you should just let some hottie slide on home and get it over with. I bet I know one person who'd happily volunteer as tribute."

I scoff. "I wouldn't give Zach another shot in his wildest dreams. Hell, if I'm honest, he never had a shot when we were together. God knows I had plenty of chances to punch my V-card with him."

It's not like I'm saving it for marriage or even love. It's not even a big deal to me. I *want* to have sex. Maybe by the time I was ready to go all the way, I was already with Zach, and something in the back of my brain could sense he wasn't honest with me, so I never took that final step.

Plus, you know, I wasn't kidding about his subpar skills. If he's that shitty with oral—which I suspect is due to selfishness and/or laziness—I'm guessing he has no idea how to use his dick either. I'm not expecting hearts and flowers or eleventy million orgasms the first time I have sex. Still, I would like to actually enjoy myself. I don't want to feel like I'm nothing more than a 'warm hole,' as Zach so eloquently put it.

"I wasn't talking about Zach. I'm talking about the dude who looked like he wanted to eat you for breakfast, lunch, and dinner."

I turn my head toward my bestie. "Who?"

Cam's lips curl into a shit-eating grin. "Mr. Tall, Dark, and Broody."

I frown. "Bentley?!"

She gives me a wry look. "Is there someone else we know that fits that description?"

"You're nuts. Bentley Fitzgerald wants to *off me*, not eat me."

She starts laughing so hard, tears are rolling down her face.

I prop myself up on my elbows. "What in the hell is so funny about that?"

"Are you in denial? Is that the problem?" Cam wipes her cheeks. "That boy wants you *bad*. Bentley Fitz-whatever-his-name-is wants to feed"—she pumps her hips like she's wearing a strap-on—"you" —another awkward thrust—"the D.

Aaaaand I'd bet my vintage Gucci bag he'd have *no problem* measuring up against his silicone predecessors. The boy is *tall*, so you know the odds are in his favor."

I roll my eyes. "You and your *if he's at least six-one, he must have a huge dick* theory."

"You know I'm right." She raises her brows. "How tall is Zach again?"

My lips twitch. "Same as me. Five-nine."

"*Exactly.*"

I have to admit that Zach has a *great* body, but his dick is average at best. Significantly below average if we're talking about girth. His peen honestly reminds me of one of those chisel-tipped Sharpies. I may or may not have shared that information with Cameron at some point.

Cam bites her lower lip in concentration. "I still have no clue how dudes walk around with those things between their legs all day, especially when they're hung. Although, it would be fun to let it hang in the breeze or slap someone's forehead with it from time to time."

I shake my head, fighting a smile. "You are the most ridiculous person on the planet. And why are you giving me sex advice anyway? You've been with *one guy*."

Cam holds up her index finger. "Ah. But said

guy and I banged like bunnies. Man, Paulo was the best."

Cam dated a model from Brazil who was in LA for a while. They were pretty hot and heavy for several months, but he went back home right before Thanksgiving.

"I swear, for a second there, I thought you were thinking about hiding in his luggage when he left."

"I was," she says wistfully. "Paulo was so pretty to look at, and damn, the things he could do with his tongue. Too bad he wasn't exactly the sharpest tool in the shed. We could've had something real."

"Yeah, too bad." I laugh. "Speaking of stupidly attractive boys... what were you saying to that Hayden guy? He looked *pissed*."

Cameron giggles. "Oh, not much. I just thanked him for giving me chlamydia and told him I never wanted to see him or his micro peen again."

"What?!" I sputter.

She nods. "Relax, Syd. I don't actually have an STD, nor have I personally seen his junk. I just said the first thing that popped into my head that would serve as payback for being such an asshole the other night."

"I stand by my previous statement of you being ridiculous." I flop back on the bed. "But I love you anyway."

"Right back at ya, bish." She taps my arm with the back of her hand. "What are you going to do about Zach? Are you going to ask him to clarify his cryptic statement?"

"I don't think he'd tell me, so I don't see the point. He said I'll find out soon enough."

"What's that supposed to mean?"

"Your guess is as good as mine." I shrug. "I suppose time will tell."

"We need to talk."

The one person I was hoping to avoid was waiting for me at the entrance to Lincoln Hall this morning. Not exactly how I wanted my Monday to begin.

I hitch my book bag higher on my shoulder. "No, we don't."

Bentley steps in my path when I try passing him. I curse my stupid body for reacting to his proximity. The second I saw him, I was instantly aroused. His brown eyes quickly flicker to my chest, no doubt noticing my traitorous nipples saluting him. This was not the day to forget my blazer. I make a mental note to always keep a spare in my locker, just in case. I have a feeling this inconvenient attraction isn't going away anytime soon, and it's not like I can wear padded bras without pushing my boobs up to my chin.

Big titty problems, am I right?

"Bentley, *move*. You're going to make me late." I lift my chin, fire burning in my eyes.

He briefly looks over my shoulder before muttering something under his breath.

"Hey, guys. Everything okay?"

I sigh in relief at the sound of Jazz's voice before turning toward her. Kingston, Ainsley, and Reed are right by her side, all eyeing Bentley strangely. When I see Bentley clenching his jaw in irritation, part of me wants to be an immature brat and stick my tongue out, but the other part feels kind of bad for him. It's apparent something is going on between this group of friends—something much deeper than you can see on the surface—and whatever that is, is causing Bentley distress.

Not my problem, I remind myself. Bentley's been a prick to me since I arrived at this damn school. He doesn't deserve my sympathy.

"It is now that this jackass is no longer in my way." I take advantage of the distraction and step around Bentley. "I'll see you in class, Jazz."

"Wait, I'll come with you." She gives Kingston a

quick peck before stepping beside me. "I'll see you guys later."

As we head inside, I can hear the deep timbre of Bentley's voice, but I don't stick around to listen. I don't know why he's suddenly so interested in talking to me, but I don't really care either. The boy's gonna learn real fast, I won't put up with his bipolar attitude. It's obvious he's dealing with some shit in his head, but who isn't? His problems aren't more important just because he's a supposed king in this school. The whole royalty thing this academy has going on is bullshit, in my opinion. I need to remember to ask my dad what he thought about it as a Windsor student.

"So... what did I just walk in on back there?" Jazz nudges me with her shoulder.

"Absolutely nothing. He said he wanted to talk. I told him I had nothing to say."

"Maybe you should hear him out."

I shake my head. "Why would I do that? He was a massive jerk to me all last week. I know he's your friend, Jazz, but I have no desire to make him mine."

She sighs as we take our seats in class. "I know it's hard to fathom considering how he's treated you, but Bentley is a great guy. He just has some... issues that he's trying to work through. Sydney, your arrival has really thrown him. It's bringing up a lot of awful memories, and he's not handling it well."

"But why? He doesn't know me, but he acts like he hates me. What am I missing? I can't recall a single reason why he would associate any bad memory with me. You say he's not generally an asshole, but that's all I've seen."

Not all, that annoying voice in my head insists. He didn't have to step into my not-so-pleasant conversation with my ex.

A crease forms between her dark, sculpted eyebrows. "What do you remember from the night you two met? At that frat party?"

"Not a lot." Now it's my turn to frown. "But I do remember brief conversations with Bentley, which I thought went really well."

Don't forget to mention the amazing kisses. You definitely remember those. Ugh, shut up, stupid voice!

Jazz opens her mouth to reply, but she's cut off by the bell. I can't say I'm not relieved by the interruption. Bentley Fitzgerald already consumes too many of my thoughts. I spent the entire weekend trying to figure out what my asshole ex was talking about Friday night and why Bentley seemed to know exactly what he was referring to. He even infiltrated my dreams because I couldn't stop thinking about Cam's comment about Bentley wanting to eat me alive. It's not the first time I've had a sex dream about him, but damn, it was one of the better ones. I place my hands on my cheeks when they flush, hoping no one in class notices.

I hate the way that boy affects me, yet I'm powerless to stop it. I really wish I could figure out why I'm so attracted to him. It's not like hot dudes are hard to come by in LA, but Bentley Fitzgerald is the one my body wants the most for whatever reason. I've never been drawn to someone like I am to him. It's maddening and, if I'm honest, disheartening because I clearly have a skewed recollection of the night we met. There's no way someone would treat me the way he has been if we truly vibed like I thought. The stubborn side of me really doesn't want to cave, but I think I need to take advantage of the fact that he suddenly wants to speak with me, so I can get to the bottom of this.

When the bell rings again, I take a deep breath, steeling my resolve. Bentley's in my next class, so I guess there's no reason to put this off any longer.

chapter fourteen

BENTLEY

Just like most of last week, by the time I get to psych class, almost every seat is filled. I approach the douche sitting behind Sydney and tell him to find another desk. The pussy can't get up fast enough, which has me fighting a smile. So does the incredulous look on Sydney's face. It's not often Kingston, Reed, or I need to assert our authority around here. People usually give us a wide berth, but we've been laying extra-low lately.

Quite frankly, after all the crazy shit we've been through over the past six months, it's refreshing. Our lives are almost dull even, but after seemingly nonstop telenovela-level drama, boring is good. Boring is *safe*, which I'm guessing is especially comforting for Jazz considering everything she's endured.

"That was incredibly rude of you," Sydney mutters as I take a seat. "Although, I'm not even a little surprised."

I lean forward, telling myself it's simply so I can speak low enough to not be overheard. "You've left me little choice. We need to talk. You can't run from me forever."

Sydney's torso twists until she's facing me. It feels like I've been smacked in the face with a brick as her ethereal gaze lands on me. "You're right."

Don't look at her mouth. Don't look at her mouth.

I can't seem to help myself. Hands down, the best blow job of my life came from that mouth. My dick jerks at the memory, quickly growing into a problem.

Yeah, a blow job she doesn't seem to remember because she may or may not have been drugged.

Fuck.

Well, that thought certainly helped deflate the untimely erection.

"Bentley? Did you hear what I said?"

Shit. Snap out of it, dude.

"Huh?"

Sydney's brows furrow. "I said, you're right. We *do* need to talk, and I can't hide from you forever."

I raise my brows in surprise. I wasn't expecting her to give in so easily. I tell myself to stop questioning why I'm disappointed by that.

"Well, in that case..."

The bell rings before I can finish my sentence. Sydney faces forward and pulls out her Chromebook like the good little student I'm sure she is. I would expect nothing less from the headmaster's daughter. I'd like to consider myself a pretty smart dude, but I've never had any sort of compulsion to excel in school. I've aced every test I've ever taken, but my effort with the everyday stuff isn't anything to write home about. Thankfully, test scores account for over half of our grades.

"Okay, class." Mrs. Brown, our teacher, claps her hands together. "If you open the classroom portal, you'll see your new assignment. We're going to study how music can affect your heart rate. We'll do this by listening to one-minute clips from several different genres of music and recording your pulse after each clip. Once you've compiled all your data, you'll write a short essay summarizing your conclusions during this experiment.

"Using a randomizer, I've grouped you into pairs and generated a list of musical genres, which you'll find posted on the discussion board. This will ensure we get the widest sampling possible. Today in class, you and your partner will decide which songs you'll be listening to from each genre you've been assigned. After that, you'll need to get together after school to complete the project. Your essays are due two weeks from today, so you'll have plenty of time to make arrangements to meet with your partner. Any questions?" Mrs. Brown's eyes scan the room, waiting for someone to raise their hand. When nobody does, she nods. "Very well. Pull up the discussion board, find your partner, and get to work."

I pull my Chromebook out of my bag and sign on to the classroom portal. As I'm waiting for the discussion board to load, Sydney's back stiffens, and she mutters something under her breath that sounds suspiciously like, *for fuck's sake.*

She turns around with an ominous look on her face. "Have you pulled up the partner list yet?"

I click on the notecard on my screen while the other students move around the room to find their respective partners.

"I'm doing it now. Why?"

The moment I see who I'm paired with, I know why Sydney has that look of resignation on her face. Of course. As if fate hasn't fucked with me enough.

I scoff. "Looks like you're really stuck with me now, princess."

"Don't call me that," she snaps.

"What? *Princess?* Would you prefer, sweetheart?"

Her eyes narrow. "I would prefer *Sydney*, seeing as that's my name. Or Syd. Anything else is off the table."

"We'll see about that, honey." I wink because I know it'll irritate her even more.

If Sydney's eyes were capable of shooting fire, I'd be a pile of ashes right now. I don't know why, but her obvious contempt makes me laugh. Besides my small group of friends, not many people talk back to me. It's as annoying as it is refreshing that someone else has joined the club. It makes this whole situation even more convoluted. If Sydney's memory of that night is as shoddy as I suspect based on what I recently learned, she may not remember our conversations. And if that's the case, she's no longer a liability.

Which also means I have no reason to push her away.

Well... that's not entirely true. If Sydney *was*, in fact, drugged that night, I might have yet another thing to feel guilty about. I need to figure out what happened to her, and this stupid assignment might be the perfect opportunity to do that.

"Hello?" Sydney waves her hand in front of my face. She lowers her voice before adding, "Are you high? Why do you keep spacing out?"

I laugh under my breath. I wish I were high. Maybe I'll take a detour to the parking lot before my next class and rectify that.

Sydney exhales harshly, blowing a dark curl away from her face. "Can we please just get this stupid playlist figured out?"

When she stands to maneuver her desk so it's facing mine, I can't look away from the swish of her plaid uniform skirt, dying to know what kind of panties she's wearing underneath.

Fuck.

This girl ties me into knots, which makes no sense because I hardly know her. One minute, I want to forget she exists, but in the next, I want nothing more than to see if she tastes as good as I remember.

I look over the list of the six musical genres we were assigned. "Yeah, sure. I don't really care which songs we use. Do you want to just split it down the middle? You can take the top half, and I'll take the bottom."

When Sydney tugs her lower lip between her teeth, my mind automatically goes to a much dirtier scenario involving top and bottom positioning. I'm pretty sure I groan as I envision Sydney's tits bouncing while she rides me. Not that I personally know what that's like—that's one thing I haven't had the pleasure of experiencing yet. What the fuck am I saying? There is no *yet* in this situation. Okay, fine. So I'll admit I wouldn't exactly turn down the offer. I'm a dude, and she's a goddamn smoke show.

"That works." She pulls her cell out of her bag and begins scrolling through something.

"What are you doing?"

"Searching through my music library." The look she drills me with makes me feel like a moron, which I've no doubt was her intent.

Despite the attitude that accompanied it, the idea is solid, so I pull out my phone and do the same.

"Okay, I've got 'em." Sydney sets her phone on the desk.

I type out my third song choice into my notes. "You wanna go first, or shall I?"

"Go for it."

I clear my throat. "Okay. So for nineties alternative, I have 'Creep' by Radiohead."

If I'm not mistaken, she actually looks impressed. "Nice."

I can't help the smirk that forms. "For sixties

soul, I have 'Dock of the Bay.' That's from Otis Redding."

Sydney snorts. "Like I don't already know that."

I raise my brows. "You're into music, huh?"

"I *love* all kinds of music. It's my favorite thing in the world." She laughs. "Sadly, as Cam likes to tell me, people would pay me *not* to sing, so dance was a good backup."

I quirk my head to the side. "Cam?"

"Cam, A.K.A. Cameron, A.K.A. my bestie," she explains. "The blonde who was with me at the Malibu party."

"Ah." I nod in understanding. "Greatest bitch of all time."

"One and the same." She gifts me with a huge grin. "Gimme your third song."

"For current rock, I have 'Bloody Valentine' by MGK." I wag my brows suggestively. "I showed you mine. Now, you have to show me yours."

"Okay." Her sea-green gaze drops to her screen. "For classical, I have 'Canon in D.' Rap, I had to go with my girl, Megan Thee Stallion. It was hard to narrow it down, but I chose 'Girls in the Hood' because that one's extra badass." She smiles again. "For pop, 'Dangerous Woman' by Ariana Grande."

And just like that, this newfound ease between us disappears.

My jaw tics. "What made you pick that last song?"

Sydney shrugs. "Dunno. I just really like it."

I scoff. "I bet."

She frowns. "What's that supposed to mean?"

Oh, I don't know. Maybe that this amnesia act you've been putting on was all a bunch of bullshit?

It's too coincidental that Sydney just happened to pick the one song we danced to right before she did her best impression of a Hoover all over my dick. The question is, what's her angle? Is this her way of telling me she *does* remember everything that happened that night, and now she's holding it over me?

I slam my Chromebook shut and shove it in my bag. "Forget about it. I need to go."

Her eyes widen. "What? We're in the middle of class. Where are you going?"

"Anywhere but here," I sneer.

The teacher calls my name twice, but I ignore her and head straight to the student parking lot. One advantage of being a king is that our untouchable nature applies to teachers as well. Occasionally, one will assert their authority, but it's all bluster as long as we make passing grades. When I get to my car, I dig through my glove box, cursing when I see that I'm fresh out of Oxy. Thankfully, I still have a few Xannies left, so I dump two of those in my palm and take a deep breath once the pills slide down my throat.

In about thirty minutes, everything should be gravy, and I can head back inside. I'm sure Sydney has already texted her new buddies, Ainsley and Jazz, about my disappearing act. I'm going to need the extra chill to deal with them at lunch today. Good thing I came prepared because all the women in my life are fucking complicated. As I close my eyes, waiting for my little white saviors to take effect, I make a mental note to hit my supplier up for some refills.

I have a feeling shit's about to get a lot worse before it gets better.

chapter
fifteen

SYDNEY

"Hey, Syd. I'm glad you could make it today."
Ainsley pulls out the chair next to her. "Why don't
you sit here so I can monopolize all your time?"

Jazz told me last week Bentley usually takes the
chair next to hers, so they're probably trying to
prevent him from being butthurt when he shows. *If*
he shows. Who knows after the runner he pulled
earlier.

"Thanks." I give her a small smile, grateful she's
trying to limit the awkwardness as much as possible.

Reed chokes on the sip he was taking. "This is
going to be interesting."

I—along with everyone else at the table—follow
Reed's gaze to see Bentley standing in the food line
with some tiny blonde chick. She's absolutely

gorgeous and hanging all over him like a baby koala. I look down, surprised when I feel the pain of my fingernails scoring my palm. Who cares if Bentley Fitzgerald has some rando on his arm? Not this girl. And I definitely don't care he's looking down at her with a sexy, satisfied grin, as if he just got off, and she's responsible for it.

That's probably exactly what happened.

Kingston groans and scrubs a hand over his face before muttering, "Fucking Bent."

Jazz looks like she's trying to murder the couple with her eyeballs. "Who is that?"

Ainsley rolls her eyes. "Rebecca Jenner. She's had a lady boner for Bentley since middle school. Girl's always watching him really intently, which is a little creepy when you think about it. I'm honestly surprised he's giving her the time of day, though. She's like the textbook definition of an airhead. I thought he was over girls with no substance."

I pinch my leg under the table, telling myself it doesn't matter. Bentley is a moody prick. I don't need dudes like that in my life.

Ainsley's sympathetic eyes flash in my direction. "Syd, you wanna take our food outside?"

"Why would I want to do that?"

I take a bite off a fry, choking back the sour

feeling in my stomach when Petite Barbie presses up on her toes to kiss Bentley's cheek.

"Um..." Ainsley and Jazz share a loaded look. "Never mind, I guess."

Bentley and the blonde approach, setting their trays on the table before taking a seat.

"Why don't you come a little closer, babe?" Bentley wraps his arms around her waist and pulls her into his lap.

She giggles. "Oh my God, I can't believe, I'm like, sitting at a royal table. On top of a king, no less!"

"Like, oh my God. Totally," Jazz mocks, earning a dirty look from Bentley.

Kingston leans over and whispers something in her ear.

"Fuck that," she spits out. "He's behaving like a dick."

Bentley scoffs. "You gotta problem, Jazzy Jazz?"

Barbie wiggles as she kisses his neck. Without checking under the table, I can't be sure, but I think his hand may be up her skirt.

Jazz puts her hand on her boyfriend's forearm as he tenses. "Yeah, I do. With *you*. You're being an ass."

Bentley laughs. "How do you figure? Because I invited the lovely Ramona to lunch?"

Barbie giggles. "It's Rebecca."

"Sure, babe. I knew that." Bentley winks at her before turning back to the angry brunette next to him. "You and Ains got to bring a new friend to the table." His eyes briefly flicker over to me. "Why can't I do the same?"

"I never said you couldn't. But that's not what this is." Jazz narrows her big brown eyes. "What are you on, Bent? This isn't you."

Now he really laughs, drawing the attention of nearby students. God, this is getting uncomfortable. Jazz is right, though. He's definitely high on something. His pupils are *huge*.

"Look, you guys obviously have some issues you need to work out, so I'm gonna go."

I start to rise, but Ainsley wraps her hand around my wrist, imploring me to stay. "Syd. Don't go. You didn't do anything wrong."

Bentley's head swings to Ainsley. "And *I* did?! What the hell is your problem, Ainsley?"

"Calm the fuck down, dude," Kingston growls.

Reed is now glaring at his friend, too. "Watch your tone. That's not what she's saying."

Rebecca pouts when Bentley picks her up and sets her on the chair next to him. "Why don't you tell me what she *was* saying then, Prescott? Since evidently being exceptionally pussy-whipped has made you a mind reader."

Reed's nostrils flare. "Maybe we should step outside, Bent."

The chair screeches as Bentley shoots out of it. "Why not? Kingston already got his cheap shot in. Might as well add to it."

Now Kingston is on his feet, and Jazz is, too, trying to defuse the situation. "We've already settled this. You fucking deserved that shit, and you know it."

Bentley's forearms flex when he holds his arms out to the side. "Why's that, Davenport? Because I offered to take care of your girl?" Bentley sneers when a collective gasp rings out. "It's not like it'd be the first time I made her come. Don't worry; I'll let you watch again."

"You motherfucker!" Kingston lunges for Bentley, but Jazz presses her hand on his chest.

"Get out of here, Bentley, before you say something else you can't take back! I swear to God, I will kick your ass myself if you don't knock this shit off." She whips her head to Kingston when he takes a step forward. "Don't. Not here."

Bentley looks Jazz over with a smarmy smile. "Don't worry about me, Jazzy. Take care of your boy. I'm out of here. Let's go, Roberta."

"It's Rebecca," she reminds him as she's hurrying to keep up with him.

"What-the-fuck-ever." Bentley waves his hand dismissively.

I think we all take a breath as Bentley and Blondie leave the dining room. Jazz and Kingston exchange a few quiet words before retaking their seats. Both of their cheeks are flushed, but I don't know if it's from anger or embarrassment. Maybe a little of both.

"Mind your own fucking business!" Kingston shouts. "Show's over, assholes!"

Nobody says a word for a solid minute.

"Jazz? What was Bentley talking about?" Ainsley rolls her lips. "About you and him, and..."

I'd be lying if I said I wasn't curious, too.

When Jazz looks up, her eyes are filled with unshed tears. She briefly glances at me before turning to her boyfriend. "I can't... can we get out of here?"

Ainsley's face falls. "Jazz—"

Kingston's jaw tics. "Not now, Ains."

Without another word, Kingston takes Jazz's hand, and they leave the dining room. Now it's just me, Ainsley, and Reed, and a whole lotta eyes staring at us.

"Um..." I blow out a breath. "As fun as all this

drama has been, I don't really have much of an appetite anymore. I think I'm going to hang at the library."

Ainsley gives me a sad smile. "I'm sorry, Sydney."

"Nothing to be sorry about." I wave her off. "I'll talk to you later, okay?"

She nods. "Okay."

Reed lifts his chin. "Later."

Instead of heading to the library, I opt to sit in my car and call Cam. She should be at lunch for another fifteen minutes or so and hearing her voice will do me a lot of good right now. I hit the button to FaceTime her, checking my reflection in the mirror as it rings. When she doesn't answer, I end the call and text her, asking her to call me back. I don't really feel like dealing with people right now, so I cue up my chill playlist, crack my window, and recline my chair.

My brain replays all the shit that just went down in the cafeteria and earlier in second period. What is Bentley's deal? And why can't I seem to let it go? I am not a girl who usually wastes time on someone who doesn't deserve it, but for some reason, I want to know what makes that boy tick. I want to get up close and personal with whatever demons he's clearly fighting. There's just something about him that tells me he's worth the effort, but for the life of me, I couldn't tell you what that may be.

The roar of an engine startles me as I'm zoning out. *What the hell?* I hate that I know which car that engine belongs to, but I do. I get out of my Audi and sure enough, three spots down, Fall Out Boy starts blasting out of a silver Porsche as it idles. *He's not about to drive somewhere, is he?* I've no doubt that boy is fucked up in some way. I don't think; I'm running on pure instinct when I jog over to his car and bang on the passenger window, right as he's shifting into reverse. Thankfully, Barbie is nowhere to be found, so at least we won't have an audience.

Bentley mutters something as he shifts back into park and turns the music off. I wait for him to roll the window down before I speak.

"Are you stupid?"

I frown when I spot a bag of weed sitting on the center console for anyone to see. Jesus, he's even dumber than I thought.

"What do you want?" Bentley follows my gaze, grabs the plastic bag, and shoves it into the glove box.

"Bentley, you can't drive."

"Fuck off, Mom. I'm fine."

"Charming." I give him a wry look, holding my cell up. "I swear to God, if you pull out of this lot,

I'll be on the phone with the cops so fast, you won't make it a mile before they're pulling your ass over."

His brown eyes narrow. "You wouldn't dare."

I shake my phone. "Try me. I may not like you, but I don't want you—or anyone else for that matter—to die just because you think you're okay to drive right now."

Bentley's stupidly square jaw tics as he stares me down, probably trying to gauge whether or not I'm bluffing. He must see the truth behind my words because he kills the engine and slams his hand on the steering wheel a moment later.

"Fuck!"

"Where were you going?"

He shakes his head. "None of your business."

"Fine. Let me rephrase. What is so goddamn important that you needed to drive while you're *clearly* intoxicated?"

"Still none of your fucking business." Bentley sniffles.

I cross my arms over my chest. "Well, you can't go back to class in this condition, so what do you propose we do?"

"*We?*" He scoffs. "*We* aren't going to do anything."

I round the hood of the car until I'm standing beside the driver's door, feeling his gaze on me the entire time. "Get in the passenger seat. If you want to go somewhere, I'll drive you. No questions asked."

He laughs. "You do realize this car costs two-hundred grand, right? Nobody drives her but me."

I roll my eyes. God, what is it with boys always feminizing their vehicles?

"I don't give a shit which car we take. If you don't want me driving your precious car, get in mine." I jerk my head to the side. "It's three spots over."

He stretches his neck like he's trying to spot my Audi, but there's a Maserati Levante right next to us. Bentley's Porsche is too low to the ground for him to possibly see over it.

"Fine."

I step back a little as he opens the car door and climbs out of the vehicle. When he gets to his full height, I subconsciously move back *a lot* more because his ridiculously kissable lips are a little too close for comfort. Not that I noticed his lips were kissable or anything. Okay, fine, so I noticed. The boy is fly as fuck, and one thing I definitely remember from the night we met is what an excellent kisser he is.

Damn it, Sydney, stop staring at his mouth.

"Why are you looking at me like that, Sydney?"

His tone is mocking, as if he knows *exactly* why I'm looking at him like this. "And why does it seem like you're two seconds away from bolting? What's the matter, princess? Afraid you can't keep your hands to yourself if I'm within reach?" When his long legs move in my direction, I have to make a conscious effort not to retreat.

My eyes narrow. "Don't flatter yourself. I was moving away in case your inebriated ass fell over. I don't need you taking me down with you and pinning me to the ground."

Bentley releases a dark chuckle as he comes closer. "I thought you said you didn't lie." Another step. "But *that...*" And another one. "Was a *big* fucking lie." His toes bump against mine as he takes one final step before caging me in against a black Escalade. Bentley runs the bridge of his nose along the slope of my neck, making me shiver against my will. I can feel his lips curving into a smile as he presses them against my ear. "Because we both know that if I was *pinning you down*, you wouldn't hate it one bit. Your pussy would be soaked, *begging* to be filled." He braces a hand on my hip. "In fact, I'll bet a thousand bucks if my fingers reached under your skirt right now, I'd find exactly that. Shall we see if I'm right, sweetheart?"

Nope. Definitely not, because I don't have the money to pay up.

I place my palm flat against his chest and push. "Get off of me, Bentley."

"Yeah, didn't think you'd have the guts to do it." I want to punch the smirk off his face as he steps back. "You still wanna drive me somewhere?"

"I'll drive you." I nod. "Just keep your hands to yourself."

As Bentley folds his large body into my passenger seat, laughing under his breath, I really hope I'm not going to regret this.

chapter
sixteen

SYDNEY

Well, I've gotta say. This is probably the last place I expected we'd wind up. When I offered to drive Bentley somewhere, I thought maybe he'd want to hit up a fast-food joint. Or go back to his house. Perhaps even the beach. But never in my wildest dreams did I think he'd want to come *here*.

"Where to?" I ask as I ease through the gates of Westlake Cemetery.

Bentley's knee is bouncing wildly. Whatever drug he took back at school has seemed to wore off, but he's still agitated. I'm guessing our location has something to do with that.

"I can just get out here and walk."

"You don't have a particular destination in

mind?" I wave my hand toward the massive stretch of green grass before us. "Or maybe I should say a particular grave?"

Bentley scrubs a hand down his face. "This was a mistake. Just let me out here."

I pull off to the side of the narrow road and shift into park. "And then what?"

"And then don't fucking worry about it," he snaps, pulling off his seat belt.

"Nuh-uh." I shake my head, pressing the button to kill the engine. "You don't get to be an ass right now, Bentley. Look. I know whatever reason we're here is personal to you—and I respect that—but you need to respect *me* as well. You don't get to treat me like shit when I've done *nothing* to deserve it. You wanted to come here for a reason, so you might as well do whatever you came here to accomplish."

"*Just leave, Sydney.* You have no business being here. You're the *last person* I should've brought here. I'll order an Uber to get home."

He climbs out of my car and starts walking away without another word. There's no way I'm letting him get away without explaining what the hell that cryptic statement meant, so I follow.

"Bentley!" I shout when he speeds up. "Stop!"

To my surprise, he stops walking and plops his

ass down on the curb, hanging his head in resignation. I approach slowly, quietly, until I'm standing right in front of him. When Bentley's eyes lift, my breath stutters. Those dark chocolate orbs are filled with misery. Pure, unadulterated agony. Shit, he really is broken on the inside, isn't he? Bentley Fitzgerald may fool a lot of people with the blasé act he puts on, but he's not hiding a damn thing right now. My heart clenches in empathy. This boy is hurting badly.

"You shouldn't be here, Sydney." His deep voice is gritty, his sentence choked off at the end like it took considerable effort to speak a few words.

I lower myself to the ground, careful not to flash him in the process. "Bentley, you've gotta give me a clue. I feel like I've done something wrong, and what you said a few minutes ago supports that, but I can't think of a damn thing that would cause you to hate me so much. We barely know each other."

"I don't hate you," he says quietly, wringing his hands together. "I hate myself."

It's not really a conscious thought when I fold my hand over his and twine our fingers together. Bentley stiffens at the contact but quickly gives into it. It's odd how perfectly natural this feels with someone who's essentially a stranger. I'm not a big touchy-feely person, but I get the sense that Bentley is and that he needs this. We just sit here holding hands on a curb in the middle of a cemetery. No words are necessary. At one point, I rest my head on his shoulder, which causes him to relax just a little bit more. Finally, after maybe twenty minutes or so, Bentley is the first one to break the silence.

"Syd, I really do need time. I wasn't kidding about catching an Uber home. There's someone... uh, here, that I need to talk to. I know that sounds dumb, or whatever, considering where we are, but—"

I squeeze his hand. "It's not dumb. But I'm not leaving. I'll wait in my car, and when you're done—however long that takes—I'll drive you home."

He thinks about that for a moment before releasing my hand to stand. He extends his arm, helping me off the curb. "I don't want to waste any more of your time."

I look him dead in the eye. "You're not wasting my time. I'll just be in my car listening to music. Take all the time you need."

Bentley nods, muttering, "Thanks."

He goes in one direction while I head in the other toward my car. I watch as he walks along the grass for quite a ways before stopping and sinking down to the ground, presumably next to the grave he came here for. I don't want to intrude, so I repeat my routine from earlier, reclining my seat and pulling up a zen playlist. I must doze off for a bit because Bentley is knocking lightly on the passenger window the next thing I know. I hit the button to unlock the door and lift my seat until it's back in the proper position to drive.

I give him a soft smile as he gets in the car. "You good?"

He gives a single nod. "Yeah."

I push the buttons on my navigation until I get to the address input section. "Plug your address in there, and I'll take you home."

Bentley types a Calabasas address into the computer and hits the "start navigation" button. I'm surprised our houses are so close together— about five miles or so—but I suppose I shouldn't be considering their proximity to Windsor Academy. Neither he nor I say a word as we drive. When I pull in front of a Spanish-style mansion, I shift into park, allowing the car to idle.

Bentley clears his throat. "Do you want to come in? Maybe we can get started on that assignment since you're already here?"

I look at the clock on my dash and shake my

head. "I can't. I'm actually teaching a class in about an hour."

"Dance, right? At your mom's studio?"

I raise my brows, wondering which one of his friends gave him that piece of information. "Yeah. Tonight, I have two lyrical classes back to back, followed by hip-hop."

He searches my eyes. "You like it? Teaching, I mean?"

"I love it." I smile.

Bentley briefly looks away before returning his gaze to me. "I guess we can figure out another time to meet, huh?"

"I don't have any classes tomorrow, but I need to cover the front desk from four to five. Maybe you can meet me after? There's actually a room in the back of the studio for private lessons that isn't used very often, and it has a great sound system. It's sort of becoming my office-slash-personal-practice-space. We can hang there if you want."

He considers that for a moment before nodding. "Okay." Bentley gets out of the car, leaning on the doorframe. "I'll see you tomorrow."

I swallow. *God, why is my mouth suddenly so dry?* "See you then."

He starts to close the door, but before he does, he says, "Thanks for being so... chill today."

I wave him off. "No biggie."

As I watch Bentley walk into his house before driving off, I question the truth behind my last statement. Because the thing is... whatever happened between that boy and me this afternoon feels like a *very* big deal.

"Okay, one more time, and then we're out of here, ladies and gents. Five, six, seven, eight!"

As I watch my beginner hip-hop class go through the first half of their spring recital routine, I zone out for what feels like the millionth time tonight. I suppose it's good I can practically do this job in my sleep because I can't stop thinking about Bentley. Wondering whose grave he was visiting this afternoon. Why he's seemingly stuck in a downward spiral, doing drugs in the middle of the school day, and being an asshole to people he cares about deeply.

I know Jazz or Ainsley would probably tell me if I asked, or at least give me a hint, but I'd feel like a gossip if I went that route, and spilling the tea is *so* not my style. Plus, I wouldn't feel like I earned the right to know if it didn't come straight from the source, and the thought of that makes me feel icky. The tiny glimpses Bentley's afforded me of the man behind the mask are of someone I'd like to know. But at the same time, do I really want to make his problems *my* problems? 'Cause, the boy's definitely got some major issues. Lord knows I have enough on my plate with school, work, and prepping for my audition next month.

Once my students finish their routine, I cut the music and clap my hands together. "Great job, everyone. I'll see you next week."

Cameron waits until every last tween and parent leaves the studio before locking the door behind them. She and I are the only ones here on Mondays, so it's up to us to close up shop once my final class ends. My bestie used to take courses here, which is how we met, but nowadays, she only dances for fun. My mom's former receptionist was leaving for college when Cam was looking for a job, so she naturally slid into the part-time position. It's pretty awesome working with her, especially since we can no longer see each other at school.

I lean against the doorjamb to our main dance room. "You need help with anything?"

"Nah." She shakes her head. "I finished about twenty minutes ago. We just need to toss the garbage in the dumpster on the way out. You wanna stick around for a bit and practice?"

"No." I pull my scrunchie out and re-do my messy bun. "I'm pretty wiped. It's been a long day."

Cam assesses me carefully. "I noticed. You wanna talk about it? Zach's not giving you shit, is he?"

I frown. "I haven't heard from him since the party. Did he say something to you at school?"

She bites her bottom lip. "After the final bell, I ran into him in the hall. He told me to give you his best and that he'd *be in touch* soon."

I wave my imaginary pom-poms. "Lucky me. Zach is delusional—or a flat-out dumbass—if he thinks I'd ever give him another shot, especially after the way he treated me Friday night."

"No shit." Cam laughs. "But to be fair, you weren't exactly dating him for his brains."

"I'm not too proud to admit that I find him attractive, but in my defense, he wasn't a *terrible* boyfriend." I avert my eyes, biting the tip of my thumb. "Until, you know, I figured out he was cheating on me."

"Well, it's his loss, and I don't think we should waste any more time talking about that idiot." Cameron sighs. "Hey, you can still cover for my dentist appointment tomorrow, right?"

"Yep, I'm good." I nod. "Although, I should probably warn you that someone is meeting me here afterward. We're going to work on a school project in the back studio."

Cam tilts her head to the side. "Why do I get the feeling you're not telling me everything? Who are you meeting?"

I shrug, trying to appear nonchalant, but I'm sure I'm failing miserably because she knows me so well. "Bentley Fitzgerald."

Her lips form into a cheeky grin. "Oh, really now?"

I narrow my eyes. "Oh, don't even go there. It's not like we'll be alone. You, my mom, and Shayna will be in the building."

She raises her brows. "But the private dance room is at the back end of this place, and the soundproofing is *excellent*."

Now I roll my eyes. "Yeah, just like it is in the other two rooms where we blast music. What's your point?"

Cameron holds her palms out. "No point, Sydney. Don't get your panties in a bunch. I'm just saying… if you and Mr. Hottie Pants just happened to get freaky back there, no one would be the wiser. You are aware that's the only room without an observation window, right?"

I'll give her a wry look. "Of course I'm aware. You do remember I've spent more time in this building than anywhere else, right?"

Cameron giggles. "I suppose we'll just have to wait and see what happens, won't we?"

"Yeah, yeah," I mutter. "Let's just get out of here, okay?"

"Sure, Syd." Her lips twitch. "Do you feel like swinging through a drive-thru on the way home? I'm freaking starving."

I nod. "Yeah, that sounds good. Do you have any place in particular in mind?"

She nods. "In-N-Out sound okay? I'm in the mood for a Double-Double. And some fries. Ooh, and a giant milkshake."

"You and your carbs."

This girl has an obsession with simple carbohydrates. I call her a carb-a-tarian because I swear carbs make up for over ninety percent of her diet. If that's not a real thing, it should be. I'm pretty sure she has the world's fastest metabolism, eating all the crap she does and still remaining tiny. I definitely can't get away with that. If I didn't dance as often as I do, my thighs would be a hell of a lot thicker than they already are. Not that I'm complaining, mind you. I love having curves.

Most serious dancers are stick figures because

you burn so many calories during each class. I may be taller than average, but my height doesn't hide the fact that I inherited my mom's large lower body muscles and boobs. The latter of which tends to be a problem during dance, but all of my leotards have built-in support bras, which help.

Cam shrugs. "I make no apologies."

I laugh. "I wouldn't expect you to."

We lock up the studio and dump the garbage before making our way to my Audi. Cameron doesn't have a car yet because even POS's are expensive, so I drive her around whenever I can. If she needs to, her mom will let her borrow the only car in their household, but considering the woman is gone more often than not with said car—prowling for a new husband, no doubt—it's not really an option all that often. I really wish Cameron's mom would get her act together, but that's a problem for another day, I suppose.

We grab food on the way, and ten minutes after that, I'm pulling into my driveway. Cam's house is only two blocks from mine, which is really convenient for carpooling to and from work. As I'm inhaling my burger at the kitchen table, I once again think about my afternoon with Bentley. I can't stop myself from wondering what he's doing right now and who he's with. Maybe Barbie showed up at his house for round two. I tell myself to ignore the pain in my chest when I think about that, but it's much easier said than done.

God, I am so screwed when it comes to that boy, aren't I?

chapter
seventeen

BENTLEY

I swore to myself that I would never step foot in a dance studio again, yet here I am, in the parking lot of one. When Sydney asked me to meet her here, my first instinct was to say no. But then I would've had to explain why I have an aversion to places like this, and I didn't want to do that either. Besides, I feel like maybe it's time to stop being such a pussy and face my demons head-on. What better way to start than this?

Yesterday was kind of a wake-up call for me. Whoever said drugs cause you to make bad decisions wasn't kidding. Benzos and cocaine are a combo I can safely say I'll never do again. The Xanax I swallowed made me sleepy, so I decided to take a little power nap under the bleachers because

Porsches are not made for stretching out. The problem with that plan is when I got there, I found that chick Rebecca, along with a few of her little cheerleader friends, doing lines of coke. When she offered me a sample straight from her ample cleavage, I figured why the hell not?

I typically stick to weed, and as of lately, a pill here and there, but cocaine never appealed to me before. I mean, why waste your money on a high that only lasts fifteen to thirty minutes? You might as well just light some Benjamins on fire. But... it was right there waiting for me to snort off the tempting swell of her tits, so I did. I may have kept my face buried in her boobs a little longer than I should've because I imagined they were attached to an entirely different person.

When my dick started getting hard—because they're tits, I'm a dude, and it's been a minute since I've fucked anyone—let's just say Rebecca noticed, and she was *more than willing* to help me take care of the problem. Sadly, the second she fell to her knees and I looked down on a head of pin-straight blonde hair instead of dark and curly locks, I completely lost interest. I had to save face, so I invited Rebecca to lunch instead, promising to take a rain check later, although I have no intention of honoring that.

And fuck, let's not even get into what happened

at lunch. I was just so on edge, I couldn't seem to help myself. Kingston has been texting and calling me nonstop with all sorts of colorful threats, saying we need to meet up. It would be a massive understatement to say he's furious with me, and it's not like I can blame him. I'm pissed at myself.

I can't believe I said what I said, in front of the entire dining room, no less. In a matter of seconds, I demolished the trust of two of the most important people in my life, and I don't know how in the hell I'm supposed to recover from that. If I were Kingston and Jazz, I sure as fuck wouldn't forgive me. I'm sure all the gossip whores at Windsor are having a field day with that one, letting their imaginations run wild with the bread crumbs I left behind.

Rumors were already flying, shipping the three of us into some ménage relationship, which is fucking comical because there's no way Kingston would ever go for something like that. Not with Jazz. And it's not like I would be interested in sharing the woman I loved either. It was one night —one of the hottest of my life because Jazz is pretty fucking incredible—but there were definitely extenuating circumstances at play, and it will never happen again. Shit, I'm lucky if either one of them will ever *talk* to me at this point.

I skipped school today because when I woke up this morning, I knew I would have to face the consequences of my actions, and I wasn't ready to do so. I know it's a pussy move, and I'm going to have to deal with it sooner rather than later, but one thing at a time. Right now, I need to deal with my present situation. I really need to get laid soon, though. I swear carpal tunnel is starting to set in from all the times I've jerked off over the last couple of months. It's gotten even worse since Sydney showed up at Windsor. Hell, last night alone, my boner wouldn't go down until after four *very* strenuous sessions because I couldn't stop thinking about her. I was afraid I was actually going to chafe the poor guy.

I curse when I look at the clock on my dash. I can't put this off any longer. I just need to nut the fuck up and get in there. I take a deep breath as I approach the front door. There might be a different name on the building, but the set-up is almost identical to the studio I'm familiar with, giving me all sorts of uncomfortable déjà vu vibes. When you first walk into the brightly lit space, there's a reception desk to the left—sans the woman I was expecting to be sitting there—and a room to the right behind a wall of windows, where a dozen or so parents are oohing and aahing over their precious little ones in pink tights.

A second, slightly smaller room with another set of windows is on the opposite wall, but that one has older children—middle schoolers, I'm guessing—dressed in black leotards and shiny black pants. I glance around, looking for Sydney, but don't see her, so I take a seat in one of the chairs to wait. It's only a matter of seconds before I get a strange sense of awareness and look up. Sydney is walking toward me, carrying a giant box. The cardboard is obscuring her face, but I'd recognize that body anywhere. God knows I've dreamed about it enough.

She seems to be struggling with the box, so I rise from my chair to assist her. Sydney startles when I place my hands on the cardboard and lift.

"Here, let me."

Her sea-green eyes lock onto mine the moment her beautiful face comes into view. A pink blush stains her cheeks when I smile, making my grin grow even wider.

"Thanks."

I raise my brows when several seconds pass without a word. "Where do you want it?"

Sydney blinks rapidly. "Oh. Um... right next to the desk would be awesome."

I set the box where she indicated and stand to my full height. I suppress a groan when I get a good look at what she's wearing. The black joggers she has on aren't revealing by any means, but she's wearing them over a black leotard that does *nothing* to hide her curves. Her tits are practically spilling out of the thing, but not in an intentional way. There's just no way to conceal them with something so formfitting. There's also no way I'll be able to concentrate on our assignment if she's dressed like that.

Fuck.

She motions to the box. "Recital costumes came in today. We need to make sure they're all accounted for, then call the parents to let them know. There's actually one more box in the back. Would you mind?" She holds her left arm out. "I'd normally be able to manage it myself, but my wrist is still a little sore from my fall last week."

I incline my head in the direction she came from. "Lead the way." I'm transfixed by the sway of her hips as she walks in front of me, down a long hallway until we reach a storage room. Damn, this place is bigger than it initially looked. "So, that's why you were wearing the Ace bandage last week? Because you fell?"

Sydney points to a large box on the floor. "Yeah... something like that."

I frown. "What does that mean?"

Her teeth press into her lower lip as if she's contemplating something. "It was more of a push than a fall."

"Someone pushed you?" I think I surprise both of us by the outrage in my tone. "Who?"

Sydney does the lip-biting thing again before answering. "I don't know. Some girl shoved me as I was coming out of the bathroom, but I didn't see her."

"What the fuck?" I throw my hands up. "Did you tell your dad what happened? Did he check the security feed?"

She nods. "Yeah, I told him, but because it happened right outside of the bathroom, he couldn't see anything. He said it's one of the few dark zones in the hallways where the cameras can't film."

"Well, that's fucking convenient, isn't it?"

Sydney's full lips curve upward. "That's what I said."

I pick up the box. "Did they say anything?"

I see her shrug out of the corner of my eye. "She called me a nasty name, but I can't say I was

183

too surprised based on how I've been treated since I arrived."

I release a heavy breath. "Jazz and Ainsley are cool, but the rest of the female population at Windsor is made up of crazy bitches." I smirk. "Present company notwithstanding."

She folds her arms. "Even Barbie?"

I raise a brow. "Barbie?"

Her eyes roll back. "Rebecca."

I set the box down and rub the back of my neck. "Yeah... about that. I suppose I should get the apology out of the way. I'm sorry you got stuck in the middle of that shit show. I wasn't exactly... myself yesterday."

Sydney leans against a shelving unit. "Why is that?"

I make a rolling motion with my hand. "Right before lunch, I... uh... decided to try powder for the first time. Needless to say, I didn't have the best reaction. I can be an asshole, no doubt. Still, I'm not usually so aggressive, and I don't typically inflict my assholery onto my friends."

"Well, it was definitely... interesting. And by interesting, I mean incredibly awkward." Sydney chuckles. "I'm honestly surprised you came here. After you were a no-show at school, I wasn't sure."

"I figured it was best to give things at least a day

to calm down on all fronts." My shoulders lift. "Did they seem... I mean, did you have lunch with them today? Did anyone say anything to you?"

My jaw clenches as I wait for her reply. The fact that I'm asking this woman for information about *my* friends confirms how quickly she's infiltrated our group. I love it as much as I hate it, and that in itself is confusing as fuck.

Christ, I'm a mess.

Her eyes bounce between mine. "Jazz and Kingston weren't there. I had lunch with Reed and Ainsley, though. Ains wasn't as bubbly as she seems to usually be, but it wasn't too bad, I guess."

I scrub a hand over my face and groan.

Sydney pulls my hand away and weaves our fingers together like she did at the cemetery. "Hey. Don't beat yourself up so much. Human beings are flawed; we make mistakes. What matters is whether or not you truly regret your actions, and it's obvious you do."

I hang my head for a moment before turning my palm over, looking at our joined hands. "Why are you so nice to me? I don't exactly deserve your kindness."

She squeezes. "Because the world could use a little nice. And yes, you've been a prick, but... I don't think that's who you really are. The night of the party... when my ex was getting pushy... if you were really *that* guy, you would've walked on by. It's a testament to your character that you didn't. The fact that Jazz and Ainsley are so fond of you is, too."

I scoff. "I don't think they're so fond of me right now, especially Jazzy."

Sydney squeezes my hand again, waiting to speak until I look up. "You were having an... exceptionally rough day yesterday. If they're true friends, they'll understand. Just talk to them, Bentley. Talk to *someone* about what's eating at you. Whatever it is, you can't just let it suck you dry."

I smirk. "Is it bad that my mind instantly went to a dirty place with that last part?"

Her eyes twinkle with amusement. "Not at all. Because mine totally did, too."

I take a deep breath when Sydney tucks her face into my neck, chuckling. When she lifts her head, mine automatically lowers until our mouths are maybe two inches apart. Neither one of us says a thing. We just... stare, trying to get a read on one another. When I can't take it anymore and move in to close the gap, her eyes widen.

"Bentl—"

"Syd?" a feminine voice calls. "You back here?"

Sydney jumps back, pulling her hand away. "Shit."

A second later, a middle-aged, darker-skinned version of Sydney stands in the doorway.

She raises her delicate brows, taking in the scene. "Well, I can't say I was expecting this." She reaches her hand out. "I'm Daphne. Sydney's *mom*. And you are?"

Fuck. I'm really glad I didn't smoke that joint before coming here. Who knew I'd be meeting the parentals today?

I clear my throat and shake her hand. "Uh... Bentley Fitzgerald. Nice to meet you, Mrs. Carrington."

She wags her finger at me. "Nuh-uh, my mother-in-law is Mrs. Carrington, and she's *old*. You can call me Daphne."

"Mom," Sydney groans. "Stop embarrassing me."

"Sorry, honey." Daphne's tone says she's not sorry *at all*. "I was caught off guard finding you hiding in the storage room with this *handsome* young man."

"Oh my God," Sydney mutters. "You're making it worse. Don't you have a class to teach?"

Her mother waves her hand dismissively. "I have two minutes. Plenty of time."

Sydney grabs my hand and pulls me out of the room. "Bentley is my partner for that psych project I was telling you about. He was just helping me carry the last box of costumes, but we'll worry about those when we're done. If you need us, we'll be in room three."

"Have fun, sweetie," her mom calls behind us. "And remember, I can walk in that room *at any time*, so no funny business. I don't care if you're eighteen. My studio, my rules."

"C'mon!" Sydney whisper-shouts, yanking on my arm. "Let's get out of here before she starts giving us *the talk*."

I'm full-on laughing when Sydney pulls me into a small room, slamming the door behind her and locking it.

She levels me with a glare. "It's not funny."

"It kind of is," I argue. "But if it makes you feel better, my mom would do the exact same thing. Let's hope they never meet because I'm pretty sure they'd be instant besties, and then we'd be really fucked."

"Noted." Sydney's lips twitch. "You ready to make this assignment our bitch?"

I smile, feeling lighter than I have in a long time. "I'm ready."

chapter eighteen

SYDNEY

"Let me pull up the instructions real quick to make sure we're doing this right."

I adjust my Chromebook on my lap and open the classroom portal. Thank God I had the foresight to stash my backpack in this room before Bentley got here, so I didn't have to deal with my mother's knowing smirk again.

Bentley's long legs are bent at the knee as he sits propped against the wall like me. "I'll open my timer for the heartbeat thing."

When the assignment loads, I read through the instructions out loud.

"Okay, so research suggests that listening to music can influence your thoughts, feelings, and behaviors. It can also have many psychological benefits like relaxing your mind, energizing your body, or even help manage pain. Today we're going to specifically focus on how different types of music can affect your heart rate." I pull up the playlist I made earlier and connect my phone to the Bluetooth speaker. "I added all six songs we chose to a playlist to make it easier for us."

"Nice." Bentley's blinding smile—and those damn irresistible dimples—are reflected in the wall of mirrors directly across from us.

I clear my throat, hoping to God he doesn't notice my skin flushing. *Again.* "I have the chart pulled up, so we can log our results. Our base rate needs to be measured after being at rest for five minutes, which I think we've been doing at this point. Then, we retake it after listening to a one-minute clip of each song. In the end, we should have seven measurements in total. It also says to notate any mood changes you feel during each song for extra credit."

Bentley fiddles with his phone. "How long should I set the timer?"

"Fifteen seconds. We'll measure the beats at our wrists and whatever number of beats we counted in that fifteen seconds, we then multiply by four to get the beats per minute."

"Simple enough." He nods. "Okay, tell me when you're ready for the first one."

I place two fingers on my pulse point. "Ready."

He places his phone on the floor between us and starts the timer. "Go."

I count fifteen beats before he calls time. Bentley gets twelve. I multiply those numbers and type the results onto the chart.

Cueing up the first song, I ask, "You ready?"

Bentley leans his head back and closes his eyes. "Yep."

I watch the time as Radiohead plays through the speakers and cut it off after we hit the one-minute mark. We measure our heartbeats, noting a slight increase for each of us. When we switch to classical music, there's a decrease. With rock and rap, there's a noticeable spike, but when we get to the Otis Redding song, our pulses slow down again significantly.

"Last one," I say.

Bentley gets a strange look on his face right before I press play, but I don't have time to question it because I need to focus on the music. I close my eyes and rest my head against the wall like he did earlier. As "Dangerous Woman" plays, I tune every-thing else out and listen to the lyrics.

Shit.

Why didn't I consider how freaking sexy this song is when I chose it? The longer it goes on, the more turned on I'm getting. The fact that a gorgeous guy who smells incredible is sitting next to me isn't helping. Oh, who am I kidding? It's not just because *any* hot guy is in this room with me. It's one-hundred-percent because Bentley Fitzgerald is that guy.

My nipples are no doubt plainly visible through my Lycra top right now, advertising my sudden state of arousal. *Ugh.* Why didn't I throw a hoodie over my leotard? I'm so used to wearing much less than this in class, the thought never crossed my mind. The sexual tension in the room is so thick, I'm almost afraid to open my eyes because then I'd have to acknowledge this pull I feel toward the boy next to me.

When the song ends, the first thing I think is *so much for that one-minute clip we were supposed to listen to.* The second thought is, *Bentley could've just as easily stopped it, but he didn't.* The room is completely silent except for the sounds of our breathing. When I feel him shuffling next to me, I take a deep breath, knowing I can't hide behind my eyelids any longer.

"Syd," he chokes out. "Look at me."

I blink rapidly from the harshness of the over-head lights before my eyes adjust. When they do, I see Bentley's face, mere inches from mine. The hunger in his expression matches how I feel inside. I don't know which one of us moves first, but the next thing I know, our lips are pressed together, and his tongue is sliding into my mouth.

There's madness in our kiss. Complete chaos swirled with desperation. A groan rattles from deep within Bentley's chest as our mouths move against each other. I crawl on top of him at some point, this blinding sense of urgency to be closer overpowering my common sense. Bentley's rock hard, and I shamelessly take advantage of that by grinding on top of him, swiveling my hips to get just the right amount of friction on my clit. His hands are every-where—my arms, my waist, my ass. I moan as his mouth moves down the side of my neck, kissing and licking and sucking until he reaches my collarbone.

"God, you're so fucking responsive," he growls against my skin. "You make me feel insane."

"Same," I pant.

Nothing about the way I feel toward Bentley is logical. I barely know him, but when he looks at me, I feel like he *sees* me like nobody else. The way he draws me in without any effort whatso-ever is unnatural. My brain knows this, but my body... God, my body just doesn't fucking care. I could chalk it up to teenage hormones, but I'd be lying to myself. This is more than just sexual attraction. This boy and I connect on a soul-deep level.

Bentley pulls back and seeks my eyes for permission. With a single nod, his long fingers slip under the thin strap of my leotard, sliding it over my shoulder at a torturously slow pace. He does the same with the other before giving the stretchy material a good yank, freeing my breasts, so nothing is barring his view now.

"Jesus Christ," he mutters before sealing his mouth over one of my nipples.

He maneuvers our bodies until I'm lying on the floor with his weight on top of me. I stretch my arm out, pawing the surrounding area until I find my phone.

Bentley pulls back with a questioning look on his face.

I pull up a playlist—*any playlist*—and press play. "It'll be suspicious if there's no music."

His lips curve into a sexy grin when The Weeknd's voice rings through the air. "Smart."

"Bentley?"

He raises his brows. "Yeah?"

"Touch me."

There's that smile again.

God, he has a great smile.

"Yes, ma'am." His eyes are locked on mine as his tongue darts out and circles my nipple.

My back bows. "Fuck."

He does it to the other one and gets the same reaction. "You like that?"

"God, yes." I stretch my arms over my head as he resumes his delicious torture. Licking and then sucking, he brings me to the precipice of pleasure and pain before alternating sides. It feels so incredible, I can't even bother to be mad at the marks his mouth leaves behind. At least they're in a spot when I can easily hide them. When I catch our reflection out of the corner of my eye, I turn my head toward the wall of mirrors to get a better look.

Sweet baby Jesus, that's hot.

My toes curl in anticipation when he abandons my boobs and begins moving south. My leotard is way too tight over my abdomen to pull it down with any sort of finesse, so he doesn't even try. Instead, he kisses a path directly over the fabric until he reaches the top of my sweatpants.

"You want me to keep going, Syd?" His fingers loop under the elastic waistband. "Because I *really* want to find out if your pussy tastes as good as the rest of you."

"If you stop before I get off, I might actually punch you in the balls."

He chuckles. "Well, we wouldn't want that to happen, now would we?"

I tap my lower lip in mock contemplation. "Hmm... jury's still out."

His eyes twinkle with amusement before briefly flickering to the door. "I'm assuming there's a key to that lock if someone wanted to get in? Namely your mom?"

"Yeah, but she's teaching a class right now." I nod. "Show me what you've got, big boy."

Bentley flashes me a wolfish grin. "Oh, I'll show you what I've got, all right."

He pulls my pants off, taking my jazz shoes with them. Bentley's large hands grip my inner thighs and push them open as wide as they'll go, which is pretty damn far considering my flexibility. When he runs the bridge of his nose right over my Lycra-covered clit, I gasp. As he moves the material to the side, exposing my bare pussy to his hot breath, I purse my lips to stifle a moan. And when he gives me one long lick down the middle, I legit have to bite my tongue so I don't scream. The soundproofing in our dance rooms is the shit; typically, you can only hear muffled bass thumping from the other side of the door. But considering there are multiple people in this building, I'm not taking any chances. I can't believe I'm even doing this right now, but I'll be damned if I put a stop to it.

Bentley eats me like mine is the last pussy he will ever dine on. He swirls his tongue, nips, sucks, and licks every bit of my hot flesh. He moans encouragingly every time I pull on his short hair or arch into him. My hips are rocking unabashedly into him, not given one single fuck how out of control he makes me feel. When he inserts two fingers into me and curls them in just the right way, my body clenches around him as I come harder than I ever have in my life. I swear to God, my vision actually blacks out for a second.

Goddamn, this boy knows how to eat pussy.

Bentley nibbles my inner thigh, sucking on my skin, no doubt to mark me down there, too. It's such a caveman move, but I don't hate it. He resumes licking me into a frenzy, his mouth and fingers working in perfect harmony. I stare at our reflection in the mirror the entire time because I'm fascinated with the image staring back at me. I don't recognize that girl. She's sex personified with her kiss-swollen lips, glowing eyes, flushed skin, and languid limbs. And Bentley, he looks damn near feral, feasting on me like he could never get enough.

After two more orgasms, Bentley grabs the bottom of his shirt to wipe his mouth before crawling back up my body and sealing his lips over mine. He's hot and hard against my thigh as I taste myself on his lips. Right as I reach down to help him take care of that, my phone starts vibrating like crazy from its spot on the floor. I ignore it at first, working the button open on Bentley's jeans, but whoever's trying to reach me isn't giving up.

With a frustrated sigh, I pull away from Bentley's mouth. "Hold that thought for a second."

"Mmm..." Bentley holds himself in a plank position, looking down at my naked chest. "Don't worry about me. I know just how to pass the time."

I roll my eyes, grabbing my phone. I frown when I see four message alerts from Cam.

What the hell?

After reading the first two, then looking at the time, I jackknife into a sitting position, knocking Bentley back on his ass.

How has it been an hour already?

"Shit!"

"What's wrong?" Bentley frowns as I pull my top back up and reach for my pants.

"That's Cam. My mom just got done teaching her class, and she's heading this way to check on us."

"Fuck," Bentley whisper-shouts, not-so-discreetly adjusting the boner in his pants.

I run to the door to unlock it, then I take a seat next to Bentley with our backs against the wall like they were earlier. I'm setting my Chromebook on my lap, right as the door handle turns, and my mom peeks her head in.

"How's the project going, you two?"

"Fine," we say in unison, a little too quickly.

My mom narrows her brown eyes, her maternal Spidey senses kicking in, no doubt. "You sure?"

Bentley and I reek like sex. We're screwed if she comes closer.

"Positive. We're just finishing up, actually." I nod, hoping like hell I'm projecting the aloofness I'm shooting for.

My mom's eyes dart across the room. They pause when she sees my discarded dance shoes in the middle of the floor, but she doesn't say anything. "Okay... don't worry about the costumes. Cam already grabbed the second box and is halfway through the call list."

"Got it."

She gives us one last suspicion-laced glance before pulling the door closed.

I thunk my head against the wall. "Jesus. That was too close for comfort."

"It's been a while since I've had a close call with someone's parents. Mine are always gone, so I usually... uh, never mind." Bentley laughs. "It's weird, being a legal adult, but still having to worry about stuff like that, isn't it?"

"Totally weird."

I smile, telling myself to stop thinking about what Bentley usually does when his parents are gone because he's probably doing those *things* with other girls. Ugh, he was probably doing them with Barbie just last night. Not that I have a claim on him or anything, so I can't be mad, but it still makes me feel icky.

Bentley rubs the back of his neck. "I should probably get going; I have something I need to take care of. Maybe we could finish the assignment later this week at my place?"

I search his eyes, trying to figure out if *assignment* is code for *let's fool around some more*. Unfortunately, the bastard isn't giving anything away.

"Sure." I nod. "I teach the next two days, but I'm free anytime Thursday through Sunday." I unlock my phone and hand it to him. "Put your number in there, and we can figure out the details later."

Bentley takes my phone, sends himself a text, and hands it back to me. "This way, I have your number, too."

"Right." Crap, why am I acting so nervous all

of a sudden? "Well, I guess I'll talk to you later then?" I stand up to walk him out.

Before I can turn the handle, Bentley braces his arm against the door and swoops in for a kiss. As he pulls away, he leans into my ear and whispers, "I'm not nearly finished with you yet, Sydney. *I can't wait* to hear you screaming my name when we're alone."

With that, the cocky ass walks out the door, leaving me to stare after him like an idiot with my mouth hanging open.

A few seconds after I hear the bell over the studio's front door ring, Cameron shows up with a container of Clorox wipes and shoves it against my chest.

I grab the canister. "What's this?"

She scoffs. "Puh-leez. Don't play innocent with me, missy. I saw the look on that man's face when he walked out of here. *This* is to wipe up any bodily fluids you two may have left behind because I'm sure as shit not doing it for you."

"Oh, shut up." I flip her off.

Cameron holds her palms out. "Hey, don't shoot the messenger. I've gotta get back up front." She jerks her head toward the room behind me. "Go clean up your jizz"—she disguises that last word with a fake cough—"then come join me."

"Yeah, yeah," I mutter. "I'll be out in a few, asshole."

"You love me, bitch." She winks over her shoulder. "Now, get to work."

I flip her off again, but I'm secretly glad she thought of it. I think it's pretty safe to say my brain isn't firing on all cylinders right now, thanks to a certain guy doling out orgasms like they were Mardi gras beads. Although, I suppose I did show him my tits, so...

I snicker at my own joke, wondering what I'm going to do about Bentley Fitzgerald for the hundredth time today. As if things weren't complicated enough before I let him get me off. Now, they're going to be much worse. The question is... why am I not bothered by that?

chapter nineteen

BENTLEY

Goddamn, this is the best head of my life.

I'm transfixed as I watch the most beautiful girl I've ever met bobbing up and down over my shaft. I should probably care that we're in the middle of a crowded room, but I don't. I should definitely care about the occasional phone I see lifted in our direction, but again, not what I'm focusing on now. Besides, it's not like we're the only people engaging in a little public foreplay. Hell, there's a couple no more than ten feet away straight-up fucking on a recliner. That's the beauty of a frat party; anything goes.

My balls tighten as Sydney's gorgeous aqua eyes

peer up at me while her full lips are wrapped around my cock. I know I'm not going to last much longer, especially when she does this swirly thing with her tongue. God, she's so fucking good at this.

"Honey, you feel so fucking good. I'm gonna come any second, so if you don't want to swallow, you'd better back off now."

Sydney moans as she takes me in deeper.

Fuck. She's going to swallow.

Out of the corner of my eye, I catch a flash of golden blonde hair. I don't know how it's possible with all the noise in here, but I swear I can hear her gasp from across the room. When my head turns in that direction, my eyes lock on her baby blues. Carissa looks like she's about to puke as her gaze falls to the woman sucking me off.

I smirk, taunting Rissa, as I fist Sydney's curls and begin thrusting into her mouth, chasing my release.

You wanted this, remember? my eyes say. *Well, take a good look because I'm finally on board with your plan.*

I hold Carissa's stare the entire time my orgasm barrels down my spine and as I shoot my load into Sydney's mouth. I stroke the indentation of Syd's cheek lovingly, showing my appreciation for her oral skills. Carissa's eyes follow every little movement. She balls her fists, looking like she's ready to charge over here and slap me across the face as I extend my hand to help Sydney up.

"You're fucking incredible, you know that?" I grab the back of Sydney's neck, pulling her into a movie-worthy kiss.

Take a good look, Riss. You're no longer the only girl I've ever kissed on the mouth.

Sydney offers me a dreamy smile, completely oblivious to our enraptured audience of one. "You're not so bad yourself. You wanna grab a drink and head out back?"

I brush a curl away from her face. "I'd love to."

As I press a kiss against Sydney's forehead, she wraps her arms around my waist and melts into me.

I look over at Rissa one last time, giving her the most disinterested expression I can manage when I see her eyes watering. I'm not a fucking robot; seeing her cry makes me feel like shit. But then I remind myself how many times *she's* made *me* feel like shit by pushing me away and fucking the first surfer boy she could find. I have no doubt the astonishing girl in my arms wouldn't screw with my head the way Carissa does. The funny thing is, I don't blame Carissa because I encouraged our toxic relationship by continuously crawling back to her. But that changes right now because I've finally found someone I want more. Someone who won't play mind games every chance she gets. And if the tears rolling down her cheeks are any indication, I'd say Rissa just figured that out.

When Carissa turns around and bolts out of the room, the thought of chasing her never crosses my mind.

"So, tell me about my competition."

I laugh. "What makes you think you have competition?"

Sydney runs her finger along my forearm. "Well, if you've only kissed one other girl on the mouth, I'm assuming she's pretty special to you. What was her name again? Marissa?"

"Carissa." I exhale heavily, turning my hat backward.

Sydney snuggles into me further. We're out back, Sydney nestled between my legs on a lounger. There are plenty of seating options, as we're the only two people in this little corner of the yard, but I couldn't stand the thought of her sitting anywhere else. The closer she is, the easier it is to touch her silky skin.

"Carissa," she repeats. "Tell me about her. You said you're single, but I sense there's a story there."

"I *am* single," I assure her. "And after tonight, I don't think you need to worry about Carissa."

She twists around until she's facing me. "What does that mean?"

I grip her thighs, wrapping her long legs around my waist. "She was here earlier."

Sydney lifts her delicate brows. "Really? When?"

When you were blowing me like it was your job.

I decide that's probably not the most tactful answer, so instead, I say, "When we were on the dance floor. She saw us together and ran out."

Confusion crosses her face. "Why didn't you go talk to her?"

Uh... because my dick was in your mouth? Wait... I probably shouldn't say that either.

I place a soft kiss right over the freckles that run across the bridge of her nose. "Because I'm right where I want to be, with whom I want to be with."

Damn, this girl's smile does things to me. "As sweet as that is, you're dodging the question. C'mon, Bentley, you can talk to me. I genuinely want to know you better, and this girl plays an important role in your life."

"Played," I correct. "She *played* an important role in my life. Carissa is..." I take a moment to think of how best to explain this. "She's not who most people believe she is. She comes across as this sweet, all-American girl next door. Which she can be. But... I see a side of her that she hides from everyone else. Even her lifelong best friend."

Sydney frowns. "And what side is that?"

"She has... issues. It's almost like she has this... compulsion, I guess. She can't stand not being the center of attention. If people don't naturally offer their adoration and put her on a pedestal, she manipulates them until they do, including me." I laugh sardonically. "*Especially* me. The older we get, the more noticeable it becomes. She's the textbook definition of a narcissist."

"How so?"

I smile, but there's no joy behind it. "That's the most fucked-up part of all. There've been so many incidents, I literally don't know where to begin. What I *do* know is that I'm done putting up with her bullshit. I'm not saying I'll never see her again because her bestie is my best friend's twin sister, but I'm ending the cycle. I can't do it anymore." I nip her earlobe. "I don't *want* to do it anymore. I want *you*, Syd."

She scoots closer until she's straddling me. We both groan as Sydney's luscious ass rubs against my denim-clad hard-on. "This is crazy, right? I'm not the only one who feels like we've known each other forever, am I?"

I frame her face with my hands and wait for her to look at me before I speak. "You're not. It's hella crazy, but I'm feelin' it, too."

She smiles softly. "But it makes no sense. Logically, I mean. We don't know even the simplest things about each other."

"So, let's fix that."

She chuckles. "What?"

"I said, let's fix that. Ask me questions. Whatever you want to know. We'll take turns."

Sydney taps her lips in thought. "What's your favorite color?"

"Blue. And yours?"

"Also blue." Her lips curve. "What's your favorite food?"

"It's a tie between pizza and enchiladas. You?"

Her eyes widen. "Shut up! Are you serious?"

"Um... yes? What'd I say wrong?"

"Nothing." Her dark curls bounce as she shakes her head. "*My* favorite food is a tie between pizza and enchiladas."

My eyebrows lift. "No shit?"

She holds her right palm up. "Bible."

"Do you go to this school?"

"No, but my cousin does. I came with her."

Sydney nibbles on her lip before continuing. "What about you?"

"Nah, just got an invite from an old high school buddy." That's one topic I don't want to expand on quite yet, so I quickly change the subject. "Favorite sport, on the count of three. One... two... three."

"Football."

"Basketball," I say at the same time.

"Well, that's a relief." Sydney chuckles. "At least I know you're not some freaky mind reader."

"I don't know..." I rub my chin. "I bet I know what you're thinking right now."

She raises a brow. "Oh yeah? What's that?"

I smile, loving the way her eyes home in on my dimples when they pop. God bless these fuckers. I haven't met a girl yet that doesn't love 'em.

"You're thinking I'm pretty dope. Also, you really want to kiss me again."

"Damn, you're cocky, aren't you?" Sydney's head falls back in laughter before returning her distinctive gaze back to me. "But you're not wrong."

"No?" I pull her closer. "Prove it."

She places her palms on each one of my cheeks. "Gladly."

chapter twenty

BENTLEY

"You're fucking crazy if you think I'm letting you in this house. I don't want you anywhere near her." Kingston pushes me out of the way, shutting the door behind him.

I follow him to the little courtyard he and Jazzy have on the side of their house. "C'mon, dawg. I came here to apologize."

His hazel eyes narrow. "You already did that. And then you fucked up again. *Even worse.* I mean, what the hell, Bent? You swore you'd take that shit to your grave. Do you have any idea how fucking mortified Jazz is? How difficult it was for her to explain to my goddamn sister? Don't you think she's been through enough shit? How could you, man? I love you like a brother, Bent, but I don't fucking like you right now. I don't know if I will anytime soon."

"I know." I slump down on a little wooden bench that sits beneath a pergola. "I don't know what I was thinking. Well... to be frank, I *wasn't* fucking thinking. It's possible the Xannie-coke cocktail I had clouded my judgment a bit."

He plops on the bench next to me. "When the hell did you start doing coke?"

"The other day, right before lunch. Ramona offered me a line, and I decided to partake."

"Rebecca."

I wave my hand. "What-the-fuck ever. She's inconsequential."

"Yet important enough to use as bait."

"Bait?" I frown. "Bait for what?"

Kingston gives me an *are you stupid?* look. "It was clearly a ploy to make Sydney Carrington jealous. My question is, why?"

I take off my hat and comb my fingers through my hair. "I wasn't actively trying to make her jealous. I was pissed that she's everywhere I turn. Ever since she showed up, I can't seem to get away from her. It's like she's fucking haunting me, man."

"I don't think *Sydney* is the girl who's haunting you."

I look up, trying to read his expression. Kingston's insanely adept at communicating with his eyes, and right now, he might as well be screaming Carissa's name at the top of his lungs.

I kick some gravel and send it flying. "Yeah, maybe not."

"There's no maybe about it, asshole." He scoffs. "I know Sydney's arrival is stirring up a lot of memories, but she's not going away, Bent, so you need to figure out a way to make peace with that."

I don't want her to go away.

"What's that?"

Ah, fuck. Did I say that out loud?

"Huh?"

Kingston whacks me on the back of the head. "You said you don't want her to go away. When did your opinion on that matter change?"

I rub the sore spot on my head, leveling him with a dirty look. "I don't know."

He goes to smack me again, but I dodge it this time.

"Knock it off, fucker!"

He smirks. "Stop lying to me, and I will. What happened between lunch yesterday and now?"

I rest my elbows on my knees, hanging my head. "Right after lunch, when I..." I swallow the lump in my throat. "She gave me a ride to see Rissa, and we kinda talked it out."

"You shitting me?" Kingston's eyebrows lift. "How the fuck did that happen?"

"She caught me trying to pull out of the lot while I was fucked up." I shrug. "Threatened to call the cops if I drove anywhere. I don't know... maybe if I wasn't so determined to see Riss so I could get some stuff off my chest, I would've thought better. But when Sydney offered to drive me wherever I wanted to go, I accepted."

"What the fuck, dude? You were buzzing on benzos and powder, and you thought it'd be a smart idea to drive?" He shakes his head, clearly disgusted with me. "You've gotta get off this wheel of self-destruction before you kill yourself, Bent. If anyone knows how toxic that can be, it's me."

"I'm just trying to quiet all the noise in my head. Nothing is working anymore. I can't tell you when the last time I slept through the night was."

Kingston blows out a breath. "I didn't want to bring this up, but you're not giving me much choice."

My head swings to him. I don't like the ominous tone in his voice. "What?"

"I know you've been bottling shit up, and again,

nobody gets that better than me, but you've gotta find a healthier way to cope with your demons. I can't have you coming around here if you're going to be like this. Belle is coming to live with us full-time next week. I can't put her at risk like that."

Well, how's that for a verbal bitch slap?

"What the hell does that mean? I *adore* that girl. I would *never* do anything to hurt her."

"I know you wouldn't *intentionally* hurt Jazz or her little sister." He rakes his hands through his dark blond hair. "But dude... we're essentially going to be her parents, which means it's our job to set the example. Think about it. Belle's only eight, but she's extremely smart, observant, and impressionable. If you come over here high as a kite, she's going to know something's up. What if you pulled the shit you did at lunch in front of her?"

He has a damn good point, so I have nothing to say.

"Not to mention the fact that Social Services is going to be up our asses for a while. Jazz filed for permanent custody, but they could drop in for visits at any time until that goes through. Shit's changing, brother. This house—and everyone who comes into it—needs to be on the straight and narrow. I know you've been bottling shit up, and again, nobody understands that better than me, but you've gotta find a healthier way to cope with your demons. I'm not going to risk fucking this up. Belle and Jazz are too important. Don't make me choose, Bent, because you're not going to like my answer."

"Oh, trust me. I'm suffering no delusions that I could ever compete with Jazzy. Shit, *I'd* pick her over me any day." I shake my head. "I still can't believe you guys are going to be raising an eight-year-old. I mean, I love it because I know how happy Belle and Jazz will be, but it's still pretty fucking crazy. I don't know how you're going to manage everything."

"It makes me pretty fucking happy, too." A genuine smile stretches across his face, which, quite frankly, is a bit jarring. I've known this guy almost my entire life, and I've never seen him smile like he does since he stopped denying his feelings for Jazz. Despite his silver-spoon upbringing, the dude's had a rough life. "We'll have some help, though, at least while we're still in school. I hired a lady—Julia is her name—to nanny part-time. She used to live in New York, working for the lead singer of Unrequited, but she wanted to move back to LA to be closer to family."

"Cool. Cool." I nod my head.

Kingston assesses me carefully. "So, what's the deal with Sydney, dude?"

I bite the tip of my thumb, thinking about it for a moment. "Honestly? I don't know. But I think maybe... eh, never mind. Let's go with I don't know."

Kingston laughs. "Well, that certainly clears it up."

Now it's my turn to laugh. "It's all so fucking confusing, man I don't know what to think where Sydney is concerned."

"But you *are* attracted to her," he prods. "Right?"

"I think that's pretty apparent, don't you?" I can't help the smirk that forms on my lips, remembering how she writhed beneath me earlier. "I mean, I'm not blind. Who wouldn't be attracted to her?"

He does the intense staring thing again. "But it's more than that, isn't it? It's not just a physical attraction."

I shrug. "I barely know her."

"Bentley, don't forget who you're talking to here. I was there the first time you met. I saw how consumed you were by her that night. I didn't think about it until just now, but you reacted to Sydney a lot like I reacted the first time I saw Jazz. Something inside of me, whether I was willing to admit it or not, immediately knew that she was a game-changer."

"I never said Sydney was a game-changer." I shake my head in denial.

Kingston gives me a wry look. "You didn't have to. I can see it now, just like I could see it then. The question is, why are you fighting it? Why are you such a dick to Sydney? And everyone else, for that matter?"

I shrug, not really knowing how to answer that without showing my ass.

Kingston exhales. "Look, dude. I know Carissa was your world for a long time. And her death really fucked you up. But it's been over two years. Don't you think it's time to cut yourself a little slack? I know when someone dies, we tend to forget about the negative, but there was *a lot* of negative, dude, at least as far as your relationship was concerned. You need to stop blaming yourself. Rissa made the decision to end her life. Not you."

I shake my head. "You don't know what you're talking about, dawg. If you knew the truth, you wouldn't be saying that."

"So, tell me."

I blow out a breath. "It's complicated."

"Then uncomplicate it."

"Hey."

I look up at the sound of Jazz's voice and see her walking down the little path toward us. Damn, I must've really been locked inside my head if I didn't hear her coming.

"Hey, Jazzy."

Jazz looks to Kingston. "Give us a minute, will you?"

Kingston stands up and points a stern finger at me. "Don't make me come back out here and kick your ass."

I scoff. "No offense, bro. But I'm more afraid of your girlfriend than I am of you. Woman is scrappy when she wants to be."

He smirks. "You might not be such a dumbass after all."

Jazz rolls her eyes as Kingston plants a kiss on her forehead before walking away. She takes a seat beside me and leans her head on my shoulder.

I put my arm around her back and pull her into a side hug. "I'm sorry about what I said, baby girl. What I *did*. If I was thinking... if I... aw, hell. I have no excuse. I'm just fucking sorry."

"What happened, Bentley?"

I scratch the back of my head. "Uh… I kind of decided to try powder for the first time right before lunch, and let's just say I didn't have the best reaction. I was already on edge... but until the high wore off, I felt extra angry, I guess. But again, it's still not an excuse. What I did was shitty, and if you can't forgive me, I completely understand. But I hope you will anyway."

Jazz pulls away from me and looks me dead in the eye. "What's going on with you? And please don't tell me nothing. I hope you know by now that you can talk to me. I understand you and the guys are close, but I also know that you idiots don't like talking about your feelings with each other. Something is obviously eating at you, and I'm concerned. I'm a judgment-free zone, Bent. You can tell me anything."

"I wouldn't even know where to start. Everything is just so fucked up." I scrub a hand down my face. "My head is not in a good place. If I'm honest, it hasn't been for quite some time."

"And Sydney being here is making it worse?"

I take a deep breath. "Yeah, I guess you can say that."

"Because she reminds you of something you'd rather forget?"

I shake my head. "I wouldn't exactly put it that way."

"Well, then how would you put it?"

Oh, fuck it.

If I'm going to talk to anybody about this shit, it might as well be the one person who never met Carissa. I know I can trust Jazzy with anything. If nothing else, maybe it will help her understand why I was such a douchecanoe yesterday.

I clear my throat. "I know your boy gave you the basic rundown of what happened that night—before, during, and after the frat party—but I think it might help you better understand things if I gave you a little history lesson first, from my point of view."

"Okay..."

"Rissa and I had an odd relationship. Turbulent is probably a better word for it. We were never officially together throughout the years because she refused to be monogamous, even though I wanted that more than anything at one point. Kingston and Reed think it's because she was insecure."

Jazz thinks about that for a moment. "How so?"

"Like, maybe she was afraid I'd cheat. Maybe she thought if I sowed my oats during my teenage years, I'd get it out of my system, and she wouldn't have to worry about me being unfaithful. Not that I ever gave her any reason to believe I'd step out, mind you but, that's the guys' theory."

"But you don't agree with that?"

I shake my head. "Not at all."

Her carefully sculpted brows furrow. "Why not?"

"I think she liked the attention I gave her. I *know* she loved the fact that I always came crawling back to her, begging her to stop the *let's see other people* bullshit. But Rissa wasn't truly happy unless she was the center of attention. Which is weird because she wasn't stuck up. She didn't have a pretentious bone in her body. But that didn't make her self-centeredness any less real.

"That's why she threw herself into ballet. Riss had a natural talent for it, and she excelled at it. When she was on that stage under the spotlight, she was in her element. That's when she really shined. It was fucking beautiful. But when she wasn't dancing—when it was just our everyday life—she was always pulling little stunts, so she was the focus. She had this freaky ability to take any situation and make it about her.

"The thing is, she was so subtle about it, I don't think anyone ever noticed. Hell, it took me far too long to figure it out. I think the only reason I did was that I was so desperate to make her want me, and only me, I would watch her when she didn't think I was looking. I would dissect her words, trying to find the hidden meaning. It was damn near an obsession of mine.

"It was no secret we didn't have the healthiest relationship, but the Rissa I knew was very different from the person she let everyone else see. Including Ainsley, her best friend since kindergarten. To an outsider, I was the bad guy. I was the joker, the partier, the guy who would never turn down pussy, which in turn, made everyone sympathize with Carissa, giving her the attention she craved."

Jazz puts her head back on my shoulder and loops her arm through mine. "Why didn't you set the record straight?"

I think about it for a moment. "Because I was in love with her. Or... I thought I was. In retrospect, I'm not so sure."

"How does Sydney tie into all of this?" Jazz asks. "Why does the mere sight of her have such a strong effect on you? *How* can she have such a strong effect on you when you were so messed up you barely remember the evening you met?"

And here we go down my rabbit hole of self-hatred.

"Because... I wasn't nearly as fucked up as I led people to believe. I remember *everything* from that night, Jazz."

She stiffens. "Why would you want people to believe otherwise?"

I shrug. "When I met Sydney, something inside of me just clicked. It's like I had been in a daze all

223

those years under Carissa's spell, and all of a sudden, I wasn't. I realized I didn't need to keep crawling back to Carissa. I didn't *want* to go crawling back to Carissa because everything about Sydney drew me in. I knew it was batshit, considering I had only known Syd for a couple of hours, but I felt it in my gut."

"That's why you feel so guilty? It seems like I'm missing something here."

I suppose I could give her some information without divulging the part that would make her never want to speak to me again.

I clear my throat. "Because while I was falling for a girl I had just met—talking shit about Riss and the toxicity of our relationship, no less—Carissa was somewhere in the same house being brutally raped by God only knows how many frat boys. And the only reason she went off with one of them in the first place was that she saw Sydney and me together. *I knew* Rissa was at that party, Jazz. I knew she saw Syd and me together, and *I goaded her.* I was angry and hurt, and all I could think about was showing Rissa how much I didn't need her after all. I wanted to make her feel the pain like I did for so long." I scoff. "I guess I got my wish and then some, huh?"

Jazz pulls back. "God, Bentley, nobody thinks

you wanted something awful to actually happen to her. Especially not *that*."

I shrug. "Yeah... well... doesn't change the outcome."

Or the fact that I'm the reason Rissa—and maybe Sydney—was drugged that night.

"Fuck," I mutter.

"I know you're flayed open right now, but I've gotta say this, Bent." Jazz waits until I meet her gaze before continuing. "You can't take your damage out on Sydney. She did nothing to deserve it. And since you evidently *do* remember the night you met her, you know damn well how awesome she is. Ainsley and I really like her." She chuckles softly. "Hell, even Kingston likes her, and he doesn't like *anybody* outside of our circle."

"This is true," I smirk. "And you can relax about Syd. I think it's pretty safe to assume she and I are chill now."

She tilts her head to the side in question. "What makes you think that?"

Oh, no big. Just the fact that she let me eat her pussy like a fiend a couple of hours ago and seemed more than willing to allow me back for seconds.

"Just the vibe she was giving off when we were hanging out earlier."

Jazz's eyes widen. "Bentley-whatever-your-middle-name-is-Fitzgerald! Did you hook up with Sydney?"

"You don't really want me to kiss and tell, do you?" I gasp dramatically, clutching my imaginary pearls.

She glares.

"And it's William, after my dad and grandpa. Bentley William Fitzgerald."

"Quit trying to change the subject. You can skip the details of your sexcapades, but I do want an explanation. Why would she let you touch her when you've been such a prick? Sydney does not seem like the type of girl who'd just let that shit slide, regardless of how pretty you are."

"Awwww." I place my open palm on my chest. "You think I'm pretty?"

Jazz rolls her big brown eyes. "Shut up, smartass. You know damn well you're hot. Now, spill the goddamn tea."

I chuckle. "We were working on our psych project together, and things just kind of happened. Chemistry *definitely* isn't our problem. And not like you'll go spreading this around or anything, but I feel I should mention we didn't actually fuck. We just fooled around a bit."

"Did you manage to ask her about what her douchebag ex said in between the *fooling around?*"

"Not yet." I swallow the sudden lump in my throat. Fuck, I was so busy being led around by my dick, the thought never crossed my mind.

Or maybe I was subconsciously avoiding the topic because if Syd confirms she was drugged, that makes me even more of a despicable human being.

"You need to ask her, Bentley." Jazz gives me a sad smile. "The tiny bit that I gleaned from her, she doesn't seem to remember much from that night, so the drugging makes sense. I also get the feeling that what happened between you two that night—the public indecency part—was *extremely* out of character for her. If she doesn't already know there are pictures of it out there in the world, she needs to."

"I know." I hang my head in resignation. "So... are we good, baby girl?"

Jazz sighs. "You know... I honestly don't think I'd be so quick to forgive if this happened a year ago."

I raise my brows. "But?"

"But... if all the shit I've been through lately has taught me nothing else, it's that life is short. You need to hold your loved ones close because you may not get a tomorrow with them." She bumps her shoulder into mine. "Just because I'm pissed at you doesn't mean I don't love you, Bent. We all do."

"Thank you, Jazzy." I stand, extending my arm

to help her off the bench. "It's getting chilly out here. My So-Cal bones can't handle it. Do you want to head inside and Netflix without the chill?"

"Sure." She nods. "Ainsley should be home from ballet any minute, and I'm sure Reed won't be too far behind. Do you want to stay for dinner?"

I pat my stomach. "Is that a real question? If you're offering food, I'm eating."

Jazz chuckles. "Of course. Why did I even ask?"

Kingston is right inside the door, leaning against the back of the couch. He's trying to appear relaxed, but I don't miss the tension coiled in his body. I'm sure it was killing him, not being able to stand next to Jazz like a guard dog while we were having our little heart-to-heart. Dude is hella protective and a control freak, but he's also smart enough to know when to pick his battles. Jazz may be tiny in stature, but she's a badass who has no problem reminding him of that if need be.

"Everything good?" His eyes briefly flick to me before settling on Jazz.

I fight a laugh when she gives him a condescending pat on the head. "Everything's copacetic, Cujo. You can stand down now."

I flat-out guffaw as she voices my thoughts from a few seconds ago, which earns me a fierce glower from the grumpy asshole in the room.

When he follows that up with a fist bump, a weight is lifted off my chest. Jazz and Kingston may not forget my recent behavior anytime soon, but that right there tells me I'm on the path to forgiveness.

chapter
twenty-one

SYDNEY

"Okay, bitch. Spill the deets."

I give her a blank stare, pretending like I have no idea what she's talking about. "Whatever do you mean?"

Cameron rolls her eyes. "Really? Are you playing dumb right now? Is that what you're doing? Tell me what happened in that room with Bentley!"

I take a bite of my pizza and deliberately chew slowly just to drive her nuts before answering. "Not much. We did our assignment—or most of it anyway—and then he left."

Cam gives me a dubious look. "I don't believe that bullshit for one second. Try again."

I sigh dramatically. "Fine. We may have made out a little bit too."

"And what else?" she asks. "Because I know that's not all. Did you get naked?"

"No, we didn't get naked!" I lie.

She scoffs. "Really? Then why were your joggers on backward when you left?"

Goddammit. I was hoping she overlooked that.

"How do you know they weren't on backward to begin with?" I challenge. "You didn't see me before we went into that room together."

I don't know why I'm giving her such a hard time. I tell Cam everything. But then again, I do like driving her crazy, so there you go.

Before she can answer, my phone buzzes on the floor beside us, and Cameron snatches it. She holds the phone up to my face to unlock it before turning the screen back to her.

"Give me my phone back, whore!"

Cameron is a squirmy little thing, so, unfortunately, I don't get my cell out of her hands until *after* she's read the message.

She looks at the phone pointedly, where Bentley's message is staring right back at me. "Well, that tells me *one thing* that happened."

Bentley: I can't stop thinking about how beautiful you are when you're coming all over my tongue. I'm counting the seconds until I can taste your pretty pussy again.

I know I'm blushing like crazy, but I refuse to give my bestie the satisfaction. Dirty-talk isn't something that's ever appealed to me before, but now I think that may have been because the guys who've attempted it in my past couldn't pull it off. Bentley Fitzgerald definitely doesn't have that problem. The boy exudes carnality like a boss. His filthy words just heighten it.

I jump a little when my phone buzzes again, this time with an incoming FaceTime call. My eyes widen in panic.

"What do I do?!"

Cameron laughs. "Uh... answer it?"

I shoot a warning glare in her direction as I answer the call. In the next moment, Bentley's too-sexy-for-words dimples are on the screen.

"I apologize in advance for anything you may be subjected to during this conversation."

Confusion is etched across his face, but only for a moment because that's when Cam plops on my bed, sticking her head over my shoulder so he can see her face.

"Hey, Bentley. Fancy meeting you here."

He smirks. "Cameron."

She gasps theatrically. "You remembered! Well, tickle me pink. Eh... actually, don't do that. I'm not into sloppy seconds. Although, it's a shame because if my girl's flush after receiving your text is any indication, I'm guessing you're pretty damn skilled in that department."

I spread my palm over my face and groan. "Jesus, Cameron. You couldn't have a little more discretion?"

Cam snorts indelicately. "Bitch, have you met me?"

Bentley's smile grows. "Is this a bad time?"

I move across the room to get away from my annoying best friend. "Not really. We were just finishing our late dinner, but I'm in my room, so the only prying ears belong to Miss Tactless over there. As long as you keep that in mind, we're good."

His rumbly laughter causes a flutter in my belly while Cam flips me a double bird.

"Show me your room."

I scrunch my nose. "Why?"

"Helps with the visual for later." He winks.

"Did you really just infer that you would be masturbating while thinking about me later?"

Bentley's shoulders lift. "I'm a dude. It's no secret that we jerk off."

"Ooh, spicy!" Cameron starts fake humping my bed. "Can I watch?"

I pan my phone to show Bentley what she's

doing before bringing it back. "See what you caused?"

Bentley releases a hearty laugh. "You know, they say you can tell a lot about a person by the company they keep."

I raise my brows. "Are you implying that I'm a slightly insane, relentlessly thirsty bitch, and have zero filters?"

"Rude!" Cameron gripes.

He smiles. "Nah, I think your girl is pretty cool. And funny as fuck."

"Mom," Cam singsongs, flopping onto her back. "Can we keep him?"

I roll my eyes. "Don't encourage her."

Bentley holds his free hand up. "Hey, I'm just sayin'."

"So, are you *just sayin'* that you think I'm pretty cool and funny?"

Bentley's full lips twitch. "I haven't experienced much of the funny yet, but I do suspect it's under there somewhere. And I definitely think you're pretty fucking dope, Sydney."

His dark eyes bore into me. It's almost as if they're simultaneously trying to see straight into my soul and melt my clothes off. Now that I think about it, that's pretty much on par with the rest of him.

"Same."

If I'm not mistaken, the boy is preening, which is pretty damn adorable. "I'll let you get back to your friend. I just wanted to see your pretty face one last time and say goodnight."

I tuck a lock of hair behind my ear, fighting a smile. "Goodnight, Bentley. I'll see you in the morning."

"See you, Syd."

I end the call and press the phone against my chest.

"Damn, girl. He's into you." Cam sits back on her legs. "Question is, what are you going to do about it?"

"I don't know." I shake my head. "He's got issues, and I don't know if I want to take that on."

She shrugs. "So? Then, just bang him and get rid of that pesky virginity of yours."

I take a moment to think of the best way to explain this. "I can't say the thought of having sex with Bentley isn't *really* appealing, but there are all sorts of red flags waving around in my head where he's concerned. There's this weird niggling in the back of my brain, but for the life of me, I couldn't tell you why. I wish I could remember more about the night we met because I have a feeling the two are related."

Cam straightens her spine and makes a *gimme* gesture with her hands. "Remind me again what exactly you *do* remember from that night. About Bentley specifically. It's been so long since we've discussed it; the details are blurry."

I grab a scrunchie and pull my hair into a messy bun before joining her on the bed. "Not much, unfortunately. I remember talking a lot, but not many details on *what* we discussed. And I remember kissing. Vividly. But for the most part, that entire night is a blur, thanks to the crap Linz put in my drink. I suppose I should be grateful I can't recall much, all things considered. The little flashes I have unrelated to Bentley aren't all that fun to think about."

I used to dabble in weed on occasion, but I swore off all drugs, natural or otherwise, the night my cousin decided to feed me what she called an Aphrodite cocktail. They were made up of two parts champagne, one part raspberry vodka, a heavy dose of Molly, and a dash of Rohypnol. Apparently, some Abercrombie model wannabe introduced her to them as *the ultimate party enhancer*. When I flipped out on Linz for feeding me date rape drugs, the bitch actually had the nerve to act like she was doing me a favor. She swears the drugs were just a trace amount to loosen my inhibitions so

I could get laid, but it wasn't enough to make me lose control of my body. Maybe if I only had one, that would be true, but I had several throughout the evening.

God, when I think about all of the awful things that could've happened, it makes me sick. I'm lucky Cora, one of Lindsey's sorority sisters, walked into that bedroom, saw what was going on, and got me the hell out of there before those assholes could take it any further. The campus had a DD service which we apparently utilized to get back to the Delta Pi house, but I don't remember that part either.

Cam gives me a sad smile as I lie on the mattress beside her. "Have I mentioned lately how much I hate your cousin?"

"I feel ya."

She frowns. "I still don't understand why you didn't tell your family about it. Or even the cops. She shouldn't get away with it."

"I know." I sigh. "I've thought about saying something so many times since that night, but when all is said and done, I got out relatively unscathed. And as reckless as she could be back then, I genuinely don't think Lindsey meant any harm or truly considered the consequences. Besides, ever since she got pregnant with Christopher, she's been a totally different person. I'm not going to do some-thing that would adversely affect that little boy. She's his everything."

A couple of months after that party, my cousin got pregnant. It wasn't planned by any means, but the second she saw that pink plus sign, she hung up her party-girl ways and became fully committed to motherhood. I don't know if I'll ever forgive her, but I can't deny how much she's changed or forget how tight we used to be. Lindsey was like my older sister growing up.

"Have you asked Bentley what he remembers?"

"No." I shake my head. "But I suppose it wouldn't hurt to talk to him about it."

"Well, there you go." Cam wags her eyebrows. "And if you happened to get a few orgasms out of it while you're *talking*, so be it."

I throw a pillow at her. "You're an idiot."

She throws it back at me. "Bitch, you couldn't live without me."

"That's debatable." I roll my eyes.

"So... if you're not going to give me all the dirty, dirty deets, at least tell me this. How many O's did you get out of him this afternoon?"

I hold up three fingers, fighting a smile.

Her periwinkle eyes widen. "Holy shit! Girl, if you don't want him, will you send him my way?"

"Who said I don't want him?"

Cam points her finger at me. "Ha! I got you to admit it."

I flip her off. "Yeah, yeah, like you didn't already know."

She shrugs. "Well... whatever you decide, you know I've got your back, right?"

I smile. "I know you do, and I love you for it."

Cam pulls me into a side hug. "They don't call me the Greatest Bitch of All Time for nothing."

"*I'm* the only one who calls you that." I chuckle.

"Eh, semantics." Her full lips turn up in the corner. "Anyway... talk to Bentley. Find out what he remembers, and go from there. Easy peasy."

"Yeah... easy peasy."

Why do I get the feeling those words are going to wind up biting me in the ass?

chapter
twenty-two

BENTLEY

"Did you know I screamed for you? In that room, at that house, when I was being violated by all those guys, while every hole of mine was bloodied and bruised, I screamed for you. But the thing is, the words wouldn't come out. It's like I was having this out-of-body experience where I could see all of these horrible things happening to me in colorful detail, but I was helpless. My limbs were useless. My voice was silenced.

"But inside my head, I was screaming as loud as I could. I was screaming your name, Bentley. I knew you were somewhere close by, and I thought that if I screamed loud enough, even if I wasn't making any noise, that you would somehow know. That you would somehow sense what was happening to me and rescue me from that hell. But you didn't rescue me, did

you? Because you were off with that girl getting your dick sucked, or God knows whatever else, while my soul was being shredded beyond repair. How does that make you feel, Bentley?"

I watch Carissa's feet dangling off the graffitied platform of Topanga Lookout, trying to formulate a response. What am I supposed to say to that? How am I supposed to ever right the ultimate wrong?

"I didn't know, Carissa. I thought you had left. As angry as I was with you, I never would have wanted that."

She laughs, but there's no humor behind it. "You could've fooled me. Because the thing is, I know, *Bentley. I know Grady was at that party because of you. I was at my most vulnerable because of* you.*"*

I throw my hands up. "I had no idea he dealt goddamn roofies, Riss. I swear to fucking God. You know me better than anyone. Do you really think that I would condone anything that would hurt a woman?"

Carissa stands, looking out at the valley. "See, that's the thing. Apparently, I don't know you at all. Because the Bentley I know would have never let me walk away. He would've never allowed me to witness him getting head from another girl. The Bentley I know would've pushed that slut off of him the moment I walked into the room."

"Sydney's not a slut."

"*Right.*" Rissa rolls her eyes. "*Chaste little princesses don't go around giving public blow jobs.*"

I shake my head. "*I think there may have been extenuating circumstances at play. She's not exactly a public blow job kind of girl.*"

"*He certainly wouldn't have come down her throat, taunting me with that fact,*" she continues as if she didn't even hear my last statement. "*Or even worse, kissed her like she was the best thing that's ever happened to him. That kiss was a dagger to my heart. I've never felt pain like that before. Well... until shortly after, anyway.*"

I cringe, thinking about the unimaginable horrors she went through that night.

"*So, how's it feel knowing you're responsible for my death? How can you live with yourself?*" Carissa fans her arm out, gesturing to the steep drop below. "*If I were you, I could never wake up every morning, knowing what I'd done. Maybe you should follow my lead. Death is the easiest way to end the pain, Bentley.*"

In the blink of an eye, Rissa jumps off the edge of the platform. I try lunging forward to catch her, but for some reason, I can't move. I'm cemented to the ground as I watch her body smack into a jagged boulder with a sickening thud. As blood pours from her skull, seeping into the red rock beneath her, the life slowly drains from her eyes. Right before Rissa takes her final breath, I hear her parting words loud and clear.

"I'll never forgive you, Bentley."

My eyes fly open, and it takes me a moment to sink back into reality.

"Fuck."

I rub my eyes with clenched fists, trying to shake the nightmare. Christ, will this torment ever end? Will there ever come a point in my life when I'm not afraid to go to sleep because I have no idea what nightmares await me on the other end? I thought I was finally turning a corner because I hadn't had a bad dream in months, but since Sydney showed up, they've hit every night. I get out of bed, walk over to my bathroom, and splash some cold water on my face. Looking at my reflection in the mirror, I rub the tight spot on my chest. When my hand falls to the side, my eyes catch on the delicate script tattooed directly over my heart.

Sleep well, Tiny Dancer

I trace the ink with my index finger. I got this tattoo the day Carissa was buried. After her attack, she had virtually no memory of the incident, but she was plagued by night terrors. Carissa couldn't remember her dreams, but she would wake up in such a state of panic, we believed her subconscious was reliving the night she was brutally raped over and over again.

As her best friend, Ainsley spent a lot of time at

Rissa's house. Riss refused to see me or even talk to me, for that matter. But according to Ainsley, she believes that was because I'm a guy, not because of who I am personally. The only man Carissa would let come close to her was her father, and even then, Ainsley said she flinched from his nearness.

The night terrors became so frequent that Carissa forced herself to stay awake as long as possible to the point where delirium was setting in. Her doctor prescribed sleeping pills, which Carissa ultimately used to end her life. According to Ainsley, Rissa seemed to be making progress. She finally agreed to set an appointment with the therapist her parents were begging her to see, which was a *huge* breakthrough. But that same night, she swallowed so many pills, an accidental overdose was out of the question. There is no doubt in anyone's mind that Carissa had no intention of waking up the following day. She never left a note, so none of us are exactly sure what she was thinking at the end, but her doctor believed sleep deprivation contributed to her fragile mental state.

I curse when I glance at the time and see that I'm late. I must've forgotten to set my alarm last night. I get ready for school as fast as possible and head out. By the time I'm pulling into the Windsor lot, I'm twenty minutes late for first period and still extremely on edge. I dig through my glove box, grab my new bottle of Oxy, and transfer a couple of pills into the breast pocket of my blazer just in case. I take a deep breath, get out of my car, and head to the office for a tardy slip.

When second period rolls around, I'm even more agitated. The moment I step into my psych class, I spot Sydney smiling up at me from her desk in the back. I attempt to return the gesture, but I'm just not able to force one out right now.

"Hey, you," she says softly as I sit down next to her. "How's your morning going so far?"

I rub the back of my neck. "Fine."

I can feel her aqua gaze burning into the side of my face, but I can't bring myself to look at her. "Is something wrong, Bentley?"

I turn my head slightly in her direction. "No. Why would you think that?"

Sydney nods to my bouncing leg. "Because you're really antsy right now like you're upset about something."

I force my leg to stop being so goddamn twitchy. "I'm fine," I snap. "I forgot to set my alarm, so I was late this morning. I'm just a little off because of it."

She considers that for a moment. "Are you sure that's all? You can talk to me, Bentley." She leans over and lowers her voice further. "Does this have anything to do with the reason you asked me to drive you to the cemetery the other day?"

My fists clench under my desk. "Don't."

Sydney straightens in her seat. "Don't, *what?*"

My narrowed eyes drill into her. "Don't go fucking sniffing around things that are none of your business. I told you it was a mistake bringing you there, and I meant it. Do us both a favor and just fucking forget it ever happened."

I can't handle the buzzing beneath my skin anymore, so I discreetly slip the pills out of my pocket and pop them into my mouth, swallowing them dry.

Sydney's eyes widen. "What was that?"

"Another thing that's none of your fucking business."

"Okay." She stretches the word out. "I don't know where the guy is that I hung out with yesterday afternoon, but this is not him. I didn't sign up for this shit."

"I didn't ask you to sign up for *anything.*" I lean into her ear to ensure no one hears this next part. I have to tell my dick to calm the fuck down when I inhale her sweet vanilla scent. "You don't have the right to know things just because you let me dine on that pretty pussy of yours. Don't mistake this for anything more than it is, sweetheart."

She scoffs. "Oh yeah? And what's that?"

My teeth briefly clamp down on her lower earlobe, making her shiver. "Lust. Wanting to fuck you doesn't mean that I want to *know* you, or vice versa."

"Duly noted." She faces forward as the bell rings and proceeds to ignore me throughout the rest of the class.

I know all the shit with Carissa was just a dream. I know it didn't *really* happen, but I can't fucking get it out of my head. I can't stop flashing back to that night and the events that actually transpired. How I used Sydney to taunt Carissa. That one action—an action driven entirely out of spite—caused a massive butterfly effect that can never be undone. Syd might not be at fault, and as I've learned, she very well may be a victim as well, but that doesn't stop my mind from racing. For some reason, I can't seem to compartmentalize the two. Being around Sydney triggers thoughts of Carissa's trauma and my role in it.

When my pills kick in, I feel like I can finally take a breath for the first time since I woke up. I feel like an asshole for treating Sydney the way I did earlier. If the way she's been stewing for the last forty minutes is any indication, she'd happily castrate me right now. When the bell rings, I grab her sleeve to get her attention, but she shakes me off and levels me with a look that would have a lesser man pissing himself.

"No. I cannot talk to you right now. I'm liable to say something that I'll regret. Unlike you, I understand the power words hold, and I don't get off on hurting people."

I have nothing to say to that, so I let her go.

Christ, why can't I stop fucking things up so royally?

She's right, though; she didn't sign up for this shit. I just need to make her hate me enough that she'll stop trying, because I've already proven I'm not strong or selfless enough to refuse anything she's willing to give. I know what it's like to be on the losing end of a toxic relationship, and I wouldn't wish that on my worst enemy.

"Hey, baby." A small hand wraps around my bicep. When I look down, I see Rebecca fluttering her lashes. "You feel like cashing in that rain check?"

We dodge a few people as we step into the busy hallway. Sydney is no more than a few feet ahead of us, giving me the perfect opportunity to set this shit straight. She's pretending like she's not listening, but I can tell she is.

"Not right now, babe. But I'd love to meet for lunch. Why don't you bring along a friend and some *refreshments*?" I touch my finger to the underside of my nose, hoping she gets the hint.

Rebecca's collagen-injected lips break into a grin. "I can do that."

"Great. It's a date."

I break away from Rebecca and toss a wink over my shoulder. I don't miss the glare Sydney's flashing in my direction or the muttered "asshole" that falls from her lips. As I'm walking away, I tell myself this is what's best for both of us.

Now, if only I could believe it as well.

chapter
twenty-three

SYDNEY

I've no desire to run into Bentley or Barbie in the dining room, so when lunchtime arrives, I head toward the library to grab a sandwich from their café. Unfortunately, my plan backfires because Bentley, Barbie, and a second blonde are leaning against the brick wall of the library just to the right of the entrance. If I want to go inside, I have no choice but to walk past them. I do my best to ignore the sharp pain in my chest when I see Bentley's strong arms wrapped around both girls. They're snuggled into his side, giggling about something he said. Bentley and I make eye contact as I get closer, and neither one of us seems able to look away. I decide to be the bigger person, so instead of pretending he's invisible, I walk straight up to him.

"Can we talk?"

I'm looking directly at Bentley, but out of the

corner of my eye, I see Rebecca glaring a hole through me. Screw her. This is a free country. I can talk to whomever I want.

Bentley's dark chocolate eyes scan my body from head to toe, pausing briefly on my breasts before returning to my eyes. "I'll pass. I'm a little busy right now, sweetheart."

I sigh, tamping down my aggravation. Of course, he's not going to make it easy on me. "Come on, Bentley. I just need a few minutes."

On his right, Rebecca rolls her eyes dramatically. "Get a clue, you dumb bitch. Bentley doesn't want you, so run along and stop being so pathetic."

I do my best to mask my surprise as the realization sinks in. I think I was too preoccupied with all the drama the day she sat at our lunch table. It's the only explanation I can think of why I didn't recognize her voice then. This is the bitch that pushed me down outside of the bathroom. I've no doubt about that.

I return her frosty glare. "Honey, I think that's for him to decide." My eyes swing to Bentley, imploring him to remove his head from his ass. "Well?"

Bentley's arms lower until each one of his hands is resting on one of each girl's hips. "Like I said, I'm a little busy." His gaze flickers to both girls. "Come on, ladies. Let's go have a little fun."

Well, so much for that idea. Fuck him. I can't say I didn't try. If he wants to be a massive douchebag, hell-bent on destroying anything good we may have shared, so be it.

I rip open the door to the library and stomp inside. My appetite is pretty much nonexistent, so instead of heading to the café, I find a table in a quiet corner and take a seat. Cameron is also on lunch, so I pull out my phone to send her a text.

Me: Hey, bitch. How's your day going?

GBOAT: Boooooring. *singsongs* I hate it here without you. I know we see each other all the time, but I miss you, boo.

Me: I miss you, too.

GBOAT: What's wrong?

Me: What makes you think something is wrong?

GBOAT: Uh... because I know you. Also, I know you've been eating lunch with your new friends, so if you're texting me right now, that tells me that something happened.

I sigh.

Me: Honestly, I have no idea what the hell happened. Today's been weird.

GBOAT: How so? Does this have anything to do with Mr. Triple O?

Me: Oh, you mean the giant douchebag?

GBOAT: Uh-oh. What did he do?

Me: Oh, nothing big. Just acted like a complete dick in psych class, telling me that just because I let him eat me out doesn't mean he has ANY interest in getting to know me. Then, I just ran into him with his arms around two girls, one of which I just figured out is the bitch who pushed me down.

GBOAT: *angry guy from *Inside Out* GIF*

Me: No shit. That about sums it up.

GBOAT: Fuck him. I don't care if he knows his way around a clit. Nobody treats my bestie like shit and gets away with it.

GBOAT: *bad bitch GIF*

Me: Thanks, girl.

GBOAT: *Fez I love you GIF*

That makes me smile.

Me: We're going to get some giant Oreo milkshakes after you get off work. And fries.

GBOAT: *My milkshake brings all the boys to the yard GIF*

I laugh, loving how easily she can turn my bad mood around.

Me: I'm heading to the studio for some extra practice/anger management after school. Do you need a ride?

GBOAT: *Yaas girl GIF*

Me: Are you capable of communicating in anything other than GIFs?

GBOAT: *Grumpy Cat NOPE GIF*

Me: *Oh, you crazy Steve Harvey GIF*

GBOAT: Love you too, babe. ;)

I put my phone back in my blazer's inner pocket and decide that I might as well get some work done while I'm here. I pull my Chromebook out of my bag and start writing the essay on our findings for this stupid psych project. There's no way in hell I'm going to meet up with Bentley to finish the assignment, so I'll just have to fudge the numbers a little bit. The sooner I can complete this essay, the sooner I can turn it in. After that, I'll have no reason to talk to that asshat.

Yeah, you keep telling yourself that, Syd.

I thunk my head on the table. Why am I such a glutton for punishment? If any other guy treated me the way Bentley has, I would've thrown his ass to the curb right away. What is it about him that makes him the exception? I sit up when it hits me, the proverbial lightbulb above my head blinding me with its intensity.

It's his eyes.

Or... more in the way he looks at me. It's like he can see me better than any other. Like he has a direct line to my soul or something. I'm not a religious person by any means, but I do embrace spirituality. And the hopeless romantic in me likes to believe that everyone has a soul mate somewhere in the world. I'm not saying that's who Bentley is for me, but I do think he's significant somehow. Like, he's in my life to serve a greater purpose.

Some people might think it's woo-woo, but I think of it more like intuition. One thing my mom has always taught me is to trust my gut. She swears that your instincts will never steer you wrong in any situation if you listen to them. *Truly* listen to them. And for whatever reason, my gut is telling me that Bentley Fitzgerald is worth my time. Hopefully, I can figure out why before I lose my mind or turn him into a Eunuch. I'd say either is a distinct possibility at this point.

I groan as an ache settles deep in my chest, thinking about Bentley *having fun* with Barbie One and Barbie Two right now. I know guys—and girls for that matter—can separate sex from emotions, but when he kissed me... it was so beyond the physical act of it. I know I didn't imagine that. I felt it last night when he called, too. So the question is, what the hell happened between the time we hung up the phone last night to this morning? Why did he go from sweet and charming to cold and vindictive?

Ugh. Boys suck.

The bell rings, startling me. I look at the clock, and sure enough, I've been zoning out for a solid twenty minutes. I gather my things, zipping them in my bookbag, and head back toward Franklin Hall, where my last few classes are located. Right before I get there, I'm surprised again when I spy Rebecca and her friend standing in front of the building with sour looks on their faces. I weave to the right, blending in with the crowd so I can pass them without notice. And okay, maybe eavesdrop.

"I don't know what his problem is," Rebecca whines. "This is the second time he's shown interest one minute and blown me off before we could get to the good stuff."

Interesting.

"Why would he do that?" her friend asks.

Rebecca huffs. "If I didn't know better, I'd say he likes the new girl. But that can't possibly be true because he's so out of her league. He's a *king*, for fuck's sake, and she's a goody two-shoes. Totally not his type."

Goody two-shoes, my ass. Just because I don't sleep around and get good grades doesn't mean I always take the moral high ground. Not that there's anything wrong with people who do, but this bitch is cray if she thinks that's who I am. I smile when I envision wrapping my fist around her ponytail and ripping her bleached hair out of her skull.

Okay, maybe that was a little over the psycho line.

I climb the front steps to the building, and when I'm sure Rebecca can see me, I flip her off before turning around and walking away with my head held high.

Damn, that felt good.

These people have another thing coming if they think I'll take their abuse lying down. And that includes Bentley Fitzgerald.

chapter
twenty-four

SYDNEY

As Beyoncé's "Halo" reverberates through the speakers, I glide across the floor with practiced ease. I know this routine like the back of my hand. I've done it so many times, my body naturally moves to the music. Today, however, while my steps may be the same, the emotion behind them is not. My frustration and anger leak through the surface from the tips of my fingers down to my pointed toes, defying the lyrics. Everything is a blur of pirouettes, pliés, and passés. I effortlessly nail every trick, but I don't take the time to set them up properly, which could potentially lead to injury.

Consequences are the furthest thing from my mind right now, though. All I can think about is dancing until I no longer feel like I want to implode, which is precisely what I do as one song leads to the next until I'm so exhausted, I slide to the Marley floor, making no attempt to get up. I'm not sure how much time passes as I lie here dripping with sweat, trying to catch my breath before the door opens.

"Whoa, baby," my mom says. "What's eating at you?"

My eyes follow the sound of her voice until I find her standing in the doorway. "What do you mean?"

"Oh, I don't know, maybe the fact that you've been back here for almost three hours, and by the looks of it, you've been dancing nonstop."

I prop myself up on my elbows. "And? This *is* a dance studio. People come here to dance."

She gives me a wry look. "Yes, that's true. But you know your limits. When you dance to the point of exhaustion, that means you're trying to work through something inside your head. So, I'll ask again. What's eating at you?"

I release a heavy breath. "Boy problems."

She walks across the room, taking a seat next to me on the floor. "Does this have anything to do with the handsome young man who was in here the other day?"

"Maybe."

My mom chuckles. "I figured as much. Do you want to talk about it?"

"He's just so hot and cold. One minute, he's sweet and charming, and in the next, he's a sullen jerk. I don't know how to handle his mood swings."

She thinks about that for a moment. "Is it possible he's going through something you might not know about?"

I shrug. "I'm almost sure of it. A couple of his friends even mentioned something, but I didn't get any details."

"Did you ever think to ask him directly?"

"Yeah." I lean forward, wrapping my hands under my arches to stretch my muscles. "I've tried, somewhat, at least. But he's not giving me anything, which frustrates me to no end. I know I should probably walk away and forget about it, forget about *him*, but for some reason, I can't do that."

My mom stands and extends her arm to help me up. "You know what I think?"

"What?"

"I think there's no time like the present to ask again, but this time, don't give up until he lets you in." She gives me a good once over and chuckles. "But maybe you should make a pit stop at home for a shower first. It might help your cause if you don't show up stinking and looking like a drowned rat."

"Gee, thanks, Mom. I can really feel the love."

She scoffs. "Please. You know you're my favorite daughter."

"I'm your *only* daughter."

"Yes, but you're still my favorite."

I shake my head, fighting a smile. "You really think I should go see him?"

"That's exactly what I think you should do. If you see something in him, Sydney, you should explore that. Maybe he *is* worth the effort. But at the same time, you need to demand respect. You need to make it crystal clear you're not a girl who will allow him to treat you poorly." She looks at me thoughtfully. "Did I ever tell you I couldn't stand your father when we first met? I thought he was an arrogant ass."

I laugh. "*What?!* No, you've *never* told me that. You two have always been so disgustingly in love."

She nods. "It's true. He was *such* a jerk. Acted like he was God's gift to women, and I wasn't having any of that nonsense. I should've dismissed his ass right away, but I saw something beneath the cocky surface, and I knew I'd regret it if I didn't explore that."

I shake my head, trying to picture them being at odds, but I can't. My dad is incredibly humble, and he treats her like a queen. He even gave up a sizable trust fund to be with her because his father didn't think she was a *suitable wife*, whatever the hell that meant. My mom once told me that when his dad issued the ultimatum, he walked away and never looked back and hasn't spoken to either of his parents since. I've never met my grandparents on his side, even though they live less than twenty minutes away. From what I know about them, I don't think I'm missing much.

"What happened after that?"

Her full lips curve into a sassy smirk. "Oh, I let him know real quick, that shit wouldn't fly. That if he wanted a chance with me, he needed to *earn it*. Quite frankly, I think I scared him a little." She laughs. "You need to understand your father grew up with a bunch of uppity spoiled brats who all followed certain societal rules. People catered to their every whim, and they valued possessions over character. It's all he knew.

"Then, here I was, this girl from Compton, who knew *damn well* what hard work and sacrifice looked like. I knew the content of a person's character was their greatest asset. He says I was like a hurricane, turning his life upside down the moment we locked eyes at that fundraiser. He swears he knew at that moment he was going to marry me one day. The ironic part is he wasn't even supposed to be at that event. Your grandfather typically attended them—

hell, it was his company that hosted it—but evidently, he had a more pressing engagement that evening and sent your father on his behalf."

"It was fate."

She smiles. "I like to think so."

"Thanks, Mom."

She pulls me into a hug. "Anytime, baby."

"I'll do my best," I assure her. "But I told Cam I'd drive her home."

"I got it." She pulls back. "Now, go clean up and make that boy talk to you."

After a quick shower, I head to Bentley's house, thankful his address was still programmed into my navigation system, and his gate code was easy enough to memorize. It kind of ruins the element of surprise if I can't get into the community without calling first. As I stand in front of the heavy wooden door to this imposing mansion, I take a deep breath before ringing the bell. No one answers after a minute, so I try again. When the thought he may be hooking up with Barbie instead of answering the door crosses my mind, I hit the bell in rapid succession. I smile when I hear a series of curses yelled from inside, telling me to calm my tits.

Ha! I knew he was home.

I know it's petty AF, but I'm pretty proud of myself as the door is ripped open so forcefully, I'm surprised it doesn't fall off the hinges. My amusement is short-lived when I get my first glimpse of the furious man standing in the doorway. Bentley is shirtless, wearing nothing but a pair of low-slung black basketball shorts. His skin is dotted with droplets of water, as is his hair, which leads me to believe he just got out of the shower. There's a strong possibility I'm actually drooling as I take in all of his finely sculpted muscles and the deeply carved vee low on his torso. When I spot the small tattoo on his chest, I reach out without thinking, but Bentley stops me from touching it by taking a few steps back.

When my eyes lift to his, my skin heats from the anger in his gaze. "What are you doing here, Sydney?"

I bristle from his abrasive tone. "Are you home alone?"

His brows lift. "Why? You offering to keep me company?"

Bentley steps back further when I push my way into the house. "We need to talk."

"Is that so?" he sneers. "And what makes you think I'm interested in doing that?"

"I don't give a damn if you're interested or not." I cock a hip. "Now, I'll ask again. Are you home alone?"

A muscle in his cheek jumps. "The parentals are in New York."

"And?"

Please don't say another girl is here.

He offers me a cruel smirk as if he can read my mind. "And I'm taking advantage of their absence with a couple of cheerleaders. They're waiting for me in my bed, so feel free to show yourself out. The ladies are probably getting started without me, and I really don't want to miss the show. Blondes are always the most adventurous in bed. It's why I prefer them."

Shit. *Don't cry, Sydney.*

I jut my chin out. "Well, tell them to leave because I'm not going anywhere until we have this discussion."

"You think so, huh?"

I glare. "I *know* so."

"Suit yourself." Bentley spins on his heels and starts walking away. "I don't care if you watch. I won't judge anyone for their kinks. Hey, maybe you should call your bestie up and see if she wants to join the party?"

I scoff. "Fuck you."

"Nah." He pauses at the bottom of a grand staircase, turning around. "One taste was *more* than enough."

I try resisting, but my eyes won't stop falling to his naked chest. God, he has an incredible body. Broad shoulders that taper down to rippled abs. Strong arms and legs, but not bulky in a 'roid freak kind of way—more like a professional basketball player. I feel a sudden urge to trace every inch of Bentley's exposed skin with my tongue, dying to know how he tastes.

"See something you like, Syd?"

Damn it.

Stupid hormones. This would be much easier if he wasn't so pretty. I think about what my mom said. How I need to make it crystal clear I won't take his shit anymore.

I straighten my shoulders. "Not especially. Your personality ruins it."

"Right," Bentley scoffs, continuing his trek up the stairs, leaving me no choice but to follow. "You keep telling yourself that."

"Where are we going?"

"My bedroom," he tosses over his shoulder.

I freeze on the top step. "Uh... yeah... no. I don't think that's such a good idea."

His lips curve into a cocky grin as he leans against the doorjamb of a room halfway down the hall. "Why not? Scared?"

"No." I climb the last step and walk down the hall so he doesn't call my bluff.

"Shit, you really are a terrible liar, aren't you?"

I give him a *who, me?* look. "Who says I'm lying?"

He crosses his arms over his chest and inclines his head toward the room behind him. "Prove it."

"Fine," I say through gritted teeth. "I'll tell the Barbies playtime is over myself. *Move.*"

Jesus Christ, I can't believe I'm really about to break up a threesome.

Bentley makes a point not to budge an inch as I skirt past him. With my double-D's, and as big as he is, there's no avoiding the brush of my boobs against his forearms as I walk over the threshold. I've no doubt the move was purposeful on his end to make me uncomfortable, so I do my best not to show it. This jackass has another thing coming if he thinks a little discomfort is all it'll take to make me go away. One way or the other, we're airing our shit out tonight.

One look around confirms that this is Bentley's bedroom. Not only does the place smell like his absurdly sexy cologne, but the décor suits him. I can easily imagine him lying in the massive bed at the center of the room. The same bed that *isn't* currently occupied by two bimbos.

"Now, who's the liar?" I sass, trying not to broadcast my relief he wasn't hooking up with someone.

"You're looking mighty pleased with that fact, Sydney."

I roll my eyes. "Hardly."

I scan the rest of the room, unable to meet his smug gaze any longer without punching him in the throat. The leather couch under the window is plush and decidedly masculine. The giant TV perched on the wall opposite his bed is currently showing Sports-Center, but the volume is muted, so it doesn't compete with the music quietly playing from the Bluetooth speaker on the corner desk. There are two closed doors which I assume lead to a walk-in closet and bathroom based on the fact that every mansion I've ever been in has master-sized bedrooms throughout.

Everything is obviously expensive, but not ostentatious. It's freakishly clean, too, but I wouldn't be surprised if a maid was responsible for that. I can feel Bentley's scrutiny as I take in our surroundings, but he doesn't say anything. He's waiting me out, almost as if he's making a game out of it. Like, the person who speaks first loses. Too bad for him, I've never been known to keep my mouth shut when I have something to say.

"What's your problem?"

He laughs derisively. "Wow... you're not pulling any punches, aren't you?"

I park a hand on my hip. "Why would I? I have no interest in playing mind games, Bentley. I'm sick of dealing with your mercurial temperament. One minute you act like you're into me, and the next, you're an epic douche. So, my question is, which version is the *real* you? Because if it's the latter, I don't want to waste my time."

His brown eyes narrow. "I never asked for your time."

I point at him. "Ah, but that's not entirely true, is it? You said we needed to talk. But that never happened because we got... distracted."

Bentley's full lips curve. "I didn't exactly hear you complaining about that distraction."

"I wasn't." I shrug. "But I also thought we would have an opportunity to talk after the fact. I assumed we turned a corner and could put the bull-shit animosity behind us. I sure as hell didn't think the person I spent the afternoon with would be someone entirely different by the next day."

"You know what they say about people who assume, don't you?"

I roll my eyes. "Yeah, yeah, I get it. Perhaps I *am*

an ass for thinking you were a good guy beneath the rude surface."

"I never once claimed to be a good guy." A vacant look crosses his face before he looks me directly in the eye. "I'm *not* a good guy, Sydney, and you'd do well to remember that."

"See, here's the problem with that: I'm not so sure that's accurate. Because the thing is... the people who love you *are* good. You said it yourself— you can tell a lot about a person by the company they keep. As far as I can tell, Jazz and Ainsley are great people. *Genuine* people. I don't know their boyfriends all that well, but they must be good ones, too, if they've earned the love of those two girls.

"And one thing I know for certain, Bentley, is that all four of them love *you*. They wouldn't hesitate to have your back, no questions asked. Loyalty like that isn't freely given. It's *earned*. So, that tells me they see a side of you not many people have the privilege of knowing. *That's* the guy I want to know. Not the entitled, playboy prick you show the rest of the world." I straighten my spine and lift my chin. "So buckle up, Buttercup, because I'm not leaving this room until I get to talk to the *real* Bentley."

A muscle tics in his jaw. "What if I don't want to talk?"

"Too bad."

His eyes fall to my lips for a moment before he speaks. "If you insist on having this no-holds-barred conversation, there's something I need to do first."

"What's that?"

Before I can even blink, Bentley closes the gap between us and grips the back of my neck with a firm hand. "*This.*"

chapter twenty-five

BENTLEY

Sydney squirms in my arms, and I laugh when she bites my lip hard enough to draw blood.

"What the hell was that?!" Her fists are balled at her sides. "I didn't say you could kiss me!"

I wipe the droplet of blood away, my eyes lazily roaming her curves, pausing briefly on her peaked nipples. Fuck, she has a great rack. I'm pretty sure her tits are bigger than they were when we met, and she already had more than a handful back then. I *really* want to slide my dick between those beauties.

I shake out of my titty-fuck fantasy. "You didn't have to. Look down, Syd. It's written all over your body. You know you wanted it just as much as I did."

She briefly glances down at her chest. "Well, that's an awfully rapey thing to say. How do you know I'm not cold?"

"Because the thermostat's set to seventy degrees, and you're wearing a thick hoodie. Although... not thick enough to hide how badly you want me, is it?"

"I *do not* want you!"

She's lying through her teeth. Her cheeks are flushed with arousal, as is the exposed patch of skin near her collarbone where the zipper parts. Her thirsty gaze hasn't left my body since she walked through the front door. If there was any question whether or not she'd consent, I would've never kissed her. If anyone is overly cautious about that shit, it's definitely me. Sydney may be pissed, but I've zero doubt she fucking wants me.

I laugh mockingly. "Liar."

She releases the cutest little growl. "I am *not* lying, asshole!"

"Prove it," I challenge. "Kiss me and *then* try telling me you don't want me. A kiss doesn't lie, Syd." I flick my finger between us. "Not with chemistry like this."

Her malachite eyes narrow. "Check your ego, bud. Don't confuse my disdain for attraction."

I wonder if she'd lose the attitude if she knew it only made my dick harder.

I take a step closer. "Ah, but therein lies the problem. The line between lust and hate tends to get a little blurry sometimes." I take another step, chuckling darkly. "Ask Kingston and Jazzy. They wrote the book on that shit."

She gasps when I run the bridge of my nose along the side of her neck. "Bentley, what are you doing?"

My tongue darts out, and I smile against Sydney's skin when she shivers. "Proving you wrong."

She pulls back and waits until I'm looking her in the eye. "Don't think for one second I'm giving up."

"Okay, baby, you're *not* giving up. Ten-four." I smile.

"Don't placate me, you ass!"

"I'm going to kiss you now, Syd." I lean closer, cupping her cheek in my palm. "Then, I'm going to make you scream. If you don't want this, say the word right the fuck now." When the only sound coming out of her are her soft breaths, I add, "Three... two... on—"

Before I can end my countdown, Sydney lifts up on her toes and presses her mouth against mine. I don't give her a chance to waver—I lick the seam of her lips until she opens for me. After that, I'm fucking done for. Kissing this woman is an experience that consumes your senses. It's the finest high, one I could easily get addicted to if I'm not careful. My hands, greedy fuckers that they are, touch everywhere they can reach while my tongue plunges in and out of her mouth.

Sydney moans against my lips as I palm her ass, tugging on the firm globes, prompting her to jump up. Without hesitation and without breaking our kiss, she wraps her legs around my waist. I take a few steps forward until we reach my bed, tossing her on the mattress. I grin from ear to ear when she pouts from the loss of connection.

"Don't worry, princess, I've got you."

She glares. "*Don't* call me princess."

"Sure thing, sweetheart." I wink.

"This was a mistake." Sydney starts to rise from the bed, but I pounce on her before she gets the chance.

"Aw, c'mon, Syd." Her back arches as I trail kisses down her neck. "We both know you don't mean that."

"Your level of cockiness is unbelievable," she mutters grumpily, but she makes no move to stop me.

"It's not cockiness when you can back it up." Sydney gasps as I press my hard-as-fuck dick into her. "I think what you meant to say was, '*Bentley, your confidence makes me so wet, I want you to drive that nine-inch cock of yours into me right the fuck now.*'"

Her body shakes with laughter she's trying—yet

failing—to hide. "Oh my God, you're ridiculous. Only porn stars have dicks that big."

I push up into a plank position and raise my eyebrows. "Wanna bet? I measured and everything."

Her gorgeous eyes widen. "Jesus. You're not kidding, are you?"

I smirk. "Not even a little."

"I think I just heard my uterus say, 'ouch,'" she mutters.

I laugh. "Don't worry, baby. I'll make you feel *real* good. No cap."

"What happened to '*one taste was more than enough*'?" She lowers her voice mockingly on that last part.

"I lied."

"Why?"

I blow out a breath. "Earlier... when I said I wasn't a good guy... despite your theory about my friends, it's true, Sydney. Straight up. I've done some horrible, unforgivable shit in my life. Things those friends of mine don't know. But if you want to get down, knowing you're so far out of my league, it's insane, then I'm selfish enough to take whatever you're willing to give."

A deep crease forms between her brows. "What kind of horrible shit?"

"The kind I don't talk about with anyone. *Ever*."

She doesn't seem to have a response to that, so I lower my head, laving kisses along her collarbone, slowly moving south. If Sydney really doesn't want to take this any further, I'm giving her plenty of opportunities to hit the brakes.

"Bentley," she pants.

"Yeah?" I unzip the purple hoodie she's wearing, carefully watching her reaction. "You want something from me?"

She nods. "Yeah."

"Fuck," I curse under my breath as I discover she's only wearing a sports bra beneath the sweatshirt. One that zips in the front, no less. Her full tits, taut abdomen, and smooth skin are calling to me like a siren, begging me to mark her as mine in any way that I can. My dick is practically weeping at the prospect. But first, there's another part of her I'd like to lay claim to.

I loop my fingers under the waistband of her leggings. "You want me to keep going, baby girl?"

"Bentley, just fucking touch me."

I couldn't prevent the smile from forming on my face if I tried. "I don't normally dig bossy chicks, but for some reason, you make it hot."

She props herself up on her elbows and lifts a

challenging brow. "You did say you'd make me scream, did you not?"

I laugh. "I believe I did."

"Then do it already!" Sydney's teeth clamp down on her lower lip. "But when we're done... we're having a talk. A *real* talk. I'm okay if you don't want to unearth every skeleton in your closet, but we will talk about you and me. You feel me?"

I yank her pants down to her ankles in one fell swoop, causing her to squeal. "Yeah, honey, I feel you."

Before pulling her pants off completely, I gently remove her Nikes and socks because fucking with socks on is just weird. From the waist down, she's wearing nothing but a pair of black cotton boy shorts. Most girls I've been with dress in fancy matching lingerie, which I can't say I don't appreciate, but with Sydney, it's not necessary. She could be wearing puke-green granny panties, and she'd still somehow make it sexy.

Everything about her appeals to me in the most primal way. I've never been more attracted to a woman in my life—I feel like a live wire whenever she's near. It was like that the first moment I laid eyes on her, and if anything, it's even stronger now. It's almost as if she was fucking made for me.

My gaze roams from her unique eyes to her

smart mouth and all around her luscious curves. I'm dying to be inside of her, but I need to feel her coming apart on my tongue first.

Sydney sucks in a harsh breath when I place open-mouthed kisses on her inner thigh. "That feels *so* good."

I smirk as I loop my fingers beneath the waistband of her panties. "It's about to feel even better."

"Less talking, more *doing*, big boy."

I laugh, but my amusement quickly fades as I pull her underwear off and see her glistening with want. I swipe a finger down the middle, teasing her entrance.

"Christ, you're so wet."

"Bentley." She moans. "Stop talking and put your goddamn mouth on me!"

I dip my index finger inside her body and curl it toward me. "Look at how you're squeezing my finger, Syd. Damn, I can't wait to get my dick inside of you."

Sydney gasps when I add a second finger, rubbing circles over her clit with my thumb. "So put it inside of me!"

I blow on her clit. "Nah, baby. A man should *always* eat his dinner like a champ before he gets dessert. Don't ever let some idiot tell you otherwise."

The thought of some other fucker down here makes me want to raze villages and shit. Feeling an irrational surge of jealousy, I jump into my mission. I'm going to fuck this girl so hard and so thoroughly, no other guy will compare. I have a steady rule of never getting off before my lady comes at least twice, but Jesus, this woman makes me want to say *screw it* and slide on home just to stake my claim. The compulsion to do so is hard to ignore. The only thing preventing me from going for it is the fact that the one time I ate her out was better than the best sex I've ever had. If Chow Town makes me this delirious, I can only imagine how euphoric actually fucking Sydney will be.

I drag my tongue over her lower lips and around her clit, but never quite going where she wants me. She makes the cutest little noises of frustration every time I get her close, then deny her orgasm.

I've always thought women should be worshipped in bed like the queens they are. Even during the most casual encounters I've had, I *never* treated a chick like a glory hole. I made *damn sure* she came so hard, she couldn't see straight before I would even think about getting off. Now, suppose a woman gets down on her knees and offers a BJ before I've had a chance to touch her. In that case,

I'm not exactly going to turn it down because, well, *blow jobs*, but I would never *expect* one, unlike a lot of assholes I know. Even Whitney Alcott was miles ahead of me on the O-count—and, let's face it, she's one of the biggest bitches alive and probably didn't deserve my generosity.

I flatten my tongue and swipe it directly over that little explosive bundle of nerves. "Patience, Syd, I said I'd take care of you, didn't I?"

"Oh my God, *just do something, Bentley!* I never thought you'd be a tease."

"It's called *delayed gratification*. It makes the end result that much sweeter."

I smile when she makes the growly sound again.

"I'd be better off going home and digging out my vibe collection at this rate."

I pull back and lift my brows. "You have a vibe *collection*, huh? Tell me more."

"Ugh! You're infuriating!"

"No, seriously. How many vibrators does a collection make? Two? Twelve? Twenty?"

She whacks me on the head. "I don't have *twenty*, you idiot!"

My lips twitch. "But you *do* have *twelve?*"

Her cheeks flush. "Shut. *Up.*"

"Interesting. You'll have to show me this collection sometime. It's only fair I know what I'm up against." I lower my head again, nibbling on her inner thigh. "But for now... I'm gonna make you forget anyone or anything else exists."

I don't give her a chance to reply before diving back in, giving her one long lick from ass to slit. I pull Sydney closer, hooking her legs over my shoulders. I lick and suck and swirl my tongue until she's a whimpering, writhing mess. Sydney's spine arches off the mattress when I circle her entrance with my index finger, once, then twice, before plunging two fingers inside of her and curling them toward me.

I devour her pretty pussy, my mouth and fingers working in tandem as she begs for more. When Syd's thigh muscles tense, I know she's almost there, so I go for the pièce de résistance that'll make her come harder than she ever has before. I wrap my lips around her slippery flesh, applying suction as I withdraw my fingers from her tight grip. Using the natural lube from her body, I apply pressure to her puckered hole before sinking my index finger inside up to the second knuckle.

"Oh God, oh God, *oh my fucking God!*" Sydney's raspy scream is music to my ears.

She comes spectacularly, and I swear to Christ, I've never seen anything more beautiful. I repeat the process until she's screaming my name before slowly easing my finger out of her ass as I lick her through the aftershocks. Once Sydney stills, I nibble her inner thighs before sitting back on my knees. Her forearm is flung over her face as she catches her breath. When her aqua gaze meets mine, the perpetual tightness in my chest suddenly loosens. I take a deep breath, and there's no strain in doing so for the first time in years.

I watch as Sydney lifts her upper body off the bed to fully remove her top. My eyes are fixed on her fingers as she lowers the zipper of her sports bra. Her brown nipples pucker when her gorgeous tits spill from their binding. Once the bra is gone as well, leaving her upper half bare, she lowers her back onto the mattress again.

Sydney smiles. "Come here and finish what you started, Bentley."

I jump off the mattress and hold a finger up. "Hold that thought."

She watches as I riffle through my nightstand drawer until I find what I'm looking for. With the corner of the foil packet clenched between my teeth, I drop my shorts to the ground, and my dick springs free. I smirk when Sydney's eyes widen and she swallows audibly. I'm hard as fuck, so everything I'm about to give her is on display.

She looks a little intimidated as I stroke myself from root to tip before tearing open the condom and sliding it down my length. Hers is not an unusual reaction the first time a girl sees me like this, but I've never had any complaints. I'm well hung, for sure, but not in an over-the-top way that would make a girl avoid coming back for seconds. I'd say my cock is a happy medium between boyfriend dick and porn star scary.

"Don't look so freaked out, Syd. It'll fit."

I ignore the voice in my head that reminds me this *isn't* the first time she's seen it, but it may be the first time she remembers it.

She scoffs. "I wasn't worried."

I rejoin her on the bed. "You sure about that?"

Sydney gasps as I rub the tip against her swollen clit. "Bentley, get inside of me already."

We both moan as I slide my dick against her a few more times before easing my hips back and nudging myself at her entrance. "So impatient."

Her shapely legs wrap around my waist, and her heels dig into my glutes, pushing me forward until the tip slips inside. My head falls to the crook of her neck on a groan, needing a second before I embarrass myself. *Jesus fuck, she's tight.* I feel the rapid beat of her pulse against my cheek as her fingers run the length of my spine. She makes a soft mewling sound when I dip my hand between us, touching the spot where we connect.

I lift my head and watch as a myriad of reactions flicker across her face as I circle her clit. "Relax, Syd. I don't want to hurt you."

Sydney's front teeth score her bottom lip as I press forward a bit more, and that's when I see it. *When I remember.* I instantly freeze.

Is it really possible she's a virgin?

"Are you..." I swallow the lump in my throat and try again. "Sydney... have you done this before?"

A curl falls over her face as she shakes her head. "Not with an actual person, but don't stop, Bentley."

I instinctively pull back, but her grip around my waist tightens, holding me in place.

"Please don't make a big deal out of this," she pleads. "I'm just a little nervous because I haven't done this before, but I *want* to do it. It's not like I've been saving myself or anything. Society's obsession with virginity is completely overrated, in my opinion. It just perpetuates this ridiculous cycle of shame and double standards. And if you're worried I'm going to be a stage-five clinger, don't. This is just phys—"

I press my mouth against hers, choking off the lie. Sydney is kidding herself if she thinks this thing between us is just physical. It's *never* been just physical. This strange connection of ours defies reason. But if she wants this, I'm selfish enough to go through with it, even though I know I don't deserve it. She softens against me as we kiss, giving me the ability to sink inside of her inch by inch until our hips meet.

I guess she's not a virgin anymore.

"You okay?" I say as I break our kiss. The urge to move is unreal, but I meant what I said earlier. I don't want to hurt Sydney in any way, despite my recent actions that indicate otherwise.

"I'm good." When I hesitate, she tilts her hips up and smiles. "Your silicone predecessors have set the bar pretty high. What's the matter? Afraid you won't measure up?"

A surprised laugh falls from my lips. She just had to go there, didn't she? I don't know a single dude on this planet who could resist a blatant challenge like that, especially when their sexual prowess is in question.

I pull out nearly to the tip before sliding back in again. My lips curve when Sydney mouths the words, *oh God*, as I do. Our bodies are flush, her breasts pressed against my chest. Our hearts beat wildly, damn near in sync, pounding beneath our skin. Her soft vanilla scent lingers in my nose, making my mouth water. As I develop a slow and steady rhythm, my body lights up with this crazy energy. I was not prepared for the emotional onslaught being with Sydney Carrington entailed. I've had a lot of sex in my life, but I've *never* felt anything like this. I have to close my eyes for a moment to mute the sensations and get a grip on my control.

"Bentley," she pants. "Please, go faster. I won't break."

I look into her eyes and see the truth in her statement. Who am I to deny this beautiful woman anything? I begin to move in earnest, and before long, a primal need sets in. An overwhelming desire to claim her, mark her as mine, kicks in, and from that point, I'm lost to it. I adjust our bodies until I'm sitting back on my knees, and she's straddling me. We take a moment in this new position to breathe, our skin glistening with sweat.

Sydney moans when I palm her breast and seal my mouth over the peaked tip. "God."

I release her with a pop. "Ride me, Syd."

A tiny crease forms between her brows. "I don't know if I know how... I mean..."

I cup her jaw and suck her lower lip into my mouth. "Just do what feels good. Don't worry about me. I guarantee anything you do will feel fucking amazing."

Sydney lifts her body a little before dropping back down again. After a few shallow slides, she experiments by going higher and lower until she's working my shaft over like a pro. Meanwhile, I'm whispering words of encouragement like *God, you feel good* or *just like that* or *fuck, right there*. My hands are everywhere they can reach; my lips are licking and sucking and biting her flesh. She'll likely want to kick my ass later when she notices the purple marks I've left behind, but for the moment, she doesn't seem to mind one bit.

Her rhythm gets choppy when I rub circles over her swollen clit, but I couldn't care less because I'm climbing higher and higher right there with her.

"Oh, God, oh, God, oh God," she chants as she comes, clenching around me like the most exquisite vise.

Once her orgasm wanes, I grab on to her hips, thrusting from below until I reach my own completion. I swear on my nuts that I see fucking stars for a second there.

I blow out a breath. "Christ."

Sydney chuckles, resting her head on my shoulder. "Tell me about it."

I'm not sure how long we remain wrapped around each other, but when I feel my dick softening, I know I need to break our connection, despite said dick's vehement protests. I'm perfectly clean, but I have no clue if Sydney is on the pill or not, so I can't take the risk of spilling any baby batter. I hold the base of the condom with one hand while I use the other to lift her off of me. I don't miss the slight wince on her face as I do, but she smiles reassuringly immediately after.

"I'll be right back."

I step into my bathroom to dispose of the rubber before returning to the bedroom with a warm washcloth. Sydney's cheeks pinken as I gently wipe between her legs, but she allows me to do this for her. Shit, it's the least I could fucking do. I'm still a little in shock about what just went down, if I'm being honest.

"You still doing okay?"

Sydney gives me a sleepy, sated smile. "I'm *great.*"

"I'm feeling pretty fucking great myself." I pull back the comforter and pat the mattress. "Get under the covers."

"Oh. Um... I should probably head home."

I frown. "Do you *need* to head home for some reason?"

"Well...no."

I pat the bed again. "Then, get in. You look exhausted, and I'm pretty wiped too. I'm not ready to say goodbye to you yet. Besides... didn't you say we needed to talk?"

Sydney crawls across the bed and slides beneath the comforter. It takes tremendous self-control not to pin her down when she moves past me, all her luscious curves proudly on display.

"I did say that, didn't I?"

I stretch out beside her, pulling her into me until her head is resting on my chest. "You did. So, let's get a little sleep, then we can talk."

I feel her jaw stretching against my chest as she yawns. "Okay."

Within a few minutes of me petting her back, Sydney's fast asleep. I'm not too far behind her, sporting a ridiculous grin as I drift off into Dreamland.

chapter twenty-six

SYDNEY

"Are you ready to talk now?"

Bentley shifts our bodies until we're lying face to face and gives me a suggestive grin. "I can think of something else I'd like to do *much* more. That nap gave me *a ton* of energy."

I smack his arm playfully. "Nuh-uh. We had a deal. Besides, it's almost midnight. I need to get home, so I'm not too much of a zombie at school tomorrow."

He sighs dramatically. "Okay, fine. Talk."

I take a moment to think about how I want to approach this.

"The night we met... what *exactly* do you remember?"

His shoulders stiffen. "Why? What exactly do *you* remember?"

"Honestly? Not a lot. I remember hanging out

with you for most of the night. Thinking you were pretty fly, but the details on what we talked about are fuzzy. I think I recall us dancing at one point, I *know* we made out quite a bit, but that's about it. I was pretty wasted."

Bentley's brown eyes bore into mine. "I don't recall you being *that* wasted."

Okay, here we go. The only people who know what my cousin did to me are Cam and Zach. It's not an experience I enjoy thinking about, so I've shoved it inside a tightly locked little box in my head.

"Do you remember meeting my cousin Lindsey? She was the one who invited me to that party."

"Vaguely. What about her?"

I smile softly, but there's no mirth or affection behind it. "Lindsey and I were really close growing up. She was like an older sister to me. But she was also... I don't know. Reckless, I guess? Back then, I don't think she gave two shits about the consequences of her actions. She was very... open-minded and enthusiastic about sex. She didn't understand why everyone else didn't feel the same. Even me, despite the fact that I was only sixteen at the time. She lost her virginity at fourteen, so maybe she thought I was overdue or something.

"Unbeknownst to me, she decided that party

was the perfect opportunity for me to get some. I didn't know this at the time, but that's why she talked me into wearing her sorority shirt. She wanted the guys at that party to think I was older. She told me if anyone asked to say I was a sophomore and leave it at that. Let them assume I meant college, so I wouldn't get kicked out of the party. It wasn't technically a lie, or that's how I justified it in my head anyway. I looked up to her. I was trying to fit in with her friends."

He traces the contour of my jaw. "Where are you going with this, Syd?"

"She... uh... started bringing me these cocktails. She thought they'd help *loosen me up*, as she put it. She'd never given me any reason not to trust her before that night, so I had no reason to suspect anything was wrong. But... it turned out, I shouldn't have trusted her. Lindsey conveniently omitted two of the drinks' key ingredients. If I had known, I would've never taken a single sip."

"Which ingredients did she leave out?"

"Um... well, it was supposedly only a tiny amount, but throughout the night, I had five or six cups, so it had a much stronger effect than what she was going for. At least that's what Lindsey claims."

"Sydney, *which* ingredients?" Bentley growls.

Damn, why is he getting so worked up about this when he doesn't even know the worst of it yet?

"Molly with a dash of roofie." I clear my throat. "Evidently, she got them from some preppy guy she was hanging out with that night. So, as you can probably imagine, I was out of it after drinking enough of them. Thank God one of Lindsey's sorority sisters found me on the verge of passing out and took me back to their place. I woke up the next morning feeling like ass with very little recollection of the whole thing."

"So you were doped up on ecstasy and Rohypnol that night? Drugs that some *preppy guy* provided?" Bentley's jaw is clenched so tightly, I'm not quite sure how he forms words.

I shrug. "In a nutshell, yes."

"Fuck," he mutters, scrubbing a hand over his face.

"Yep." I pop the P. "That night is the primary reason why I stay away from drugs, even weed. And I won't ever accept an open drink at a party from *anyone*. I... that night could've gone so much worse. I never want to be in such a vulnerable position again."

Bentley sits up, swinging his long legs over the side of the bed. His elbows are propped on his knees as he takes a deep breath in and then out.

"Bentley? What's wrong?"

Another deep breath. "Just... give me a second, okay?"

I'm a little confused why he seems so bothered by my story, but I get the sense this is another one of those moments where Bentley could use a reassuring touch, so I sit up behind him and place a soft kiss right between his shoulder blades.

Bentley twists his torso until he's scooping me into his lap. With my bare thighs bracketing his, our fun parts are in direct alignment, which doesn't go unnoticed by either of us. I moan as his growing erection presses into me, and he briefly takes my lower lip between his teeth. I also wince a little because, despite my extensive collection of silicone boyfriends, they're nothing compared to Bentley Fitzgerald.

"What's this about?" I trace the delicate script inked right above his heart.

Sleep well, Tiny Dancer

I watch his Adam's apple bob as he swallows. Since when are Adam's apples so sexy?

"It's a reminder."

"Of what?"

Bentley's brown eyes bounce between mine for a

moment. "Of why someone like you is way too fucking good for someone like me."

"Care to elaborate?" I lift my brows.

Bentley shakes his head. "No. It's my cross to bear."

I frown. "Does this have anything to do with the person you visited in the cemetery?"

"I said, *no*, Sydney," he snaps, grabbing on to my hips when I try pulling away. "Look, I'm sorry. I'm not trying to be a dick. I just... *can't* talk about it. I need you to respect that. Can we please change the subject?"

"Okay..." I say, treading lightly. The vibe in this room is getting way too intense for two naked people who recently had mind-blowing sex. "Can I ask what *you* remember from that night?"

Bentley's fingers flex infinitesimally over my breast. If he wasn't touching such a sensitive spot, I probably wouldn't have even noticed it. His head falls to my chest, his forehead resting over the dip between my clavicles.

I gasp as his thumb brushes back and forth over my nipple while his warm breath skitters across my skin. "I'd say about as much as you. I partied pretty hard that night."

Damn it.

I was really hoping he could help decode Zach's

cryptic statement about that night. I thought for sure Bentley remembered something based on his reaction, but it's possible he was just hyped up from rescuing me from my handsy ex.

"Can we be done talking now?"

I think about something else that's been nagging me ever since it was brought up.

"I have one more question." I lift his chin with my finger. "At lunch that day... when you referred to Jazz... and letting Kingston watch... can you explain *that?*"

He groans. "Do I have to?"

"No..." My brows lift. "Bentley, I know you have a past, and that's okay. I would seriously never judge you for that. The thing is... I like Jazz. I think she could become a really good friend, but I feel like I'm missing something between you two. Something *significant*, and I'd be lying if I said it wasn't bugging me. I'm a big fan of transparency, and I was hoping you'd respect that."

His eyes bounce between mine for a few beats before he speaks. "Jazz and I... uh... fooled around a couple of times a while back, but we never actually slept together." He clears his throat. "Kingston was there both times, and I can guarantee it'll *never* happen again. Jazzy and I are just friends. Always have been, and always will be."

I'm not going to lie to myself and say my gut doesn't clench thinking about Bentley being sexual with that gorgeous girl in *any* capacity. It's a little awkward because they're close, but at the same time, Bentley doesn't look at Jazz like he wants to screw her. There's definitely fondness, but it's *very* different from the way he looks at me. Plus, I have no doubt Jazz only has eyes for Kingston, and it's not like Bentley was a virgin when we met.

Unlike me.

I blow out a breath. "Thank you for telling me."

"*Now* can we be done?" His pillowy lips surround my nipple, sucking briefly before pulling back. "Because I can think of something much better I'd like to do."

"Bentley, I really should get home." I moan as he gives the same treatment to the other side. "Besides... as much as I hate saying this because your BDE doesn't need the boost, I'm way too sore for round two right now. I think you may have broken my vagina."

His chuckle reverberates against my skin. "As much as I'd love being inside of you twenty-four seven, there are plenty of other ways to chase an O."

My body is *so* on board with that plan, but my head overrides it.

I place my hands on each side of his jaw, lifting his gaze to mine. "Bentley, I know it's a little late to be having this conversation, but I don't do casual hookups. No judgment to anyone who does, but that's not me. I know I have no right to ask you this, but if there's going to be a repeat of what happened earlier this evening..." I groan when he moves beneath me just enough that my swollen—and very interested clit—glides over his shaft. "I'm not asking to be your girlfriend or anything, but... I need to know that when you're not with me, you're not out there banging every blonde in sight. I like you, Bentley. I think there's something special here. But if you can't agree to that, I totally understand."

His lips part as if he's going to say something, but they snap shut again. God, it's really freaking awkward having this conversation in our current position, but I know I need to be true to myself, or I'll regret not doing so. That's another one of my mom's life lessons that haven't steered me wrong yet.

A wrinkle forms between his eyebrows. "Syd."

I shake my head. "Forget about it. No hard feelings, right? I'm a big girl. I knew what I was getting myself into." I try pulling out of his hold, but his grip tightens.

"Sydney. Will you let me talk, please?"

I stop struggling to get free. "Go ahead."

Bentley grabs a wayward curl, running it between his thumb and index finger. "I don't want anyone else, so you have nothing to worry about."

What? I couldn't have possibly heard him correctly.

"Huh?"

His mouth kicks up in the corner. "I said I don't want anyone *but* you, so you have nothing to worry about. I've had my fair share of casual hookups, but the truth is... I lost interest in them a while ago. And I haven't been with *anyone* in *any* way, in a few months, so..."

I frown in confusion. "But... what about Barbie? Erm... Rebecca."

"Yeah... about that. I may have been using her to piss you off. But nothing actually happened." Well, at least he has the sense to look ashamed.

"Why? And while we're on the topic, why were you such a jerk all those times?"

He briefly looks over my shoulder. "Because I was trying to push you away. But I'm sick of feeling so fucked up all the time. I'm sick of pretending like I'm okay. I don't even think I know what happiness feels like anymore, but being with you, like this... it's the closest I've been in as long as I can remember. Like you said earlier... you're a big girl. If you want to do this—be with me—despite my issues, knowing there are certain things I won't talk about, then I'm not going to deny myself any longer. I'm not going to push you away anymore."

"We all have issues. Some of them are bigger than others, but everyone's got something they're dealing with. That doesn't mean you're not a good per—" I yelp when he lifts me off his lap, throws me on the bed, and covers my body with his own, all in less than two seconds. "Bentley! What the hell?"

He smiles. "Less talking. More kissing."

His lips find mine before I can protest. When his tongue slides into my mouth, mingling with mine, any objections I may have had go out the window. And as that tongue glides down my body, in between my thighs, Bentley enthusiastically gives me several more reasons to scream his name before the night is over.

chapter
twenty-seven

BENTLEY

"Whassup, man?" Kingston lifts his chin in greeting as he exits his vehicle.

I mimic the gesture. "'Sup?"

Kingston rounds the hood of his matte black Koenigsegg Agera right as Jazz opens her door on the passenger side. When she climbs out of the car, she smiles as he pulls her into his side. For the first time since they hooked up, I don't feel the little pang of envy that usually hits when I see them together. Don't get me wrong; it's still a little nauseating seeing them so loved up all the time, but it's easier to tolerate this morning. I suspect the reason behind that is the woman who just pulled into her own parking space about half a dozen spots over.

I'm not oblivious to the stares as I make my way over to the black Audi, nor my friends walking behind me, but I ignore them. I know what I'm about to do will cause a big splash in the Windsor gossip mill, which is why I chose to do this in the parking lot in front of as many witnesses as possible. I know Sydney has reservations about us being together, despite telling her I didn't want anyone else. I can't exactly blame her—my reputation and recent behavior warrant a little hesitation—but I'm going to do what I can to squash her doubts. And since I'm doing this in front of half the student body, it'll also send a message to them.

If this woman will have me, I'm all in.

I don't waste a single second as Sydney gets out of her car. The moment her feet touch the ground, I'm advancing with a single mission in mind. Her beautiful eyes widen as I approach, likely because she can sense something big is about to happen. She gasps in surprise as I slam my mouth against hers, which allows me to deepen the kiss. I'm vaguely aware of murmurs and catcalls from the crowd gathered around us, but mostly all I can focus on is her taste—a little bit of iced coffee mixed with cinnamon—and the breathy moans that are making my dick hard. When we finally break apart, we're both breathing heavily, under a thick haze of lust.

Sydney blinks a few times. "Whoa. What was that for?"

I brush a curl behind her ear. "Just needed to kiss you. I'm going through withdrawals. It's been too long."

Her lips curve. "It's been less than seven hours since the last time."

"Like I said, too long. Plus, I wanted to remind you about what I said last night."

She tilts her head to the side. "Which part?"

"That I don't want anyone but you." I jerk my head toward the crowd of gawking students. "And now they know it, too."

"Oh." I'm tempted to throw her in the back seat of her Audi when she bites her lip. "Okay."

A throat clears. "Uh, guys. We have less than five minutes before first period begins. Syd, you wanna walk with me?"

Sydney's cheeks flush as her eyes follow the sound of Jazz's voice. "Um... sure." She turns her attention back to me. "I guess I'll see you in psych?"

I take a step back and hoist my bag over my shoulder. "I'll be counting the seconds until then."

She laughs. "That was cheesy. Really, really cheesy."

"Doesn't mean it's not true."

Sydney steps out of my hold and joins Jazz. "Later, guys."

"Later," Kingston, Reed, and Ainsley say in unison.

"I'll see you at lunch." Ainsley lifts on her toes to peck Reed's cheek before she heads toward Franklin Hall, the building where her first class is.

The guys and I let Sydney and Jazz get ahead of us a bit before we head toward the center building where our classes are located.

"You gonna tell us what that was all about?" Kingston gestures to the two beautiful girls stepping through the doors of Lincoln Hall.

I shrug. "Not much to tell."

"Bullshit," Reed scoffs. "When did you and Sydney Carrington get so cozy? How the fuck did you convince her to forgive your ass after your epic douchebaggery?"

I punch his arm. "Shut the fuck up."

"What? You know it's true." Reed smirks. "So, what gives?"

"I'm sick of being so goddamn miserable all the time. After last night... I decided to man the fuck up and get over my shit. For whatever reason, Sydney can see past my dickish behavior and wants to give me a shot. Who am I to look a gift horse in the mouth?"

Kingston's brows rise. "What happened last night?"

"A gentleman never tells."

He gives me a wry look. "In other words, you fucked her."

I know the look on my face gives it away, but I don't verbally confirm anything.

"So, what?" Kingston presses. "Are you two a thing now?"

"I don't know," I answer honestly. "We didn't exactly give it a label, but I guess you could say that. I don't want anyone else, and I wanted to prove that to her."

"That's what the parking lot scene was about?" Reed questions. "To send a message to the female population of Windsor that you're not interested in hooking up?"

I laugh. "I may have also been publicly claiming Sydney so the dudes would back off, too. I see how they look at her, and I don't fucking like it. Two birds, one stone."

The three of us stop in front of my class since this is where we usually part ways.

Kingston's staring at me like he's trying to do his freaky mind-reading thing again. "Huh. Well, I'll be damned."

"What's that supposed to mean?" I frown.

He grins. "It looks like our little Bentley is finally growing up."

Reed and Kingston laugh as I flip them off.

"Fuck you. There is *nothing* little about me, and you pricks know it."

"Sure, buddy. You keep telling yourself that." Kingston's tone couldn't have possibly been more condescending. "Later, asshole."

They're still laughing as I mutter, "Fuck off."

I take my seat right before the bell rings and begin my countdown of when I can see my girl again.

"So, do you have your audition piece all ready to go?" Ainsley takes a bit of her pasta.

"I do," Sydney replies. "How about you?"

She clenches her fingers over mine to stop the hand that's on her thigh from wandering too high. I'm not about to slip my fingers inside of her—as awesome as that thought is—but I can't stop touching her now that she's finally within my reach. Her skin is so fucking soft, I can't resist.

Ainsley blows out a breath. "I don't know. I mean, I think so. Madam Rochelle loves the routine I've come up with, but I feel like something's missing."

"But you don't know what?" Syd takes a sip of her soda.

"Nuh-uh." Ainsley shakes her head. "It's frustrating."

"Maybe my mom could pinpoint it," Sydney suggests. "You're welcome to come by the studio if you want."

Ainsley's hazel eyes round. "Seriously? Oh my God, that would be amazing!"

I watch as they go back and forth for a bit, throwing around dance terms I don't understand. Jazz meets my eyes and gives me a knowing grin. Probably because I'm sitting here smiling like an idiot. Ainsley took Carissa's death pretty hard, which is understandable considering they were besties since kindergarten. Until Jazz came around, I didn't think Ains would ever have a relationship like it again.

With Sydney here and their shared love of dance, I can see Ainsley coming out of her shell even more. My circle of friends is tight. We're all pretty guarded and don't easily let newcomers in. But Sydney fits in seamlessly. She and Ains have the dance thing in common, and they're applying to the same performing arts college, while Syd and Jazz have that strong, badass-but-can-be-soft-when-it's-needed personality. It all seems a little

chapter twenty-eight

)NEY

"Oh my God, oh my God, oh my God. I can't
·ve *the* Daphne Reynolds is standing right in
t of me!"

look at Ainsley out of the corner of my eye
smile. "You do know she's just a regular person,
? I'd think someone who grew up in LA would
nmune to celebrities at this point."

"This isn't just *any* celebrity. That's Daphne
1olds!" She throws her arms out, gesturing to
nom through the observation window, where
currently teaching a pointe class.

shake my head. "She's just Mom to me.
les... most people outside of the dance
d have no clue she even exists. I don't think
ever been recognized by some rando in
ic before. At least not while she was
me."

too good to be true, but I can't say I don't fucking
love it.

When lunch is over, I walk Sydney to her next
class.

"You know, we never did finish our assignment."
I smile against Sydney's ear as she shivers. "You
should come by my place after school so we can
work on it."

"I have to work." She gasps quietly as my hand
grabs on to a hip over her plaid skirt. "But I could
probably swing by after. Are your parents still
gone?"

I nip the shell of her ear. "They are."

"Whore," a familiar voice mutters, making
Sydney tense.

I immediately snap back to find the source.

"You got a problem, Whit?"

Whitney's over-collagen-injected lips pull up in
a snarl. "What if I do, *Bent?*"

"Bentley, don't." Sydney grabs onto my
forearm.

Fuck that. If I don't put this bitch in her place,
she'll consider Sydney an easy target.

I glare at Windsor's supposed queen bee.
Whitney Alcott has always been a Grade-A cunt,
but ever since Peyton Devereaux was ousted and
subsequently sent to a boarding school in France,

she's been worse than ever. "Then I'd say you need a reminder of your place. If you have a problem with me—or anyone I care about—then *we're* going to have a problem. You feel me?"

Whitney's eyes narrow. "Whatever. Everyone knows this bitch is just a shiny new toy you'll use up and toss aside soon enough. It's not worth my trouble." She turns her gaze to Syd. "Good luck with that, honey. The ride may be fun while it lasts, but don't think you're the one who's going to tame him. If I couldn't do it, no one can."

"Get fucked, Whit—"

Sydney's nails are now scoring my skin. "Bentley. She's not worth it."

"I give it a month, tops." Whitney flips her brown hair over her shoulder and walks away.

My nostrils flare as I watch her go. There's no way I'm going to allow Whitney to subject Syd to her bullshit. After the crap she and her little posse pulled with Jazz, I don't trust her one bit. I used to think she was nothing more than Peyton's little puppet, but Whit's proven she has no issue stirring up her own drama. I make a mental note to have a little chat with her later.

Sydney pulls on the lapels of my blazer. "Bentley. Seriously. I know how to handle catty girls. Don't worry about it."

I lean down to close the gap betw ping the Whitney subject for now. Aft I say, "Get your sexy ass into class. I'll front after the final bell."

She smiles. "'Kay."

I wait until she walks into the heading down the hall for Lit, countin until she's off work and in my bed agai

Ainsley gasps. "That's like saying Michael Jordan doesn't exist!"

"*So* not even close to the same thing." I laugh, wiping a tear from the corner of my eye. "You're not going to make me regret this by going all single white female, are you?"

She rolls her round hazel eyes. "Oh, shut up. I'm not that bad."

"You kind of are." I scrunch my nose. "You're lucky I think it's kind of adorbs."

"Crap, class is ending." Ainsley takes several deep breaths. "I can do this. I can meet my idol and not make a complete fool out of myself." More breathing and mumbling. "Don't freak out, Ainsley. *Don't* freak out."

I look over my shoulder and smile at Cam, who's sitting behind the desk. She's clearly thinking the same thing I am: *This is going to be fun to watch.*

"Great job, ladies," my mom calls to her departing students. "I'll see you next week."

After the dancers file out of the room, I take Ainsley's hand and lead her into the studio.

"Hey, Mom. I wanted you to meet my new friend from Windsor. This is Ainsley Davenport."

My mom finishes sipping from her water bottle and offers Ainsley a big smile. "Nice to meet you, Ainsley Davenport."

"Uh..." Ainsley shifts from one leg to the other. "It's nice to meet you, too. I mean... it's an *honor* to meet you, Miss Reynolds. Big, *big* honor. I'm a *huge* fan. I think I have, like, every one of your performances on YouTube memorized. Wait... should I call you Mrs. Reynolds? Mrs. Carrington?" Her eyes flicker to me right before she stage-whispers, "*What do I call her?!*"

"Daphne's good." My mom chuckles. "So, you're a ballet fan?"

Ainsley nods enthusiastically. "It's my life. I've been taking classes at Diamond Dance Company since I was little."

"With Rochelle Laurent?" my mom asks.

"Yep," Ainsley confirms.

"Well, I'd love to see you perform sometime. Rochelle and I go way back. You're in great hands with her."

My friend's eyes brighten. "Wow... um... yeah, I could do that. Perform, I mean. Whenever's good for you. I'm sure you're very busy."

My mother's chocolate eyes twinkle in amusement at Ainsley's awkwardness. "You just let me know. I can always make time for one of Sydney's friends."

"Ainsley is applying to the LASPA like me," I offer, deciding to put the poor girl out of her tongue-tied misery. "We're actually going to run through our audition pieces in the back room for a bit. You don't have another class coming in for an hour, right? Care to watch? Ainsley feels like something's missing from her routine, but she can't quite pinpoint it. Since it's a ballet piece, you might have better luck than me."

Ainsley is practically vibrating with nervous energy, waiting for my mom's reply.

My mom smiles. "I'd love to. Is that okay with you, Ainsley?"

"Are you kidding?! Um... I mean, *of course*. It's your studio, right?" Ainsley makes this bizarre half laugh, half groan noise. "I mean... I'd be honored, Miss...er, *Daphne*. Totally honored."

Cameron giggles softly behind us, prompting my laughter. Not gonna lie; Ainsley's fangirling is the funniest thing I've witnessed in a while.

My mom inclines her head. "Well, let's go then."

"Ugh, why did I have to be so extra?" Ainsley groans.

"It wasn't that bad," I assure her.

Her eyebrows lift. "Really?"

"*What* wasn't that bad?" Jazz asks as we approach the counter.

Calabasas Coffee, the shop where Jazz works, is only five minutes away from the studio, so Ainsley, Cam, and I decided to drive here since Jazz's shift is almost over. I have to admit, I was surprised when I found out Jazz is a part-time barista. After seeing where she lives, I'm pretty sure she doesn't *have* to work like I do. My parents bought my car for me on my sixteenth birthday, but they did so on the condition I pay for its expenses. Luckily for me, my mom needed an extra instructor at the studio around the same time.

Ainsley cringes. "I met Sydney's mom this morning. She gave me some really great feedback on my audition piece, but I'm pretty sure the woman thinks I'm an idiot. I was so nervous, I could barely spit out a word. *Thank God* dancing is so natural for me. I would've bawled if I screwed that up in front of her."

Jazz's lips twitch. "Oh, I'm sure you were fine." Her eyes swing to me. "She didn't make a *total* ass out of herself, right, Syd?"

I hold my index finger and thumb an inch apart. "Maybe just a little."

"Ugh." Ainsley's face lands in her palm. "I'm

never going to be able to show my face around Daphne Reynolds again."

Cam laughs. "Guuuurl, Mama D has been putting up with my ridiculousness for over ten years now. Trust me when I say anything awkward you may have done today, wouldn't faze her in the slightest."

Ainsley's lips twist. "You're just saying that to make me feel better."

I shake my head. "She's *really* not."

All four of us laugh.

"I'm about to clock out," Jazz says. "Do you guys want drinks before I do?"

"Uh, yeah." The *duh* is clearly implied in Ainsley's tone.

"Okay, I know what Ains wants." Jazz's eyes shift to Cameron and me. "What about you two?"

"Um... iced chai latte for me, please." I jerk my thumb toward Cam. "Iced mocha for her."

"I'll get those two," Jazz's co-worker offers before grabbing two plastic cups and filling them with ice.

Jazz nods to the blonde beside her. "Sydney and Cameron, this is Alley."

Alley gives a little wave. "Nice to meet you."

"You too," Cam and I say at the same time.

Jazz nods. "Why don't you guys grab that table in the back, and I'll bring these over?"

A few minutes later, the four of us are sipping delicious lattes while filling Jazz in on our morning.

"So..." Cameron pauses until she has our rapt attention. "I heard there's a party tonight at this place in Bell Canyon. You in?"

"Can't." Jazz shakes her head. "My little sister is officially moving in with us tomorrow, and I still need to do a few things to get ready for that."

I tilt my head to the side. "Can I be nosy and ask what that's about? You said she's eight, right?"

"Yep, she turned eight last Christmas." Jazz takes a long sip of her drink before continuing. "Well, you already know my mom died last summer. Belle—that's her name—has been living with her dad since then. He decided to sign over his parental rights, and since I'm her only remaining relative, I'm filing to become her legal guardian. A judge granted a temporary order for us to have her until all the paperwork goes through. We still have to jump through some hoops, but my attorney says everything should be okay soon enough."

"That's a tremendous responsibility," Cameron says. "Raising a little girl, I mean."

Jazz shrugs. "When our mom was alive... she worked *a lot*. Don't get me wrong; my mom was the best. She spent every minute she wasn't working with us, and we never questioned her love, but I've been helping raise Belle since I was about ten. Me and my mom... we were a team." She pauses for a moment before clearing her throat. "It really won't be that big of a difference. That little girl's been my number one priority since the day she was born."

"And Kingston's okay with taking that on?" I take a sip of my chai.

Jazz and Ainsley both smile.

My brows scrunch. "What's that dreamy look for?"

"My brother might be a grumpy ass to most, but he's a big softy around a select few. Especially Belle. She has him wrapped around her little finger." Ainsley giggles. "He's the reason Jazz is getting custody so easily."

"How so?" I ask.

Jazz's bronzed cheeks pinken. "He... uh... paid Belle's dad to sign over his rights."

Cam's jaw drops. "Seriously?"

"Yeah." Jazz nods. "But it wasn't exactly hard to convince him. Kingston made him an offer, and the dude couldn't collect his money fast enough."

"And your sister is okay with everything? Not being around her dad?"

Jazz gets a sad smile on her face. "Jerome,

Belle's dad, is a dick. He never wanted her in the first place, and she's old enough now to pick up on that. She actually asked if she could live with us instead, which prompted Kingston to visit Jerome. Before talking to me, my stubborn boyfriend made the deal because he knows how uncomfortable I get when he spends money on us. But I didn't fight him on it because I truly believe he wanted this, too. Belle... me... one big blended happy family. And money can make that happen faster than any legal battle."

I think about that for a moment. "Wow... not exactly a decision a normal eighteen-year-old would make. You weren't kidding when you said you guys had to grow up fast, huh?"

"Not even a little." Jazz shakes her head. "And I'm going to do everything in my power to ensure Belle doesn't have the same experience. She deserves to be a kid as long as possible."

Cam leans forward. "So, are you and Kingston, like, engaged?"

Ainsley laughs. "If Kingston had his way, they'd be *married* already. There's no better way to piss circles around someone than putting a wedding band on their finger."

Jazz's lips twitch. "To answer your question, Cameron, no, we're not engaged."

"But?" Cam challenges.

"But... we talk about it. And he knows I'm in this for keeps. I just want to at least graduate high school first. Ya know? It's one of the few normal teenage experiences I have left that's within my control. Kingston's as alpha as they come, but I can be just as hardheaded, and he respects me enough to taper his inner control-freak when need be."

"God, you two must have the hottest sex," Cameron muses. "I'd love to be a fly on that porno's wall. Are you guys by chance into exhibitionism?"

Jazz practically chokes on the sip she was taking, making the rest of us laugh. "Uh..."

Ainsley plugs her ears. "Nope. Don't answer that. We may have shared a womb, but I do *not* need to hear about my brother's sexual preferences."

I throw my balled-up straw wrapper at Cam. "They don't know you well enough to know that you're joking, asshole."

Cam's lips curve into a sly smile. "Who said I was joking? They're both smoke shows. And he looks at her like he wants to rip her panties off with his teeth." She fans herself dramatically. "Like I said, *hot*."

"She's joking," I assure Jazz, kicking my wildly inappropriate bestie under the table.

"I really wasn't," Cameron laughs.

I groan, rubbing my temples. "I can't take you anywhere."

Cam waves her hand dismissively, totally ignoring my jab. "So, anyway, about this party. Jazz, you're out, but what about you, Ainsley?" She turns to me. "Syd, I need a wing woman, so you don't get a choice."

I flip her off.

"I think I'll sit this one out. I've barely seen Reed all week. But you should totally ask Bentley if he wants to go." Ainsley winks at me.

"Ooh, good call!" Cameron points to Ainsley before turning her gaze to me. "Get on that, bish. And don't even pretend you don't want to see him."

I roll my eyes as I pull out my phone to text him. "Yeah, yeah." It only takes Bentley a few seconds to respond.

Bentley: If you're there, I'm in. Text me your address, and I'll pick you up.

I smile as I reply, telling him I'll drive to his house instead, and we can go from there. I'm supposed to be spending the night at Cam's, and this way, if I happened to stay with Bentley, my parents wouldn't question why my car is still at home. When I look up, Jazz and Ainsley are watching me intently.

"What?"

They give each other a strange look before Jazz speaks up. "You really like him, don't you?"

"I don't think I know him well enough to say that."

But well enough to give him my virginity, it seems.

"But you met over two years ago." Ainsley pulls her hair into a ponytail.

"Yeah, but neither one of us remembers much from that evening. It's more like a feeling I get than actual details."

"How do you know what Bentley does or does not remember?" Jazz inquires.

"He told me." I shrug. "He drank a lot that night—among other stuff—and hardly remembers a thing."

She narrows her eyes, cursing under her breath. "*That's* what he told you? That he doesn't remember anything?"

"Pretty much." I swallow the sudden lump in my throat when I start getting a weird vibe from her. "Why?"

She nibbles her lower lip. "No reason. Just wondering."

"You sure?"

Jazz takes a sip of her latte. "Yep. Totally."

I feel like there's something she's omitting, but I don't want to accuse her of anything by pushing it.

I glance at the time on my phone. "Well, I guess we should get going so we have time to get ready for the party. Thanks for the drinks."

"Anytime." Jazz replies. "See you later."

"Bye!" Ainsley adds.

Cam and I wave goodbye before heading to my car.

Once we're inside, I buckle up and face my bestie. "Is it just me, or did it seem like Jazz was holding herself back from saying something?"

"Not just you." Cameron frowns. "The vibe got really strange all of a sudden. Any idea what it could be about?"

I shake my head, pushing the ignition button. "No clue."

"What does your gut tell you?"

"That she's withholding information to protect Bentley." I shrug. "I totally respect her loyalty to him, but it kind of sucks, too. I don't know... maybe I'm reading too much into it."

"Maybe."

I shift into reverse and pull out of the parking spot. "Bentley and I are just getting to a good place. These last few days have been... amazing. The last thing I want to do is accuse him or his friends of anything, especially with only a hunch to back it up."

"Right," Cam agrees. "I guess time will tell, huh?"

"Guess so."

"And in the meantime..." I can see her Cheshire grin out of the corner of my eye. "You get your freshly devirginized puss-ay tongued and dicked by that gorgeous man as often as possible."

I laugh. "You're ridiculous."

She blows me a kiss. "Love you too, babe."

chapter
twenty-nine

BENTLEY

"Welcome to a Cambridge party," Cameron shouts over Dua Lipa's "Levitating" blasting through the speakers.

"You wanna find the drinks?" Syd asks.

I nod. "Sure."

As we walk toward the kitchen, I take note of all the differences between this and a Windsor party. Although most are rich, Sydney mentioned that Cambridge kids aren't nearly as entitled as Windsor kids, which is evident here. It's obvious by the cars parked out front and the way people are dressed, they like flashy things, but the party itself isn't a big production like I'm used to.

Whereas a Windsor party host wouldn't dare throw a rager without hiring a professional bartender, this party has your standard self-service booze setup: a couple of coolers filled with beer and hard ciders, with an array of liquor bottles, red cups, and mixers littering the counters. Instead of a professional DJ booth stationed in the corner, music blasts from an overhead speaker system.

"What's your poison?" I jerk my head to the counter.

The ladies start digging through the coolers.

"We only drink from sealed bottles," Syd explains. "Past experiences and all that."

Shit.

I try to stop the wave of guilt that hits me from the reminder, but it's a futile attempt.

Sydney scrunches her delicate brows. "You okay?"

I give her my cocky asshole smile. "Of course. Why wouldn't I be? I'm at a party with the two most beautiful girls here."

Sydney snorts. "Laying it on a little thick there, don't you think?"

I lean down a bit so I can speak into her ear. "If you want *thick*, I can certainly help you out with that if we can find an empty room."

When I pull back, Sydney's cheeks are flushed. Fuck, I love how easily I can make her blush.

"Ooh, you just totally said something dirty, didn't you?" Cameron pries. "C'mon, now. Share with the class."

Syd whacks her bestie with the back of her hand. "Shut up, bitch."

Cam laughs. "I'm just sayin'. God knows I'm not getting a good dicking anytime soon, so I might as well live vicariously through you."

"Cameron!" Syd shouts while I laugh.

I take a sip of my beer. "Why is that? It couldn't be for lack of options."

While my dick only has eyes for Sydney, I can still appreciate the fact Cameron is fine as fuck. Hot girls do tend to travel in packs, and these two certainly live up to that stereotype.

"Aw, well, aren't you sweet?" Cameron flashes a toothy grin. "To answer your question, I guess you could say I'm... selective. I mean, I'm not opposed to a drunken make-out sesh with some hot guy at a party, but when it comes down to putting the P in my V, I reserve that for dudes I *really* like. Technically, there's only been one dude who's had the honor, but sadly, he was from Brazil and had to go back home. Cambridge guys are kinda douchey, plus with work and my lack of a vehicle, I don't get many chances to scope out prospects."

I take a moment to think about that. It's refreshing to meet a chick who doesn't bang every dude in sight. Don't get me wrong, I am the *last* person who should be slut-shaming anyone. But these last few days have proven to me that I don't need someone who fucks like a pro to have a good time. Sex with Sydney is hands down the best I've ever had. And considering the fact she was a virgin less than a week ago—which still blows my mind, by the way—really says something. Her inexperience doesn't even factor into the equation. I'm hard as a fucking rock when she just *looks* at me. I'm pretty sure there's nothing she could do that wouldn't turn me on. Plus, the fact that she wants me for *me*, not because of my money or the fact I'm a Windsor king, is a bonus.

She wouldn't want you if she knew you lied to her.

"Fuck," I mutter, scrubbing a hand down my face.

Sydney grabs the same hand. "Hey. Are you sure you're okay? You seem a little... off."

"Yeah," I add yet another lie to the pile. "Totally fine. You know, I think I need a smoke. It doesn't look like anyone's doing that in here, so I'm going to head out back. You ladies care to join me for a round of puff, puff, pass?"

"Oh. Um... no, I stay away from drugs. Remember? Same with Cam." Syd's eyes widen. "I mean, I'm totally okay if *you* want to smoke some weed. No judgment from either of us, I swear. It's just not our thing."

Christ.

I'm fucking up all over the place tonight, aren't I? And the night's barely begun. Still, I really need something to help me chill. My head is spiraling into a rabbit hole I don't want to go down.

I clear my throat. "Cool. Will you two be okay if I step out back for a few?"

They both nod and say, "Sure."

I weave my way through the crowd, feeling like a first-class asshole, but that doesn't stop me from my mission. The second I step into the backyard, I pull the pre-roll case out of my pocket and duck into a shadowed corner before opening it. This entire area is filled with skunky-scented smoke, so there's no reason for me to hide a joint, but I require something extra that I don't want to draw attention to. I grab the little white pill from the case and dry-swallow it, looking around to make sure no one witnessed me popping opioids. I don't care what these randos think, but I do care what Sydney thinks. Despite her insistence she was okay with me smoking ganja, I doubt she'd be as cool knowing about my little Perc habit. I'm honestly surprised she hasn't pushed the issue after watching me take one in class.

I pull out a spliff and light it up. I take a long drag, holding the smoke inside my lungs for a few beats before blowing it out again. After a few tokes, the tightness in my chest loosens a bit. In about twenty minutes, the Perc should kick in, which will have me feeling *really* good. Nobody wants to party with a guy who constantly feels like he's suffocating, right?

By the time I head back inside, the party has grown in size. Thankfully, my height allows me to see over the mob, so it doesn't take too long to find Sydney and Cameron dancing with each other. They look like they're having a good time, so I prop my foot against the wall and watch for a bit. My eyes automatically scan the room—a habit I developed after spending so much time helping my best friend investigate his late father's shady-as-fuck lifestyle—and pause when I spot two familiar faces.

Sydney's dickbag ex appears to be macking on the tiny blonde who's constantly trying to jump on my dick. As if she can sense someone watching her, Rebecca's eyes search the crowd until she gets a lock on me. The second our gazes meet, her lips form into a sinister smile that seems out of place on her peppy cheerleader face. In the next moment, she fists the asshat's shirt and pulls him into a kiss. The guy instantly responds, deepening their kiss while his hands do their best impression of an octopus all over her body.

I scoff, immediately returning my attention back to the only woman I came here for. If Rebecca thinks that little show she put on will make me jealous, that bougie bitch is even dumber than I thought. The crazy magnetic pull I feel toward Syd lures me in, having me close the distance between us in a few long strides.

I slide in behind her, placing my hands on her hips. She immediately relaxes into me, no question on who's grinding against her.

"Mind if I cut in?"

Since my lips are already pressed against her ear, I take advantage and dart my tongue out to lick her sensitive lobe, causing goose bumps to pebble her bare arms. I don't know if I'll ever get over how responsive Sydney is to me. It's the biggest fucking ego boost as well as a huge turn-on.

Cameron gives us a knowing smile before shouting, "I'm going to go find a boy to play with for a while. You two have fun."

I feel Sydney's chuckle vibrate in her throat as I trail kisses down the nape of her neck. That quickly morphs into a moan as I press my dick into her luscious ass.

My hand grazes the bare skin her crop top leaves exposed. "Have I told you how amazing you look tonight?"

"Mmm. Maybe once or twice. But feel free to keep saying it."

I smile against her neck. Sydney's style is effortlessly sexy. More often than not, she seems to favor cotton tops and a pair of jeans. She's not afraid to put her gorgeous curves on display, but she's also not dressing for attention. I know firsthand how toned her entire body is—likely from a lifetime of dancing—but she doesn't flaunt it like the girls I usually hook up with.

No words are exchanged as we continue dancing from one song to the next. I'll occasionally check on Cameron to make sure she's doing okay out of the corner of my eye. When I catch Cam eagerly making out with some dude in a corner, I decide to give them a little privacy so I don't feel like a creeper and focus one-hundred-percent on the incredible woman in my arms. I'm not sure how long we dance, but it gets to the point where our skin is slicked with sweat. I could really use a drink, and I'm sure Sydney can, too, so I reluctantly unglue myself from her body.

"You wanna grab a drink and get some fresh air?"

She smiles, which momentarily stuns me. "Probably not a bad idea. But let me tell Cam where we're going first."

I nod, taking her hand to lead the way back into the kitchen after checking in with her girl. Once we each have a new bottle in hand, we head through the doors leading to the backyard. The dark corner I was in earlier is occupied, so I pull Syd toward the pool deck, where several empty loungers are stationed. I lie back on one while Sydney settles between my legs, reclining on my chest with a soft sigh.

Neither one of us speaks; we just stare at the glowing blue lights of the pool for a while, occasionally sipping our drinks.

"I have the strangest sense of déjà vu right now." Syd takes another pull from the bottle in her hand. "Weird, right?"

I shift uncomfortably, thinking about the night we met. We talked for hours in this exact position, which apparently, her subconscious remembers.

I wrap my arms around Syd and squeeze gently. "Nah... I get that feeling a lot with you."

"Mmm, yeah, me too." She sighs wistfully. "I really wish I remember more from the night we met. At least the parts with you in it."

I hum in agreement, not wanting to incriminate myself any more than I already have tonight.

"Do you—"

"Well, look who we have here. Isn't this cute?"

I stiffen the moment I hear the deep voice from behind us. Before I get a chance to shift to find the source, Zach, Sydney's ex, takes the empty chair next to us.

"Do you mind?" I snap. "We were having a private conversation?"

Zach's mouth curves into a smug grin. "The chair was empty, bro. Correct me if I'm wrong, but this isn't your house, right? That means you have no say where I sit, doesn't it?"

Sydney swings her legs to the side, straightening her spine. "Zach, go away. Nobody wants you here."

He takes a swig of beer. "*I don't care what you want*, Sydney."

I start to get up, but Syd's firm grip on my thigh stops me. "Don't, Bentley. He's not worth it. Let's go grab Cam and take off."

"Nah." Zach releases a caustic laugh. "Your slutty friend probably isn't in any hurry to leave. She was too busy sucking some dude's face off, last I saw. She's probably moved on to sucking *other things* by now. You know how that goes, don't you, Syd?

Your new man here, and I, both know how much you *love* sucking cock."

"Excuse me?!" Sydney screams.

Fuck this.

I move her aside and stand, towering over her ex. "You got a problem, asshole? I suggest you apologize right the fuck now."

He slowly stands as well, looking far too confident for someone who's about to get his ass kicked. "Why would I do that? I'm not saying anything that isn't true." My fists clench as his slimy gaze travels over my girl's body. "Isn't that right, Syd?"

"*Fuck you*, you tiny-dicked piece of shit!"

We've gathered a bit of an audience by now, so a round of snickering begins as Sydney's insult rings out through the crowd.

Zach's eyes narrow. "Fuck *you*, whore."

My fist goes flying toward his face without thought. The fucker stumbles back from the force, cursing under his breath. Sydney gasps but doesn't try stopping me.

"I suggest you leave unless you want more," I warn through gritted teeth.

Zach's nostrils flare before he spits blood on the ground. His eyes flick to Sydney as he starts backing away. "Remember this moment, Syd, so you know who to blame for what happens next. Payback's a bitch, *bitch*."

I lunge forward as he walks away but stop when my girl's hand wraps around my wrist. "Bentley, let him go." She looks around pointedly. "As much as I'd love to see you kick his ass, there are a shit ton of witnesses right now. I don't want you getting in trouble because of me. He's not freaking worth it." I don't give a fuck about consequences if it means teaching that prick a lesson, but when she adds, "*Please*, Bentley. Just let it go. *For me*." I take a deep breath, willing myself to calm down. I've quickly come to realize there's not much I won't do for this woman.

Except tell her the truth that'll make her hate me.

Now, *that* is something I can't do, no matter how badly the guilt eats at me. Because losing Sydney after I just found her again, isn't an option.

chapter
thirty

SYDNEY

"I've been dying to touch you all night." Bentley's warm breath dances over my skin as he nips my earlobe.

"Me too." I groan as he unclasps my bra with expert precision and pulls one of my nipples into his mouth.

"Next time either one of us is invited to a party, let's skip it and get to the good part instead."

I laugh. "Is this the good part?"

He pinches my side, causing me to squirm. "Smartass. Now get naked."

"Yes, sir," I sass.

We fumble on the mattress to remove the clothing from our lower bodies until we're both blissfully naked on his bed.

Bentley's large hands knead my breasts, pushing them together as he peppers kisses over them.

"I love your tits so much. I *really* want to fuck them, Syd."

I can't say a guy hasn't asked for boob sex once or twice, but the idea never appealed to me before now. With Bentley, the thought of it causes wetness to pool between my thighs, which I'm sure he can feel since his fingers are now down there working their magic.

"So do it."

He releases my nipple with a pop. "Seriously?"

"Why not? It sounds hot." I gasp. "Oh, God. Right there."

Bentley smiles, working his fingers faster while the pad of his thumb rubs circles over my clit. "I've got you, baby."

And he does. When his body slides further down the mattress and his mouth goes to town on my pussy, I detonate in record time. His tongue and fingers work in tandem through two more orgasms until I'm so sensitive, I can't take anymore. Bentley climbs up my body until he's straddling my abdomen. He rubs his thumbs over my nipples, causing them to tighten even more than they already were.

"You're so fucking beautiful, Sydney. Every inch of you."

He bends down to lick the valley between my

breasts before sitting up again and spitting into his palm. That in itself shouldn't be sexy, but it totally is, especially when he coats his shaft with saliva. I'm mesmerized as Bentley strokes himself up and down, down and back up again, before scooting up just a little bit further. He squeezes my boobs together, then pulls them apart, almost methodically, as if he's formulating a plan. Right when I'm about to ask him what the holdup is, he lines his impressive cock up in the center of my chest and glides it through the tunnel he's created with my tits.

His jaw clenches. "Jesus. So fucking good."

As Bentley falls into a rhythm, he continues playing with my nipples, sending lightning bolts of pleasure straight to my core. His thrusts are slow as he pushes the tip of his cock closer and closer to my mouth. I flick my tongue out as he approaches again, licking the salty bead of precum off the end.

Bentley's lids fall closed on a groan. "Shit. You keep that up, this'll be over a lot faster than I'd like."

I smile. "Aw, c'mon, Bentley. Don't hold out on me."

His eyes open as he flashes me a blinding smile. "Yeah? You want me in your mouth, Syd?"

My body's on fire as he inches closer with each

thrust. I'm writhing beneath him as he fucks my boobs. Rubbing my thighs together to ease the ache. I would've never imagined this position could be so arousing, but holy crap, it *is*. Instead of answering him verbally, I wet my lips and form them into a perfect O. Bentley eagerly takes the hint and slides his dick past my lips on the next pass. He's rock hard yet velvety smooth. With each thrust, he goes deeper and deeper into my mouth until he abandons my boobs altogether and starts straight-up fucking my face.

"Fuck. Fuck. Fuuuuuuck. Goddamn, your mouth is heaven."

I lift my head off the pillow, changing the angle so I can take him deeper. I moan enthusiastically around Bentley's girth, assuring him I'm enjoying this just as much as he seems to be. I can tell he's getting close as his breathing grows ragged, and his thrusts become a little less coordinated.

"Shit. Sydney, I'm going to come, baby."

I moan, grabbing his muscular ass, clearly communicating my intentions. In the next breath, Bentley's chanting my name through his release, shooting salty cum down my throat. After one long shudder, he carefully withdraws from my mouth and falls to the side in a heap of sweaty, sated limbs.

I swallow, taking a moment to catch my breath as he does the same.

Bentley drapes his heavy arm over my torso, pulling me into him. "Jesus fuck, Syd. That was incredible. I'm pretty sure I went blind for a second."

I laugh. "Wow. Who knew one could go blind by orgasm? Maybe we should rent out a billboard to warn others. Perhaps write a book. A cautionary tale, if you will."

I squeal when he clamps his teeth around the skin where my shoulder and neck meet. "Girl's got jokes."

"See?" I smile. "I may not be over the top like Cam, but I can be funny sometimes."

Bentley tucks a damp curl behind my ear. "I think you're pretty fucking perfect just the way you are. You don't need to *be* anything for anyone. Just be yourself."

I tilt my chin up until our gazes meet, aqua to deep brown. Neither one of us says a word for a solid minute; we just look into each other's eyes while breathing softly. The spark between Bentley and me is otherworldly almost. I feel *whole* when we're together. I didn't even realize something was missing until he came back into my life. It makes no sense considering we barely know each other, but it's true nonetheless.

"Why do I feel like you're the missing piece I've been looking for my whole life?" My voice is so quiet, I'm not sure if he hears me at first. "How is that possible?"

Bentley presses his forehead against mine. "I don't know. But I'm right there with you, Syd. Same page. Same fucking sentence."

He leans into my touch as I cup his jaw. "It's crazy, though, right?"

He gently shakes his head. "Who says it has to be? Why do we have to overanalyze it? Why can't we just enjoy it for what it is? Take it one day at a time?"

"Do you honestly think you can do that?"

"I already do." He presses his lips against mine. The kiss starts out innocently enough, but it quickly escalates until we're both gasping for air. "Can we table the heavy shit for now? I have plans for you."

I have a pretty good idea what plans he's referring to when I feel him hardening against my thigh, but I ask anyway. "Oh yeah? What kind of plans? Tell me all about it."

Bentley starts kissing his way down my body. "I'd rather show you instead."

Ugh, why am I so hot? I peel my lids open to find a head of dark hair draped over my chest. Well, that explains the heat. Bentley's big body is wrapped around mine, my boobs serving as a pillow for his head. I carefully slide out from beneath him, not wanting to wake him. He stirs slightly as I get out of bed, but instead of waking, he grabs the pillow my head was on, hugging it to his chest.

I smile as I watch him for a moment. There is nothing boyish about Bentley's looks, but he has this childlike innocence about him in slumber. I think he spends so much time thinking about whatever's constantly haunting him or trying to pretend like nothing's wrong, the hard set to his jaw never seems to fade. His posture is usually stiff as if he's resisting the urge to tighten every muscle in his body. But right now, his limbs are languid. His expression is... peaceful, almost. It's nice to see him so at ease.

My bladder is screaming at me, so I duck into the en suite to take care of it. After washing my hands, I give my teeth a quick finger brushing, then wrap my unruly hair into a bun. I pad back into the bedroom, step into my underwear, and pull the T-shirt Bentley was wearing last night over my head. Because I'm so tall, it only hits me mid-thigh, but my ass isn't hanging out, so I'm calling it good. Plus, it smells like his ridiculously sexy cologne, which I don't mind one bit.

I head downstairs to grab a glass of water, but when my bare feet hit the bottom step, I freeze. The beautiful woman standing directly before me looks about as shocked as I am.

"Well... hello there," she says.

I stand here like an idiot, blinking for a moment before replying. "Uh... hi."

I know this is Bentley's mom. There are framed pictures of her throughout the house. But considering this is the first time we've met, and it's incredibly obvious I spent the night having sex with her son, it couldn't possibly be more awkward. Oh my God, why didn't Bentley warn me his parents were back in town? I automatically assumed they were still gone when he suggested we come here after the party last night.

Mrs. Fitzgerald's long, dark hair falls over her shoulder as she tilts her head to the side. "I'm sorry, I didn't get your name."

"Oh..." I fidget with the hem of my borrowed shirt. "Um... I'm Sydney. I'm a... *friend* of Bentley's."

She lifts a delicately sculpted brow. "It's nice to meet you, Sydney. I'm Lani. If you haven't already figured it out, I'm Bentley's mom. Where is my dear son, by the way?"

I jerk my thumb over my shoulder. "He's uh... still asleep."

"Well, in that case, why don't you join me in the kitchen? I can make some breakfast, and we can get to know one another." Her coffee-colored eyes give me a quick once over. Eyes I'm just now noticing are identical to her son's. "Maybe you'd like to get dressed first? And while you're up there, perhaps you should wake Bentley and invite him to join us."

"Oh, um... that's really not necessary. I'll just get out of your way."

I turn, intending to bolt up the stairs, but halt mid-step when she says, "*I insist*, Sydney." Damn, the woman has the *stern mom* tone down pat.

"Okay." I hurry up the stairs and slam the door to Bentley's room the moment I'm inside.

He shoots up in bed. "What the hell?" His gaze scans the room, stopping when it lands on me. "What's going on?"

I pad across the plush carpet, pulling on my clothes as fast as possible. "Oh, not much. Just getting dressed so I can go have breakfast with *your mother*. You know, the woman who just caught me doing the walk of shame down your staircase?"

His eyes widen. "Oh, shit. I didn't realize they were back."

I exchange his shirt for my own. "Bentley! How could you not know when your parents were coming back?" I gasp when a thought occurs to me. "What if they heard us? *What if your parents heard us having sex?*" My cheeks heat. "Oh my God. I'm mortified. This is so much worse than when my mom almost caught us fooling around at the studio. There is *no way* your mom thinks we weren't screwing like bunnies under her roof."

His full lips twitch. "Syd. Calm down. They must've come back this morning. There's no way they heard us."

I throw my hands up. "How can you be so sure? You didn't even know when they were due back!"

I tell myself not to ogle his body when he gets out of bed, but it's kind of hard not to when he's sporting impressive morning wood.

Bentley winks when he catches me checking him out. "Easy. My dad's car wasn't in the garage when we got here last night. I'm guessing they got in this morning."

He digs through some drawers, grabbing a pair of basketball shorts, a T-shirt, and some boxer briefs. As Bentley gets dressed, I use the mirror above the dresser to wipe away the dark smudges under my eyes from yesterday's makeup. Jesus, I'm a hot mess. What a great first impression I made.

I sigh. "What are we going to do, Bentley? We can't go down there and act like nothing's wrong! I think I should just go home."

He laughs, but for the life of me, I can't fathom what he could possibly find funny right now.

"Yeah... hate to break it to you, Syd, but there's no way in hell that's happening. I can guarantee my mom has eagle eyes on the staircase right now, waiting for us."

I perch my butt on the end of his bed and groan.

Bentley grabs my hand and pulls me back up. "C'mon, Syd. My mom's actually pretty cool. It'll be fine. I promise. And she's a fucking amazing cook, so if she offered to make us breakfast, we definitely want to cash in on it."

Despite his assurances, I feel like I'm walking to my execution as Bentley leads me down the stairs. When we reach the ground level, just as he predicted, his mom is waiting for us.

Bentley releases my hand to hug his mother. "Hey, Mom. When did you get back?"

"This morning." She props a hand on her hip. "I don't even know why I bother sending you our itinerary if you never check it."

Bentley quickly glances over his shoulder and gives me an *I told you*, look. "Where's Dad?"

"The office." She rolls her eyes playfully. "Have you met your father? Now, quit hiding that pretty girl, and come have breakfast with me."

Bentley grabs my hand as we follow his mom into the kitchen. I reach into my back pocket to pull out my cell before taking a chair at the breakfast bar. It vibrates with an incoming text before I have a chance to sit down.

Moms: Is there any chance you could take a pre-ballet class at 11? Shayna has food poisoning. I'd do it, but my pointe girls are coming in at the same time.

I smile as I type out my reply. If there was ever a time to get called into work, this is it.

Me: Of course.

Moms: Thanks, kid. Love you.

Me: Love you too, Mom

When I lift my head, Bentley and his mom are looking at me expectantly.

I hold up my phone. "Um, I'm going to have to take a rain check. One of our instructors called in sick, so I need to teach some little kids ballet this morning."

Thankfully, my car is parked out front because I couldn't exactly leave it at home when my parents think I spent the night at Cameron's. Which, as I'm now realizing, Bentley's parents likely saw it when they came home this morning.

Lani's eyes sharpen with curiosity. "You teach ballet?"

I shake my head. "Not usually. Mainly lyrical and jazz, but I fill in on other classes when need be. My mom owns a studio, so I've been dancing my whole life."

"Well, it's great your mom has you to help out. I have two left feet myself, but I've always loved watching other people dance. Bentley's dad and I have season tickets to the Los Angeles Ballet. However, he's such a workaholic, someone else usually accompanies me to performances."

Bentley clears his throat as his mom gives him a pointed look. Weird. I wonder what that's about.

Lani clasps her hands together. "Well, I won't keep you, Sydney, but I am going to hold you to that rain check."

I nod. "Okay."

Bentley places his hand on my lower back. "Mom, I'm going to walk my girlfriend out. Be right back."

My jaw drops, but I'm too stunned to formulate any words as he guides me to the front door. My brain finally connects to my mouth as we get to my car.

"Girlfriend, huh? What's that about?"

He grins. "Well... the way I see it, neither one of us have any intention of seeing other people, and we're banging, so naturally, that makes you my girlfriend."

My eyebrows reach for my hairline. "Shouldn't I get a say in this?"

"Nope." I lean into him as Bentley cups his hand around my jaw.

I stretch up on my toes to meet his lips. "What are you going to tell your mom about why I was here?"

"The truth." A deep chuckle rumbles in his chest. "Well, the G-rated version anyway."

I groan. "God. I still can't believe she caught me wearing nothing but your T-shirt and sex hair."

Bentley presses one last kiss on my lips before pulling back. "It's a good thing you look so great in my T-shirt with sex hair, then, isn't it?"

"You're an idiot." I lightly smack his arm. "I'd better go. I need time to stop by my house to shower and change."

He waits for me to get behind the wheel before leaning against the doorframe. "Text me when you're done with class."

"Okay. See you later." I smile.

Bentley closes my door and steps back to allow me room to drive away. I catch him waving in my rearview before sticking my hand out the moonroof and doing the same. As I'm making the short trip home, I can't stop grinning, thinking about my night with him. God, I'm falling so hard for that boy, which scares the shit out of me, but I'm quickly learning there's not a damn thing I can do to stop it.

And even if there was, I'm not sure I'd want to.

chapter thirty-one

BENTLEY

"Bentley William Fitzgerald, don't even think about trying to get out of this conversation."

Damn it, she knows me too well. I blow out a breath as I ditch my plan to sneak up to my room and make my way back into the kitchen.

I make a gimme motion with my hands as I take a seat at the breakfast bar. "All right, lay it on me."

She pops a few slices of bread in the toaster oven before turning back to the stove where she's cooking eggs.

"Look. I'm not dumb. I know you're sexually active, but I thought you knew better than to invite your conquests into our home for a sleepover."

I shake my head. "Sydney's not a *conquest*, Mom. She's my girlfriend. And I *do* know better. Syd's the *only* girl who's ever spent the night in my bed before."

I don't think she needs to know what's gone down in the pool house. Now *that* bed has seen plenty of action with more girls than I'd care to admit. It's always been my fuck pad, even with Carissa. Which is the exact reason why I never even thought about bringing Sydney there.

My mom looks at me thoughtfully. "You're trying to tell me you *never* snuck another girl into your room at night? Not even... your last girlfriend?"

I appreciate the fact she doesn't say her name. Both of my parents know what a sore subject Rissa is for me. Right after she died, I didn't bother hiding my drug or alcohol use from them. There were plenty of nights when I would get blitzed and run my mouth off about our toxic relationship. They threatened to toss me into rehab multiple times, but I don't think they ever followed through because they assumed I stopped when the grief no longer overwhelmed me.

Little do they know, guilt makes me use more often than grief ever did. The main difference now is that I've been using so heavily for so long, I've learned how to function exceptionally well while high. The only time anyone can even tell I'm fucked up anymore is when I've gone overboard. Which, admittedly, seems to be happening a lot lately.

I shake my head. "Not even her. And technically, she wasn't my girlfriend."

My mom frowns. "Bent, you don't need to downplay—"

I hold my hand up. "Mom. Don't. We're not discussing her."

She plates the toast, flipping the fried eggs on top of it before placing it in front of me with a fork.

"Okay... I'll agree to that. *If* you tell me about Sydney."

I pop the yolk, moving it around the bread before cutting off a piece with my fork. "What do you want to know?"

"Let's start with her age. Because if you brought a minor into my house to do God knows what, I swear, Bentley—"

I don't even finish chewing before I stop that trainwreck of thought. "She's *eighteen*, Mom. Relax."

Right before I turned eighteen, my dad made damn sure I familiarized myself with California's statutory rape laws. They're insanely strict, so once I became a legal adult, I decided I wouldn't stick my dick into some chick who wasn't one as well. I'm not even willing to risk the close-in-age exception because, in the eyes of the law, it's just that: *an excep-*

tion. As much as I love fucking, no pussy is worth being labeled a sex offender.

"Well, it's good to know you have some sense," she mutters. "How long have you known her? Where did you meet?"

"Sheesh. What is this? An interrogation?"

Her eyes narrow. "Don't get smart with me, mister. You know, I'd like to think of myself as a pretty laid-back parent, but if you're going to bring a girl into my house, I have the right to ask questions."

I take another bite and finish chewing before I answer. "Technically, we met at a party a couple of years ago, but we recently reconnected when she transferred to Windsor. Her dad's the new headmaster."

My mom releases a surprised laugh. "Felt like playing with fire, did you?"

"Haha," I grumble. "Anyway... I think Syd's pretty fly, and fuck if I know why, but she likes me back, so I'm running with it."

"Language," she scolds. "But in all seriousness, Bent, if she makes you happy, I'm happy. Just nix any future sleepovers, will ya?"

"Yeah, sure."

I have no intention of honoring that, but I sure

as shit will be checking their itineraries from now on whenever they leave town.

"I have one more question, then I'll drop the subject."

"What's that?"

She blows out a breath and crosses her arms over her chest. "Are you being safe? Because I'm sure as hell not ready to be a grandma."

I nearly choked on the damn bite I was taking. "Christ, Ma. Really?"

"Yes, *really*. Look, I don't like this any more than you do, but if you're old enough to be having sex, then you should have no problem *talking* about sex. So, I'll ask again. *Are you being safe?*"

"Yes!" I scrub a hand down my face. "Fuckin' A."

"Bentley..."

"Yeah, yeah," I cut her off. "I know. Language. Sorry. Can we be done now? This is awkward AF, Mom."

"Fine. Speaking of grandparents... have you given any thought to visiting yours during spring break? Flights are filling up, so I'll need to book tickets soon."

Usually, I'd jump at the chance to go to Hawaii, but I'm not exactly in any hurry to be two thousand miles away from Sydney for a week.

"Can Sydney come too?"

I don't know if I've ever seen my mother look so shocked before.

"You're that serious about this girl? You want to take a vacation with her? Introduce her to your grandparents?"

I don't even need to think about it before I nod. "She's different, Mom."

A smile stretches across her face. "Well, in that case, I'd love to have her come with us. *If* her parents are okay with it. And I'm not just taking your word for it. I know she's eighteen, but I refuse to take someone else's daughter across an ocean without personally verifying they know where she's going."

"Fine. I'll talk to Syd, and if she's game, I'll hook you up with her mom's digits."

"Okay. Talk to Sydney, and we'll go from there." She leans over the counter and kisses my cheek. "I need to run a few errands. Do the dishes while I'm gone?"

"Yep."

After stacking the breakfast dishes in the dish-washer, I head back to my room to get ready for the day. While I'm pulling up a playlist to blast some music while I shower, a text from Jazz comes in. A sense of dread fills my gut when I read her message.

Jazzy Jazz: I've given you twenty-four hours to come to me, but since you haven't, this is me coming to you.

Me: About what, Jazzy? I wasn't aware I was on the clock for anything.

I watch as the dots start bouncing, indicating she's typing a reply. It takes forever for the message to come through, and when it does, I see why.

Jazzy Jazz: I had an interesting conversation with Sydney yesterday. Imagine my surprise when she informs me your amnesia about the night you met is back. C'mon, Bentley. You're better than this. Why would you lie to her? She is literally the ONE PERSON ON EARTH who deserves to know the truth about what happened at that frat party. And YOU have that truth. Kingston thinks I should stay out of it, but I'm having a hard time doing that, Bent. She's a good person, and you're acting like a goddamn fool. I'm so disappointed in you. I'll give you time to pull your head out of your ass, but if you don't man the fuck up and tell her soon, I will.

Fuck.

I toss the phone on my bathroom counter and head to my walk-in. I reach up to grab the shoebox off the top shelf and riffle through its contents until I find what I'm looking for. I shake a pill into my palm and toss it back. Right before I put the box away, I grab another and swallow that one, too. *Fucking hell.* What am I going to do now? I know Jazz isn't bluffing. Frankly, I don't know why the fuck I didn't realize this was going to happen before now. Shit, I don't even know why I lied to Sydney in the first place when I had the perfect opportunity to talk to her.

Yes, you do. You were scared shitless she would leave you.

I pace the length of my room, trying to figure out what the hell I'm going to do. I must've been racking my brain for a while because the Oxy kicks in, flooding my veins with relief. I head back into my bathroom, turn the shower on, and grab my phone to send a message to Jazz while the water warms up.

Me: Don't do anything until you talk to me. I'll find a way to fix this.

Jazzy Jazz: How?

Me: I don't know, but I'll think of something.

Jazzy Jazz: We all love you, Bent. You don't need to do this alone. We can figure it out together.

I exhale.

Me: Thanks, Jazzy. Just give me some time to think, and we'll talk soon.

Jazzy Jazz: Okay.

I strip out of my clothes, feeling a little better knowing shit won't hit the fan anytime soon. I grab my phone and send one more message before hopping in the tub.

Me: I'm getting low. When can you meet? Double my usual.

Cody: 9:00 – my place

Me: Word. See you then.

I love my friends to death, but I'm going to need a little more help than they're able to provide to get me through this.

chapter
thirty-two

TWO YEARS EARLIER

BENTLEY

"Whoa, the sky is spinning."

I laugh. "The sky is *always* spinning."

Sydney stretches languidly, reminding me of a cat. "I think cocktails are my new favorite thing." She twists her body just enough to boop me on the nose. "You're a close second."

"Ouch. Taking second place to booze. You wound me."

She giggles. "But I feel *good*, so you'll get over it, right?"

"Sure." I give her a little squeeze. "You're a lightweight, aren't you?"

The girl switched to water almost an hour ago, but I swear she gets more buzzed by the minute. I think that last one really tipped her over.

"Guess so." Sydney shrugs. "This is the first time I've been drunk."

My jaw drops. "How is that possible?"

"I didn't say it was the first time I've drunk alcohol." She leans back and gives me a *duh* look. "I usually don't have more than a drink or two, though."

I figure this is the perfect segue to ask something that's been on my mind all night. "All you've had tonight are the drinks your cousin made for you? Nothing else?"

"Like what?"

"Take your pick. There's a lot of shit floating around. Weed, Molly, coke..."

Her dark curls bounce as she shakes her head. "Nope. I've smoked weed before, but it's not really my thing. I never tried anything besides that. Does that make me totally lame?" She clears her throat and lowers her voice. "Drugs are bad, Sydney." She giggles again, rolling her eyes. "My dad is a school administrator. When he's really serious about something, he gets this super stern voice. I think he's trying to be scary, but he's a big softy, so it doesn't really have the effect he's going for. Anyway... I can't even tell you how many times I've been lectured about the dangers of drug use in my life."

"Funny, those lectures have had the exact opposite effect on me. There's not much I haven't tried."

"Meh." She rolls her hand breezily. "I won't hold it against you. You only live once, right?"

I smile as I tuck my face into her neck. "Good to know."

"Hey, man." When I pull back, I see Grady holding his fist out for a bump. "Thanks for inviting me to this place. You're right; it was a fucking gold mine. I'm completely tapped out. I even offloaded product people don't usually ask for."

"Like what?"

He shrugs. "Mainly Scooby Snacks, which I guess isn't all that uncommon nowadays, but about a dozen different people were looking for Circles, too. Most don't have the balls to ask for that unless they're already a client. I'm glad I decided to bring 'em."

What the fuck? I didn't know this asshole dealt that shit.

"What are Circles?" the beautiful girl in my lap asks.

Grady's blue eyes widen as he glances at Sydney like he's just noticing she's here with me. "Oh, hey. Wait a second... I know you."

Sydney frowns. "Um... I'm sorry, but I think you must be mistaken."

"No, I'm not." Grady shakes his head. "Maybe I should back up. I was hanging with your cousin earlier, and she pointed you out. I would've said hello, but you were a bit... *occupied*."

The way this fucker is leering at her makes me want to punch him. It also tells me exactly what was happening when he first noticed her. A quick glance at Sydney tells me she knows what he's referring to as well. Her cheeks are flushed more than they already were from the alcohol, and she's fidgeting. Now that I'm starting to sober up, I sorta regret allowing her to blow me in front of other people. As much as I wanted her, and as awesome as it was, I should've tabled it until we could find someplace more private. I can't say I haven't engaged in public foreplay before—or group sex for that matter—but the more I get to know Sydney... the worse I feel about the whole thing. Like I've cheapened the experience, maybe. Don't even get me started on how shitty I feel about using her to provoke Rissa.

It's not like I can take it back now, though, right?

I incline my head toward Grady. "Sydney, this is Grady, a... *friend* of mine." Friend, dealer, same thing, right?

"Nice to meet you, Grady."

"Trust me; the pleasure's all mine, babe." I swear to God, if he doesn't stop staring at her tits,

I'm going to deck him. Grady *finally* stops ogling her and returns his attention to me. "Anyway, Bent, I'm out of here. Hit me up if you get an invite to another one of these things."

I nod as he starts to walk away. "Sure."

Yeah, not gonna happen.

If I had any clue the dude dealt fucking roofies, I would've never invited him here. In fact, I think it's time to find another supplier. Call me crazy if you will, but I do believe there's a difference between selling drugs for recreational use versus giving a person the ability to render someone else defenseless. The latter is straight-up shady, and I don't want to give my money to someone like that.

"That guy's totally a drug dealer, isn't he?"

I nod. "Uh... yeah."

"Huh. I've never met one in person before. I wasn't expecting someone so... yuppie." Sydney tilts her head to the side. "What are Circles?"

Fuck.

"It's one of the many terms for... uh..." I clear my throat. "Rohypnol."

"I need to pee." Sydney stands from the lounger but stumbles backward, almost falling into my lap. "Shit."

I grab her elbow to help steady her, grateful for the sudden change in topic. "You okay?"

Her glassy eyes twinkle as she gives me a lazy smile. "I'm good. I'll be right back, okay?"

"You sure?"

She waves me off. "Positive. I just got light-headed for a sec, but I'm fine now."

Yeah... no. Her speech is starting to slur.

I stand up and place my hand on her lower back to guide her into the house. "Humor me, okay? I just want to make sure you get there safely."

We weave through the crowd until we get to the line outside of the lower first-floor bathroom, which is a mile long, so I lead her upstairs to check the one I saw earlier.

"Crap. I'm going to pee my pants if I have to wait in that line." Her long legs are doing a little dance to demonstrate her point.

I laugh. "Hold on, one of these bedrooms has to have an en suite."

We check two rooms and get an eyeful of bare skin, but there's no attached bathroom. We move onto the third, which is thankfully empty and does have an en suite.

"Oh, thank God!" Sydney flips on the light and slams the bathroom door behind her. As she's doing her thing, my phone vibrates with a message from Reed.

Reed: Where're you at? Peyton is

straight-up belligerent at this point. It's time to go. Kingston just called an Uber that'll be here in a few.

Fucking Peyton.

That girl has a knack for ruining everyone else's good time.

"Everything okay?" Sydney's back, nodding at the phone that I'm white-knuckling.

"My friend's girlfriend is trashed. They want to take off, but I think I'm going to tell them to go without me."

She gives me a sleepy smile. "It's okay. I totally understand. I'm actually really tired all of a sudden."

"Yeah? You want me to drop you off somewhere?"

She shakes her head. "I'm staying at the sorority house tonight, but I don't have a key. I need to find my cousin."

I curse when my phone buzzes again.

Reed: Dude. Seriously. We need to go. Peyton just tried to bitch slap some girl she thought was looking at Davenport.

I shoot off a quick reply to my friend.

Me: Give me a sec.

I can't say I'm not bummed, but it's late, and

she does look really wiped. "Okay, well, let me help you find her first."

We've barely made it into the hallway before Sydney's cousin appears. "There you are. I've been looking for you."

"Well, here I am." Sydney stumbles a bit. "Oh, man, I really think I should lay down."

"Let me just text my friends to tell them to go without me." I dig my phone out of my pocket and open the text window.

"Don't worry about it. I've got her." Lindsey motions toward the room we just left. "Syd, why don't you lie down for a bit? I'll be right here with you."

My brows lift. "You sure?"

"Bro." Lindsey waves me off. "She's my cousin. I'll take care of her."

Reed and Kingston are now blowing up my phone, asking what's taking me so long. Fuck. I don't like the idea of leaving Sydney like this, but what can really happen with her cousin right here?

I guide Sydney to the bed and help her to the mattress. "Just get some rest, and text me when you get back to Delta Pi tonight, okay?"

She stretches. "Okie dokie."

With one last kiss on her forehead, I reluctantly exit the room. As I'm passing her cousin, I ask,

"You're really going to stay with her the whole time?"

Lindsey holds up her hand in a Boy Scout salute. "Scout's honor, Champ. I'll even lock the door if it makes you feel better. Now, go. I'll make sure she texts you later."

I nod. "Thanks."

I wait for her to turn the lock before walking away to find my friends. It's not until I'm halfway home that I realize Sydney and I never exchanged numbers. Oh well. I guess I'll just have to make a trip to her cousin's sorority house sometime tomorrow.

chapter
thirty-three

SYDNEY

"I can't believe his mom caught you doing the walk of shame." Cameron bites off the end of a Twizzler. "Only you, Syd."

I palm my face and groan. "Tell me about it. It was so awkward."

She laughs and makes a lewd gesture with her tongue in cheek. "At least she didn't catch you in the act, I guess."

I shove Cam's shoulder playfully. "Shut up."

"Girl, he invited you to Hawaii." Cameron sighs. "I'm so jelly."

"I didn't say I was going."

She gives me an *are you kidding me?* look. "Yeah, right. You'd be a major dumbass to turn that down, and I know you're not one of those."

"I don't know." I shrug. "Don't you think it's a little too early to start planning vacations together?"

"His mom and grandparents will be there, right? What's the worst that can happen?"

I think about that for a moment. "True."

"You should totally stash me in your luggage."

I snort. "You're little, but you're not *that* little."

Cam gasps. "Rude!"

I point my Twizzler at her. "Enough about me. What's up with you and that Hayden guy?"

Her head falls with a groan. "He's *such* a dick. He's always so smug, like 'Look at me, I'm stupid hot. All girls should worship the ground I walk on. And I'm not just a god on the football field. I'm also apparently a genius—top of my class, in fact.' My mom won't stop yammering about what a perfect child Hayden is and how I could learn a thing or two from him. Ugh! It's infuriating!"

I try fighting a smirk, but I don't think I'm succeeding.

Cam's brows furrow. "What? What's that look for?"

"Oh, nothing." I wave my hand. "Just can't help but notice how one of the first things you say about him is how *stupid hot* he is."

"Oh, c'mon, Syd. You saw him. I'm not blind. But like I said before, his personality totally ruins it. I wish our parents would stop trying to push us together like we're some big happy family. They just started dating, but they're acting like they're getting married or something."

"Didn't you say they knew each other before?"

"Yeah, like eleventy million years ago. I'll admit, Archie—that's Hayden's dad—doesn't seem so bad beyond his douchey name. I actually feel sorry for the dude being with my nutcase mom. But even if they were high school sweethearts, or whatever, they can't possibly be the same people they were back then. Hell, I know my mom's not. She adopts a new personality with each guy she hooks. She's gone through over a dozen of them since I was born. This time around, she's totally rockin' the Stepford vibe. It's really creepy."

"Maybe that's what he's into." I shrug. "Someone to look pretty and keep her mouth shut."

Cam snorts. "Well, if it is, I'm sure there'll be a ring on her finger in no time."

I poke her side, making her squirm. "Ooh, and when they get married, you'll be fantasizing about banging your stepbrother. Kinky."

She shoves me, damn near knocking me off the Jacuzzi's bench. "Gross. I do *not* fantasize about Hayden-freaking-Knight."

"Methinks the lady doth protest too much." I giggle when Cameron flips me off.

"Bite me, bish." She throws a piece of licorice

at me, which bounces off my nose into the bubbling water. "Besides, there's no way our parents would even make it to the altar. My mom can only keep the façade going for so long. Hence, why she's been engaged five times and married zero."

I shrug. "I guess time will tell."

Her eyes roll. "Anyway... can we please stop talking about my mom's love life? I wanna hear more about yours. I'd much rather picture you and Bentley doing the dirty than a couple of oldies."

I give her a wry look. "And *I'd* rather you *never* picture Bentley and me having sex. You have serious issues with boundaries, Cameron."

Cam laughs. "Well, how the hell am I supposed to live vicariously through you if you won't give me details? It's not like I'll be getting any anytime soon. At least tell me this: Does he know how to use that big beautiful D of his?"

My shoulders lift. "Well, I don't really have anyone else to compare, but yeah... I'd say he definitely knows how to use it. Last night, I came without any kind of external stimulation. I honestly thought vaginal orgasms were a myth. Lord knows I tried enough times with all the Bobs."

Cameron holds up an index finger. "You know, I read an article in Cosmo that said your clit is like an iceberg."

"What?!" I sputter.

"You know how like ninety percent of an iceberg is underwater?" She dips most of her arm underwater to demonstrate. "It's the same thing. If you wanna talk about myths, it's the G-spot that's a myth. That's actually the internal part of your clitoris, which you can't see, hence the iceberg. So, there's really no such thing as a vaginal orgasm because it's your inner clit that's being stimulated. Inside your body or out, they're both clitoral orgasms."

"Wow..." I take a moment to contain my laughter. "Thanks for the biology lesson, Professor Pryce. What do you have planned for extra credit? Shall I grab a banana from the kitchen so you can demonstrate how to properly roll on a condom?"

"Pft! Forget the bananas." Her lips curve upward. "We both know there are plenty of phallic-shaped objects in your closet to choose from. Speaking of... is Bentley aware he has competition? Are you planning on introducing him to your *other* boyfriends?"

My cheeks warm as I picture doing just that. "Yes, he knows I own a few vibrators."

"*A few?*" Her jaw drops. "If you have a *few* battery-operated boyfriends, then I have a *few* romance books on my Kindle."

Cameron *lives* for her book boyfriends. The girl has completely unrealistic expectations of men thanks to the billion-dollar industry. She's been on this sexy barbaric alien kick lately. The way she describes it, it's equal parts fascinating and horrifying.

"So I like variety." The silicone kind anyway. "Sue me."

She holds her hands up in surrender. "No judgment here, *chica*. Although... if you and Bentley decide to break out the toys, I want video proof, or it didn't happen."

"Boundaries, Cameron. Boundaries." I shake my head.

"You and your damn boundaries, always ruining my fun." She sticks her tongue out. "I guess I'll have to rely on my good pal, Pornhub."

"You do you, boo. Just keep my sex life out of it." She flips me off, so I return the gesture.

Cameron narrows her eyes. "You're lucky I love you, bitch. God, I really need to get laid. How much do you think a plane ticket to Brazil costs? I bet Paulo would be D-T-F in a heartbeat."

"You know..." I rub my chin in mock contemplation. "I bet Hayden wouldn't mind helping you out with your little problem. Where'd you say he lives? Beverly? That's *much* closer than South America."

She scoffs. "He wishes."

Oh, I have no doubt about that. I saw the way he was eyeballing my best friend. The thing is... whether she's willing to admit it or not, Cameron was looking at him the exact same way. I'd say it's only a matter of time before Cam and Hayden funnel the energy they used to argue into something much more fun. And I can't wait to give her shit about it.

I mean, what kind of bestie would I be if I didn't?

chapter thirty-four

BENTLEY

"Why do you keep bringing me here?" I trace a bright blue tag with the tip of my finger.

I smirk when I read the artist's name: Misfit. How very fitting I chose this spot to sit on. On the surface, most people probably wouldn't associate that word with me, but some days, on the inside, I feel like I don't belong anywhere anymore.

Carissa leans back on her hands, arching her face into the sun. Her golden hair falls down her back, nearly touching the concrete. I was obsessed with running my fingers through those thick strands, but I've recently begun to favor darker locks. "Why wouldn't I? It's our place."

We used to love coming here just to chill. The view is incredible, with endless mountain views high above Red Rock Canyon Park and a sliver of ocean in the distance. People like to bitch about all the graffiti that's taken over this old fire lookout, but Rissa and I always thought it was pretty fucking *sick. There's a bunch of random artwork that shouldn't make sense together, especially when it's surrounded by such natural beauty, but it does.*

"It was *our place,*" I correct. "Not so much anymore."

"Oh c'mon, Bentley, be a good sport." Carissa crawls toward me on her hands and knees with a wicked gleam in her eye I know all too well. "We have this whole place to ourselves. I think we should take advantage of that."

I grab on to her arms when she tries climbing onto my lap. "Carissa, what are you doing?"

"What does it look *like I'm doing?" When I refuse to allow her to come any closer, her glossy lips form into a pout. "Since when do you turn down pussy? Especially mine?"*

"Since I got a girlfriend." I gulp. "I'm not about to do anything that would fuck that up."

She throws her head back, laughing. "Don't you think it's too late for that? You've already *fucked that up. What harm can a little nostalgia fuck do when you've been lying to your so-called girlfriend's face all this time? The damage is done, Bent; you've broken her trust. She just doesn't know it yet." Carissa winks. "But don't worry; she will soon enough."*

My eyes narrow. "What's that supposed to mean? What are you planning to do?"

Now she's straight-up cackling. "I *don't need to do anything, lover boy.* You're *the one who set things into motion. And when it all goes down in flames, you'll have nobody to blame but yourself. When are you going to learn, Bentley?"*

I shake my head, running my finger over a new design. "You're wrong. I'll find a way to make Sydney forgive me."

"Impossible."

My head snaps up when I hear the raspy yet feminine voice. I look around, trying to locate Carissa, but she's nowhere to be found. Sydney now occupies the spot where Rissa was only seconds ago.

"Syd. How'd you get here?" I try inching closer to her, but I'm glued to the cement.

Fuck. Not this again.

When Sydney stands, her long legs extend toward the edge of the platform, one after another, with grace only a dancer could possess. My eyes widen in panic when she gets to the lip, bouncing on the balls of her feet. I try moving again, but it's like my body is ingrained into the cement.

"Syd. Don't move. For the love of God, please step away from the edge." My heart is beating so wildly, I feel like I'm going to implode.

She turns toward me, her back to the valley below. Now her heels are suspended in the air while her toes balance on the platform. If you're careful and take it very slowly, you can climb off the platform onto the ground below. But if you're not exercising great caution, the steep slope combined with large jagged boulders can be deadly.

"You had your chance, Bentley, and you made the wrong

choice. Now you have to live with the consequences of your actions." A strong breeze blows through the valley, lifting Sydney's dark curls. As she pushes some hair out of her face, she adds, *"I will never forgive you, Bentley."*

Before I can utter another word, Sydney stretches her arms out, falling backward. I scream her name, watching helplessly as she falls, her body slamming against a boulder, bending at an unnatural angle, before rolling off and falling onto the dirt below.

"No!"

I don't know if it's through divine intervention or sheer force of will, but I'm finally able to move. I hang off the edge of the platform, dropping carefully to the ground, desperate to get to Sydney. I slide across the dirt, nearly falling a few times before I finally reach her. I drop to my knees, cradling her in my arms.

"I've got you, baby. I'll get you to a hospital. You'll be okay."

As I take in the dark sticky puddle beneath her head and the wheezing in her breath, I know I don't have much time. Her eyelids flutter closed right before her chest expands with a shudder, and she starts hacking up massive amounts of blood.

"Fuck!" I tilt her to the side so she doesn't choke, careful not to jostle her too much. *"Hold on, Syd. Just hold on. Just... give me a second to figure out how to get you out of here without making it worse."*

Sydney's long lashes lift as her aqua eyes meet mine. "It's... too... late."

"No!"

I brace my arms beneath her, trying to cradle her body into a bridal position. Blood splatters across my face as she begins coughing again, some of it getting in my eyes, creating a red haze. I blink rapidly, trying to clear my vision, so I can get us out of here somehow.

"Hold on, Syd." I start to lift her. "I've almost got it."

"Bentley..." More garbled wheezing. "Stop. You're... too..."

My body goes rigid when I feel hers go slack. Just like that, she's hanging limply in my arms, no longer wheezing or coughing.

Or breathing.

"No-no-no-no-no!" I carefully set her down, brushing blood-soaked hair away from her face. "Sydney, baby, stay with me." Tears are pouring down my face, blurring my vision almost entirely. "Just fucking stay with me!"

When I clear the curls away from her eyes, her words ricochet through my brain.

It's too late.

Her lids are slightly open, but the vibrancy that once lived behind them is nonexistent. Her beautiful blue-green eyes are completely lifeless.

So is she.

I fall over her motionless body, clutching on to her as if that will somehow breathe life into her again. When her chest refuses to rise and fall against mine, an ear-splitting wail echoes throughout the canyon. It takes me a moment to realize the sound is coming from me. I scream and cry until my throat is raw. Until the sun descends over the ocean, casting us into darkness. Until I finally succumbed to the exhaustion, however many hours later.

Right before I slip into unconsciousness, I whisper, "I'm so sorry, Sydney. I'm so fucking sorry."

I slide into the parking spot right next to Sydney's Audi and bolt out of my car the second I cut the engine.

She smiles as she sees me. "Hey, you."

I loop my fingers around her wrist and drag her toward Jefferson Hall. "C'mon."

Sydney speed-walks to keep up with my pace. "Whoa, Bentley. What's going on? Where are we going?"

"Auditorium," I tell her.

Jefferson Hall is the arts building where there's an auditorium, and I happen to know from experience, it has no morning classes and several conveniently dark nooks.

"What? Why?"

"Need you."

I'm struggling, trying so desperately not to freak the hell out from the worst nightmare I've had yet, I'm incapable of saying much else. With the image of Syd's death burned into my brain, I need a physical connection with her more than I need my next breath. I need solid proof she's okay. That she's mine, at least for now.

With Jazz's threat looming in the back of my mind and no idea how to fix it like I said I would, part of me knows I'm going to lose Sydney sooner rather than later. She's too fucking good for me; there's no way she'll forgive me for lying. Obviously, my subconscious was reminding me that I'm on borrowed time in a way that's pretty damn hard to ignore.

I fling the auditorium door open and drag Syd down the slanted aisle until we reach the stage. I jump up, then turn around to offer a hand and help her up as well. Her expression is hesitant, but she doesn't refuse. I push the heavy black curtain aside, allowing us to move behind it, giving us some semblance of privacy should someone wander into the room. I doubt that'll happen, but I feel like I should do what I can to protect her modesty, considering how spectacularly I failed to do so when we first met. Sure, not fucking her *at all* in public would be best, but desperate times call for desperate measures and all that.

"Bentley, what's going on?" Sydney pulls out of my grip. "What's wrong?"

"Need you," I repeat, pushing her up against the back wall.

Her eyes round when I grip the backs of her thighs, lifting until they're wrapped around my waist. Lucky for me, Windsor's uniform options don't include pants for the ladies. It may be sexist as fuck, but you won't hear me complaining about the easy access, especially not now. My pulse is thumping in my ears as my hand finds its way beneath her skirt. I shift Sydney's panties aside, silencing her moan with a kiss as I slide a finger into her tight cunt.

"Wait," she pants. "This is crazy. We're at school. Someone might see us."

"Won't happen." I kiss the slender curve of her neck as my thumb rubs circles around her clit. "There aren't any classes in here until after lunch."

"How do you know that?" She groans as I add a second finger.

"Just do. Don't worry; I've got you." I pump my fingers in and out, getting impossibly hard imagining how incredible she'll feel around my dick. "Now undo my fucking pants, Syd, because I need inside of you within the next thirty seconds and my hands are a little occupied."

"This is crazy," she repeats, reaching between our bodies to unfasten my belt. Sydney wastes no time once she gets my fly open, reaching into my boxers and wrapping her delicate hand around my shaft.

"Don't care." I line myself up against my beautiful girl's soaking entrance.

She whimpers as I push forward, bottoming out in one smooth thrust. "God, Bentley."

My head falls to the crook of her neck on a groan. "Fuck. Nothing feels better than this. No. Fucking. Thing."

The sound of skin slapping skin and labored breathing fill the otherwise silent room as I begin moving in earnest. I growl in approval as Sydney angles her hips, meeting me thrust for thrust. She fists my hair, spurring me on even harder, faster. I grab on to her round ass with bruising force, loving the thought of leaving fingertip-shaped bruises behind.

I've never been a particularly possessive guy before—not even with Rissa—but this woman makes me feel crazed. Everything about Syd calls to my inner Neanderthal. The need to claim her— own her, consumes me. The thought of marking her, even if it's in a place where only we'll see, makes me so fucking hot, I know I won't last much longer.

"Bentley..." Sydney's grip on my hair tightens. "Shit. I'm going to come."

"C'mon, baby. Give it to me."

I widen my stance, using the wall to help support her weight. I band my forearm beneath her ass, and I grasp the front of her neck with my newly freed hand. Our gazes lock as I give a little squeeze —not enough to cut off her air supply, but enough to make my point. This woman is mine. She knows it, I know it, and if I have my way, every fucking person on Earth will know it.

Until she uncovers the truth, anyway.

When Syd's pussy starts clenching around me, my balls tighten, and lightning shoots down my spine. A few thrusts later, I'm following her into blissful oblivion, where nothing exists beyond us. Our eyes are locked as I reluctantly pull out, set Sydney back on her feet, and tuck myself into my pants as she straightens her clothes. It's not until we're put back together that I realize we didn't use protection. Suddenly my mom's lecture about babies comes back to me in full force. I've *never* had sex without a condom before.

"Fuck."

Sydney frowns. "What?"

"No condom."

She reaches up and cups her hand around my jaw. "I'm aware. My uncomfortably moist panties are a bold reminder."

I smirk. "Am I a complete asshole for being happy about that fact? And did you really just say, 'moist'? I thought all women had some weird aversion to that word."

"It's a *terrible* word unless you're talking about cake." She scrunches her nose. "If it makes you feel better, I'm on the pill. Have been for years to regulate my cycle, and you know I haven't been with anyone but you, so... if you're okay, we're okay."

"I'm okay. I've never gone bareback before, and I was tested shortly before you showed up at Windsor." I lean into Sydney's touch, kissing her palm. "Sorry, though. I wasn't really thinking before... just *had* to be inside you."

Her teeth press into her pillowy lower lip. "What happened, Bentley?"

I wrap my arms around her back, tucking my face into her neck. "Don't worry about it. I'm better now."

"Talk to me, Bentley. Something clearly upset you before you came to school." She presses on my chest to pull out of my hold. "Don't you trust me?"

I damn near laugh at the irony. "Of course I do."

"Well?" Syd's eyebrows lift expectantly. "Are you going to tell me what's bothering you then?"

I shake my head. "I can't."

She frowns. "Why not?"

I take a few steps backward, kneading the suddenly tight muscles at the base of my neck. "Because."

"Because *why?*"

I look her dead in the eye. "Because if you knew, you would despise me!" I lower my voice and add, "I have more than enough self-loathing for the both of us. I can't have you hate me, too."

Sydney's face falls. "Bentley..."

"No." I point at her. "Don't do that. Don't pity me."

"I don't *pity* you. I want to *help* you." She throws her hands up. "But I can't do that if you won't let me in. *Let me in*, Bentley!"

My jaw clenches as I pace back and forth like a caged lion. Sydney waits me out, doesn't say a word as I sort through the mess in my head. Fuck, I need a pill so I can think clearly. I can't focus when the chaos is this deafening. I reach into my pocket, fingering the little baggie I stashed there. I know if I take this in front of her, it will cause a whole host of questions and even more concern on her end. And I don't want that. She shouldn't have to worry about a piece of shit like me.

But I can't breathe. The tightness in my chest is unbearable. Sweat beads across my forehead, and I'm getting more agitated by the second. I feel like I'm losing my goddamn mind.

"Fuck it," I mutter, retrieving the pill and popping it into my mouth. The moment I swallow, I feel a tiny bit of relief, knowing it'll all be better soon. Until I catch the look on Sydney's face.

"*What was that?!* What did you just take?" She tugs on my arm. "Bentley, answer me."

"Fuck!" I slam my fist through the canvas backdrop that's propped up off to the side. I'm sure the drama club will not be happy when they see the gaping hole I left behind.

She jumps. "Bentley, calm down. You're scaring me."

Our gazes meet, and I see the truth behind her statement.

"Shit." I rake a hand through my hair as I take deep breaths.

"Bentley." She grabs my hand, weaving our fingers together. "What did you just swallow?"

Goddammit. Why couldn't I have waited until she went to class?

I exhale harshly. "It's not a big deal. Just some painkillers."

Technically, that's not a lie.

Her aqua eyes narrow. "Like Tylenol?"

"Not exactly." I shrug. "More like the prescription variety."

"A prescription in *your* name?"

I wince, knowing there's no way out of this. It's not like my drug use is a big secret, but besides occasionally taking E, pills are a new thing for me, and I don't want Syd to think I'm a junkie or something.

"They help quiet all the shit going through my head."

Sydney sighs. "Bentley, there are other ways to cope with whatever you're going through. I wish you would just talk to me. Or talk to *anyone*, for that matter. I think you'll be surprised how therapeutic it can be."

I have to bite back my scathing reply. If I told Syd or anyone important to me what I did, they'd kick my ass to the curb so fast, my head would spin. I'd hardly call losing them therapeutic.

"It's not like I'm addicted; I can stop at any time. I just take 'em because weed no longer does the job anymore. It's not a big deal, Sydney. I'm in control."

She considers that, skepticism plainly visible in her expression. "Okay."

My brows lift. "Okay? Really? You're not going to press for more?"

"No." Sydney shakes her head. "Just know that if you ever feel like you're slipping, or if you decide you do need to talk, I'm here, ready to listen. Okay?"

My words get lodged in my throat. I pull her into me, placing my lips on her temple. "I don't deserve you, Syd."

She wraps her arms around my waist and squeezes. "Maybe you don't give yourself enough credit. Because the way I see it, you deserve the world, Bentley."

God, if only that were true.

chapter
thirty-five

SYDNEY

"Bitch, you're legit living my dream. If I didn't love you so much, I'd hate you."

I laugh when I see the sour look on Cam's face. "What are you talking about?"

"This morning with Bentley." Cameron reaches under the reception desk to empty the little garbage bin. I'd taught back-to-back classes all afternoon, so the first chance I'd had to tell my bestie everything was after closing the studio. "I'd do some shady shit to have a guy *need* me like that. Especially someone as hot as Bentley. Not only do you get great sex out of the deal, but you have the knowledge you're so vital to his life, that he craves you so badly, he can't possibly wait for another second to have you. It's hot as fuck and great for the ego."

I blush, thinking about our morning quickie. I swear, every time Bentley and I are together is hotter than the last, but today, there was something primal about it, driving things to new heights. I've had my fair share of attention from the opposite sex over the years, but I've *never* felt such... reverence. So much *relief* from merely being close to me. Bentley acted like I was some magical balm that could soothe every ounce of pain festering inside of him.

"I just wish he'd talk to me, Cam. He's holding on to something that's messed him up pretty badly." I sigh, debating whether or not I want to share this next bit. Part of me feels like I'm violating Bentley's privacy, but the other part really needs to talk it out with my best friend. "There's something I left out earlier... something that's been bugging me. *A lot.*"

She frowns. "What?"

"So, Bentley smokes weed and... does other stuff recreationally, right?"

"And?" Cameron shrugs. "Not many people our age don't."

"What if it's more of a *need* than letting loose at a party?"

She tilts her head to the side in question. "Like an addiction?"

I nod my head.

"Isn't it super rare to be dependent on Mary Jane?"

"I'm not talking about herb." I swallow the

lump in my throat. "I saw Bentley swallow a pill two different times now, but he was cagey about it. And both times, he was really on edge, like he was jonesing for it."

"Any idea what he took?"

I plop down into one of the lobby chairs. "This morning, he said it was a prescription painkiller but didn't specify which one. I don't know about the first time."

Cam takes a seat beside me. "You think he's hooked on pills?"

My shoulders lift. "I honestly don't know. He says he's not. And I actually think he believes that."

"But?" Her brows climb toward her hairline.

"But... sometimes, he gives me these little glimpses of the pain he's harboring. I think he's been wearing a mask for a long time trying to conceal it, but whatever it is, has to be pretty intense."

"And this is the same thing he refuses to talk about?"

"Yeah." I blow out a breath.

Cam bumps her shoulder into mine. "Syd, you know I'm not trying to be a dick when I say this, but why are you putting up with all these secrets? You're better than that."

I think about that for a moment. "Because I don't think his secrets are hurting anyone but him."

"Do you really believe that?" she challenges. "What about that weird moment with Jazz at the coffee shop? You said you felt like she was covering up for him."

"And I still think that's entirely possible. But... I think if it were something malicious, she wouldn't do that. It's pretty obvious Jazz is nobody's doormat, don't you think? We both know Bentley can be a supreme asshole, but my gut is telling me when he acts like that—at least toward people who don't deserve it—it's because of whatever's haunting him. I think it's eating him alive, Cam. Sometimes, when he thinks people aren't looking, he has this expression of pure, unadulterated agony on his face."

"I hope he figures his shit out, Syd. I don't want you becoming collateral damage."

I hold my finger up, pausing when my phone buzzes with a text alert. I dig it out of my pocket and immediately scowl when I see who it's from.

"Oh, what the hell does he want?" I mutter, showing Cam my phone before opening Zach's message.

Zach: I think I've been more than patient with you, Syd. It's time to pay up.

"What the fuck is that supposed to mean?" Cam asks.

"My thoughts exactly."

I should probably just block his ass, but I'm curious enough to reply.

Me: I have no clue what you're talking about.

He must've been waiting for my reply because he answers right away.

Zach: Sure you do.

Me: Uh, no, I DON'T.

I watch the dots bounce as he takes his sweet time typing a reply.

Zach: You want me to spell it out for you? Fine. I've waited long enough to fuck you, and I'm not waiting any longer. And before you try pulling the blushing virgin card, don't forget who you're talking to and what I know. The innocent act might make your new fuckboy hard, but I'd rather have you take it like the whore you are.

Cam gasps as she reads over my shoulder. "That motherfucker!"

I feel like steam is literally about to start pouring out of my ears. "Who does this douche think he is?"

I angrily pound my thumbs onto the screen as I give him a piece of my mind.

Me: Since you're clearly having trouble remembering we're no longer together, let me remind you. YOU'VE BEEN CANCELED, ZACH, because you are a lying, cheating piece of shit. I will NEVER fuck you. If I had my way, I'd never see your smug-ass face again. But since I'm feeling generous, and I feel sorry for any girl you manage to sucker into bed, I'll give you a tip. That pencil dick of yours doesn't impress ANYONE. If you have any hope of keeping a girl, I suggest you learn how to eat pussy, because honey, your current skills are a joke. I faked it EVERY SINGLE TIME you went down on me, then afterward, I'd get myself off while thinking of anyone BUT you. So, FUCK OFF, Zach. Don't bother trying to contact me again because I'm blocking your number.

Zach: You're going to regret that, slut. Don't say I didn't warn you.

I scream as I pull up his contact card and block him.

"I can't believe him." Cameron scoffs. "I mean, I *can*, considering it's Zach, but holy shit, that idiot is delusional."

I throw my phone on the empty chair beside me. "No kidding."

Cam stands up, offering me a hand. "C'mon. Let's finish closing this place down, then pick up milkshakes on the way home. My treat."

I smile because, in my opinion, there's not much a milkshake can't fix. "Deal."

After a restless night stewing over boys—past and present—I decided I wouldn't let negative thoughts get to me anymore. I'm going to take this new day as an opportunity to move beyond my asshole ex. To focus on the things I can control, like nailing my LASPA audition or enjoying time with Bentley and my friends. If Bentley feels comfortable talking about whatever mental baggage he's been lugging around one day, I'll be ready to support him. But I'm not going to force him to unearth any demons he's not ready to face, no matter how badly I'd like to help.

Speaking of my ridiculously sexy boyfriend... I smile when I see Bentley and his friends leaning against Jazz's SUV in the Windsor parking lot. I slide into the empty spot beside them, shift into park, and kill the engine. Bentley's opening my door

LAURA LEE

before I even get the chance to do it myself, pulling me into a kiss.

"Well, good morning to you, too," I say as I pull back.

His brown eyes twinkle with equal parts amusement and lust. "Hi."

"Hey, Syd," Jazz calls from behind Bentley. She's so tiny, he's blocking her entirely.

Bentley steps aside, allowing me to finally see her. "Hey."

Kingston and Reed give me dude nods while Ainsley says, "Morning, Sydney."

"Mornin'," I echo. "Were you guys waiting for me?"

Bentley flashes his panty-dropping smile. "I told 'em to get lost, but they wouldn't listen. Well, Jazz and Ainsley at least, and the other two losers go wherever they go, so..."

"Fuck off, Fitzgerald," Kingston mutters.

At the same time, Reed and Jazz flip Bentley off.

Ainsley rolls her eyes. "Oh, shut up."

"Can you believe the crap I have to put up with?" Bentley jerks his head toward the group. "I need better friends."

I laugh. "Well, I happen to think they're pretty great."

Jazz and Ainsley smile before sticking their

400

tongues out at Bentley. Their boyfriends are still doing the silent broody thing, but I know they're totally gloating on the inside.

Bentley swings an arm over my shoulders, inclining his head toward the building where our first classes are held. "Shall we?"

As the six of us cross the parking lot, I smile, thinking about how I got to this place in my life. When my dad first mentioned he wanted me to transfer to Windsor, I fought him on it. I had no interest in completing the second half of my senior year at a new school. But as angry as I was when he told me it wasn't up for discussion, I can't help thinking maybe this was how it was meant to be.

If I hadn't come to Windsor, Bentley might have never come back into my life. He would've just been a fuzzy yet fond memory from once upon a time. I may have always wondered if he was the one who got away. And I would've never met Jazz or Ainsley, both of whom I felt an instant connection with, just like when Cam and I first met in the third grade. The only way this could be any better was if Cameron were here right now.

Just as we reach the fork where Ainsley breaks off for a different building, a series of text tones ring throughout the crowd of students, causing most to stop in their tracks, including us. My expression probably mirrors the confusion on every-one's faces, wondering why we're all simultaneously getting an alert. As I dig through my bag, I start to get this weird sense of foreboding.

"Oh, fuck," Kingston and Reed both mutter, looking down at their phones.

Jazz looks at her phone, tears forming in her eyes. "Oh my God."

Ainsley gasps as she peers at her friend's screen.

"What's it say?" I ask, digging through my bag.

Bentley goes rigid beside me as he opens his messages. "Sydney. Don't. Let's just get out of here, okay? We need to talk."

I frown. "What? Why?"

Bentley tugs on my arm. "I'll explain in the car. Let's go."

I pull out of his grip. "Bentley, stop it. What's going on? Why are you acting so strange?"

Right as I unlock my phone, a wave of catcalls, insults, and laughter surrounds me. When I look up, I see dozens of eyes directed my way. Barbie, A.K.A. Rebecca, is standing front and center with a smug smile plastered on her face.

What the hell?

Bentley reaches for my phone, but my hold is solid, so it remains in my hand. "Sydney, seriously.

Don't. Let's just get out of here." His panicked eyes flick to Kingston. "Dude."

Kingston nods. "I'll call my tech guy and get it wiped."

Jazz steps forward, covering my hand with her own. "Sydney. You need to get out of here. Don't let them see your reaction. We'll take care of this." She motions to the crowd.

"What are you guys talking about?" My voice is rising with my panic. I know that whatever's on this phone is not good, and I suspect it's related to me somehow. I gently remove Jazz's hand, looking down at my phone. I nearly drop my cell in shock, my eyes instantly watering. "What is this?! Where did this come from?"

Right there on my phone—and everyone else's, I'm guessing—is a picture of Bentley and me from the night we met. I feel nauseous as it triggers a memory from later on in the evening.

"C'mon, baby," the first guy says, pawing at me, completely ignoring my feeble attempts at pushing him off. "You know you want to suck me off, and lucky for you, I'm in a giving mood tonight."

"No," I mumble. "Don't... want... this. Where's... Linz?"

"Honey, you owe us. You made us so hard when you were blowing that guy earlier. You can't just leave us like this," the

second one says, stroking himself as he looks down on me. "We don't have a lot of time, sweetheart, so why don't you be a good girl and use that pretty mouth for much better things than talking?"

I try shifting away as he kneels on the bed, coming closer with his erection in hand, but I can't move a muscle. I'm too tired. Dizzy.

"No," I whimper, making them both laugh.

"Don't worry, babe. We'll make it real good for you."

I shake out of the memory, tears streaming down my face. The need to flee is overwhelming, so that's exactly what I do. I hear someone running behind me, calling my name, but I don't pay them any attention. I just need to get to my car and get the hell out of here.

"Sydney, wait!" Bentley pulls my arm, spinning me around as I open my car door. "I'm coming with you."

I nearly fall as my knees buckle when I think about what Zach said to me at the party in Malibu, and the realization of what this picture means, kicks in. The stab of betrayal is so sharp, it takes my breath away.

"How could you not be an easy lay after seeing what you did with him in the middle of a crowded room? I mean, if you did that shit in public, you had to be a freak in bed, right? I guess the joke's on me, isn't it?"

Bentley stiffens at my side, making me wonder what that's all about, but I have bigger fish to fry at the moment.

"I'm lost. What are you talking about? I've never done anything with anybody in public. What evidence do you supposedly think you have?"

"Oh, that's right; you have no idea, do you? Because that's the same night your cousin spiked your drinks. Maybe that's my problem. Maybe your inner slut only comes out when you've been drugged."

Bentley lunges for him. "You motherfucker."

I step in the middle of these two assholes, determined to figure out what the hell is going on. I don't even care about the audience we've gathered at the moment.

"Bentley, stay out of it. This is my *problem, not yours."*

Bentley's jaw clenches in irritation, but he's smart enough to keep his mouth shut.

*"*Explain, *Zach."*

He laughs. "Nah, I don't think I will. You'll find out soon enough, and I'm going to really fucking enjoy it when you do. Later, Syd. I'm gonna go see what Liv's up to."

Bentley lunges for him again when Zach starts to walk away, but I grab onto the back of his shirt. "It's not worth it."

Bentley's nostrils flare. "The fuck it's not."

I narrow my eyes. "Why do I get the feeling you know what Zach was talking about?"

"You don't?" He stares at me for a moment. "Seriously? You have no idea?"

Bentley's reaction to Zach's statement confirms he knew about it back then. Sure, we got interrupted shortly after that, so maybe I could overlook the fact he didn't tell me that evening. But... he's had *plenty* of opportunities to fess up since then. The bastard's been lying to my face this whole time, playing me for a goddamn fool, while I was falling for him.

I toss my bag in my car and shove Bentley with as much force as I can manage, not even caring about our audience at this point. "The hell you are!"

He holds his palms out. "I am not responsible for blasting that picture! I swear to fucking God, Syd."

I sniffle, wiping the remainder of my tears with my sleeve. "That *is* you in the picture, is it not?"

Bentley closes his eyes briefly. "Obviously."

My eyes swing to Kingston and Reed. "Where did it even come from? Did one of your buddies take it? *Did you ask them to?*" Kingston's jaw tics like he's pissed I'd accuse him of anything, but I couldn't give a flying fuck right now.

"No!" Bentley adamantly insists. "I didn't even

know pictures existed until after the fact when random people started sending them to me!"

Oh, God, there's more than one of these out there?

"Ah, but you *did* know, though, right? To be clear, that *is* what you're saying, correct?"

He nods solemnly and croaks, "Yes."

"And you didn't think this was something *I* should know at any point? When I told you I had virtually no memory of that night, you had the *perfect* opportunity to fill in some gaps! You should've told me that we'd... hooked up like that before, and God, in front of tons of people, no less! You could've warned me there were pictures of us... of me... of *this*, yet, you chose not to. Why is that, Bentley?"

I tell myself to ignore the liquid welling in his eyes. "I don't know."

"How could you do this to me? Are you really that cruel? You know, I thought we might've had something really good here. What a dumbass I've been, huh?"

How could I have been so wrong?

"No!" he shouts. "Syd, you're the best thing that's ever happened to me. I meant to tell you. I just—"

I held my hand up, cutting off whatever lie he was about to spew. "Was the whole thing part of some sick game? Were you and those two assholes who tried assaulting me in on it together? Is this some fucked-up version of notches on a bedpost?"

Bentley's espresso eyes widen. "What?! No! What assholes? *You were assaulted that night?!*"

"Don't play dumb with me, Bentley."

"I'm not," he insists. "I swear I'm telling the truth, Syd."

I belt out a sardonic laugh. "Why would I believe you? Because you've been so truthful up until this point?" When he says nothing, I shake my head, getting behind the wheel. "Stay the fuck away from me. You're not who I thought you were."

He grabs hold of my door when I attempt to close it. "No! You don't understand! Just please, give me a chance to explain."

"Go to hell, Bentley."

"Sydney, wait!" Jazz calls.

I shake my head. "Can we please not do this right now? I need to get out of here."

Jazz nods. "I know you need to get out of here —trust me, I know more than anyone what you're going through right now. I'll take you wherever you want, no questions. I just don't think you should be behind the wheel right now."

I know she's right. I shouldn't be driving when I'm this upset. But can I really trust her? Or was she in on this whole thing? I decide to err on the side of safety. What harm can come from her driving me somewhere?

I sigh. "Fine."

I unlock the doors and round the front of my car to get in on the passenger side. As I do, Bentley reaches for me again, but Jazz and Ainsley block him, their voices too low to make out what they're saying.

Ainsley hops in the back while Jazz adjusts the seat and mirrors. "Is it okay if I come, too?"

"I don't care as long as we get out of here."

I see the guys talking animatedly out of the corner of my eye, but I refuse to look in Bentley's direction.

Jazz shifts my Audi into reverse. "Where am I going?"

"Cambridge Prep." I plug in the location on my nav, then grab my phone to text my bestie. "Just please, get me to Cameron."

The nav says we're about twenty-five minutes out with traffic, so I lean back, put my shades on, and hope neither one of them will try talking to me on the drive there.

chapter
thirty-six

SYDNEY

"Shit!" Jazz slams on the brakes, causing my body to jerk forward before the seat belt locks up. "Where the hell did she come from?"

Cam, who darted off the front steps of Cambridge's main building—getting damn near run over in the process—spots me sitting in the passenger seat and makes her way to my side. I don't even think Jazz has a chance to shift into park before I'm tearing out of the car, running to her. Thank God classes are currently in session, so it's just the four of us.

"Shh, Syd." Cam strokes the back of my head as I proceed to lose it again on her shoulder. "It'll be okay. We'll figure out who sent those pictures out and make them regret it."

Wait a second...

When I texted Cam, I told her I needed her,

and she said she'd meet me in front of the school. I did *not* go into any detail as to *why* I needed her.

I pull back, wiping my eyes. "You know?! *How?*"

Her brows crinkle in confusion. "The entire Cambridge student body got a text about two minutes before the tardy bell rang. Well, I assume everyone got it, but I'm not positive because only a couple dozen were still outside at the time. I was just about to call you when your text popped up. I stayed out here to wait instead of going to first period."

"Oh, God." I sink down, planting my ass on the curb, feeling sick to my stomach. Cambridge begins their school day only five minutes after Windsor, which means the texts were sent out one after another.

Cam takes a seat beside me. "That's *not* why?"

Jazz and Ainsley joined us after Jazz pulled my car off to the side.

"Everyone at Windsor got it first." I cover my face with my hands. "I'm so mortified. I can't believe I did that. I'm pro-sex positivity and all, but that's so... not something *I* would do. And the fact there's photographic evidence proving I was obviously into it, regardless of our audience? *God.* Who knows how many people have seen some variation of that picture over the last two *years?*"

Cam rubs my back. "Honey, you were drugged. And not just any drugs. Ones that pretty much obliterated your inhibitions. Don't beat yourself up over it."

I give her the side-eye. "That's easy to say when you're not the one who unwillingly became an amateur porn star. *Thousands* of people have seen me with a dick in my mouth, Cameron." I groan. "Jesus."

She gives me a soft smile. "At least you looked hot as hell doing it."

I snort-sniffle. "Only you would pull that out of it, nerd."

Cam shrugs. "I'm just sayin'. You've gotta look at the positives."

I sigh. "I don't see how *any* of this could be considered positive."

Jazz comes over to my side. "Sydney, remember how I said I know what you're going through?" She waits for my acknowledgment before continuing. "When I first came to Windsor... there was a party. I was talking to a guy from UCLA who roofied my drink while I was in the bathroom. I should've known better not to drink from that cup after walking away from it. I mean, I *did* know better, but I wasn't exactly thinking clearly that night." She gives me a rueful smile. "I was pissed at Kingston and couldn't think about much else. He had a way of consuming my thoughts back then."

Ainsley snorts. "*Just* back then, huh?"

Jazz flips her off. "Anyway... I wound up, uh... making out with two guys at the same time, and... I may have been topless for part of it. They didn't know I was drugged until well after it happened, but that's beside the point. From what I could tell from the video sent out to the entire Windsor student body the following Monday, I was pretty damn into it. Like, really, *really* into it. As you can imagine, that really set the gossip mill and mean girls into motion."

My eyes widen. "What'd you do? Did you ever find out who was responsible for sending it out?"

If I'm not mistaken, Jazz and Ainsley both cringe. "I feel like I should preface this by saying he had a reason for doing what he did. A *misguided* reason, mind you, clouded in a vendetta. And it still pisses me off to this day, but I understand now where he was coming from, and he's more than made up for it since then."

I shake my head. "I'm not following."

Jazz nibbles on the corner of her lower lip. "*Kingston* released the video, plus some still shots. He and... uh, Bentley were the guys I was making out with. And Reed filmed the whole thing."

"Whoa," Cameron mutters under her breath. "Didn't see that one coming."

My jaw drops. "Um... I'm not really sure what to say to that."

I already knew Jazz and Bentley had fooled around before, which I've made peace with, but the fact there's photographic proof of it, *and* he was involved in some plan to hurt Jazz? That's a little harder to swallow.

"It's pretty tough to digest." She scrunches her nose, wringing her hands together. "And it took me a while to move past it. I don't trust people blindly, and when someone violates my trust, I don't usually give them a second chance. Those boys had to work *hard* to make it up to me, but they did. Sometimes good people do bad things, Syd. I know Bentley's made some really shitty decisions lately, but he's still one of the best people I've ever met. I genuinely mean that."

I shake my head. "It doesn't matter. Whatever Bentley and I had is over."

Jazz quirks a brow. "Do you really believe that? You've gotta know Bentley had nothing to do with sending those pictures out."

"How can you be so sure?" I challenge. "He had no issue sending out intimate photos of *you*."

Jazz shakes her head. "That whole situation was

Kingston's doing. Yeah, Bent and Reed are big boys who were perfectly capable of saying no, but at the time, their allegiance was to Kingston, one-hundred-percent. They may not have agreed with him, but they knew Kingston believed he had a valid reason, and that was good enough for them. If nothing else, those three are loyal to a fault. Once you have their devotion, it's infallible. Sydney, I have no doubt Bentley has strong feelings for you. He would never intentionally hurt you."

I frown. "He deliberately kept something important from me. An omission is still lying, in my opinion, if it's something a person deserves to know. And I *sure as fuck* deserved to know what happened that evening. Every interaction I've had with Bentley since coming to Windsor is tainted. I flat out asked him what he remembered from the night we met. *I told him* I was drugged and had almost no memory of it. He had *the perfect opportunity* to come clean, but he didn't. I can't just forgive *or* forget that, Jazz. I can't be with someone I don't trust."

"We're not saying what he did was right," Ainsley pipes in. "But I *do* think you need to talk to him. It's not my place to give you details, but something happened the night you and Bentley met. Something *life-changing and awful*, and it's been messing with his head since he found out the next morning. We were all affected, really, but Bentley took it harder than the rest of us. If you knew the truth... if you know what's driving him... I think you might feel differently."

"I *know* something's haunting him," I admit. "And I've tried getting him to open up because I wanted to help. But Bentley refused to talk to me, and I can't force it out of him. You can't help someone who doesn't want to be helped. I know he's your friend, and I appreciate what you're trying to do, but I need to focus on myself right now."

Jazz bumps her shoulder into mine. "We're your friends, too, Sydney. Neither Ainsley nor I am taking sides here. We want you *both* to be happy. You just need to figure out how to get past this."

"How am I supposed to show my face at Windsor ever again?" I groan, jerking my head toward the school behind me. "And since they got it, too, coming back here isn't an option either. Shit, what if that picture got sent to the faculty?"

The thought of my dad seeing it makes bile rise in my throat.

"Syd, if your dad isn't currently blowing up your phone, there's no way the faculty got wind of it," Cam offers.

I sigh in relief, knowing she's right. "It still

doesn't change the fact that every single student saw me like that. *In both schools.*"

Jazz takes my hand, squeezing. "I know it won't be easy, but you need to walk into school tomorrow morning like nothing happened, with your head held high. Don't let those assholes have any kind of power over you. Ainsley and I will be with you the whole time."

I squeeze her back, grateful for the offer. "I still don't understand why anyone would do this to me. What were they hoping to accomplish?" I clench my fists when it hits me. There *is* someone who has the motive to do something like this, and he's a big enough asshole to actually go through with it. "Zach."

"That shithead!" Cam shouts. "It *has* to be him! After those texts he sent you last night... what else could he have been referring to?"

"What texts?" Ainsley and Jazz both ask.

"That prick sent a few cryptic messages to Sydney last night, actually trying to blackmail her into sleeping with him, telling her she'd regret turning him down." Cameron stands as if she's getting ready to march into the building. "I'm going to kill him. Or at least knee him in the balls so hard, he'll be eating testicles for dinner."

I stand, pulling her back by her navy blazer.

"Hold up there, Killer. I'm not going to let you get suspended, or worse, for fighting my battles." The bell rings, indicating the start of passing time.

Cam throws her hands out. "I don't give a shit about being suspended. Let me at him, Syd. I bet I can find him in the halls."

I pull harder when she tries charging off again. "Sit down, Cameron. If it *is* Zach, I'll make him pay for it somehow."

"Fine." She plops down with a huff.

Right before I take a seat again, the front doors to the school open, and none other than the prick himself walks out with a smug smile on his face.

"Well, well, well. Look who we have here: LA's newest porn star." Zach walks toward us, completely ignoring the fire shooting out of my eyes. "You're the trending story at Cambridge today. I'm guessing the same applies to your new school, too, thanks to my lovely friend Rebecca who so graciously used her office assistant position to give me access to their directory. I bet you wish you took me up on my offer now, don't you, Syd?"

I can hear shuffling behind me and Cameron swearing up a storm, but I pay her no mind because I am laser-focused on the dickhead in front of me. When he's no more than a foot away, I am so furious, my fist immediately shoots out, slamming directly into Zach's nose with a satisfying crunch.

"You fucking bitch!" he yells, cupping his hands over his nose while blood pours down his face.

"Fuck you!" I scream, shaking my hand out. *Ouch.* "I hope it's broken, you son of a bitch!"

There's more shuffling behind me until Cam runs forward, props her hands on both of Zach's shoulders, and thrusts her knee right into his balls, making him double over in pain. As he's huddled into the fetal position on the sidewalk, Cam kicks him in the shin for good measure, making him yelp.

"You stupid, micro-dicked motherfucker!" She slams her pointed shoe into his other shin. "How's it feel getting your ass beat by a girl?"

People must've heard the commotion from inside because dozens of students are now spilling out of the front doors. Cameron is a flurry of motion, my own little blonde Tasmanian devil, kicking and screaming, while Zach whimpers like the pathetic piece of shit he is on the ground. She nails him in the nuts again, causing a collected *"Oof!"* from our gathered audience. As satisfying as this is to watch, I don't want my best friend to get expelled, so I need to break this up.

"Let's go, Cam." I grab her arm, pulling her back. "We need to get out of here."

"You're not getting away with this, skank." Zach seethes, glaring at my best friend. "You know Headmaster Aldridge has a zero-tolerance policy on violence."

"Go right ahead, fuckface. If you get me expelled, I'll easily find another school to graduate from. But what do you think will happen to *you* when I report your ass for distributing revenge porn featuring a minor? Because you do realize she was a minor when those pictures were taken, right?" Zach blanches, making Cameron smile. "I don't think the police take too kindly to that stuff, and I'm sure it'll be no problem whatsoever to trace those pictures back to you. And since you're a legal adult, I'm sure the D.A. would *love* to make an example out of you, don't you think? You'll be someone's prison bitch before you know it.

"If you don't want to see that happen, I suggest you deny any and all involvement from any of us." Cam flips her blonde hair over her shoulder, gesturing to me, Jazz, and Ainsley. She looks up at the crowd. "And you'd better start thinking about how you're going to convince *them* they saw nothing either. Tootles!" She gives him a finger wave before taking my arm and walking with me toward my car.

As we pull away from the curb, I rest my head on Cam's shoulder, grateful for her friendship. I think about what Jazz said about Bentley and his friends being infallibly loyal to one another. That's what Cameron and I have. She's the girl I'd call to help me hide a body, no questions asked. The two girls in the front seats have that potential, too, and I believe them when they said they wouldn't take sides. But can I really maintain a friendship with Jazz and Ainsley if Bentley and I aren't together? Can they really respect my decision to cut one of their best friends out of my life?

I guess time will tell.

chapter
thirty-seven

BENTLEY

"I fucked up so bad." I take a swig of Beluga, notes of vanilla and sage sliding down my throat. "I bet that doesn't surprise you one bit, though, does it? That's what I do because I'm a fuckup. No one knows that more than you, huh, Riss? You paid for it with your life." I trace the letters and numbers denoting the day she left us forever and raise the bottle in a morbid toast. "No higher price than that."

I gulp down the remaining vodka and set the bottle on the smooth black granite, watching as it rolls across the surface before falling into the perfectly manicured grass. No ordinary gravestone was good enough for Carissa Marquart. Instead, her parents chose an ornate full-sized ledger, her eternally sixteen-year-old face etched into the stone right above some trite poem she would've hated.

I lie back on the ground, staring at the moon as it blurs in and out of focus. "Why won't you stop haunting me? I can't live like this anymore, Rissa."

I check my phone as it buzzes for the millionth time since I've been here, but it's not the one person I need to talk to, so I toss it to the side. I've been calling and texting Sydney all day, but it goes straight to voice mail now, like she turned off her phone. I just wish she'd let me explain. Jazz called earlier to let me know what went down when Syd ran into her douchebag ex, confirming my suspicions he was the one who put that pic on blast. She wouldn't tell me anything else, though, other than stating I need to give Sydney time.

Fuck time.

Time is only going to give Syd more opportunity to think about all the reasons why she should stay far away from me. And it's not like they wouldn't be true. But if she'd just give me a chance to explain where I was coming from... maybe she can find a way to forgive me. I can't fucking lose her. I just *can't.*

Should've thought about that before you lied to her face, asshole.

My cell buzzes again, and this time Davenport is calling instead of sending a colorful text, threatening to ask my mom to track my phone if I don't answer him. Well, the joke's on him because I disabled the Find My Phone feature. The call goes to voice mail but starts ringing again two seconds later.

Christ, give it a rest, will ya? Can't a guy sob over his dead ex's grave in peace?

I groan when he calls for the third time in a row, deciding to get this over with. I would just power it down, but I don't want to risk missing a call from Sydney.

"Chill the fuck out, man." I bend my legs, knees pointed at the night sky.

"Where are you?"

"Doesn't matter," I slur, my gaze wandering aimlessly.

Damn, graveyards are creepy as fuck at night.

There's silence on the other end for so long, I have to check to see if the call's still connected.

"Is there a reason you called me, dude, or did you just want to jerk off to the sound of my breathing? Because if that's the case, I gotta say, buddy, I love you, but I'm way too into pussy to be down for th—"

"Bent. You've been gone for over twelve hours. I think you've had enough time to wallow in self-loathing, don't you?"

I belt out a derisive laugh. "It's been a helluva

lot longer than twelve hours since I've been doing that, dawg."

Kingston's harsh exhale echoes through the phone. "You're at the cemetery, aren't you?"

Fuck.

I knew it wouldn't take long before they figured it out, but I hoped to have a little more time before they found me and put the kibosh on my fun. I mean, how am I supposed to drown my misery with premium spirits and the finest Oxy money can buy when my well-meaning-but-total-buzzkill-friends are hovering over me, waiting for me to go off the deep end?

Whoa, this is some good shit.

My supplier was fresh out of my usual thirty-milligram order, but I can't say I hate the enhanced buzz from the sixty he gave me instead. He told me to cut 'em in half, but I needed extra after the morning I had. Besides, I think I'm building up a tolerance to the lower dose, so it's time to step it up anyway. Hence, why I popped another pill about thirty minutes ago.

"Bent. Did you hear what I said?"

"Huh?" It takes me a second to remember what I was doing.

"What did you take? And don't even try

insulting my intelligence by telling me you're not fucked up."

"Don't worry 'bout me, bro. It's all good." I'm pretty sure I blended all of those words into one. Meh, he'll get the gist.

"Bentley," Davenport says with more force. "What the fuck did you take, and *where the hell are you?!*"

I hear talking in the background for a few seconds before a much more feminine voice takes over.

"Bentley. Tell me where you are, and we'll come to get you."

"Nah, Jazzy Jazz. Everything's hella cool. Swear."

I hear the distinct sound of an engine starting; I'm guessing Jazz's vehicle over Kingston's since the sound isn't making my skull rattle.

"C'mon, Bentley." Her tone is pleading, anxious. "Are you by Carissa's grave? Kingston says we'll be there in... twenty minutes max. We just need confirmation."

I sit up, or at least I try to. I close my eyes as my face presses against the cool marble ledger. I just need a minute to clear my head.

"Yeah, I'm here. But I was just leaving."

"What?!" Damn, that was loud. "No, Bentley.

Stay where you are. We're coming to get you. Hold on, I'm switching to hands-free."

My head moves from side to side. "I'ma letchu go. I gotta get out of here."

"Fitzgerald, don't you fucking move an inch." Kingston's tone is part scolding, part worry. I'm sure the latter wouldn't be there if he knew the truth.

"I'm the reason she's dead," I mumble.

I hear Kingston blowing out a breath. "Dude. We've been through this. You can't blame yourself. It's not your fault."

I start to nod but think better of it when a wave of dizziness washes over me. "You don't know, man. Whatever happened to S-Sydney that night's my fault, too. Maybe R-Rissa's right. Can't hurt someone else if I'm not around to do it."

I somehow manage to stand up and start walking across the grass to get to my Porsche.

"Bentley, did you just start moving around? Don't leave that cemetery, goddammit!"

"Bentley..." Jazz's tone is much softer. *Did she just sniffle? Or was that me?* "Please stay right where you're at. We'll be there soon, and we'll get this all figured out."

"Ain't nuthin' to figure out, Jazzy Jazz. *I'm* the reason the roofies were at that party. Which means *I'm* the reason those fucking frat boys got a hold of them so they could drug Riss. That's how Syd's cousin got 'em too, I'm sure. Nuthin' confusing about that, baby girl." My lips curve when I'm met with complete silence on the other end. "Weren't expecting me to drop that bomb, were ya? So, now ya know why I don't deserve anyone's forgiveness. You're all better off without me."

I open my car door and fall into the driver's seat. *Damn*, talk about a head rush.

Kingston clears his throat. "I don't know what exactly that means, but it doesn't matter, bro."

"The fuck it doesn't."

"Why don't you explain it to me then? So I can understand."

I push the start button on my car and rev the engine.

"Get out of your fucking car, Fitzgerald," Kingston barks. "We're halfway there. Jazz and I will take you anywhere you want to go."

Why would I do that when I have a perfectly good car here?

"Nah, dawg. It's all good." I end the call, turning off my phone before tossing it on the passenger seat.

I blink a few times to clear my vision before shifting into gear and pulling away from the curb, heading for the old fire lookout. If Carissa won't talk to me from her grave, maybe she'll be chattier at her chosen location for all my recent nightmares. There's gotta be a reason why she keeps taking us there, right?

I shake my head.

Damn, I'm losing my marbles.

Look at me, trying to talk to a dead girl like I'm a psychic or some shit. Not that I believe in that crap, mind you. Or maybe I do. I don't fucking know jack anymore, other than what a worthless, selfish piece of shit I am. I start laughing at the painful truth behind that statement. I've been floating for so fucking long now, numb to everything around me, I really am just a waste of space. I mean, really, the only thing I seem to accomplish anymore is hurting people. Look at what I did to Sydney. I had every opportunity to come clean, but I chose to take the chicken-shit way out.

God, Sydney.

I don't know if I'll ever forget the way she looked at me when she figured out I lied. The complete devastation in her eyes mirrored what I felt on the inside. What I *feel* on the inside. Why does losing Sydney hurt so badly when it's barely been a minute since I've had her?

My Porsche handles beautifully, hugging the

pavement through each twist and turn down this dark and windy road.

Shit, I'm tired.

I roll my windows down to get a nice breeze going, hoping it'll wake me up a bit. I smack each one of my cheeks a few times to help speed the process along. This section of Mulholland is nice and empty, so I push the pedal a little harder. I wonder what Sydney's doing right now. Is she angry? Sad? Or worse, is she the type of girl to go after a revenge hookup? I mean, I don't think she is, considering she was a virgin before me, but who knows? It would definitely be the ultimate *fuck you* to get back at me for my dishonesty.

I scrub a hand down my face, groaning at the thought of Syd being with someone else. Why does that make me so crazy? After what I did to her, I couldn't exactly blame her. I've gotta figure out a way to make her forgive me. Maybe I should head to her place instead, refuse to leave until she lets me explain. Or until her parents call the cops, whichever comes first. *Ah, fuck it.* I won't know unless I try, right? I've gotta fucking try.

I stretch my neck from side to side, feeling good about this decision. Jesus fuck, my head is spinning. I blink rapidly, trying to focus as I approach a U-shaped curve. I take the corner a little too tightly, my teeth clacking as my low-profile racing tires bump along the narrow dirt shoulder. I yank the wheel to the left and ease off the gas as I start to fishtail, but I'm heading directly for a large berm, so I have no choice but to slam on the brakes. The smell of burning rubber assaults my nose as I skid across the double-yellow. The screech of crumpling steel and the loudest bang I've ever heard ricochets through my ears. I grunt, head snapping back as the airbag kicks me in the face. The last thing I grasp before losing consciousness is Carissa sitting in the passenger seat, completely unharmed, with utter despair written across her face.

chapter
thirty-eight

SYDNEY

I tell myself not to look for a certain silver Porsche as I pull through the Windsor gates, but I do it anyway. I frown, disappointed he's not here yet, then I remind myself Bentley Fitzgerald lost his shot with me, so I don't need to see him anyway. Maybe if I say it enough times in my head, it won't feel so wrong. I drive through the lot, sliding into the spot next to Jazz's Range Rover. As I shift into park, I'm surprised to find Ainsley in the passenger seat and Jazz behind the wheel. Huh. Kingston must not be coming to school today for some reason because he's usually behind the wheel with Ainsley in the back.

I take some deep breaths, giving myself a mental pep talk. I'm a few minutes earlier than usual, but if I hide out in my car, it'll defeat the purpose of what I'm trying to accomplish here. I need to show the assholes who were laughing at me and calling me names that I won't let them bring me down. A bunch of elitist pricks who don't even know me aren't going to shame me for my behavior while I was unknowingly drugged.

I wish I could say I regretted my actions with Bentley, but I can't. I mean, sure, I wish it wasn't so public. I definitely wish there wasn't photographic evidence of it, but seeing that picture jarred my memories a bit. My enthusiastic participation is evident. I could blame the ecstasy or the fact that several spots throughout the frat house had live-action porn, but that'd be a lie. Maybe my inhibitions were lowered from the drugs, but I now recall feeling so overwhelmingly drawn to Bentley at that moment, wanting more than anything to connect with him on a physical level, consequences be damned. It was the exact same feeling I had the day he went down on me in the dance studio, and I was stone-cold sober then. Without a doubt, I am the one who instigated the blow job that'll forever live in infamy. I think Bentley may have even tried talking me out of it at one point, but that part's still a little fuzzy.

I felt like I had made peace with what happened later that night after my cousin left me alone and vulnerable so she could go screw some rando. But after yesterday, I've realized I haven't put it behind me nearly as much as I thought. Every time I closed my eyes last night, trying to get some sleep, I would get flashes of those two guys pawing my breasts, voicing the vile things they had planned. I couldn't shake the phantom feel of their hands on me.

They didn't get any further than that before my cousin's sorority sister walked in, and they ran off, but that didn't stop my imagination from continuing the scene, playing all sorts of horrific possibilities on a constant loop. I was nauseated and awake almost all night because of it. I think it's time to see the therapist Cam's been hounding me to talk to. The thing is, I don't think I can pull that off without telling my parents why because I'm on their insurance. But if that's what it takes so this isn't haunting me for the rest of my life, I guess I'll have to suck it up. It might make things awkward next Thanksgiving, but what other choice do I have?

The girls exit their vehicle once they notice me getting out of my Audi. I instantly know something's wrong when I get a good look at them. Not only are they not in uniform, but they both have dark circles under their eyes like they haven't slept a wink.

I frown. "Hey. What's going on?"

Ainsley frees her lower lip from her teeth.

"We've been trying to reach you, Sydney, but your phone kept going straight to voice mail."

Ah, shit.

Bentley wouldn't stop blowing up my phone, so I eventually shut it off, then shoved it deep in my backpack to avoid the temptation to answer. I should just block his number, but I'm not ready to do that yet for some reason.

I dig through my bag to locate my cell. "What's up? You guys aren't going to school today?"

It's a dumb question because it's obvious by their choice of apparel, they're not.

Jazz's head shakes. "No. We've gotta get back to the hospital."

"Hospital? Why?"

She swallows. "Bentley was in a car accident last night. A pretty bad one."

My bag slips from my hand, falling to the ground. "What?!"

"He's okay," Jazz assures me. "Or... he'll *be* okay, physically. He's pretty banged up, but he got really lucky considering he totaled his car."

"What happened?" I croak.

Ainsley's hazel eyes begin to fill when she sees my eyes doing the same. "He took a corner too fast, lost control, and ran his Porsche into a rocky dirt ridge along the side of the road. Thankfully, his airbags deployed, so most of his injuries are from the force of that. He told Kingston he slammed on the brakes, which significantly reduced his speed before impact. If he hadn't... the officer on the scene said he probably wouldn't be here."

My gut clenches. "Which hospital?"

I don't know why I asked. The thought just kinda flew out of my mouth.

"The one right by your house, actually, off of Mulholland." Jazz clears her throat. "Did you... do you want to come with us? I'm sure he'd love to see you. I know we said we'd be here for you today, bu—"

"I get it. You should be at the hospital." I wave her off. "Thank you for telling me, but I think it'd probably be best if I stayed away. I can't..." I shake my head. "Please don't think poorly of me, but I just can't."

"We totally understand, Syd." Ainsley smiles and nods reassuringly. "Seriously."

"Thanks." I pick my bag off the ground, hoisting it over my shoulder.

I can feel several sets of eyes on me as more students arrive, but I don't give them the satisfaction of acknowledging them.

Jazz jerks her thumb over her shoulder. "We

should get going. Call or text if you change your mind about coming."

I nod. "I will."

I wait for them to drive away before getting back in my car. I type a quick text to my dad, telling him I'm not feeling well, which isn't exactly a lie. Then I send another to Cam, asking her to meet me in the Cambridge parking lot, hoping she gets my message before going to her first class. I feel bad asking her to skip a second day with me, but I really do need my bestie, and it's not like her mom ever acts like a parent long enough to care about her attendance.

When Cam sends me a thumbs up in reply, I start my car and head over to meet her. I'm not sure where we're going or what we'll do, but I know I won't be able to focus in class today, so I've gotta get out of here.

"Are you sure you want to do this?"

I nod, bracing myself as we exit the hospital elevator onto the fifth floor. "I know you think he doesn't deserve my sympathy."

Cameron's brows arch. "But?"

"But... I can't stop thinking about the fact

437

Bentley could've *died* yesterday. And if he did... I don't think I would've ever forgiven myself for leaving things the way we did." I take a deep breath and let it out. "I can't deny the connection we share. I feel it in my bones, Cam. Regardless of whether or not Bentley will be a part of my future, I've no doubt my time shared with him—no matter how limited—has changed me. Plus... I know in my heart Bentley's a good person. That doesn't mean I can overlook his terrible decisions, but I believe Jazz and Ainsley's assertion that he would never intentionally hurt me."

Cameron grabs my arm and pulls me to the side of the hallway. "Wow, you really fell hard, didn't you?"

I shrug. "I don't think I could've avoided it no matter how much I tried."

She pulls me into a hug. "Honey, I'm so sorry."

"It is what it is, right?" I blink back tears as I pull away. "Okay. Enough of this. I need to get in there and see that he's okay with my own eyes. Maybe then I can move on."

"Are you sure you don't want me to go in with you?"

I shake my head. "I need to do this alone."

Thankfully, when I texted Jazz asking for Bentley's room number, she mentioned she and

Kingston were heading home to relieve the nanny. Ainsley and Reed were going to grab some dinner, so we should have privacy.

Cam jerks her head toward the waiting room on our left. "I'll be right here if you need me."

"Thanks, boo."

I checked in with the nurse's station and head in the direction they pointed me. Right before I approach room five-ten, Bentley's mom steps out, closing the door behind her, looking weary but still gorgeous.

Her whiskey eyes widen in surprise. "Sydney, hi."

"Hi." I shift awkwardly on my feet. "Um... is it okay if I visit Bentley for a few?"

"Of course." She smiles softly. "He's resting right now, but he's been asking for you quite a bit, so you should go in. Don't be surprised if he's a little out of it, though. His nurse recently gave him a new dose of Morphine for the pain."

"Oh. Um... okay. I won't take too much time."

Lani gently squeezes my shoulder. "Take as much time as you need. I'm heading home to grab a few things that'll make Bentley more comfortable while he's here, so I'll be gone for a couple of hours."

"How long..." I clear my throat. "I mean, if you

don't mind me asking... how long do they think he'll be here?"

"Probably no more than a few days. His concussion is mild, but two of his ribs are fractured, and he has a bruised lung, so they want to keep an eye on him to make sure he doesn't develop any complications."

My chest tightens. "Oh, God."

"All things considered, we're fortunate these are his only injuries." She hitches her designer bag over her shoulder. "I'd better get going. I hope to see you soon, Sydney."

"Okay. Bye." I ignore the pang in my chest when I think about how that's probably not going to happen.

I wait until Bentley's mom is out of sight before stepping closer to the door leading to his room. I shove my fist against my mouth, choking back a sob as I get my first look at him through the tiny window. Bentley's big body is stretched out on the much-too-small-for-him bed, his upper half propped up by a series of pillows. There's dark bruising around both of his eyes, and the bridge of his nose is bandaged. His lids are closed, but his brows are pinched together as if he's in pain.

He's hooked up to a bunch of monitors with one of those plastic things in his nostrils, with an IV needle taped to the back of one hand, while the other is wrapped in an ace bandage going halfway up his forearm. I got a glimpse of how mentally damaged Bentley is the few times he dropped his mask long enough for me to see, but now his outsides seem to match the inside. I would've never thought someone so physically imposing could appear so frail, but there's no denying how broken he looks right now. I cringe as the door creaks when I open it, but the sound doesn't cause him to wake.

Bentley's lids flutter as I approach the bed. It takes him a moment, but his eyes round slightly when he notices me. "Didn't think you'd come."

"That makes two of us." I don't want to get too comfortable because I won't be here long, so I stand behind the plastic chair closest to him, with my hands curling over the top of it. "How are you feeling?"

"Prolly 'bout as great as I look." Bentley's speech is a little slower than normal, but he's surprisingly lucid considering the painkillers his mom mentioned.

My fingers clench around the hard plastic when I realize that's probably because he's built up a tolerance to opioids. "What happened, Bentley?"

"Oh, nothing new." He chuckles, but it's choked off by a wince. "Just your standard case of me making godawful decisions." When I don't say anything, he releases a sigh and adds, "Turns out Perc, vodka, and German sports cars aren't a great combination."

"Was anyone else... hurt?"

Please say no.

Bentley's head slowly slices left. "Nah. Just me and the side of a mountain."

I swear I just felt my heart stop for a second, thinking how disastrous that could've been. "I talked to your mom on her way out. She said you have a concussion and some broken ribs?"

"Plus a sprained wrist, couple'a black eyes, swollen nose, and a side of nasty bruises. No big. I'll be good as new in no time."

"Don't downplay this," I snap. "You could've *died*, Bentley. What were you thinking?"

I'm not trying to kick the man while he's down, but I need to know. Bentley's not dumb; I *know* he knows he shouldn't have been driving.

His chocolate gaze bores into mine for several long beats. "Why're you here, Sydney? Thought you were done with me."

"Just because I'm angry with you doesn't mean I don't care. I'm not a freaking robot."

"I know you're not a robot. But you *are* done with me, right?"

I sigh, briefly closing my eyes to ward off the tears. "Right."

"Better for you that way. It was stupid of me to think I had a chance." A pained groan falls from his lips as he shifts in bed. "Not like I'll be around for a while anyway."

I frown. "What does that mean?"

Bentley's full lips kick up in the corner, but there's no mirth behind it. "Funny thing about driving while fucked up... it seems the cops don't like that, especially when you crash."

I hold my breath, waiting for more information. I don't know why I didn't consider the possibility of legal ramifications, but it makes sense there would be some.

"What's going to happen to you?"

"My attorney says the judge should accept a plea deal since no one else was involved. Rehab, community service, shit like that. Prolly won't have a license for a while. My mom found this place in Ojai... they have a thirty-day program. She's tryin' to get me in." He clears his throat. "I'm sure detox is going to be a fucking blast, and I'll have to listen to a bunch of psycho-babble, but it might not be such a bad idea. Better than being in jail or six feet under, right?"

I swallow audibly. "Do you think you *need* rehab? You said you had it under control."

Bentley stares at me for a few beats. "I thought I did."

"But now you don't?"

His shoulders lift slightly. "I don't remember the last time I spent a whole day fully sober. I think... maybe that was like, my new normal, or whatevs, so it didn't *feel* like I had a problem. But wrecking my car was kinda a big wake-up call, ya know?"

"I bet." I nod. "So... after you get out of here, you'll go there for a month?"

"If it all works out, yeah." Bentley's lids close.

I jerk my thumb over my shoulder. "I should probably get going so you can rest. I'm glad you're going to be okay."

I start backing out of the room but pause when he says, "Syd. Wait." His eyes are wide open now. "Can I... while I'm in rehab... if they let me have my phone... can I call you? Or text?"

I sigh, my eyes filling with water. "I don't think that's a good idea, Bentley. You should focus on getting better."

I fight the urge to take it back when I see the crestfallen look on his face. "Right. Yeah. Dumb idea. Sorry."

"It's not a dumb idea," I insist. "But... I think I

need some time, too. I've got issues of my own to work through." I stop over the threshold. "Take care of yourself, Bentley."

He inclines his head. "You too, Syd."

As Cameron and I head to my car, I tell myself this is for the best. Bentley and I each need to work some shit out, and we can't focus on ourselves properly if we're trying to repair this rift between us, too. I don't know what our future holds, but I do know it's not healthy for either one of us to continue the way we've been.

chapter
thirty-nine

BENTLEY

I should be in Hawaii right now with the girl of my dreams. Instead, I'm one day away from graduating from a swanky wellness spa, which is really code for *rehab for the rich folk*. I don't even want to know how much money my parents ponied up to get me here. I've met a couple of A-list celebrities roaming through the meditation garden or hanging by the juice bar, so I know it ain't cheap. I'm not complaining, though. In fact, I'm grateful I've had this opportunity. I knew I had been using drugs and alcohol to cope with my demons, but I don't think I truly understood the extent of it before coming here.

My first week was hell. Detox was nothing like I expected and made me feel like complete ass. They used the term medically supervised, so I assumed they'd give me some sort of drug to prevent any withdrawal symptoms. While I did have meds to reduce the severity of my symptoms, I still experienced them in spades. I can't imagine how bad it would've been had I tried doing this on my own. If I wasn't nauseous or puking—the latter of which is ten times worse when you have cracked ribs—I had cold sweats, massive anxiety, and insomnia. I lost ten pounds because my appetite was pretty much nonexistent.

I wanted nothing more than to pop a pill or smoke a few bowls to make it all go away. I was ready to check myself out dozens of times, but then I'd picture the devastation on my parents' faces when they first saw me after the accident. Or the disappointment and worry radiating from my friends as they practically held a vigil by my bedside. The betrayal in Sydney's eyes as she realized I'd repeatedly lied to her or the pity she clearly felt for me during her brief visit at the hospital.

I knew I had to grow some fucking balls and get over this, no matter what it took. It wasn't easy, and there were so many ups and downs, I felt like I had vertigo at times, but I made it. Here I am a month later, feeling like a completely different person. A better person. I won't lie and say I haven't had cravings, but the counselor I've been seeing said those will be around for a while. I just have to focus on taking my meds, avoiding triggers, and continuing therapy to prevent a relapse.

My doc prescribed an anti-anxiety/anti-depressant combo which I probably should've been on for a while now. I scoffed when he first suggested it, thinking only pussies needed that shit, but I've come to see the error of my ways. I can't deny how much better I feel since it's worked its way through my system. I don't feel out of it or anything, but the constant buzz beneath my skin that kept me on edge is no longer there. My therapist likes to remind me anxiety and depression are genuine chemical imbalances, not a weakness or figment of one's imagination. Just because you can't see mental illness doesn't mean it's not very real.

The 12-Step program is no joke; that's for damn sure. I've learned a lot about myself during my stay here, and I can't say it was all sunshine and roses. Losing Carissa didn't put an end to the toxicity in my life like I had thought. In reality, it festered, morphed into something much more encompassing and destructive. It took hitting rock bottom finally see how much pain my fears and selfishness brought onto others. I certainly have a lot to atone for.

On the flip side, I'm now able to look at the past from a different perspective. I had been using drugs

"Hey." The pressure in my chest eases as her full lips curve into a soft smile. "This is a surprise."

"I hope it's okay. I—"

"Of course, it's okay." I instinctively step closer to pull her into my arms, but I catch myself and take a seat in the chair opposite from her instead. "I'm happy you're here."

I'm transfixed as she licks her lips. "You look good."

"I *feel* good," I say. "Better than I've felt in as long as I can remember."

Her dark lashes fan her cheeks as she takes a deep breath. "I'm glad to hear that, Bentley. Truly."

I lean forward, elbows propped on my knees. "I'm grateful you came all this way, but can I ask why? You said you didn't want to talk to me while I was in rehab. What changed?"

When Sydney opens her eyes, they're filled with unshed tears. "I got your letter. I'm sorry it's taken me so long to respond. It was... a lot to digest. I needed time to process."

I shake my head. "You don't owe me an apology for anything, Syd. Seriously."

She thinks about that for a moment. "Well... regardless. I think maybe I wanted to see you with my own eyes. Jazz said you were coming home tomorrow, but I couldn't wait. I needed to make sure you were okay."

Well, that's promising, right?

"I'm getting there." I smile.

She nibbles on her lower lip. "For what it's worth... I'm proud of you. For sticking it through."

"Thanks. I've had a lot of time to self-reflect in here. It's been a pretty eye-opening experience. I've got a long road ahead, but... I have a great support system in place. I feel good about things. Enough about me. How are *you?*"

"I've been doing a lot of thinking lately, too." Her face flushes. "I've been talking to a therapist... about what happened to me that night. Better late than never, right?"

I swallow the lump that's suddenly lodged in my throat. "Will you... will you tell me about it some-time? I know I don't deserve it, but not knowing is killing me. I can't seem to stop myself from imag-ining horrible things."

"It's nothing like what happened to Carissa, Bentley." Sydney shakes her head. "Not even close. I got out in time. I can explain more later."

"Thank fuck." I exhale harshly.

"I should get going."

I fight the urge to reach out when she stands. "Already?"

"Yeah." She nods. "I don't exactly know what the rules of recovery are, but when you get settled at home... if you want... I'd love it if you called me. If you're open to it, I think I'd like to try being friends."

I honestly don't know if I could ever be just friends with Sydney, but I'm smart enough to try.

"I'd like that, Syd."

Her beautiful face lights up in a smile. "Take care, Bentley. I'll see you soon."

As much as it hurts watching her walk away, I find myself smiling like a loon with a warm feeling in my chest. It's something I haven't experienced in so long, it's damn near foreign, but there's no doubt as to what's causing it.

Hope.

chapter
forty

SYDNEY

The first day back from spring break usually has me longing for at least one more day off, but this year, I'm anxious... yet, not necessarily in a bad way. Bentley came home over the weekend, and much to my surprise, he's already returning to school. Ainsley told me he made arrangements with my dad to do all his coursework online while in rehab so he could stay on track for graduation. I'm a little shocked my dad never mentioned it to me since he knows we were together, but then again, maybe there's some sort of student confidentiality agreement he has to abide by.

I'm honestly impressed Bentley was able to maintain his studies while he was undergoing treatment. The determination it must've taken for him to do that confirms he's serious about getting better.

I just hope it lasts now that he's back in the real world. Whether Bentley and I are involved romantically, I genuinely wish him well, and I hope we can be friends. Jazz and Ainsley have been such rocks for me over the last month, filling in during school hours when Cameron can't, and selfishly, I don't want to lose time with them. It's much easier for everyone if Bentley and I can coexist peacefully.

I perk up when I see Jazz's SUV pull into a lot. She had mentioned Bentley's license was revoked for a year, so he'll have to rely on others for transportation for a while. Since she has the roomiest vehicle, I assumed he would ride with them, so I'm a bit confused when only Kingston, Jazz, and Ainsley exit the Range Rover, heading toward me.

"Hey, Syd." Jazz tucks a swath of dark hair behind her ear.

"Hey." I try not to be too obvious who I'm looking for, but she quickly reads my mind.

"Reed's picking him up since their houses are closer together," Kingston explains, swinging a proprietary arm around his girlfriend.

Okay, evidently, he could read my mind, too. Not that I'm surprised. The boy's freakishly observant. Possessive, too. I swear Kingston couldn't be more so if he tried. I've spent quite a bit of time with them over the last month, and every move he makes lays claim to Jazz. It doesn't seem to matter whether or not there's a perceived threat in the vicinity.

I don't think he realizes he's even doing it unless Jazz calls him out for behaving like a caveman, which often happens. I think the whole thing's hilarious while Cam thinks it's hot as hell. I will never forget the look on Kingston's face when my bestie asked him if they ever considered starting an Only-Fans account, not-so-subtly suggesting she'd happily subscribe to their page.

"Look!" Ainsley nods over my shoulder. "There they are."

I turn, watching as Reed's flashy car comes rumbling through the gates, sliding into a spot two spaces down. When Bentley steps out, donning his black sports coat emblazoned with the Windsor crest, all eyes turn to him. There's chatter throughout the gathered crowd, no doubt talking about the return of one of their kings. I suppress an eye roll for about the millionth time at the stupid royalty thing this school has. I will say I haven't seen it get to the guys' heads much, but that Whitney chick is a total wench, and her royal counterpart, Imogen, isn't any better. Ainsley says they're salty because they think we stole their men, but she also says Bentley and Reed never committed to those girls, so they're full of shit. Plus, you know, Bentley's technically not mine anymore, so it should be a non-issue.

Bentley raises his head, taking in the crowd. I can tell he's anxious, but he masks it really well. I honestly don't think anyone outside of his inner circle sees it. When Bentley spots me standing with his friends, all nervousness seems to dissipate as a genuine smile stretches across his face, making his dimples pop.

Damn, why does he have to be so pretty?

Jazz nudges me with her shoulder. "You okay?"

I take a deep breath. "Yeah. Why wouldn't I be?"

Ainsley stands on my left. "You don't need to do that, Syd."

I honestly don't feel all that comfortable discussing this in front of her brother since he and Bentley are so close.

I straighten my spine, hitching my bag higher on my shoulder. "I'm good. Really."

I think.

Sure, it's weird having Bentley back, especially considering the last time he was here was the same day we broke up right in this very parking lot. But his near-death experience and my ongoing counseling sessions have changed my perspective. Not to mention everything he divulged in the letter he sent to me while he was in rehab. I may not know what battling an addiction feels like firsthand, but I think I have a much better understanding of what Bentley was dealing with day in and day out. His betrayal cut deep, but I can now see his actions weren't malicious. He was just scared and so very, very sad.

I'd be a pretty awful person if I didn't have empathy for anyone who suffered like Bentley did, but because it was him, it pulled on my heartstrings even more. On my drive home from Ojai the other day, I decided holding our past against him wasn't doing either of us any favors. I believe Bentley's sorry for his actions and wants to be a better person going forward. Maybe one day we can return to something more than friends, but for now, I think setting that expectation aside is what's best for both of us.

When Bentley approaches our group, he shares a bro-hug-backslap-thing with Kingston, followed by quick side hugs with Ainsley and Jazz. Bentley may be greeting the others, but his eyes are on me the entire time. I barely notice the four of them heading toward the school because I'm trapped in Bentley's unwavering gaze, unable to focus on much else. When it's just the two of us, he finally speaks.

"Hey, Syd."

"Hey." Damn it, I can feel my cheeks flushing. "I mean... welcome back. How are you?"

"I'm good. How've you been?"

"Uh... same. Good, I mean, for the most part." I startle when the warning bell rings.

His lips twitch, probably because I'm being incredibly awkward. "Can I walk you to your first class? Friends do that, right? Unless you changed your mind about trying the friendship thing."

"No." I shake my head. "I definitely didn't change my mind about that."

"Well, all right then." Bentley rubs his thumb along his lower lip.

Ugh. Why is it so freaking sexy when a guy does that? Bentley's not making this just friends thing easy on me, that's for sure.

Puh-leez, Sydney. Like it was ever *going to be easy?*

I incline my head toward the center building. "I guess we should get in there, huh? You ready?"

He smiles. "Let's do this."

461

Thank God I got over my nerves by the time second period rolled around, and Bentley took the desk next to mine in psych. I won't pretend I wasn't hyperaware of his every little movement—and okay, I may have sniffed him at one point, too—but for the most part, I played it cool. I keep telling myself to woman up—I'm the one who suggested this friends thing, after all—but my body isn't cooperating. It remembers all too well why Bentley Fitzgerald walks around with big dick energy, unlike anyone I've ever known. It also knows my vibe collection is a piss-poor substitute. I went from virgin to sex maniac in zero-point-five seconds, and it's all his fault.

Stupid hormones.

"I don't know. I was thinking maybe some shade of pink. What color are you getting, Syd?"

I was spacing out during the first part of this convo, so I have no clue what Ainsley's trying to ask me. "Color?"

Jazz gives me a knowing smile. "For prom. I told Ainsley I'm going with a black dress, and she's thinking of doing pink. Do you have a color in mind? We're going shopping this weekend so we can get a jump start on others. You're more than welcome to join us if you'd like."

Oh.

"Um... I haven't really thought about it. I'm not sure if I'm going to prom."

Ainsley practically chokes on the sip of iced tea she was taking. "What?! Why not? You can't not go to your senior prom!"

"Here we go again," Jazz mutters. "It's like homecoming two-point-oh."

The boys chuckle while Ainsley gives her bestie the finger.

"What am I missing?" I ask Jazz.

She smirks, dragging a fry through ketchup. "At the beginning of the school year, I had the *nerve*—" she rolls her big brown eyes as if to say: *insert sarcasm here*—"to tell these guys I wasn't going to the home-coming dance. It'll probably come as no surprise to you that was unacceptable to the twins." Jazz gives said twins a pointed look.

Kingston grabs the back of Jazz's neck and pulls her closer. Whatever he's whispering into her ear has her sighing with a dreamy look on her face.

Bentley clears his throat from the chair beside me. "Do you want to go? I mean, would you go if someone asked you?"

Crap, why didn't I see this coming?

God, I hope he doesn't ask me because prom is

a pretty big deal, and I don't want to give him false hope.

"Uh..."

"We should all go as a group," Ainsley enthusiastically suggests.

I flick my finger between her and Reed. "How does that work if four of the six of us are coupled up?"

I really don't want to miss out on prom, but I don't see how it could work when Bentley and I are the only singles. We'd automatically be thrown together, and that goes directly against the no-pressure friendship thing we're trying to establish.

Bentley shifts in his chair, obviously picking up on my hesitation and why. "Maybe you could see if Cameron wanted to come along?"

I consider it for a moment. "She was planning on skipping Cambridge's prom, but I doubt she'd be opposed to the idea of going to ours." I pull my phone out to message my best friend. It takes her less than five seconds to reply.

GBOAT: *Snoop Dogg *HELL YEA!* GIF*

GBOAT: *Jersey Shore *You can't do a party without the most valuable players* GIF*

GBOAT: *Napoleon Dynamite dancing with Deb GIF*

Me: Have I told you lately how ridiculous you are?

GBOAT: *Loki You know you love me GIF*

Bentley's lips twitch as he reads over my shoulder. "Her GIF conversationalist skills are on point. You've gotta give her credit where credit's due."

I tuck my phone back into my blazer's inner pocket, shaking my head.

I point a stern finger at him. "Do *not* repeat that in front of her. The girl does not need encouragement."

He holds his hands up, eyes lighting up with mirth. "You have my word."

I don't miss how easily we banter as if the last month never happened. Nor how intently the other four people sitting at this table are watching us. Being around Bentley is easy. His charm certainly hasn't lessened in his time away. But I need to remember not to allow that to lure me into a false sense of security.

"So, it's official then." Ainsley claps her hands together excitedly. "We're all going to prom!"

I study my lunch tray, trying to sort through how I feel about that.

Bentley bumps his shoulder against mine and

whispers, "We'll figure it out, Syd. Because losing you entirely doesn't work for me."

I smile softly, secretly loving how well he can read me. "Me neither."

I can see his grin forming out of the corner of my eye. "Then I'd say we're off to a good start."

God, this boy.

chapter
forty-one

BENTLEY

Growing up with two hardcore ballerinas in our tight-knit group, I've attended many dance recitals, and for the most part, they're all the same. You sit in an uncomfortable tiny-ass chair for three to four-hour stretches, watching performances of varied skill, from precious preschoolers tripping over their own two feet to older teenagers gliding across the floor with unfathomable grace. The steps and music may change, but if you've been to one, you've been to them all.

Or at least that's what I thought before I saw Sydney Carrington take the stage.

I've watched this girl bust hella impressive moves on a dance floor, but I've *never* seen anything like what I'm witnessing now. Hozier's "Take Me to Church" blasts through the auditorium's speakers, its evocative melody providing the perfect soundtrack to complement the way her body moves. I'm so entranced by Sydney's performance, I barely notice the tight leotard and sheer skirt she's wearing. Considering how often I surreptitiously perv on her, that's a damn miracle in itself.

Sydney's a tornado of twists and leaps and twirls. Her long limbs seem impossibly longer as she gracefully extends them, effortlessly blending one move to the next. The sheer athleticism she exudes is astounding. But even more remarkable is her ability to pour so much emotion into this piece. She's passion in its rawest form. Heart bleeding, dripping onto the floor with each step she takes. I knew Sydney had talent, but this is upper echelon shit right here. The fact that she choreographed this routine and can execute it in a manner so beautiful half the audience is literally crying is mind-blowing. It's no wonder she got her acceptance letter from the Los Angeles School of Performing Arts merely days after her audition. The panel probably would've accepted her on the spot if they could've gotten away with it.

I blink rapidly as the song ends, too stunned to do much else as Sydney heads backstage.

"She's pretty amazing, right?"

I nod dumbly. "Incredible."

"I think greatness runs through her blood. She

is the child of one of the best ballerinas in the world after all." I wince when Ainsley digs her nails into my forearm. "Oh, speaking of... here she comes now!"

Sydney's mom walks to the middle of the stage, mic in hand. "Ladies and gentlemen, before we get to our finale, I'd like to take a moment to thank each one of you for coming out..."

Ainsley snickers. "As if I'd miss a chance to see *the* Daphne Reynolds in the flesh."

I bite back a laugh as Daphne finishes her speech. Syd told me Ainsley is a major Stan around her mom, but I hadn't seen it in action before today. Every time the woman came on stage to address the audience, Ainsley leaned forward and legit stared so hard, her eyes watered.

Adorable little psycho.

A few minutes later, the finale is done, and the dancers take a collective bow before the curtain is drawn. Baby Davenport and I stay put as the others leave, knowing we have a bit of a wait before Sydney emerges from backstage. She asked us to wait for her up here as they get everyone cleared out.

"I think it's really cool you came today, Bent. I know it's probably bringing up some tough memories."

Surprisingly, it's not nearly as bad as I had anticipated. I was worried coming to a dance recital would trigger me, considering the previous ones I've attended were for Carissa, but I wanted to see Sydney perform so badly, I knew I couldn't pass up this opportunity. Besides, it's nearly impossible to avoid every trigger, so when I encounter them, I need to focus on what my counselor calls exposure therapy.

"I didn't have a choice. I couldn't miss seeing you get your fangirl on!" I press an open palm to my chest and gasp dramatically.

"Har-har, very funny." Her hazel eyes roll back. "Seriously, though. I know Sydney appreciates it."

I shrug. "I guess."

"She notices the effort you've made, Bentley, with her and your recovery. We're proud of you. All of us are."

I wave her off. "It's no big."

"Oh, shut up. Since when are you so modest?" She gives me a playful shove. "You should own that shit. You've been home for a few weeks now, and you've stayed sober. That's huge!"

I pull my hat off and flip it around. "It hasn't been easy. I want to get high all the fucking time, Ains."

A couple months ago, I would've never

admitted that. I would've put that shit on lock and thrown away the key. But my counselor says hiding your cravings from those you trust is lying by omission, which can lead to destructive behavior. If I don't have anyone to talk me through it, I'm much more likely to cave.

Ainsley leans her head on my shoulder. "I know, Bent. But you're doing all the right things. You're seeing a therapist. You're going to N.A. meetings. Things you should be proud of, no matter how difficult it's been."

I'm not sure if proud is the word I'd use to describe my struggle with sobriety. I don't know what to call it, honestly. Because no doubt, it's an uphill battle. I'm just trying to take it one day at a time—hell, one minute at a time—and not succumb to this crushing weight that's constantly hanging around. I will say spending these last few weeks with Sydney has definitely helped ease my anxiety. We're only together in a group setting, but I'm okay with that because it's what makes Syd comfortable. Her bestie has even infiltrated our crew which I love because that chick's hilarious. And you know, anyone who beats Sydney's piece-of-shit ex's ass is okay in my book.

I bolt out of my chair when I see Sydney and Cameron step out from behind the curtain, grabbing the bouquet I had resting in the chair beside me. Ains and I make our way down the stairs until we meet them in front of the stage.

I hand the bouquet of Casablanca lilies and roses to Sydney. "You were incredible up there, Syd."

She smiles as she sniffs the flowers. "Thank you."

"Damn, playboy, you're laying on the charm thick today, aren't you?" Cameron teases. "I wonder what else around here is thick?" She taps her chin in contemplation.

Sydney's eyes widen as she smacks her friend's arm. "Jesus Christ, Cameron!"

Ainsley and I both laugh. Never a dull moment with this one around, that's for sure.

"Oh my God, don't freak out," Ainsley mutters. "Do. Not. Freak. Out."

I look down at her, brows drawn together. "What are you talking about?"

"Hey, honey." Sydney's mom glides up to her, squeezing her in a quick side hug. "Great job out there today."

"Thanks, Mom."

Ah, now Ainsley's behavior makes sense.

Fine lines form around Daphne's eyes as she

smiles. "Ainsley, nice to see you again. I hear you got into the LASPA as well. Congratulations."

Ainsley stares for a good five seconds before replying. "Uh... you too. Very much so. I mean... yeah. Totally. *Crap, why am I so freaking awkward?* Ugh. Let me try again. What I meant to say was, *thank you*."

Sydney's and Cameron's lips curve as they watch Baby Davenport make a fool out of herself.

"And Bentley," Syd's mom continues, graciously brushing off Ainsley's fangirling. "Nice to see you again as well. Thank you for coming to the recital."

I incline my head. "It was my pleasure."

Her sharp gaze makes me wonder how much Sydney confided in her about me. Then again, Syd's dad knows why I was gone for a month since he's Windsor's headmaster, so does that mean Daphne knows as well? I can't imagine she'd be all that enthusiastic about her daughter hanging out with an addict.

A recovering addict, I remind myself.

Daphne looks between her daughter and me. "Well, I didn't mean to interrupt. I'll see you at home, Syd."

"Bye, Moms," Sydney says.

"Later, Mama C." Cam claps her hands together. "Who's hungry? Because I'm hungry."

Ainsley and Sydney raise their hands while I say, "I'll never turn down food."

Cam loops her arm through Syd's. "How about that retro diner on Ventura? They have amazing shakes."

I nod. "Sounds good to me."

"Great. We'll meet you guys there." Syd smiles.

Fifteen minutes later, Ainsley and I are parking in front of Mac's Diner with Sydney's Audi pulling in next to us. Just as we're about to go inside, Cameron pulls up short and curses.

"What's wrong?" Syd asks.

Cam sighs. "I just remembered I promised my mom I'd come home straight after the recital. She said she had something she wanted to discuss."

Sydney eyes her bestie dubiously. "Really? It can't wait an hour?"

"Nope." Cameron shakes her head. "She's going somewhere with Archie tonight. She said it has to be *immediately* after I get off work."

"You know what?" Ainsley pipes in. "I'm not very hungry. I can drop you off at home, Cam."

"Really?" Cam smiles. "That'd be awesome. I've always wanted to ride in a Lambo."

"Uh..." Sydney's blue-green eyes flicker my way. Her hesitation in being alone with me couldn't be any more apparent.

"It's all good," I assure her. "We can do this another time."

Syd's gaze flickers between her best friend and me before settling back on me again. "No. You know what? It's fine."

"Syd, I don't—"

Her dark curls bounce as she shakes her head. "I'm serious, Bentley. We're friends, right? There's no reason we shouldn't grab a bite together. We're already here, so..."

"You sure?"

"Positive." She nods. "If you're cool with it, I'm cool. I can give you a lift home afterward."

Ainsley gives me a look that says, *Are you okay with this?*

I nod, answering both girls. "Okay, then."

Ains opens the door to her yellow Lamborghini mouthing, *good luck* when Syd turns away to head inside. Cameron sends me a saucy wink before ducking into the car, making me wonder if this was all a setup. If it is, on the one hand, I'm grateful because that means more time with the girl of my dreams, but on the other, I'm irritated because I don't want Sydney to feel pressured into spending time with me. I want her to *want* to spend time with me.

Fuckin' A.

When did interacting with girls get so complicated? I used to be a goddamn master at this shit. Then again, the stakes were never this high before. Plus, you know, all the drugs I had floating through my bloodstream probably helped mute my anxiety.

"Hey, welcome to Mac's." A middle-aged brunette—Barb, according to her nametag—grabs two menus from the hostess stand. "Two today?"

"Yes, please," I reply.

As Barb guides us to a booth in the back, I tell myself not to stare at Sydney's perfect ass on the way, but c'mon. She's wearing yoga pants, and it's hard not to when I know how those round cheeks feel in my hands. It's been almost two months since I've touched this gorgeous woman. And considering how much has happened during the last two months, it feels more like two *years*. Jerking off is so unsatisfying in comparison, sometimes I wonder why I even bother. But then I worry my nuts might literally explode from all this pent-up frustration. Google says that wouldn't actually happen, but I'm not willing to risk it.

Sydney and I peruse the menu—a bacon cheeseburger for her and chicken strips for me—and tell our waitress what we'd like.

"Have you ever been here before?" Syd takes a sip of water.

"Quite a few times. Ainsley and Jazz love the milkshakes here."

"I don't know how those two stay so tiny eating the way they do. Cam, too. If I even *think* about a milkshake, I swear, my ass gets bigger."

"I don't see the problem," I smirk.

Syd laughs. "Ah, there he is."

I quirk my head to the side. "What's that supposed to mean?"

"Flirty Bentley," she explains. "I was wondering when he'd make a comeback."

I clear my throat. "Sorry, it just slipped out."

She taps my foot under the table. "I wasn't complaining, Bent. Quite frankly, if you kept up this proper gentleman thing much longer, I was going to get really concerned something was wrong with you."

I smile when she uses the shortened version of my name. I'm fairly certain it's the first time she's done so.

"Since we're being so frank... can I say something?"

Sydney inclines her head. "Go for it."

I fuss with the brim of my hat before looking her directly in the eye. "I'm not sure I know how to be your friend, Syd. I'm trying. I'm *really* fucking trying. But no part of me wants to be *just* your friend."

"I know you're trying, Bentley. And I really appreciate it." She tucks her chin for a moment with a grin tugging at the corner of her lips. "And since you're so transparent, I think it's only fair for me to say you're not alone in feeling that way." Syd holds an index finger up when my eyes widen at her admission. "*But* that doesn't mean I can just jump back into a relationship with you either. Plus, aren't new relationships a big no-no in the first year of recovery? I thought I read that somewhere."

My eyebrows rise. "You've been reading about recovery?"

"Yeah." Syd shrugs. "I was curious what you were going through."

"That means a lot, Syd. Probably more than I could ever articulate. And coincidentally, my therapist and I were just discussing this yesterday."

"How so?"

I sit up straighter. "Well... she knows a lot about our past. Since... you know, being open and honest is all part of the 12-Step thing. Anyway... to answer your question, no, they don't recommend getting into a new relationship until you've been sober for at least a year."

"Why do I feel like there's a *but* coming?"

"*But...*" My lips curve. "Since we have history and you weren't... uh, enabling my addiction... she thinks it would be fine, provided there's no more dishonesty between us."

She chews on her lower lip. "That was never a problem on my end."

Ouch.

"I know." I wince. "I also know actions speak louder than words, so I'll need to earn your trust, but I can safely say it won't be a problem for me anymore either. I mean... you've seen me at my worst, right? What's left to hide?" I knead the tense muscles at the back of my neck. "I don't ever wanna be that guy again, Sydney."

She thinks about it for a moment and sighs. "I believe you, Bentley."

"So, where does that leave us?"

"I think... we take it one day at a time. I don't want to be with anyone else, and I enjoy spending time with you. I want to continue that." She hooks her foot around mine. "I just... I'm not ready for *more* right now. And I don't know when I will be. Can you handle an unknown wait?"

For this girl? I'd wait a fucking lifetime.

I nod. "You're worth the wait, Syd. Always."

A toothy smile stretches across her beautiful face. "Well, okay then."

chapter
forty-two

SYDNEY

"Oh, honey, you girls look so beautiful!" My mom places a hand over her heart. "Don't they look beautiful, Tim?"

My dad smiles as Cameron and I twirl in front of the mirror above my dresser. "Always. Although, you look a little too grown-up for my comfort. Don't get me started on all the boys seeing you two looking like that."

I give him a wry look. "Dad, don't start."

He holds his hands up, laughing. "Hey, don't blame me. It's dad DNA in action. I'm powerless against it."

"Oh my God, so cheesy." I roll my eyes.

He points to me. "Science is not a myth, Sydney."

"Mom," I whine. "Make him stop."

"Maybe if you wouldn't have made such a big stink about me attending, I wouldn't be so worried." He lifts his eyebrows.

"Uh... I'll take the worry any day."

As headmaster, my dad usually attends prom. He and my mom get dressed up and go every year, calling it their "annual fancy date night." But this year, since it's *my* senior prom, I begged him to send his assistant in his place. He gave me a lot of grief, but my mom eventually talked him into it. I don't want to know what she promised because there was a lot of whispering and giggling on her end, so I'm sure it'll gross me out.

"Get out in the living room so I can take pictures of you two in front of the fireplace before your friends get here." My mom makes a hurry-up gesture.

"Give us just a few, and we'll be out."

My mom nods before grabbing my dad's hand and leading him out of the room. She yelps as they get farther down the hall, and I'm pretty sure it's because my dad just pinched her butt.

Cam makes a gagging sound. "They're so cute, but at the same time, I wanna puke a little in my mouth."

I snort. "Try living with them."

"Uh... I practically have been for the last ten years," she points out. "I am *well versed* in your parents' over-the-top PDA."

"Touché."

"Okay, bitch, enough talking about your parents' raging hormones." Cam laughs when I make a face. "Let's do a quick lip touch-up and get out there."

I smile as I take in our reflection. Cameron's wearing a canary yellow chiffon dress that hits the floor with a lacy sweetheart fitted bodice. Her long blonde hair is professionally done, sitting in a pile of elegant curls on the top of her head. My dress is similar in style, though in aqua—a shade freakishly similar to my eyes—and rhinestones cover the bodice instead of lace. I extend my leg, exposing the dramatic slit that hits me at mid-thigh, showing off my dancer's calves and strappy silver sandals. My hair is in a half updo, pinned back by rhinestone clips, but most notably, it's straight as a board, giving me several extra inches of length. I rarely flat iron my hair because it takes so long, but I felt tonight called for something different.

Cameron smacks her lips together after refreshing the pink gloss. "I need to say something before everyone gets here. But you need to let me get it all out before you start brushing off the idea."

My eyes flick to hers in the mirror. "Well, that's not ominous or anything."

She places her hands on my upper arms, turning me toward her. "Sydney, as your best friend, I feel obligated to force you to stop getting in your own damn way."

I frown. "Will you stop talking in code and spit it out already?"

"Okay. I won't be offended if you spend the majority of your night with Bentley. Or... if you happened to sneak off to one of the rooms in the hotel for the whole night. I don't want you to worry about me."

"Cam. I'm not—"

She holds her hand up. "Nuh-uh. Let me finish."

I fold my arms over my chest. "Go ahead."

"As I was saying... I'm a big girl. I appreciate the invite, and I'm sure tonight's going to be lots of fun, but I don't want you thinking you have to stay glued to my side."

I take a seat on the edge of my bed. "Where is all this coming from?"

Cam lowers herself to the mattress beside me. "The last few weeks have been great, right? Specifically with Bentley, since you guys had that talk at the diner?"

"Yeah. And?"

"*And...* you said you've been getting closer as you spend more alone time together."

I shake my head. "We're not—"

"*I said*, let me get this out." Her blue eyes narrow. "I know you're just friends." She uses air quotes on the last two words. "And you're keeping things G-rated. But don't you think it's time to put both of you out of your misery? It's been almost three months, Syd. And look how far you've both come in that time."

She's right. Bentley and I have grown so much these last few months, as individuals and together. Therapy's been beneficial for both of us, and Bentley's remained sober. We talk a lot—sometimes for hours on end—and he couldn't be more upfront about his thoughts or feelings. No topic is off-limits. If Bentley needs to unload something, he will. Our conversations aren't always easy, but they *are* productive. They've definitely bonded us together more.

"I know. But we're taking it one day at a time, Cam. That way, there's no pressure."

"Oh, don't—"

"Girls," my dad calls. "The limo's pulling up."

Cam's blue eyes narrow. "This conversation isn't over, lady."

"It is for now," I sass, walking backward out of my bedroom.

When we make it to the other end of the house, my tiny living room is overcrowded with people dressed in formal wear. Jazz and Ainsley smile when they see us, both looking gorgeous as ever in their fancy gowns. Their boyfriends don't look too shabby either, wearing black tuxes. When Bentley steps out from behind Kingston, I almost embarrass myself by blurting out something totally inappropriate in front of an audience.

Ho-ly shit, he looks good.

It should be illegal to be that fine. Like his friends, Bentley's dressed in a sharp black tuxedo, but whereas Reed and Kingston opted for standard ties and vests, Bentley chose a more traditional bow tie and cummerbund. He looks very old Hollywood, and I can't say I hate it. When he smiles—*God, when he smiles*—my lady bits light up like the Fourth of freaking July. It's gotta be the dimples. Oh, who am I kidding? Bentley Fitzgerald would be equally fly without 'em.

They certainly don't hurt, though.

I can see Cameron's knowing smile out of the corner of my eye, and I swear, I hear her voice in my head saying, "Get it, girl!"

Bentley's Adam's apple bobs as his brown eyes

travel the length of my body. Rubbing a hand over his jaw, he says, "Wow. Syd, you look... stunning."

I grin. "Thank you. You look great, too."

Understatement of the year, right there.

"Uh... hello?" Cam waves her hands. "Why do I suddenly feel invisible? Can you guys see me?"

Bentley chuckles while I say, "Oh, shut up. You know you look good. Our purpose in life isn't to constantly stroke your ego, Cameron."

She sticks her tongue out. "Well, it should be."

"You look beautiful, Cam," Bentley offers.

I stick my tongue out at him. "Suck up."

"Okay, children," my mom chides. "Everyone, stand in front of the fireplace so I can annoy you with pictures before you leave."

"Um, if I gave you my mom's number, would you mind sending some of those to her?" Bentley asks. "She'd kill me if she missed out on this."

"I'd be happy to, honey. Us moms gotta stick together." My mom winks.

"Oh my God," I groan. "Did you really just wink at him?"

My mom, dad, and Bentley all laugh.

"Don't let her fool you, young man." My dad points a stern finger at my mom. "That one's taken."

Bent holds his hands up in surrender, smirking. "I wouldn't dream of it."

"I have the most embarrassing parents ever," I mutter.

"Oh, shush you," my mom says. "Now, everyone, stand together and smile."

We indulge my mother through a few dozen photos before piling in the limo and driving to the hotel where prom is being held. My jaw drops as we walk inside the grand ballroom. Every single wall is covered in a thick curtain of icicle lights. Ribbons of white and gold tulle hang from the ceiling, covered in even more lights. The sizable dance floor is already packed, surrounded by dozens of round tables adorned with white tablecloths, gold chairs, and ornate flower arrangements. The entire space is classy elegance, which I suppose I should've expected from a Windsor prom.

Ainsley gasps. "It's so pretty."

"It is," I agree.

Cam squeals when "Best Friend" by Saweetie and Doja Cat starts blasting through the speakers.

She practically yanks my arm out of its socket. "Bitch, they're playing our song. Let's go shake some ass."

"Oh... um, okay." I damn near trip trying to keep up with her.

"Later, boys!" Ainsley calls as she drags a bewildered Jazz behind her in the same aggressive manner as my bestie.

The four of us move to the beat, rapping along with the lyrics in between bouts of laughter as Cam attempts to twerk in her dress. My face hurts from smiling so much as one song bleeds into another. I can feel the weight of Bentley's gaze on me as the girls and I are dancing, but he makes no move to interject until the D.J. slows the tempo down with Andy Grammer's "I Am Yours."

Bentley and I are nearly the same height with my heels, so when he pulls me into his arms, our mouths are mere inches apart. I lay my head on his shoulder to resist the temptation to close that minuscule gap between our lips. I sigh as Bentley's strong arms embrace me tighter when Andy sings about freefalling through life until he meets the woman he loves. Toward the end of the song, my beautiful broken boy presses his mouth to my ear, singing along about how he was lost, but now he's been found. He knows who he is now. He is mine, and he wouldn't dream of being anything more.

Tears prick at my eyes as I pull back to look at him. The galaxy of emotion swimming in Bentley's gaze steals my breath. He may have used someone else's lyrics just now, but there's no questioning the sentiment was coming from *him*.

"Bentley." My voice is shaky.

I hold my breath as he cups my jaw and leans closer. "Syd, I—"

I hate myself when I see the pain I've caused as I abruptly pull away. "I need some air."

I don't explain further. I make a beeline toward the French doors on the back end of the room, grabbing Cam along the way. Once we're outside, I lean against the marble railing, taking several deep breaths to calm the panic inside of me.

"Sydney." She pets my back soothingly. "Honey, what's going on?"

I fan my face, looking up to ward off the tears. "I almost kissed him, Cameron."

"Bentley?"

"Of course, Bentley!" I spin around, throwing my hands up. "Who else would it be?"

"Whoa there, *chica*. Slow your roll. I was just making sure because I don't understand why almost kissing Bentley would upset you so much."

"Because Cameron! If I go there... there's no turning back. Not after everything we've been through."

"And that's a bad thing?" she asks cautiously.

"I don't know!"

My best friend takes a deep breath to counter my riotous emotions. "O-kay... let me ask you this. Do you like Bentley? Enjoy spending time with him? Does he treat you well?"

"You know I do." The *duh* is implied in my tone. "I *more* than like him, Cam. And he treats me like I'm the center of his universe."

"All right. I won't even bother asking if you're attracted to him because anyone can see the answer to that is a resounding yes. So, if you more than like him, he treats you like a queen, you enjoy spending time with him, and you want to jump his bones at any given moment, what's the problem?"

"I'm scared."

"Oh, babe, I know you are. But do you know what that tells me?"

"What?" I sniffle.

She smiles softly. "That he's worth the risk."

I think about that for a moment. "You're right. God, you're *so* right. What would I do without you?"

Cam swings her arm around me. "Dunno, and you're never gonna find out because I'm not going anywhere."

I lean into her. "Love you, boo."

"Love you too, babe."

Cameron and I startle when someone starts golf-clapping from a darkened corner.

What the hell?

When the tall figure emerges from the shadows, Cam immediately stiffens. "What in the hell are *you* doing here?!"

Hayden, the boy she loves to hate, is dressed in a collared shirt and dark jeans, so I highly doubt he's here as someone's prom date.

He smirks. "Listening to a couple of sappy girls, apparently."

Cameron makes a growly noise that would probably be more threatening if she wasn't a tiny blonde wearing an evening gown. "You're such an asshole!"

My thoughts exactly.

"What are *you* doing here?" he counters. "According to the sign in front of the ballroom, this isn't your prom."

Cam glares. "Not that it's any of your business, but I'm here as Sydney's plus one."

His gaze wanders to me briefly. "Huh. Didn't peg you for a lesbo. I'm usually spot on with these kinds of things."

"Oh my God, you stupid piece of sh——"

I latch on to Cam's arm when she lunges toward him. "Hold up there, Scrappy. As much as I'd enjoy watching you kick some dickhead's ass, you're not dressed for it. " I give Hayden a once-over, not doing anything to conceal my contempt. "And this guy's not worth ruining your pretty dress."

"Just gimme one punch," Cam begs, trying to break free from my hold like a feral cat. "It's all I need."

Hayden holds his arms out, arrogance seeping from his pores. "Let her go. This I have to see."

I actually consider it for a moment.

"Everything okay out here?"

My head whips to the right when I hear Bentley's deep voice. He's assessing the situation, clearly thinking Hayden's a threat as he positions himself between us. If only he could see Cam in action when she lets the crazy loose, he would know she didn't need his protection.

"No problem here, playboy." Cameron cracks her knuckles. "I'm just about to kick some pretty-boy ass, that's all."

Hayden flat-out grins at Cam's statement, which confuses the hell out of Bentley. Me, too, when I think about it.

Bent turns to me. "Syd, care to explain what the hell is going on right now?"

"This asshat" —I gesture to Hayden— "is Cam's mom's boyfriend's son. Needless to say, they don't get along very well, but I'm pretty sure he's harmless."

Hayden leans casually against the railing to demonstrate. Oddly, that only seems to incense my bestie further.

"*Dick*less is more like it," Cam mutters.

The asshat narrows his eyes. "Just say the word, and I'd be happy to prove you wrong."

Cam scoffs. "As if."

"Syd?" Bentley questions. "I gotta be honest; I'm not quite sure what to make of this situation. Am I supposed to kick this guy's ass, or..."

Cameron smirks when she sees Hayden's expression change from cocky to concerned. Although both guys are pretty equal in size; I'm guessing it'd be a somewhat even match.

Cam looks at her wrist pointedly. "You can let go, Sydney. I'm not going to go apeshit on his ass." I release her from my grip but remain focused in case she changes her mind. "And Bentley, no worries. Syd's right. Dickless over there is a prick, for sure, but he wouldn't touch me. Why don't you two go back inside while I deal with this?"

Both mine and Bentley's gazes flicker between Cameron and Hayden. The latter is back to being cool as a cucumber, while the former looks like she's planning world domination.

"You sure?" Bentley and I ask at the same time.

Cam nods. "Positive. Go enjoy your prom. You two need to talk anyway. I'll be inside in a bit."

"Syd?" Bentley reaches out his hand. "You cool with that?"

I hesitantly take his hand. "Yeah."

"Go, you guys. Seriously. I'll be fine. I just want to have a few choice words with my pal, Hayden, here."

Oh, boy. Asshole or not, I kinda feel sorry for the guy.

As Bentley and I walk inside, he asks, "What the hell was that?"

I look over my shoulder, seeing Cam wasted no time getting started on delivering those *choice words*. "I don't know. But it was certainly *something*."

He follows my gaze, lips curving into a smile as he reads between the lines. "Is it weird that I kinda feel sorry for the dude?"

I shrug. "Hope not. Because I was literally just thinking the same thing."

He inclines his head toward the dance floor. "You wanna dance some more, or..."

Cameron was right about one thing. I need to

stop being such a scaredy-cat because Bentley *is* worth the risk.

I nod. "I'd love to."

Bentley's dimples pop. "Well, okay then. Let's get over there before you change your mind."

I laugh as I struggle to match his pace because there's no way that's gonna happen.

chapter
forty-three

SYDNEY

"So, why is Cameron not with us exactly?" Jazz asks, leaning her head on Kingston's shoulder.

"Evidently, her mom was having dinner at the hotel's steakhouse with her boyfriend and his sons," I explain. "When her mom found out they were at the same hotel, she insisted Cameron join them."

"That's weird, right?" Ainsley pipes in. "I mean, who cares if it's not her school's prom? She was still at *a* prom."

I smile when Bentley shifts a little closer along the bench seat and our thighs touch. He hasn't tried kissing me again, but he was definitely more touchy-feely throughout the rest of prom. Not that I minded.

"Cam and her mom have a... difficult relationship. They always have. Honestly, Chelsea—that's her mom—isn't my favorite person. She's incredibly selfish and ignores Cam more often than not. But for some reason, Cam can't stop hoping her mom will change. She thinks if she caters to her mom's whims, maybe that'll help."

"That sucks," Ainsley frowns. "What about her dad?"

"She's never met him." I shrug. "Her mom got pregnant from one night with some rando, never to be seen again."

I wouldn't normally divulge Cam's personal business like this, but I know she wouldn't mind me telling this group of people because their curiosity stems from concern. It's not like Cam hides her messed-up relationship with her mother. She just doesn't broadcast it to the public.

"That blows," Reed says. "We all can relate to shitty parents, that's for sure." He nods to Bentley. "Well, except Fitzgerald. His parents are freakishly normal."

"Don't be a hater." Bentley flips off his friend. "Besides... from what I've seen, Sydney's parents are even more stable than mine. They're actually present even." His eyes widen. "Imagine that concept."

Half the limo's occupants chuckle, though I'm not sure why. I'd be sad if my parents weren't around much. As cheesy and nauseatingly in love as they are sometimes, they're good people.

"So, what's it like being the headmaster's daughter?" Kingston asks. "Weird?"

"I'm used to it." I shrug. "My dad's honestly pretty cool for an oldie. He can be strict or stubborn at times, but he's mostly chill. And on the rare occasion he is irrational, my mom keeps him in check. She's definitely not afraid to tell it like it is."

Bentley bumps his shoulder into mine. "So, that's where you get it from."

I roll my eyes playfully.

"He does seem pretty laid back." Kingston leans over to kiss Jazz's temple. "It's strange having a headmaster walking around campus who doesn't have a pole permanently lodged up his ass. That's all we've ever had."

"Great." I cringe. "Now I have a visual in my head of my father I could've gone a lifetime without."

Everyone laughs at that.

The car comes to a stop, and when I peek out the tinted windows, I see we've arrived at their house in Malibu. Jazz and Kingston needed to get back for her sister, so we're dropping them off first even though their home is the farthest from the prom hotel.

"Night, guys." Jazz unfastens her seat belt and gets out of the limo behind her boyfriend.

"Night," Ainsley echoes as she exits the vehicle.

When Reed gets out as well, I'm a little surprised since he lives close to Bentley, but considering his girlfriend lives here, I suppose I should've expected it.

"Night, bro." Bentley offers Reed a fist bump, to which he replies with a nod.

I've never met someone who talks so infrequently. I guess it's better than a person who never shuts up.

My nerves kick in as the door closes, sealing Bentley and me inside the now far-too-roomy limo. I don't know why. It's not like we haven't spent time alone together recently. But tonight feels... different. The air inside this car is rife with sexual tension all of a sudden.

Bentley takes my hand as the limo pulls out of the driveway. "Relax, Syd."

Tell that to the shiver coursing down my spine.

He pulls his phone out of his coat's inner pocket and checks the time. "We still have the limo for two hours. Do you want to head home... or maybe cruise around for a bit?"

"I'm good with cruising for a while."

Bentley presses the button to lower the partition. "Hey, Eddie. Do you mind cruising PCH for a bit?"

Our chauffeur makes eye contact with Bentley through the rearview. "No problem."

"Thanks, man." Bentley raises the partition again before shifting his torso, so he's facing me. "Did you have a good night?"

I raise a brow. "Night's not over."

"Smartass." His lip kicks up in the corner. "Have you had a good night *so far?*"

"Yeah, Bent. I have." I pull my lower lip between my teeth. "Barring my mini freak out while we were dancing."

He takes a strand of my straightened hair, running it through his fingers. "This has been tripping me out all night."

I pat my head self-consciously. "Do you not like it?"

"*I love it,*" he assures me. "But it's gorgeous in its natural state, too. Let's be honest, though, you could shave your head, and I'd still think you were hot as fuck."

"I don't think that's happening anytime soon." I laugh, taking a moment before continuing. "Thank you for not making a big deal out of earlier. I wasn't trying to be rude—swear. And it's not that I didn't want to kiss you. I just panicked."

He cants his head to the side. "Why? I didn't make you uncomfortable, did I?"

"God, no." I shake my head. "It was all me overthinking things like I usually do."

"Overthinking what?"

"I feel like there's so much riding on this, ya know? I don't want to screw it up."

Bentley smiles softly. "Yeah, I know exactly what you mean."

"But then Cam said something that really resonated with me."

"What'd she say?"

Here goes.

I look him straight in the eye. "She said it's okay to be scared because that means you're worth the risk."

"Yeah?" My eyes are drawn to Bentley's mouth as he rubs his thumb across his lower lip. "And you agree with her?"

"I do."

"What are you saying, Syd?"

I take a deep breath. "I'm saying I don't want to be just friends, Bentley. If you're game—and it won't jeopardize your recovery in any way—then I'm all in. I want to be with you."

My heart feels like it's going to burst out of my chest as I wait for him to say something. My nerves get the best of me when he just sits there and looks at me, obviously deep in thought.

I groan. "You have nothing to say to that? Really?"

"I'd rather show you instead."

I don't have time to ask him to elaborate because, in the next moment, his mouth is on mine. I moan, fumbling with my seat belt as he licks the seam of my lips.

Bentley rips his mouth away. "Wait. Don't."

"Huh?" I blink through the cloud of lust.

"Your seat belt. Don't take it off while the car is moving. I... uh..." He grabs the back of his neck. "After my accident, I..."

"Enough said. I'm sorry; I wasn't thinking."

Shit.

I should've known better. He already told me riding in a car makes him think about the accident and how he's glad it'll be a while before he can get behind the wheel again.

Bentley's body instantly relaxes as I fasten my belt. "But that doesn't mean we can't do things while still remaining in our seats."

My nipples perk up at his suggestive tone. "Oh yeah? What kinds of things?"

Bentley grips the back of my neck, pulling my face toward his. "Well, to start, *this*."

I thought he was moving in for another kiss, but he diverts his mouth at the last second, kissing a trail down my neck.

I gasp, craning my neck back to give him better access. "That's a good start."

Bentley's hand grips my leg, searching for the slit in my dress. Once he finds it, he dips beneath the chiffon, gliding his fingers up my naked thigh. "This okay, Syd?"

I automatically widen my legs. "Uh-huh."

If he goes any further, he's going to find out real fast how okay it is.

He groans as his fingers land on my center, pushing his thumb against that overactive bundle of nerves through the tiny scrap of satin. "Fucking hell. You're so wet."

"Bentley?"

He raises his head from my neck. "Yeah?"

I smile. "Kiss me."

I feel him smiling lasciviously into our kiss as he pushes my panties to the side and glides his fingers through my pussy lips. Bentley pushes one digit inside me, pumping in and out a few times before adding a second finger. He expertly works me over with his hand, curling his fingers just right to hit that perfect spot on the inside while the heel of his palm rubs against my clit. My hips tilt up on their own accord, chasing his hand on each withdrawal like the shameless hussy I give zero fucks about being right now.

It doesn't take long before I'm a writhing, panting mess, scoring Bentley's forearms with my nails as an inferno builds inside of me. I come violently, albeit silently, no matter how desperately I yearn to scream Bentley's name. I'm sure the driver has heard plenty of sex noises throughout his career, but I refuse to add to the collection.

Bentley withdraws his fingers, bringing them to his mouth and sucking them clean. God, why is that so hot? I grab his face with both hands and pull him into a kiss, tasting myself on his lips. He groans into our kiss before pulling away, resting his forehead on my shoulder.

"I want to be inside of you so badly, Sydney."

"So, let's go to your place."

Bentley sits up, scrubbing a hand down his face. "Can't. My parents have been spending a lot more time at home since my accident. My mom, mainly, but they're both there right now."

"Crap. My house definitely isn't an option. My parents are there, and there's not nearly enough square footage to sneak you in."

His whiskey eyes bounce between mine. "We could always get a hotel room."

I bite my lip. "My parents do think I'm spending the night at Cam's."

Bentley adjusts my dress, so I'm decent before lowering the partition a smidge. "Hey, Eddie. Can you take us to the Beverly Wilshire, please?"

Eddie nods. "Sure thing."

"Bentley, we don't need to go anywhere fancy. I'm sure that hotel is ridiculously expensive."

"Don't care." He takes my hand, placing a kiss in the center of my palm. "I'm not taking you to some budget chain when I can afford otherwise. You deserve the best, Syd."

I don't like the idea of anyone spending that kind of money on me, but I decide to let it go. Bentley can definitely afford it, and it's only one night.

"Beverly Wilshire it is."

I barely have a chance to take in the room before he's on me. We stumble across the floor as we kiss, fumbling to remove our clothing piece by piece. When we're down to our underwear, I pull back to get a good look at him.

"God, you're so beautiful."

"Isn't that my line?" He chuckles. "'Beautiful' isn't nearly masculine enough to describe me."

"Too bad." I shake my head, giggling. "Have you seen your bone structure?"

He releases a full belly laugh, leaving me momentarily stunned. I thought Bentley's smiles made me breathless before, but since he's been sober, they've become even brighter. More genuine.

My hands explore his chest, all hard muscles, and broad shoulders, lightly tracing over the script above his heart. Bentley's irises darken with lust as they track my movement, his pupils blown wide when I reach the thin trail of hair below his belly button.

He groans as I stroke him through the cotton boxer briefs he's wearing. "Fuck, Syd. I need you."

I press up on my toes, nipping at his chin. "So, take me."

Bentley gives me no time to change my mind. He pounces on me, kissing me deeply as my back hits the soft mattress. Our tongues duel as our joint need becomes an inferno. He deftly unfastens my bra, groaning as my breasts are freed.

"I missed you so much," he whispers before pulling a nipple into his mouth.

I gasp when he uses his fingers to tweak the other. "Are you talking to me or my boobs?"

I can feel him smiling against my skin. "Both."

I rub my thighs together as Bentley lavishes attention on each breast, alternating between licking and sucking each peak. My spine bows when he kisses down my torso, palming each one of my boobs as he circles my belly button with his tongue. He hesitates when he reaches my panty line, prompting me to sit up on my elbows.

"What's wrong?"

There's that breathtaking smile again. "Nothing. I just want to take my time loving on you."

"Oh, my *God*," I pant as he runs the bridge of his nose right down my center before hooking his fingers beneath the flimsy straps and pulling them down.

Once I'm laid bare, his tongue sweeps out, following the path of his nose. I moan as my beautiful boy eases a finger inside of me, my hips rising up to meet his touch. Bentley's eyes never leave mine as he devours me, hooking my knees over his shoulders. My fingers claw the bedding as he teases me relentlessly, kissing everywhere but my bundle of nerves. I shudder when he finally—*finally*—gives me one long lick up my center, swirling his tongue where I need him most.

"Swear to Christ, I could eat this pussy all day every day," he murmurs against me.

"Oh fuck, right there." My chest heaves as he lazily draws patterns on my clit. Wait a second... *"Are you spelling your name?!"*

His throaty chuckle makes my toes curl. "Are you really surprised?"

"Oh my God," I groan. "I thought Kingston was the only caveman in your trio."

"Can you save talking about another dude for a time when I'm not eating you out?" The fingertips on Bentley's free hand bite into my inner thigh. "Matter of fact, let's skip it altogether."

"Aw, what's the matter? Insecure in your manhood?" I smirk.

He pinches my ass, making me yelp. "You know damn well I have nothing to be concerned about in that area."

My eyes cross when he sucks me into his mouth. "Jesus. Carry on, good sir."

Bentley adds another finger, curling it inside of me. "Like this?"

"Just like that!" My body is taut as tension builds in my spine.

"C'mon, Syd. Give it to me so I can get inside of you."

I don't know if it's the incentive or sheer coincidence, but in the next moment, a supernova explodes behind my eyelids as I scream his name.

Bentley continues licking me gently as I come down until my quivers cease. My limbs feel like Jell-O as he slowly climbs up my body, leaving biting kisses along the way.

My thighs part for him as he fits himself in between them. I somehow missed when he ditched his boxers, but I'm not exactly complaining as he fists his length, gliding it through my sensitive flesh. Just when I'm about to tell him I can't take it anymore, Bentley lines himself up at my entrance and pushes forward.

"Fuck," he grunts. "So good."

"So, *so* good," I agree.

His large hands bracket my hips as I reach up to kiss him. I suck his full lower lip, and he returns the favor. Bentley's hands move to my ass, tilting my hips upward, his strokes long and sure. I'm so wet, he thrusts inside of me with ease, stoking a new kind of fire. The suite is filled with the sounds of our heavy breathing, bodies coming together, whispered promises, and cries of ecstasy.

Bentley slows, cupping my face and leaning down for a soft, sensual kiss. When our mouths disconnect, I'm overwhelmed by emotion. I've never felt closer to another person than I do right now, and I know Bentley feels it, too. This man has the power to destroy me, but I know deep in my heart, he'd do everything he could to avoid that. The road that led us here may have been riddled with potholes, and I know Bentley has a long way to go in his recovery, but I don't think our connection would be nearly as strong if it had been easy.

"I'm scared," I whisper, pressing my palm over his heart, feeling its steady beat.

"Me, too." He kisses the sensitive spot behind my ear before placing his hand over mine. "But you're in here, Sydney. I didn't understand it at the time, but I think I've been in love with you since the moment we met."

I briefly close my eyes, savoring his words. "Bentley..."

"I don't expect you to say it back. I don't *want* you to say it back right now." He presses his palm over my racing heart. "But I know I'm here. You saw me at my absolute worst, and you didn't give up on me. I don't need the words, Sydney, because you *show me* every single day." I moan when he speeds up, hitting just the right spot. "And as long as you'll have me, I intend to do the same."

I trace his jaw with my index finger. "Show me, Bentley. Love me."

My beautiful broken boy easily understands what I'm asking for, hitching my legs above his hips. Bentley starts moving in earnest, pressure building higher and higher until we're both falling over the edge with each other's names on our lips. As the tremors wane, we lie chest to chest, sleepy and sated and so very happy just to be near one another. I've never been more content.

My lids flutter as he presses his mouth to my ear and whispers, "Always."

chapter
forty-four

BENTLEY

"What is this place again?"

My palms sweat as I lead Sydney down the dirt trail, and it has nothing to do with the late May temperature.

"It's an old fire lookout." I point to the cone-shaped hill up ahead. "It's right up there. It doesn't look like it from here, but there's actually a large platform on top."

The closer we get, the more nauseated I feel. I know I have to do this, though. Jackie, my therapist, says I need to make new memories at this place. Good memories. I need to prove to myself that my nightmares don't control my reality.

When I asked Sydney to come with me, she enthusiastically agreed before I could even finish telling her why. I don't know how I got so lucky, but

Sydney couldn't possibly be more supportive. I've been careful not to use her as a crutch—that's one area Jackie suggested I focus on when I told her Syd and I were together. It's a tricky balance between being dependent on Sydney versus having her encouragement, but so far, I think we're managing.

We've learned the key to finding that balance is open communication. I swear, I have never spent so much time with a woman simply talking, but my girl has a way of making it easy. Plus, our deep discussions usually lead to me being deep inside of *her*, which I can never get enough of, so it's a win-win in my book. When Syd and I reach the part that requires a semi-vertical climb, I go first, reaching my hand out to assist her once my feet touch the platform.

She gasps when she gets her first glimpse of the colorful concrete overlooking the canyon. "*Oh my God.* How have I lived this close to this place my whole life and never known it existed? This is incredible, Bentley."

I try seeing it through her eyes and have to admit, it *is* pretty spectacular. You genuinely feel like you're on top of the world up here, even though it's only about twenty-four hundred feet in reality.

"It's a well-hidden gem." I gesture to the edge

of the platform. "You wanna take a seat over there and watch the sun go down?"

Sydney follows my gaze, immediately connecting the dots. That's the exact spot I was sitting on in my nightmares as first Carissa, then Sydney jumped to their deaths.

She rolls her lips. "Only if you feel comfortable doing that."

I swallow hard. "I kinda feel like I need to."

She extends her arm. "Let's go then."

We walk down the slight slope hand-in-hand, stopping right before the elevated section. Sydney squeezes my hand, giving me the courage to step up and walk across the rectangular platform until we reach the end. We both slowly lower our bodies to the ground, legs hanging over the ledge. My gaze is drawn to the giant boulder on the right, half expecting to see a dead body lying next to it. I release a harsh breath when I find dirt and brush instead and really take in the scenery.

Countless trees surrounding the scattering of boulders, and houses down below, are now bathed in shadows. The sun casts a golden pink glow over the mountains as it sets, giving the whole thing a spiritual vibe. Spray-painted designs from some truly talented artists sit beneath us in a rainbow of colors. Every time I come here, the platform looks different. It's only a matter of time until the next person paints over it, but part of the allure is the anticipation of what new artwork awaits you.

"You doing okay?"

I look to my left and find Sydney's sea-green eyes brightened with unshed tears. "What's wrong? Why do you look like you're about to cry?"

She smiles, curls bouncing as she shakes her head. "Nothing's wrong, Bentley. After what you told me about your nightmares... I can't imagine how hard this must be for you. I'm proud of you for doing this. I'm grateful you asked me to come with you."

This girl.

I grab the back of her neck, pulling her lips to mine. "I don't deserve you."

"You deserve the world, Bentley."

Sydney's said that to me once before, but I wasn't in the right headspace to hear it. But as the most beautiful girl I've ever known smiles back at me, framed by some of the best Mother Nature has to offer, I'm more hopeful than I've been in a long time. Maybe I *can* be worthy of her after all. The one thing I know for certain is I'm sure as hell going to try.

And just like that, a good memory is formed, and Topanga Lookout is no longer so scary.

"Bentley!"

I grunt as a tornado with braids slams into me when Syd and I walk into the mini graduation party being held at Kingston's house. I pick Jazz's little sister up and boop her on the nose.

"How's my favorite eight-year-old today?"

Belle rolls her eyes in the exact same way her older sister does. "I'm pretty sure I'm the *only* eight-year-old you know."

Sydney laughs. "Ooh, she told you."

"Don't encourage her." I narrow my eyes, tickling Belle's side, making her erupt into girlish giggles. "This one does not need more sass. She's already got enough to last her a lifetime."

"Kingston!" Belle shouts. "Bentley's bein' rude!"

My jaw drops. "You little sh—"

Kingston swoops in like Belle's very own knight in shining armor, taking her into his arms. "Go ahead, Fitzgerald. I dare you to finish that sentence."

Belle clings to Kingston's side with a smug smile on her face.

"Belle," Sydney interrupts. "I love your pretty pink dress!"

Belle squirms until Kingston sets her down before grabbing Sydney's hand. "Come with me!"

"Oh!" Sydney's eyes widen as Belle jerks her forward. "Okay, then. I guess I'm going with the munchkin."

Kingston and I laugh watching Belle drag Sydney to the back deck, where I can see Jazz and Ainsley sitting on loungers.

"Dude, between Jazzy and that little girl, you are *fucked*."

"Absolutely." He smiles. "But I wouldn't have it any other way."

Reed joins us, handing me a bottle of water. "'Sup?"

"Thanks, man." I crack the bottle open, taking a large swig. "Is it just me, or was graduation not such a big deal? I always thought walking across the stage, doing the whole hat-throwing thing would feel much more important than it actually did."

"Not just you." Kingston shakes his head. "But to be fair, this has been one helluva year for all of us. Getting our diplomas is pretty insignificant comparatively."

"True," I agree.

It really has been a crazy year. Between everything Kingston and Jazz went through during the first half of our senior year and my downward spiral into rock bottom during the second half, a piece of paper saying we made it through high school doesn't mean shit.

"Although, if we hadn't seen it through, we wouldn't be going to UCLA in the fall," Reed adds.

I point my bottle at him. "*You guys* and Jazz wouldn't be going to UCLA."

Reed shrugs. "You'll get there, dude."

"Maybe."

The guys and I have talked about going to UCLA together for years now, but unfortunately, my grades slipped, and I missed the application deadline because I was too stuck in my head to give a shit. So, for now, getting my core classes out of the way at community college is the plan. I don't think that's a bad thing, though, because UCLA is a notorious party school. Even if I wasn't living on campus, I don't think it's the best place for me at this point in my recovery. I won't lie and say I don't have major FOMO because five out of the six of us got into our dream schools, but I do think it worked out this way for a reason. And we're all staying in LA, so there's that.

"Are we done caressing each other's balls?"

Davenport asks. "Because I want to get back to Jazz. I'm sick of being away from her."

I laugh. "When do you ever want to be separated from her? I think your obsession with Jazzy is borderline unhealthy, bro."

He raises his light-brown eyebrows. "Oh, fuck off. You gonna pretend you don't feel the same about Sydney?" When Reed laughs, Kingston's gaze snaps to my other best friend. "Or my sister?"

"No," Reed and I reply simultaneously.

"Exactly," Kingston says. "So, what the fuck are we standing around here for?"

"I have no idea," I admit.

We join the girls outside, shooting the shit while Kingston mans the grill. As I look around at all the smiling faces, I think about how damn right this feels. These people are my family. My foundation. They've proven their love and loyalty time and time again, and for that, I'm grateful. Hell, these days, I have a lot to be thankful for. I'm sober. I'm healthy. I feel better than I ever have, and I couldn't possibly ask for anything more.

I amend that thought when the beautiful girl on my lap turns to me and smiles. One day, I'm going to ask this woman to marry me. And when that day comes, I hope she says yes.

Sydney taps her finger against my temple. "Whatcha thinking about in there?"

"You."

"Oh yeah?" Her eyes fill with mirth as she lowers her voice. "Something dirty, perhaps?"

I laugh. "Well, that's a given. But no, that's not exactly where my thoughts were headed."

She assesses me carefully. "Care to share?"

"Oh, no big," I wave my hand breezily. "Just thinking about how I'm going to spend the rest of my life with you."

Sydney's not surprised by my declaration in the least. I don't exactly hide my feelings from her anymore. But what she does next surprises *me*.

"I love you." When I look in her ocean eyes, I see the conviction behind her statement.

I don't know why I'm so shocked; I feel Syd's love every single day. But this is the first time she's actually said those three little words. Maybe I'm more surprised by how much they affect me.

I press my forehead to hers. "I'm going to show you every damn day how happy I am that you came back into my life."

"I can't wait." She palms my cheeks and releases a sigh. "And I'll be right there with you doing the same."

"But just to be clear... part of that *showing* I'll be

doing will be incredibly dirty. I'm talking about some mind-blowingly filthy shit here, Syd."

Sydney throws her head back in laughter, drawing the other's attention. "I look forward to it, playboy."

Me too, baby. Me too.

epilogue

SYDNEY

"There! All done." Ainsley turns to me and asks, "What do you think?"

I roll my lips, biting back a laugh. "I think it's really weird there's a poster of my mother in our dorm room."

Ainsley's jaw drops. "Weird?! Why is it weird? She's a ballet legend, and this is a legendary dance academy! It makes perfect sense."

I certainly didn't consider this when we requested a shared dorm room at the LASPA. As much as I love the girl, ordering an old promotional poster off the internet from one of my mother's old productions is a bit much. I wonder if it's too late to switch roommates.

"Because she's my *mom*?" I widen my eyes. "Ainsley, put yourself in my shoes. What if Bentley comes over? Would you want to have sexy times with your boyfriend while that thing is staring at you from across the room?"

She shakes her head as if I'm ridiculous. "Oh, c'mon, Sydney. You know damn well if you and Bentley have *sexy times*, odds are it'll be at his apartment."

Bentley and Reed have an apartment about fifteen minutes away, which works out really nicely because it's centrally located between our respective schools. Kingston and Jazz will commute from Malibu each day because they have Belle to consider, but there was no reason the rest of us shouldn't live closer to campus. Plus, as much as I love my parents, I want the experience of living in a college dorm. Not dealing with traffic after a day of physically grueling classes is a bonus, too.

"That's true," I agree. "But it's still freaking weird."

"Well, get over it." Ainsley sticks her tongue out, making me laugh.

"Speaking of the boys... we should probably head out if we want to make the movie in time."

She looks at the clock on the wall above our small twin desks. "Oh crap. You're right."

As I grab my purse, someone starts pounding on our door, scaring the shit out of me.

What the hell?

"Sydney!" Cameron yells from the other side of the door. "Are you in there? Open up!"

Ains and I share a perplexed look as I cross the room to open the door.

"Oh my God, this is a literal nightmare!" Cameron shoves me aside as she storms into our room and plops on the end of my bed. "How can she do this to me?"

Uh-oh. Nothing good ever happens when my bestie is worked up like this.

Ainsley and I both take a seat on her bed across from mine.

"Cam, what's going on?" I ask cautiously. "How can *who* do *what* to you?"

"My mother!" She throws her hands up. "My selfish as fuck mother! I can't believe her!"

"What'd she do?" Ainsley sits back against the wall, pulling her legs in.

Cam's wild eyes find mine. "She got married!"

Ainsley and I both gawk.

"Um..." I clear my throat. "Back up a little. I wasn't aware she was engaged."

"She wasn't!" my bestie shouts. "But she and Archie went off to Vegas over the weekend and eloped! Can you believe that? And now that she's living in wedded bliss, we're moving into his Beverly Hills mansion. *His mansion, Syd!* Do you know what this means?"

"Uh..."

She doesn't give me a chance to figure it out. "It means that Hayden-freaking-Knight is now my new stepbrother! *And I'm going to have to live with him!*"

"Oh, shit," I mutter.

The contention between Cam and Hayden has only gotten worse the few times they've been thrown together over the summer. Putting them under the same roof is just asking for trouble. Or, you know, a homicide.

"Exactly!" Cam throws herself backward on the mattress. "What am I going to do? This is the worst thing my crappy mother has ever done to me."

"Um..." Ainsley raises her hand. "Can I play devil's advocate for a moment?"

Cam screams into my pillow before saying, "Oh, why the hell not?"

"Do you think your mom and Archie may be actually in love? That she's not doing anything *to* you, but she's in love with this man and genuinely wants to blend your two families together?"

"No," Cam answers.

"Doubt it," I reply at the same time.

Ainsley's never met Chelsea, so it's understandable why she doesn't get what's happening here.

"I *think* my mother is a gold digger who cannot fathom being without a man, and she's finally landed herself a big fish after years of failed attempts. I also think she didn't take me into consideration *whatsoever* when she decided to get hitched. Nor when she said I'll be transferring to Beverly Prep for my senior year, so I can't even escape the stepbrother from hell during the daytime!" She throws an arm over her face and groans. "What am I going to do, Syd?"

I sigh, preparing myself to deliver the hard truth. "There's not much you can do, Cameron. You're not eighteen yet, and even if you were, it's not like you can afford to get a place of your own and still go to school. I think you're just going to have to somehow make the best of it."

She whimpers. "Can't you guys just hide me here? I have no problem sleeping on the floor."

Ainsley shakes her head. "I'm fairly certain the R.A., and the school, would not be chill with that."

"Ugh!" Cam rolls to her side, facing us. "This is the freaking worst! How am I going to survive my senior year?"

I have no clue. But it's going to be interesting to see how this pans out, that's for sure.

You didn't think this was goodbye, did you? Sure, the Windsor Academy series might be over, but that's what spin-offs are for, right? I couldn't just leave my girl, Cam hanging, so Cameron and Hayden's story, book 1 in the Boys of Beverly Prep series, is coming early 2022!

Did you miss Jazz & Kingston's story? Check out **WICKED LIARS**, the book that started it all!

also by laura lee

Dealing With Love Series (Interconnected standalones)

♥Deal Breakers (Devyn & Riley's story)

♥Deal Takers (Rainey & Brody's story)

♥Deal Makers (Charlotte and Drew's story)

Bedding the Billionaire Series (Interconnected standalones)

♥Billionaire Bosshole

♥Billionaire Bossman (Formerly Public Relations)

♥Billionaire Bad Boy (Formerly Sweet Temptations)

Windsor Academy Series (Books 1-3 <u>must</u> be read in order)

♥Wicked Liars

♥Ruthless Kings

♥Fallen Heirs

♥Broken Playboy (Bentley's story-can be read as a standalone)

Standalone Novels

♥Beautifully Broken

♥Happy New You

♥Redemption

GO TO:

https://www.subscribepage.com/LauraLeeBooks to sign up for Laura's newsletter and you'll be the first to know when she has a sale or new release!

about the author

Laura Lee is the *USA Today* bestselling author of steamy and sometimes ridiculously funny romance. She won her first writing contest at the ripe old age of nine, earning a trip to the state capital to showcase her manuscript. Thankfully for her, those early works will never see the light of day again!

Laura lives in the Pacific Northwest with her wonderful husband, two beautiful children, and three of the most poorly behaved cats in existence. She likes her fruit smoothies filled with rum, her cupboards stocked with Cadbury's chocolate, and her music turned up loud. When she's not chasing the kids around, writing, or watching HGTV, she's reading anything she can get her hands on. She's a sucker for spicy romances, especially those that can make her laugh!

For more information about the author, check out her website at: www.LauraLeeBooks.com
You can also find her "working" on social media quite frequently.
Facebook: @LauraLeeBooks1
Instagram: @LauraLeeBooks
Twitter: @LauraLeeBooks
Verve Romance: @LauraLeeBooks
Reader's Group: Laura Lee's Lounge
TikTok: @AuthorLauraLee

acknowledgments

To my husband, Tad: You are the love of my life, and I'm so grateful every day to have you. Now that this book is FINALLY done let's freaking go to Maui!

To my beautiful children: I love you to the moon and back.

To my author besties, Alley Ciz and Julia Wolf: This book really tested me. Without your personal and professional support, it would've never made it out into the wild. I cannot possibly thank you enough for always being there.

To my lovely beta Crystal and my sensitivity reader, Jasmine: Thank you for being among the first people to read Broken Playboy. Your feedback was invaluable.

To Christine, my proofreader, P.A., and GIF Conversationalist Extraordinaire: *Fez I love you GIF *Maya Rudolph & Kristin Wiig Soulmates GIF *Jim & Pam from The Office high-fiving GIF *Evil Elmo GIF

To Britt, my social media guru: Thank you for taking so much time off my plate so I can write and for making me look like slightly less of a hot mess.

To my editor, Ellie McLove: Thank you for not firing me after I delayed this book eleventy million times. Your flexibility, efficiency, and overall awesomeness are greatly appreciated.

To my publicist, Amanda: Thank you for getting my name out there as much as possible and for being such an enthusiastic cheerleader when life was overwhelming me.

To my agent, Bethany, of Weaver Literary & Management: I'm so grateful you took a chance on me, and I can't wait to see all the great things we can do together.

To all the seriously awesome book influencers: Thank you for all you do each day to help spread the love of reading. Your gorgeous edits astound me.

Last but never least, to my readers: For those of you who've been waiting A LONG TIME for Bentley's story, thank you, thank you, thank you for sticking with me. I wrote this book during a highly challenging time in my life. As you can probably imagine, after reading it now, it took a toll on my emotions, so I had to put it aside many times.

As much as it killed me not to release Broken Playboy earlier in the year as planned, I genuinely feel I could not have done this story justice had I rushed it, so I greatly appreciate your patience and understanding. If you found me through Broken Playboy, thank you for gambling on a new author; I know you have a lot of options out there. Regardless of whether you've been with me for a while or you're new to my words, I appreciate your support more than words could ever say. If you've taken the time to send me a message or leave a review on one of my books, please know that I personally read each and every one. I will always value and welcome your feedback because I couldn't do what I love for a living without you. XOXO